Mystic Passage

C.L. Carhart

MYSTIC PASSAGE

Book 2 of *His Name Was Augustin* series

Copyright © C.L. Carhart 2021

First edition: June 2021

All rights reserved. No part of this publication may be used or reproduced in any manner whatsoever without permission in writing from the copyright owner except in the case of brief quotations in a book review. For inquiries, please direct all mailed correspondence to PO Box 186, Pacolet, SC 29372, USA.

This is a work of fiction. Names, places, characters, and events are fictitious or are used fictitiously. Any similarity to real persons, living or dead, is coincidental.

ISBN: 978-1-954807-02-0 (paperback)

ISBN: 978-1-954807-03-7 (eBook)

https://www.clcarhart.com

Edited by Elizabeth Johnson

Cover Design © J. L. Wilson Designs | https://jlwilsondesigns.com

For Catherine
a victorious survivor
who made the bravest choice

Other Books by C.L. Carhart

Arcane Gateway
His Name Was Augustin, Book I

Brief Pronunciation Guide

Augustin – Au-GUS-tin
Bayerisch – BEYE-rish (eye is pronounced like eyeball)
Bayern – BEYE-urn (eye is pronounced like eyeball)
Eihalbe – EYE-hahl-buh (eye is pronounced like eyeball)
Freia – FREYE-yuh (eye is pronounced like eyeball)
Isar – EE-zahr
Muniche – MYOO-nih-khuh
None – Nohn
Swanhilde – Swan-HIL-duh
Thaden – TODD-n
Torstein – TOR-stein (stein is pronounced like a beer
    stein)
Wuotan – VOH-tahn

Table of Contents

Prologue

When Augustin finished perusing the first book of my story, reading over my shoulder in silence, I turned around on my stool to regard him, curious about his impression of my tale thus far. He eyed my pile of pages with his arms crossed, his expression appearing dissatisfied. When he saw me looking at him, he shook his head slowly and made a disquieting noise, his bright blue eyes alight with mockery. I frowned at him, knowing that it was time to defend my writings, though I knew not why. "What's with the vampirical smirk?" I demanded, laying down my pen and folding my own arms in tacit frustration.

He chuckled darkly and shook his head again. "You certainly are not a chronicler, Swanie, and this proves it," he said, leaning over the desk to tap my stack of papers with an incriminating finger. "Your tale reads like a novel, not like a historical event."

I snorted at him and countered, "Not too many 'historical events' happened in this part of my story."

"Your discovery of the Torstein," Augustin rejoined, still smirking. "The unveiling of the gates of time, the harrowing trip through the dark currents. Also, the death of Bertha Lohr, your era's Lady of Muniche." He nodded sagaciously, looking satisfied. "Historical events."

He was right, as usual, but I shrugged at him. "I don't care. I'm writing this for my son, not for some Teuton historians like *some* people. If Max wants to read our history, he can crack open some of your own tomes. But this is *my* story, and you shouldn't criticize the way I'm writing it." I stuck my nose up at him, contorting my expression into one of wounded pride and great abandon.

Augustin looked thoughtful for a moment. Then he tilted his head at me and added, "Your grammatical errors . . . ."

"Oh, give me a break!" I retorted, grasping the pen once more and squirting a black splotch of ink onto his tunic. "My English is far better than yours."

Augustin muttered a few choice words and dabbed at the ink spot with his fingers. "I cringe to consider how you intend to portray me in Book II," he said, rubbing his now-black fingertips together, peering at the ink stains.

I almost cringed at that idea as well, but I made a shooing motion at him and turned back to my work. "Get out of here," I told him shortly. "How am I supposed to write with you breathing down my neck?"

I heard him snicker, and his footsteps receded in the direction of the door. But he paused before exiting the chamber and called to me again. "Swanhilde?"

I did not turn around. "Yes, Augustin?" My tone betrayed a little annoyance.

There was a short silence and then, to my surprise, I heard him say, "So far, your writing is excellent." An instant later, I heard the door creak open and shut. I glanced back at the door, sensing the heat of Augustin's fire departing the room with him. Then I spun on my stool to face my work once more, a triumphant smile spreading across my face . . . .

Chapter One:
Arrival in the Past

The harrowing ride through the obscure currents seemed to last forever this time around. On my trip to 1978, I estimated that it may have taken about a minute or less according to my own internal clock. Truthfully, I believe that getting pushed backward through that awful darkness does not register at all, as far as time itself is concerned. But during our journey to the eleventh century, I felt sure that my body remained helpless to those jostling currents, pulled in all directions, pushed forcibly against a powerful undertow for an infinite eternity. I could hardly form a conscious thought during the traumatic passage, but I did think briefly of Beth and Joel, wondering how they were tolerating the experience. They had come with me—I knew that—but I could not sense them. I was alone.

Shortly after stepping into the currents, I began to hear those bothersome whispers all around me demanding my attention and my understanding. Since the journey seemed lengthier this time, I concentrated a bit more effort on trying to interpret those voices, wanting to discern of what exactly they sought to warn me. But they spoke a language I did not know. It was not German, English, Bayerisch, or

French, nor was it Latin or Teutonica. It sounded older, more rudimentary, yet also more profound. The whispers continued throughout my entire journey, insistent, warning, *warning* . . . .

Just as I began to believe that I could pick out a word or two, a dismal moan crept up from the depths, breaking my concentration. I may have discerned a shift in the whispers at that point, a hint of mockery mingling within their unknowable warnings. I struggled to focus entirely on the voices, trying to ignore how helpless my body felt with the moans seeming to work their way deep inside. At last I caught just two words, both sounding similar to Latin: *obligure* and *damnere*. Obligate, perhaps, or obligation? Damnere . . . that was easy enough. To condemn, to consign to hell. Fear washed over me at the potential meanings of those two words. The realization struck me again that I should not have opened the gateway, not at all. I should not have used the Torstein twice, not after learning about its true nature from the forbidden writings. This time, I feared I would face serious repercussions.

The fact that I could see nothing but whirling darkness and intermittent bursts of light and color—nothing solid, nothing that would have a mouth or speak with a voice— disturbed me. While the persistent moans wove their way upward from somewhere below, it seemed that those niggling whispers came from every direction at once. Some spoke directly into my ears, close enough that I should have been able to reach out and touch *something*. But my hands remained immobile. I could not move any part of my body, for the currents were far stronger than me. A burgeoning terror overtook me, convincing me that this time there would be no end to these currents, to this darkness. I had chosen—*knowing* the writings—to go back to a time before the Torstein had been created. Would I never make it there alive? Would I remain entangled in the strands of time until the end of infinity? What about Beth and Joel? They were innocent outsiders. What had I done?

Suddenly that horrible, abysmal laughter rang out again from the darkness in a tone so deep it could not have been human. Panic raced through my veins at the thought of the alternatives. *If it's not human . . . then it must be a demon . . . Wuotan . . . ?* The laughter increased, piercing my soul, grasping at my heart with hands as black as the depths of the ocean. I tried to react, but I held no power against the forces that drove me backward, and even less power to smother the laughter. *Damnere . . .* the word crept into my brain again.

Finally, I found myself falling forward, bursting from the portal onto soft brown leaves in the sheltering shade of a forest. I heard two *oofs* as my companions landed beside me, and I pivoted quickly to confront the gates, raising the Torstein in my left hand, silently ordering them to depart before that wretched, laughing demon reached out to take me. They responded properly, fading much more swiftly than they had come. I sighed in relief and collapsed onto the ground, flopping down on top of my leather bag, the Torstein still clutched in my left hand. I closed my eyes and chuckled foolishly at nothing, the twittering sounds of birds and buzzing insects soothing my frightened soul. I did not think to question why I had landed in a forest rather than on the streets of medieval Muniche. My gratitude at my safe arrival impeded my judgment.

"Swanie?" My cousin's voice pulled me out of my reverie of relief. I opened my eyes and looked toward her, where she stood in the brush on the opposite side of Joel. She clutched the strap of her bag with both hands, the skin of her face as white as a sheet. "That . . . that was *way* worse than you described," she accused in a trembling voice, her wide eyes locking with mine.

I felt oddly jubilant at the fact that the three of us had survived the journey, and I heard my own voice chuckling again. "Guess our mental images of Muniche were a bit off," I commented, glancing around at the trees. I recognized white oak and birch interspersed with brambles, ferns, and moss. Maybe the medieval version of my city had a woodsy section like the modern Englischer Garten. I heard no sounds that indicated human activity, though. It was quiet in the glade where we stood, a soft summer breeze rustling the leaves overhead.

"So," Joel interjected more loudly than necessary, "I'm going to make an assumption here and say I'm dreaming."

I lifted myself off the ground and turned to regard Joel, who stood upon a massive birch root several paces behind me with his bag on the ground before him, his eyes dazed as he stared at our surroundings. I exchanged a quick look with Beth, knowing that we could no longer keep everything to ourselves. After all, we were *here.* "Well, Joel," I began, trying to discern how I should explain what had happened. "Actually, we're not dreaming. We're in the eleventh century."

Joel focused on me, confusion in his hazel eyes, then looked around again. "No, I *have* to be dreaming this," he insisted, appearing thoughtful. "I must have fallen asleep while Beth was in the shower. She said we were supposed to meet you outside at ten-fifteen. I really need to wake up. I'm going to be late." He started smacking his arm, pinching his face. "Wake up, wake up," he muttered.

I gawked at him, shaking my head at the ridiculousness of it all. Beth took it upon herself to march up to him and take hold of his right arm. "No, Joel, I promise you, you're not dreaming. This is real. You wouldn't be wearing those clothes in a dream. You'd never seen them before." She gestured at his linen tunic and pants.

Joel continued slapping himself with his left hand, ignoring his girlfriend's words, still murmuring that he needed to wake up. Then his gaze traveled down to his shoes and the root where he stood, and he scooped up a small stick with a sharp point. Waving it at Beth and me in an ingenious manner, he announced, "*I* know how to wake myself up." Before either of us could yell at him to stop, he stabbed his own palm with the stick, drawing blood.

Beth screamed and grabbed for the stick, ripping it out of his hand before he could do any more damage to himself. I heaved an aggravated sigh and plunked my bag onto the leaves while she urged him to sit down. "For heaven's sake, Joel, listen to me!" I ordered as his girlfriend fairly shoved him down onto the root. "You are *not* dreaming, and you need to stop trying to hurt yourself, because we are *in* the eleventh century! You could give yourself blood poisoning with a cut like that." Joel cringed and stared down at his bleeding palm as I turned to Beth. "He's got the gauze and alcohol in his bag. We'd better get that wrapped up before it gets dirty." His blood had started dotting the moss below.

"Right," Beth said, crouching down to unclasp his bag and dig for our very small batch of medical supplies. Annoyance washed over me at the idea of wasting some of it now, two years before the siege. Maybe we should have left Joel at home.

"That really should have woken me up," Joel said while Beth dabbed his left palm with alcohol, softly chiding him as she worked. She began to wrap his wound, and he shook his head, disbelief still written all over his face. "But time travel is impossible. There is no way . . . ."

"Just think about it for a minute," I admonished him, watching my cousin work to repair what he had done. I wished again that Hans had agreed to teach me blood control. If I knew how to tap the full powers of my Teuton blood, I could have stopped Joel's bleeding already. Maybe here in the eleventh century, where ancient traditions still flourished among my people, I could finally learn the things that Hans was so loath to share. I smiled to myself at that idea, then focused on Joel, trying to discern the best way to convince him that we had traveled time. "If you're being honest with yourself, you'd have to admit that there is no possible way your unconscious imagination could have come up with what happened just before we got here," I pointed out. "Similar to what Beth said before about your clothes. You can't dream up something you've never seen before."

Joel's countenance paled, dull fear creeping into his eyes. "Those gigantic gates . . . those whispers . . . those awful moans . . . ."

I nodded at him in agreement. "My nightmares could never come up with something like that," I said, and it was true. Beth finished dressing his wound and tucked the remainder of the gauze back into his bag. Then she got to her feet again and retrieved her own bag, looking toward me with a determined nod. "That place in the darkness after we stepped through those gates? Those were the currents of time," I explained to Joel while pulling the strap for my bag back over my right shoulder. I moved to stand beside my cousin, feeling more at ease now that our crises seemed to be winding down.

"That was an incredible journey we made," Beth remarked, bumping lightly against my left shoulder. "And I'm kind of hoping that the journey forward will be a lot less terrifying." I did not meet my cousin's gaze, preferring to concentrate on her boyfriend, who was in the process of regaining his feet. *No, Beth, the trip forward is just as terrifying as the trip back,* I thought.

"The currents of time," Joel repeated, realization dawning in his eyes at last. "Is that why it felt like I was being pushed against a tornado or something?" He rolled his shoulders a bit and situated his bag beneath his left arm, flexing his fingers around the gauze binding his hand.

"Yes, we were flying backward through the currents of time," I clarified, thinking back to those moments in the darkness. "It's kind of crazy, but it seemed like it took *forever* that time." I shared a look with my cousin and explained, "The first time I did this, I just went to 1978, and it wasn't quite so bad. *That* trip . . . ." My voice trailed off, and I shuddered.

"I guess an extra nine hundred years would make the trip a lot longer," Beth said, and Joel murmured in agreement. He seemed to have accepted the fact that we had traveled time.

I opened my left hand and looked down at the Torstein, glowing a muted ruby in the shade. Its powers over-whelmed me again at the thought of what we had just done. Then just as abruptly, my mind turned at last to the forest and to the medieval city of Muniche. *We were supposed to arrive . . . there . . . .* I stared at the Torstein, then around at the trees, then back at the rock. "Why did you bring us *here?*" I whispered to it in Teutonica, fear seeping into my veins again.

"Is that the rock you said would take us back in time?" Joel inquired, stepping forward to peer at it himself. He reached his unwounded hand down to touch it, but I closed my fingers around it quickly. "How does it work?"

I pulled away from him and looked around again, taking note of the ancient trees, the sunlight filtering through their branches, the dried leaves beneath our feet. "It's a long story, but I can't tell you yet. We have a problem. We were supposed to get here in the Teuton city of Muniche, but we're in the woods." I looked at Beth and saw that a touch of worry had creased her brow.

"Muniche. That's right," Joel repeated, apparently remembering what I had told him when we stood on the path to the gazebo. "What's a Teuton?" he asked, the word finally having made him take notice.

I gave him the shortest possible explanation. "The Teutons are one of the old German tribes from before the Christian era. This rock was created by one of them." I held up my left hand significantly and finished, "I am one of them."

Joel nodded, following along. "Barbarians," he said, and I frowned at him. Beth giggled in an impish manner.

"Maybe to the Romans," I allowed, "but that's not important right now. I'm trying to figure out why we're in the forest. Were you thinking about the city of Muniche when we leaped through the gates, like I told you?"

Joel's face clouded over, and he put one hand to his chin as he considered. "I was thinking of the eleventh century, like you said . . . but I guess I was picturing some medieval battle in a field or in the woods, like Middle Earth. Remember when we were talking about *Lord of the Rings?*" He grinned crookedly at me.

I groaned in despair, realizing that it was the fault of Joel's foolish imagination that we had arrived in a forest. "Sounds like we'd have been better off if you'd gone back to bed," Beth observed in a scathing tone. "*I* was thinking about the city of Muniche, Swanie."

"At least you listened to me, but your boyfriend had to be an idiot thinking about elves and hobbits, and who knows where we may have ended up?!" I snapped. "I don't have a map, and I don't have a compass. We may be on the wrong continent for all we know. We're going to have to do this again." Terror seized me at the idea of reopening those gates again and confronting those voices and that laughter. And Wuotan knew that I knew that it was he who laughed. He would try to take me . . . .

All at once, Beth clutched at my left arm. "Swanie!" she gasped in a low voice laden with horror, "I think there's someone out there!" Her eyes scanned the trees around us. Joel followed her example, moving to stand before us.

I froze, my element sweeping into my veins at the possibility of immediate danger. I endeavored to keep my ice out of my eyes so it would not ruin my contacts, but I allowed it to sharpen my other senses. My keen ears picked up the distinctive crunch of twigs snapping, and a moment later a man stepped out from behind one of the ancient oaks not five meters from where we stood. In the dimly lit clearing, I could see that his clothing was brightly-colored, his complexion darker than expected, his hair jet black. And in his right hand he carried a spear.

The man stopped short when he saw us—two young, dark-haired girls standing behind a youthful blond-haired boy with three bags between them. He stared at us, confusion crossing his face. Apparently he had not expected to encounter the likes of us in this forest, but as I glanced again at his spear I felt a rush of sympathy for whatever—or *whom*ever—he sought. Three, then four more men, each looking about the same as the first, also emerged from the brush, all bearing spears. They halted as well, ogling us, and then began speaking excitedly amongst themselves in a language I did not understand.

I had a strong feeling that this would not end well unless I played the role of the peacemaker. I raised my right hand slowly, non-threateningly, disregarding the warning tug of Beth's grip. "Do you speak Teutonica?" I addressed the question toward the man who had first appeared, pronouncing every word distinctly.

There was a short pause, and then all of the brightly-dressed men began speaking at once, to each other, the word *Teutonica* on every pair of lips. That was when the first man leveled a furious gaze upon me. He slammed the base of his spear upon the leaves as he spat one word, an accusation. *"Teuton!!"*

I cursed, hesitating just one second longer. Then I grabbed Beth's hand to yank her into the forest and shouted, *"Run!!"*

Chapter Two:
Heartbreak

My cousin and I charged into the trees, running as swiftly as we could in our linen dresses. I hiked my skirt up a bit with the fingers of my left hand while my thumb pressed the Torstein against my palm. My bag banged against my right hip, and I pushed myself faster, trying to rein in my ice for fear that its verve would prompt me to outrun Beth. But my blood felt frigid, and the hairs on my arms had begun to stand up. I could hear the bellowing voices of our adversaries not far behind.

"Joel?" my cousin gasped out after we had run for at least half a minute. She was out of breath and had begun to slow. "Sw . . . Swanie . . . Joel?"

"Come on," I urged her without looking back.

"Wait!" she panted, desperation tainting her tone. "Joel . . . isn't . . . here."

I slowed my sprint, thinking again that maybe we should not have brought her boyfriend along at all. Maybe he felt the need to be a hero and defend us from the spear-bearing foes—but he had no weapons aside from the knife in his bag. And he did not yet know about that. I felt Beth's fingers tug at my right sleeve, an attempt to bring me to a complete stop. "Please . . . we have . . . to go . . . back . . . ." I heard Joel's voice shouting amongst those of our antagonists, and I slowed my pace, taking a deep breath before pivoting around a spruce tree. There I halted and turned to face my cousin.

Beth had stopped several paces away, her chest heaving, her face flushed and damp with sweat. Her tawny head covering had slid down around her neck; it must have gotten caught on something during our flight. She bent over, her hands pressed to her knees, and raised her head to meet my gaze, her lips parting to say something . . . .

And just at that moment, a burly man converged upon her from behind, pushing her into the dirt. A strange squeak escaped her lips, and the man drove his spear deep into her back.

My ice erupted in my veins, my bag and the Torstein falling to the ground as I flung myself at the man like a feral animal. I did not think; I reacted. I shoved him away from my cousin and closed my icy fingers around his throat. One of his comrades appeared while I wrestled him to the ground, but he stopped short at the sight of me. I screamed in fury at the attacker, whose face had begun to turn blue, his hands struggling in vain to release my grip on his throat. But it was far too late for him now, and I glared into black eyes that slowly glazed over. His body slumped backward, and when I loosened my fingers I saw that I had broken multiple blood vessels on his neck.

I spat an icy globule of saliva upon his face and stood up, realizing suddenly that I had killed a man, and that it had been the first time. I looked from his corpse to my cousin, who had twisted onto her side, groaning softly. Her back was facing me, dark blood pooling around the shaft of the spear. The bastard had likely pierced her heart, and a sense of dread washed over me. I raised my eyes to the other man who stood in the brush with his own spear in hand, his expression clearly implying that he would rather run than fight. But rage churned in my veins, stoking my element's power, and I took one step toward him, clinking my icy fingers together in an ominous fashion. "So. Do you still think it's wise to fight a Teuton?"

I could tell that he understood me, though the one who had stepped out from the trees first had not. He hesitated one more second, looking again at me, then at the one I had killed. "No," he responded, his accent quite odd.

"Then get out of here, and tell your friends to leave the boy alone."

The man nodded fearfully at me, hitching up his belt around his brightly colored robes, and dashed away. I watched him go for a count of five, trying to pull my element back just a little and calm my racing heart. Part of me feared to confront what had happened to my cousin, for I knew that rubbing alcohol and gauze would do no good against a stab wound of that magnitude. But I had to find my courage and go to her, to let her know that she was not alone.

My stomach twisted when I saw that the spear's blade had passed through her torso completely. Its grimy edge protruded just below her left breast, the front of her dress stained with ever-increasing crimson. I fell to my knees before her, a deluge of guilt destroying all of my dreams. "Beth," I choked on her name, a solid lump forming in my throat as I reached for her right hand. "Oh . . . Beth . . . I'm . . . sorry . . . ." The words came in Bayerisch; I could not recall any other language. My eyesight blurred, and tears of ice seeped from my eyes. I had brought her here, and now she would die. I had caused my cousin's death.

Shallow pants breezed from her lips, her brown eyes roving around vacantly, all of the color having drained from her face. Her entire body shivered, in shock, and I clasped her hand to my chest, the prominence of my ice likely doing little to ease her suffering. I whispered meaningless gibberish to her and stroked her forehead with my free hand, wishing that I could undo the events of the past hour. If I had drilled Joel more thoroughly on the concept of picturing the city of Muniche, this would not have happened. All of the adventures I had planned to share with my cousin had evaporated into smoke.

Beth's eyes finally seemed to focus on my face, her brows crinkling in what appeared to be hopelessness. A small cry broke from her throat, and she gasped more sharply as she choked out her final plea. "H . . . help . . . Joel . . . ." Her right hand had not returned my grip at all, but I felt it twitch, and then she exhaled one last time, her eyes darkening into a void. It consumed me like the currents of time, destroying my confidence. I moaned in anguish, bowing my head over her hand.

And then I felt it vanish from me.

I blinked against the icy tears that had caked my eyes, a sense of utter loss dragging me to the depths. *But she told you to help Joel,* I reminded myself, trying to get a handle on my tangled emotions. *You can't help him if you sit here bawling all day. You can grieve later. Now is the time for action.*

I pushed myself to my feet and focused on my element, awakening its full magic to enhance my senses and stamina. When I looked down at the place where Beth had fallen, I saw that naught but the spear and blood remained. Her body had vanished along with her bag. That must mean that the writings were true, that only Teutonic ritual suicide could send a time traveler into eternity. "Okay. Get it together," I told myself. I retrieved my bag and the Torstein from where they had fallen at the outset of my struggle, then paused for one final moment to look at the man I had killed. I knew that at some point I would have to face what I had done. It was wrong for a Christian to kill, so I needed to rescue Joel some other way.

I shut my eyes and stretched my icy spirit forth to scan the forest, searching for some way to escape this band of spear-wielding freaks. I felt four empty souls not far off, and I hoped that meant that Joel had somehow killed one of them. If he had died too, I would have to use the Torstein to send me home. My ice swept over innumerable trees, and finally I sensed a familiar presence—running water, a river nearby about the length of an American football field away. If I could get Joel there, I could use my ice to agitate its waters like I had done upon the Leutascher Ache, and we could escape.

As I raced for the sounds of conflict, using my ice this time to push me faster and give me endurance, another disquieting thought struck me. I had killed a man, and I had done it *in the past.* Did that mean I had changed something in history, or did it mean that I was supposed to be here, that I in fact had been fated to kill that man? A cold hand grasped my heart at that awful concept, for I had chosen to come to the year 1064, to spend two full years with my people before witnessing their demise. How many others would I kill, how many others would I change, how many would I ruin before I could leave? I whispered a silent prayer to God while I ran, that somehow I could influence at least one person in a positive way here in the eleventh century.

At last I came upon Joel and the other three men at the edges of the same clearing in which we had met them. One man lay still near a bush, bleeding from a deep gash in his throat. Joel had stolen that man's spear and now battled one of the others, each of them trying to outmaneuver the other, attempting to plant their respective spears home. The third opponent, to my consternation, was using Joel's distraction to his advantage. He crouched over Joel's bag, sorting through its contents with the hands of a professional thief. A frustrated scream escaped my lips, prompting all of them to pause, and I threw myself upon the scrounger, the man who had confronted us first. Since I had no other weapons ready for use, I dug my icy hands into his robes, into the flesh of his back, ripping as hard as I could. "Get *off* of our stuff, you scoundrel!" I screeched at him in Teutonica.

The man squealed and jerked. I leaped off his back and swatted him across the face when he turned to stare at me, leaving four bloody streaks. He yelled something at me in his own language, putting a hand to his cheek and looking around for his spear. I saw it first, lying nearby, and kicked it sharply into some brush. Then I let my claws loose on his robes, tearing them from his body, for I knew that he had pocketed some of our valuables from Joel's bag. The man cried out in rage as his clothing hit the forest floor, leaving him quite naked. He was ugly.

By this time, Joel had finally gotten the upper hand with his opponent, having knocked him senseless with the shaft of his spear. He raced over to where I was attempting to roll the leader's clothing into a bundle and jammed his spear into the man's back. He groaned, and the booted kick he had aimed at me fell short as he sank to his knees. Joel bent down to retrieve his bag, and I thrust the wounded man's bright clothing into his hands, scooping my bag and the Torstein up from the leaves where they had fallen. "Okay, we need to get out of here *now!*" I snapped at Joel, jumping to my feet once more. "And this time, make sure you keep up!"

Joel just stared at me as I adjusted the bag onto my right shoulder, gripping the Torstein in my left hand again and snatching his hand with my right. I dragged him into the forest, running in the direction of the river. "What happened to Beth?" he asked in a huffing voice. His green tunic was drenched with sweat. He had the man's clothing stuffed under his right arm, balancing it atop his bag.

I winced but knew that I could not hide the truth from him. "The other two attacked us while you were fighting with those three. One of them stabbed her in the back."

"What?" Joel ground to a halt, prompting me to do the same since our hands were joined. "Stabbed her in the *back?*"

I tugged on his hand, but he remained standing in place. "We need to keep moving. There could be more of them."

Joel dropped my hand, wriggling his own with an accusatory look. I noticed that his gauze bandage had disappeared at some point during the fray. "Wait. Did you move her to someplace safer or something? Is that where we're going now?"

I sighed and placed my hands against my temples, working to block terrible images from my brain. "We can't talk about this now, not if we want to get away from those freaks. I think they're Gypsies probably looking for new slaves."

"Swanie." Joel crept closer to me and bent his head down to look directly into my eyes. "Is my girlfriend dead?"

"Her body vanished, so technically, no. She's back in the twenty-first century. But we're here, and we need to keep moving."

Joel blinked at me, his cheeks going pale. "Wait . . . *what?*"

At that moment, a spear parted the brush behind us, embedding itself firmly into a tree trunk not two steps away. "Here they come," I announced, snatching his hand again. "Unless you've got an element I don't know about, *run*. I can't beat all of them myself." I set off in the direction of the river again. I could sense its waters flowing some thirty meters distant.

"I should have . . . brought some . . . arrows . . . ." Joel panted, obviously still exhausted from his earlier fight. He had a good point. I wished that we had been able to find a suitable bow and arrows for him before striking out on this journey. The one store we had visited back home had stocked only modern bows.

We reached the river's banks a few seconds later, poised on a hillock about a meter above a glorious expanse of light green. The river was shallow, but I watched its currents churn in response to my element, choppy ripples rising up to meet me. I called all of my ice out of my soul, disregarding what Joel might think, and wound my frozen fingers around his muscular arm in an unbreakable hold. I looked him straight in the eye and stated in no uncertain terms, "*Don't* let go of me." I sprang forward, my frozen shoes merging perfectly with the waters. Then I pointed my toes downstream, shooting that direction with the current. Joel yelled in horror, trying to tear his arm from my grip. "*Stop* fighting me, or you're going to die!" I roared at him, stretching my ice out behind us to arouse the river's currents. I wanted to be sure that the Gypsies could not follow our path.

I had had quite a few new experiences that day, I realized in passing while we flew down the river. I had killed someone with my element, and now I fled from an army of Gypsies, also using my element. Though I had danced upon both the Isar and the Leutascher Ache, I had never *fled* down the Isar or any other river for that matter. In some ways it was similar to dancing. I rode upon the water like I would during a dance, my feet barely wet, ice flaring out behind me. There was certainly glory in this, I could sense that, but there was no beauty. I made no ice sculptures in the water around me, nor did I bother to glide gracefully. This flying resulted from pure fear, and my element responded expertly to my bidding, pushing me faster, reinforcing my strength.

We had gone at least a kilometer downstream before I judged it safe enough to slow down and consider our options. Here I stood in the center of a river, an icy Teuton woman holding a total outsider out of the water. We were supposed to be in Muniche, but I had no clue where we were, or which river we rode. The presence of the Gypsies reassured me that we must be in Europe, particularly since one of them had understood the Teuton language. The color of the water beneath me was similar to that of an Alpine river, so I hoped that we were not too far from Muniche. About that time I caught sight of a large log floating a little farther downstream. "We're going to get on that log and decide what to do next," I informed Joel, who clung to my waist like a lost puppy, his hazel eyes wide.

Less than a minute later, we climbed onto the log, which looked to be the length of a house. It had probably come from one of those huge oak trees in the forest, I figured. At first I did not bother to fully observe the log, for despite my ice my endurance was nearly spent. I simply sank down upon it and placed my leather bag onto my lap, concentrating on abating my ice at long last. When my hands and hair had fully melted, my eyesight returning to its natural blurriness—so much for that pair of contacts—I grinned at Joel. He crouched at the far end of the log, slightly wet, panting and shaking his head. "So, what did you think of that?" I asked him, thinking that now we may actually have time for full explanations.

"I think I've gone insane," Joel answered, still shaking his head and staring down at the colorful robes and leather bag that he held. "I think I just rode an iceberg down a river."

I laughed out loud. "Is *that* what you think?" For some reason I found myself giggling, as though my subconscious wished to put off remembering Beth's fate for as long as possible.

Joel's eyes met mine for an instant before focusing on something behind me, alarm registering on his face. "I think we're not alone," he said.

Chapter Three:
Trapped

I frowned, recalling a vague memory of something occupying the downstream end of the log. I had assumed it was just a tangle of branches. Slowly, I turned my upper body around and discovered that Joel was right. Standing behind us at the edge of the log, leaning against a crooked branch that curled upward, stood a young woman no older than me. She wore ragged clothing similar to the Gypsies', stained with water and debris from the river, but her complexion was pale and her long hair a striking blond, shining golden in the brilliant sunlight. Her pale green eyes shone with fear and resolution, her arms brandishing a rather flat stick that she had likely been using as a paddle before we had disturbed her. When she saw me looking at her, she barked something at me in a menacing voice, shaking her stick.

Not again, I thought in despair, but I tried the traditional peacemaking tactic once more. Raising both hands, palms out, I stated slowly, "I'm sorry I don't speak that, but I do speak Teutonica."

The young woman's eyes widened, a bit of their fury dissipating. She lowered her stick just a little and said haltingly, "My Teutonica . . . is not very good."

Relief washed over me, and I gathered my courage, smiled at her kindly, and replied with a shrug, "Neither is mine."

The young blond woman nodded at my words and looked me over, casting her gaze briefly upon the still-crouching Joel, then back to me. At length she sighed, bringing her arms completely down, placing the base of her stick upon the log beneath her. "You are Teutons?" she questioned, sounding curious.

I turned my body a bit more toward her from where I sat on the log, wanting to appear courteous. Though I knew that Joel also had many questions for me, my instincts told me that I ought to finish befriending this young woman first. "I am a Teuton, yes," I answered cautiously, wracking my brain for a plausible eleventh-century explanation for Joel. At last, I jerked one finger in his direction and said, "He is from England and does not speak Teutonica."

The blond woman seemed to accept this without fuss, sitting down upon the log herself, laying her stick across her lap. "I am from the Rhineland," she told me, her words still sounding unsure.

Her strange dialect must be an old form of Rhenisch. "The Rhine is a beautiful river," I commented, and the young woman smiled at me, an almost wistful smile. I began to wonder how she had gotten here, on a log in the middle of a shallow Alpine river. Her countenance seemed so refined and so innocent. I figured I might as well tell her a portion of the truth about Joel and me, so I said, "We just escaped from some Gypsies. They attacked us further upstream."

Her green eyes darkened considerably, a frightened frown creasing her pale forehead. She glanced upstream herself, then drove her flattened stick toward the sandy river bottom, pushing our log forward. She met my gaze and murmured in a low voice, "I escaped from them also. I've been their prisoner for almost one year."

"Oh . . . ." That explained a lot. I turned around again to face Joel, who was pawing through the brightly colored robes from the Gypsy leader, retrieving food and the sock of jewels I had placed inside his bag before we had come. "Hey Joel, this girl here says she just escaped from the Gypsies, too," I told him, switching back to English. "She was their prisoner for about a year. I bet they were looking for her when they found us in the forest."

"That makes sense, I guess." Joel continued searching through the robes, not bothering to look up. "Maybe that's what these were for," he added, pulling a pair of iron fetters from the clothing.

The blond woman backed away at the sight of Joel holding the chains. She grasped her paddle tightly once more, likely fearing that we might consider returning her to her former captors. I waved at Joel frantically, indicating that he should cast the fetters into the river. "You don't want to scare her. Get rid of those."

"If you say so," Joel replied, dropping them into the water with great abandonment. A moment later he pulled a shiny knife from beneath the robes. "Hey, this is pretty nice." He held it up to the sunlight, studying every angle.

I rolled my eyes at him and turned back to the young woman, motioning for her to relax. "Just ignore him," I admonished her. "We won't send you back. We killed two of them ourselves."

Her green eyes widened with surprise, shooting from me to Joel and back again. "You fought them?"

"They attacked us first, and they killed my cousin. He was her betrothed." I gestured at Joel again, then shrank into myself a bit, wrapping my arms around the bag in my lap. Grief clawed at me afresh, and I shook my head and blinked, trying to hold back the tears that threatened to blur my vision further.

I felt a light touch on my left shoulder, and when I looked up, I saw that our female companion had moved much closer to me, sympathy shining in her eyes. "I'm so sorry," she said. "The Gypsies are a terrible people."

I did not know whether I agreed with her assessment or not, but I could not spurn the judgment of a former slave. I took several deep breaths as I tried to get my sorrow back under control, looking around at the trees lining each bank. Perhaps our companion may have a better idea as to where we were, for she may have heard the Gypsies discussing their location. I gestured back at Joel and said, "We should be in the Bavarian city of Muniche, but we ended up slightly off course."

"Ah, Muniche?" the young woman repeated, her eyes aglow with recognition, "It's just a day's journey downstream. This is the Isar. We will be there soon."

I sighed, satisfaction pulsing through my veins at long last. Thank goodness we had not ended up in some other European country, even though Joel had not thought of the city itself before we had leapt through the gates. We were not far away; soon we would be among my people. A shiver of nervous anticipation ran up my spine, and I turned partially around to regard Joel again. "We're actually on the River Isar right now," I informed him happily. "Muniche is just a short journey downstream of here. That's the best news I've heard all day."

"Excellent." Joel did not sound quite as thrilled as I felt, probably because he still had not received a full explanation from me. He was also likely thinking of Beth, for I had heard him sniff a few times as he pawed through the Gypsy's robes. Now he was in the process of stuffing all that he had found into his leather bag. "Should I keep these clothes or chuck them in the river?" he inquired, looking up at me with a grin that looked forced.

"I don't think they'd fit you," I observed. I recalled the image of the stout, naked Gypsy and failed to repress a snort of laughter. Joel guffawed in response, and I turned back to the young woman. She had moved back to the end of our log, her posture much more at ease now while she stroked her paddle into the water and out again. Favoring her with a friendly smile, I finally made introductions. "My name is Swanhilde, and this is my friend Joel."

The blond woman smiled back at me, a warm breeze brushing long locks of her sunshine hair across her face. "I am Freia," she answered.

I smiled and twisted back around to face Joel. His visage appeared unhappy, and he fiddled around with the strap of his bag, his eyes on the trees that bordered our path. "Hey Joel, you really don't have to worry about Beth," I assured him even though part of my brain had begun to doubt the writings. "When you travel back in time using the Torstein, you return in the same instant that you left. You don't age at all, and if you die in the past, you return—" I broke off, a terrible realization coming over me. I looked down at my left hand resting against the red-violet fabric covering my hip, gradually turning my palm upward. It was empty.

The Torstein was gone.

The cold hand of fear clutched my heart, and I closed my eyes, thinking back to everything that had happened since I last remembered holding the Torstein. I had picked it up from the ground when Joel and I had fled from the Gypsies. Somewhere between that clearing and here—a good distance down the Isar—the rock had sprung free. It had likely ended up in the river when I conjured the elemental storm upon its waters, and our chances of finding it there were slim to none. I had lost the ability to open the gates of time. I had lost our way out. We were stuck here now.

"Swanie? You're saying that when Beth died, she went back home? Back to that place by your gazebo?" I opened my eyes to regard Joel again. He favored me with a doubtful look, his hands now pressed against the bark beneath him.

"She did, if all of the writings about time travel are true. But we have a new problem. I screwed up. I really, *really* screwed up."

"What?" Joel's eyebrows came together, his tone thick with worry.

"I had the Torstein in *this* hand." I opened my left hand, wiggling its fingers at him. "I had it when we ran away from the Gypsies. I don't remember putting it anywhere else. I haven't opened my bag once since we got here. Now it's gone."

Joel looked even more confused. "The rock?" he asked.

I stared at him, tears welling up in my eyes again. "Yes. The rock is *gone*. It must have fallen out of my hand somewhere between the clearing and this log. And it was our only way back unless we want to follow Beth's example." I unclasped my bag to comb through its contents even though I knew that I had not put the Torstein there. Clothing, socks, jewels, blanket, thermos, contacts, solution, Bible, brush, soap, knife, camera, batteries, toilet paper, food packets. No mystical ruby stone. And Beth's bag had returned to the future with her, which meant that our vitamins were gone too, along with her sock of jewelry and the raisins and crackers.

"Are you saying," Joel began, pronouncing each word carefully, "that we can't get back to our own time without that rock?"

"Yes." The word barely escaped my lips. My voice trembled, and my tears spilled over as I choked, "I can't open the gates of time . . . without it. That's why . . . it was created. We . . . we're stuck here . . . ." I buried my face in my hands, my self-confidence taking an enormous hit.

Joel simply sat on the log in silence while I cried, apparently in shock himself. As I wiped my tears on the flared sleeves of my dress, working to get my emotions back under control, I heard him comment, "Well, that's just perfect. Guess I'm going to miss my flight back to Philly tomorrow."

"Really?" An irrational anger arose inside of me at his words, so irrelevant to the situation at hand. "Were you even *listening* to what I said? It doesn't matter how long we stay here in the grand scheme of things. We'll still go back to the same moment that we left, even if we're stuck here until we die of old age. I was planning on staying only until 1066, and now we might be here for the rest of our lives!"

Joel appeared thoughtful now, but all I could think of was the Torstein and how foolish I had been to lose it. I should have heeded the writings of that Black Priest Wolfgang in spite of his curse. He had warned time travelers to not go back further than the creation of the rock due to an escalated probability of losing it. I was an idiot, and now my stupidity had trapped both me and an innocent bystander a thousand years in the past. And my cousin had died an awful death less than an hour after our arrival.

"Hey, Swanie, look on the bright side," Joel advised as I dipped my fingers into the light green waters of the Isar, silently begging their chill to reassure me. I met his gaze, and he patted the bag on his lap. "At least you packed all this clothing and food, just what we would need," he noted, "and the jewels ought to help us out a lot once we get to Muniche. We could probably find some sort of work there . . . medieval work couldn't be so bad . . . maybe I could become a knight, if I can get a bow and arrows somewhere. I could protect you like a good lord." He winked.

His silly remarks made me snicker, and I wiped the final tears from my eyes and managed to smirk at him. "Are you going to try to woo some noble maiden by playing a lute outside her window?"

Joel cocked his head, dipping one hand into the river, then dampening his brow with its waters. "Well, I do play guitar, you know," he pointed out.

"I'm going to have to teach you to speak Teutonica if nothing else, or you'll never get by in a Teuton city," I reminded him. "Maybe that'll help you with your German." I raised one eyebrow at him.

"Or lack thereof," he appended, and I snorted. Maybe Joel belonged on this adventure after all. At least he was being a good sport about it.

When the sun sank toward the west that evening, Joel—who had ultimately taken over the duties of paddling the log—steered us toward the bank opposite of the Gypsies' camp so we could rest until morning. Though I knew that the section of the Isar upstream of the modern

München held little or no dangerous rocks or rapids, it would be far safer to continue our journey in the daylight, for the river could have changed quite a bit in a thousand years. We made camp several meters from the water underneath a group of tall evergreen trees. While Freia walked a wide circle in search of wild fruit, I opened both Joel's pack and mine, pulling out and unrolling the blankets so that we could sleep a bit more comfortably. Joel spent several minutes securing our log to the riverbank with a length of twine he had found amongst the Gypsy's robes. Then he climbed to where I worked on our campsite and muttered that he probably ought to light a fire. "Good thing I was in the Boy Scouts, or I wouldn't know how to do this," he said, sauntering off in search of dry sticks.

I emptied the contents of both of our sacks onto one of the blankets to help me remember what exactly I had brought. I refolded both of our extra outfits and placed them back into the bags, along with the underwear and woolen socks. I laid all three knives onto the blanket, deciding that we might as well be armed at all times in case we encountered Gypsies again. I set aside all of the remaining food—beef jerky, dried fruit, and peanuts—and took a swig from one of the metal thermoses, grateful that I had filled them with bottled water back at home.

I smiled when I found the digital camera at the bottom of my bag along with the extra batteries. After glancing around at our campsite and the riverbank, I decided to hold off on picture-taking until we reached Muniche. I should have snapped a few shots of the Gypsies, if they had not attacked us so suddenly. Though I did not take any snapshots, I did lift the camera from the bag and push the *on* button to assure myself that it still worked even though we were almost a thousand years in the past. It beeped its usual beep, and the green light clicked on, followed by the digital screen, showing the soft pine needles and tree roots of the forest floor. I turned the camera off and stashed it back in my bag, satisfied.

In Joel's bag I found the few items he had pulled from the Gypsy's robes. Along with the broad knife and his sock full of jewels, he had retrieved two gold chains, a rabbit's foot, and what looked like a set of olden Tarot cards. I rolled my eyes at this and determined to toss the cards and the foot into the fire once Joel got it going. We did not need to start messing with necromancy, especially since we had doubtless already bothered Wuotan by traveling to the past. The threatening tenor of his laughter haunted me as the landscape grew ever darker.

Joel eventually returned with a pile of branches and sticks in tow, dumping them in a stash beside where I had laid out the blanket. "This ought to do it. Now we just need to dig a pit so we don't burn the forest down," he said, taking up one of the larger branches to use as a shovel.

I watched him prepare the fire without speaking, the adrenaline overload from the day's events having left my system, filling me instead with a bleak emptiness. I had not expected my medieval adventure to start off with my cousin's death and the loss of the Torstein. Though my body and mind were weary, I knew that it would be a long and torturous night for me. Images of Beth's mortal wound and her brown eyes growing vacant would surely stalk my dreams.

Freia returned with a decent stash of wild fruit in her skirt, and I helped her distribute the food for dinner. Each of us had a handful of crab apples and wild cherries along with a bit of the dried beef and some peanuts. We drank only a small portion of the water since we had only two thermoses for all three of us. Freia remarked that the water tasted very fresh, and I made up an ambiguous tale about filling our bottles at a pristine stream early that morning.

Freia took the first watch that night since Joel and I were truly exhausted. Joel muttered to me that he felt like he had jet lag, for we had departed our century around ten-thirty and gotten here in the daylight. I agreed to take the final watch, and it took me a while to fall asleep, though I heard Joel start to snore almost instantly. My thoughts drifted from musing about Freia, a former slave, to Beth's dismal fate, to the looming fall of Muniche, and finally to Hans, the man I loved, the one I had left behind. Now that Joel and I were trapped in the eleventh century, when would I ever see Hans again? Would we still be able to relate to each other so well now that I had become a mad time traveler?

I awoke suddenly while the sky was still dark, panting from a nightmare in which I had taken Beth's place, feeling the agonizing stab of a spear stifling me, shackling my diaphragm. I sat up on the blanket and pressed a hand against my chest, trying to force my brain back to the present. Yes, I could breathe. No, I had not gotten stabbed in the chest. Yes, Beth was alive, back at home.

My eyes raked over the entirety of our campsite—Freia lay curled into a ball not far from where I sat, her blond eyebrows wrinkled in what looked like pain. I may not be the only one among us who suffered from nightmares. Then I looked to my left, to where the embers of our fire smoldered, and I saw Joel looking back at me, his face appearing concerned in the reddish-orange glow. "You okay?"

I rubbed my chest firmly and shut my eyes, counting slowly to ten in Latin. "Just a nightmare," I said at last, keeping my voice down. "I get those a lot."

"I had a scary one earlier," he disclosed, shifting around where he sat against a larch. "Went to visit Beth's grave, and the year of her death was listed as 1066."

A short laugh escaped me, and I shivered all over, standing up to get a good stretch. "She's not actually dead. If she had actually died, her body wouldn't have disappeared right in front of me. But it's gone along with her bag. There were more jewels and vitamins in her bag." I made a face and headed for where he sat beside the fire, noticing that he held the Gypsy's knife in his hand, his fingers stroking its blade in an absent-minded fashion.

"This wasn't really part of the plan, was it?" Joel looked up at me from where he sat, a wry expression crossing his face. A slight growth of facial fuzz had appeared along his chin, and I realized that I had not thought of bringing a razor for his sake. Out of the five Gypsies, four had sported beards, though, so maybe shaving was not the norm for men in this era.

"Plans never seem to go the way we hope," I said, gesturing for him to take my place on the blanket at Freia's side. "You might as well get some sleep. I need some time to cool down and think."

"An iceberg doesn't need to cool down," he joked as he climbed to his feet. I snorted quietly and eyed the embers. Now I had two outsiders under my charge, neither of whom could grasp all of the minutiae of our situation. I needed to unload most of the truth to Joel later on, but how much should I reveal to Freia?

Chapter Four:
Approaching Muniche

We arose shortly after sunrise and ate some more fruit before packing up and heading back to the river. Joel softly complained about the lack of coffee; he said that he had woken up with a headache. "Once we get to Muniche, we can find out how the locals deal with things like that," I responded, thinking again that I needed to learn a few things about herbal medicine while in the past, along with all of the Teuton secrets hidden away from the common people.

The radiance of the morning sun prompted me to think positively again. The weather was warm, the birds were singing, and it was obviously summer. Perhaps we would reach Muniche later that day and the next step of our adventure would begin. I had spent quite a bit of time thinking everything through early that morning, concluding that in spite of the Torstein's loss, hope remained for us yet. After all, we were bound for the greatest of the Teuton cities, Muniche—and its Keyholder was that noble Prince from our histories, Otto von Bayern. It had been he who had created the Torstein, and he also had discovered the organ song that could open the gates of time. If Joel and I could befriend him somehow within the next two years, maybe he would give up the secrets of his song so we could return that way. Of course, that would be a foolish plan if we remained commoners throughout our time in Muniche. Thus I resolved to present myself as an educated, noble-born lady who had come upon hard times, and I felt certain that Freia could do the same. That might give us a better chance to establish ourselves in the city, and perhaps we could someday gain an audience with the Prince himself.

Joel once again took up the position as rower, while Freia and I sat toward the front of the log as we drifted downstream. When I was not teaching Joel some useful statements in Teutonica—such as "hello," "my name is Joel," "I come from England," "my Teutonica is poor," "could I rent a room," "could I buy some food/beer," "are there nuts in this dish," "please," and "thank you"—I exchanged more words with Freia in a mixture of Teutonica and her own dialect, which shared quite a few similarities. I discovered that she had joined the Gypsies willingly but that afterward they had used her terribly. "Once we had gotten far enough away from my people, the Gypsies put me in chains like a dog," she told me, her comely face darkened by the memory. "They forced me to perform at many villages and manors, painted me like a heathen, ordered me to dance like a harlot. No one recognized me, and they abused me when I tried to speak out. They are a terrible people."

I shivered at her story, silently thanking God that He had rescued us from those heathens, even if it had meant committing murder. "I doubt all Gypsies are like that," I remarked, thinking of the few I knew in my own era. There had been one Gypsy girl in my high school, and aside from her occasional fantastic outfits, I had never noticed anything amiss.

Freia shook her head at me, negating my attempt to redeem them as a whole. "I'll never have dealings with them again," she stated shortly. "The Teutons are right about that." She glanced at me a bit uncertainly.

Her statement piqued my curiosity, and I wondered what my people were right about concerning the Gypsies. "Are those Gypsies going to stop at Muniche?" I asked her, considering the propinquity with which they had camped.

She shook her head again, brushing some of her hair back from her face, looking startled that I did not know. "Gypsies never perform at Teuton cities. They aren't welcome. That group passed by Augsburg a few weeks ago and did not stop. They're headed for Slavic lands." Her lips turned downward in a slight sneer.

Perhaps that explained why the Gypsy leader had reacted so strongly when I had asked him if he spoke Teutonica. But I frowned at Freia's words, knowing that while my people had never been the most tolerant, they were also not the most bigoted, at least regarding those they allowed to dwell in their communities. Teuton histories claimed that there had been both Jewish and Slavic sections in many of the ancient settlements. "Why aren't Gypsies welcome at Teuton cities?" I asked, honestly curious.

"You're a Teuton. You should know." Freia eyed me guardedly.

I thought fast, then gave her my best excuse. "I've been away from Teuton settlements for quite a while. I've forgotten many things."

She glanced toward Joel, who was ignoring us, then lowered her voice as she replied, "When you burned the fetish and the Tarot cards last night, I thought you knew everything. Gypsies practice sorcery; they do not worship God. The Teutons have been a Christian people for centuries, yet they still have their own . . . traditions." She paused, looking at me significantly, and continued, "You used your ice when you came to me on the log yesterday. That sort of sorcery is beyond what the Gypsies understand. They do not trust the Teutons. The Teutons, also, do not trust Gypsies, for they consider their sorcery to be divination"—she spoke the word in Latin, to my surprise— "and Teutons forbid such things, so it is said."

I had comprehended most of Freia's explanation, and it surely gave me a lot to think about. I had also caught her wary tone of voice as she discussed my people and their abilities, and I realized that I had to find out one thing from her, at least. Looking her straight in the eyes, I inquired, "And what's your opinion on Teutonic sorcery?" I hoped that she did not hold me in the same light as the Gypsies.

She kept silent for a long moment, breaking away from my gaze to look at the waters beneath our log, her expression pensive. At last, she raised her eyes to mine once more and answered in no uncertain terms, "It doesn't frighten me any longer. Abuse is far worse than sorcery."

Joel and I also exchanged several lengthy conversations in English while we drifted toward our goal. I finally explained our situation to him, and he listened closely, hardly interrupting even to interject a touch of humor. I described the Teuton tribe and their history as well as I could, noting that I had chosen to come to this particular era in order to see both the triumph and the downfall of the Teuton people. I had figured it would be a learning experience, I told Joel, especially since few people in modern Germany properly appreciated Teuton history.

I related the tales of Prince Otto von Bayern, the one who had discovered the methods of bending time. I also described the upcoming fall of Muniche, which had led to the Prince's mental breakdown and ultimate suicide. "We will likely see how having everything crumble in one's fingers drives a man insane," I concluded, beginning to consider for the first time what it would be like for Prince Otto when it came to pass. Though I was nowhere near as power hungry as the typical man, I could imagine the agony of such a defeat.

Joel nodded thoughtfully as he steered us down the River Isar with strong, steady strokes. "So, since this Prince Otto was the one who made the rock," he said at length, his eyes on the water, "and you say he also wrote some sort of song that made time travel possible"—he looked at me briefly, and I nodded—"maybe we could . . .

convince him . . . to share his song with us." His hazel eyes gleamed with possibilities, a rather nefarious smile spreading across his face.

I heaved a frustrated sigh, knowing that Joel had a lot to learn about the Teuton people. "*If* we ever get to see him, that is," I said. "We're commoners at this point, and I doubt we could get an audience with the Prince, even if we pawn all of our jewelry, which I'd rather not do. If we can find refuge with the nobility, we may end up meeting Prince Otto one day. *But* I strongly urge you, in spite of your self-confidence, to not try to force him to tell you anything." Half of my mouth quirked upward in a wry smile as I clarified, "He's a Teuton priest, a member of one of the strongest castes of Teutons. The priests are the ones who guard our traditions, who learn how to control all of the elements, who know all of our 'sorcery' as Freia calls it. A man has to go through torture to become a Teuton priest in the first place. If Prince Otto doesn't want to give us any information on his song, I doubt you or I could ever convince him otherwise."

Joel huffed, muttering something about witches and warlocks. "So I guess that means we're still trapped here unless we die," he translated.

"That's right, and I'm not really wanting to try that out just yet. And either way, we can't do Teutonic ritual suicide if we want to get back home alive." I had to explain the concept to Joel, who gawked at me, looking disturbed.

"So just because Prince Otto happened to find out the secrets of time travel, that means anyone who dies the way he did ends up bound for heaven or hell?"

"Something like that." I shuddered a little at the way he had phrased it. "Our best bet for getting back to 2000 would be to get Prince Otto's song. I'd honestly rather not attempt any type of suicide, just to be safe." Joel agreed and remarked that we may very well die in the upcoming battle if it held any similarities to what he had read in *Lord of the Rings.* I rolled my eyes at his apparent fascination with Tolkien's works and turned my attention back to Freia.

We ate an early dinner on our log when we saw that the forests beside the Isar had begun to thin out, interspersed now with cropland and grazing livestock. Several times we saw laborers in the distance, and once Freia pointed out a manor high on a hill surrounded by a low stone wall. Civilization was fast approaching, and I continued to rehearse our fabricated story in my mind. We were noble adventurers returning to Teuton lands after many years abroad. We sought asylum and were willing to learn any sort of necessary work or trade.

We began to encounter more and more small boats as we paddled on, most of them manned by fishermen. Joel tried to steer us clear from them as much as possible, not wanting to provoke any resentment or disturb their work. I suggested that they probably caught trout to sell at the manors and the city. Freia affirmed my assumption, adding perch and carp to the list. I told Joel that it was a pity I had not thought to bring the proper tools for fishing, or to catch some of the many geese and ducks we saw floating along the Isar as we drew nearer to Muniche. Overall, the fishermen ignored us when we passed through on our log. A few of them threw confused looks in our direction, and one of them called out to us in a rather plebian-sounding form of Teutonica, asking if our boat had sunk. I chuckled and advised Joel to wave at him companionably on our way by.

The sun had already set, the sky transitioning to a deep blue, when we first spotted the stone towers of Muniche in the distance. I rose up onto my knees to get a better look, not trusting my balance to allow me to safely stand. I invoked my ice into my eyes to sharpen my vision, taking in the extent of the ash-colored walls, built from solid stone, stretching at least twenty meters into the air. The turrets at each corner and above the gates stood higher than that, dotted with tiny windows and ornamented with curling walkways and ivy. Though I could not see the buildings of the city itself due to the height of the walls, I did catch a glimpse of several tall towers in the midst of its borders. One resembled the steeple of a cathedral, and the others looked like part of a castle, probably the Bayern fortress. A soft orange glow rose above the city as the night deepened, the light of countless torches and oil lamps assuring the weary traveler that life beckoned from within.

When we neared the closest corner of the city walls, my eyes picked out a drawbridge fast approaching, leading to the nearest gate into Muniche. I pointed it out to Joel, suggesting that he land our log for the last time close to the dirt road that followed the Isar to the bridge. He drew us up to the riverbank and held out his hand to help Freia and me dismount safely before retrieving our bags. "I doubt they'll let us enter the city this late at night, but maybe we'll find someone who can tell us where to find shelter until morning," I suggested.

Joel grunted, shouldering both leather bags with the comment that he had to start playing the role of the proper gentleman. Freia and I took the lead once we reached the road, walking together like good friends. Though her face betrayed just a hint of fear as we progressed, probably due to some wariness of walking outside of a city at night—and a Teuton one at that—she carried herself with poise and calmness, looking relieved that she drew near to freedom at last.

The certainty had begun to grow within me that Freia and I would become close friends before my time in the eleventh century was up. She was so beautiful and refined, kind and cheerful in spite of what she had been through in the past year. I wanted her to be my friend. While we walked that deserted road to the raised drawbridge, my element cautiously testing each shadow to ensure that no thieves awaited us, I began to consider what the repercussions would be if I told Freia that Joel and I were from the future. I wanted to know more about her, and it was only fair that I should tell her about myself in return. Would telling someone that I was from the future be counted as interference with history?

As we neared the place where the drawbridge of Muniche obviously rested when it was lowered, I saw what appeared to be a guard shack right at the edge of the river, with a light glowing in its window. I gestured at it pointedly and said to Joel, "Maybe the toll taker will lower the bridge for us."

"Toll?" Joel gave a silly smirk, one leather bag hanging from each of his shoulders. "How much is it going to be? I only have a couple bucks with me."

I rolled my eyes, wondering if he had actually stuffed some U.S. dollars into the pockets of his trousers. Then I turned to Freia with a serious question. "Do you think the toll taker would lower the drawbridge at this hour?"

Freia frowned thoughtfully, shaking her head, obviously well versed in the traditions of medieval cities. "Not after dark," she replied. "He may be able to give us some advice on where to safely spend the night, though. Bridge keepers usually know such things."

I nodded, and we stopped at the door of the small, wooden shack. I elbowed Joel, indicating that he should be the one to knock. He gawked at me in obvious disbelief, then stepped up to the door, dim light seeping through the cracks in the wood. He knocked sharply, twice, and called out "Hello?" in decent Teutonica. He glanced back at me, and I whispered the correct words for "Is anyone there?" slowly and distinctly. He repeated them, slurring the phrase a bit. I pursed my lips.

Footsteps sounded within the guard shack, followed by the noise of a latch being unfastened. A moment later, the door swung open inward, revealing a rather plump, friendly-looking man, about thirty, with brown hair and beard and shiny blue eyes. He wore a tunic and pants bearing some similarity to those which I had sewn for Joel. I congratulated myself silently on my success in style. His hands were thick, and from his belt there hung a rather formidable mallet. He looked at each of us in turn, quickly determining that we were travelers and posed no obvious threat. Then he asked in Teutonica as strangely accented as the fisherman's, "How may I help you?" training his gaze on Joel.

Joel stared blankly, and I realized that I would have to do all of the talking, though that may be improper for a woman. After choking out the words I had taught him earlier, "My Teutonica is poor," Joel gestured at me, and the toll taker's blue eyes locked with mine.

I took a deep breath, praying that I would sound articulate. "Forgive me. My companions have never been to a Teuton city before, nor are they familiar with our language," I began, speaking as properly as I knew how. "We have journeyed a long distance and seek refuge for the night. Could you grant us any assistance?"

I could tell from the toll taker's expression that he thought that my Teutonica sounded as strange to him as his did to me. He recovered himself quickly, however, and bowed at me, the symbol of medieval propriety. "I should be able to help you, my lady, although I can't lower the bridge for you at this hour without official permission."

I waved my hand dismissively. "That is quite all right, but my companions and I would like to enter the city in the morning, if possible. How much does it cost to make the crossing?" I asked, glancing at his mallet, knowing that he likely wore it to discourage toll evaders.

"Only two *Thaler* to enter Muniche, my lady," he responded, bowing again. "To exit it is free. Each gate charges the same fee."

Thaler must be the local currency, I figured, and I wondered what the toll taker would think if we paid him with one of the Gypsy's gold chains. It may be worth a shot. He looked like an honest man; I could see it in his pleasant expression. "Hey Joel, get one of those gold chains out of your bag," I told him, then turned back to the toll taker. "Would you allow us to pay you in advance?" I asked, speaking the words *in advance* in Latin, as a test. I heard Freia give a quiet gasp beside me.

The toll taker's eyes bugged and he took a step back, especially when he saw the golden chain that Joel had pulled from his bag. "Oh, my lady, I could not," he said, the words tumbling out. "My boss would have my neck. If you'd like somewhere to stay for the night, take that road to the first manor over the hill." He pointed one thick finger at the crossroads beyond us, jerking it toward the southeast. "My wife's uncle owns that estate. His name is Count Helmut von Meldorf. Tell him Garin Zeuner sent you. He certainly will let you stay the night."

I nodded and indicated that Joel should put the gold chain back into his bag. "Thank you kindly for your help, Mr. Zeuner," I said brightly, dropping a quick curtsey. "We'll gladly relate the tale of your graciousness to the count, should we meet him this night. Thank you." I ducked my head and stepped toward the crossroads as Freia and Joel echoed my thanks. The toll taker nodded at us as we left, replying profusely that no thanks were required, wishing us safety and a comfortable evening.

Moments later, the three of us entered the path to the Meldorf estate, and I filled Joel in on the majority of my conversation with the toll taker. He complimented me, saying that I had handled myself well, and I commented that everyone we had met so far around Muniche seemed to speak with a strange accent. As the flickering lights of the manor appeared over the hill, I gave a contented sigh, looking forward to a restful night before confronting the issues of tomorrow.

Chapter Five:
Count Helmut von Meldorf

Morning broke bearing the gray skies of impending rain, and I arose rather late from my slumber, having slept decently in spite of the lumpy bed I had been given. When we had knocked upon the count's door the previous night, a male servant opened the door, the count himself having already retired for the evening. The servant, a withered old sort holding a melting candlestick in one hand, had accepted my explanation concerning Garin Zeuner without a second look. He invited us in and served us mint tea and flatbread before calling a maid to guide us upstairs to our quarters. Freia and I had taken one guest room, while Joel occupied the smaller one beside it. Before we said goodnight, Joel and I devised a signal involving several sharp knocks on the connecting wall. He insisted that he was not about to go downstairs alone the next morning. "I don't want to have to talk to anybody without you there to translate," he said.

Our room included two thin beds with coarse blankets and mattresses that felt like they were stuffed with straw and wool, quite unlike the beds I had become accustomed to in the twenty-first century. An empty wardrobe occupied one corner, with a table and washing basin resting nearby. A chamber pot sat beside the table with its accompanying rag—just one, so I would have to share it with Freia. The idea of that had disturbed me at first, for I had faithfully used my roll of toilet paper during our journey downriver. But while lying in bed the previous night, I had realized that I had no clue how she had wiped over the past two days. Had she used leaves, the river water, or part of her dress? It was high time to start assimilating with society, so when I woke that morning, I used the chamber pot and its rag without complaint, though my squeamishness likely showed on my face.

A fireplace stood against the outer wall of our room, flanked by a window with a view of the count's fields. I headed there after relieving myself and invoked my ice into my eyes to sharpen my vision. I saw quite a few peasants at work in the fields, some tending sheep, others harvesting some type of grain. I smiled at the sight and then glanced back at the room behind me, wondering vaguely where my Rhenish companion had gone. I stretched and yawned, looking forward to meeting the count that day and finding out more about my people as well as life in Muniche in general. My qualms about being trapped in the past had begun to dissipate even further at the knowledge that in two years, Muniche would fall to the Saxons. Joel had already hinted that we may not survive the siege, and he was probably right about that. Though that sort of death frightened me, I took comfort in the fact that sooner or later, we would escape this primitive realm into which we had fallen.

Freia reentered the room while I sat at the window, having clothed herself in one of the two extra dresses I had brought in my pack. I rose to my feet and turned to face her, and she greeted me with a smile and a friendly "Good morning" in her native Rhenisch. She had brushed out her gorgeous blond hair, which hung down almost to her waist; the light green fabric of the dress and head covering she wore matched her eyes almost exactly. I smiled back at her and stretched again, then said good morning in

Teutonica, commenting that she looked a lot more relaxed in my dress than she had in the Gypsy clothing.

"I'm going to throw those rags in the cooking fire this morning," Freia told me, her green eyes drifting to where they lay in a colorful pile by the door. "Your dresses may be a bit flimsy, but they're much better than a slave's clothing."

"If we can buy some decent fabric, I'll sew both of us some better dresses," I promised, retrieving the other extra dress from my bag, one of deep blue linen. I washed my face and hands at the basin after clothing myself, noticing that one of the servants must have brought in fresh water while I slept. After running my brush through my tangled black hair and adjusting my clothing as well as I could, I put on another pair of socks with my shoes and took a good look around the room, the familiar veil of blue still enhancing my vision.

Freia stood near the window, gazing out at the cropland with a contented expression. I suddenly realized that since we were free, she would probably wish to return home to the Rhineland as soon as possible. Sadness gripped my heart at the likelihood of losing my potential best friend of the eleventh century so soon. I sighed and crossed the wooden floor to where she stood. "Well, I guess we might as well go out and meet the count, so Joel and I can find out how to become citizens of Muniche," I said, a bit of melancholy tingeing my voice. "And you can probably find someone to take you back to the Rhineland."

Freia replied shortly, without looking at me, "I'm not going back."

I started in surprise, tilting my head at her. I remembered the longing in her eyes when I had mentioned the beauty of the Rhine that first day on the log. I had simply assumed that she would want to return. "Why not?" I asked, curiosity overtaking me while I contemplated why a young woman with such a pure and innocent countenance would not want to go home.

Freia turned from the window to favor me with a tragic smile. "My father is the ruler of the village of Eisenwald on the Rhine," she related quietly in her mixture of Rhenisch and Teutonica. "I'm the eldest of three daughters. He has no sons, and he wished to marry me to a man who could take his place one day as the ruler of our settlement. I ran away with the Gypsies a year ago because I couldn't bring myself to marry the man he chose." Her sad eyes searched mine for understanding.

My eyes widened, and I took one step toward her. "What sort of man did he chose?" I asked, fearing the worst.

"A young man, one aspiring to greatness," Freia responded, her expression downcast. "He wanted me for nothing more than my beauty and my position. He never would have truly loved me, and I don't want to marry a man who would use me and destroy everything I love for his own glory." She paused and shook her head with a sigh, looking frustrated with herself. "I suppose I am ridiculous. Marriages are made for convenience, not love. But I'd rather not be forced into something so permanent when my instincts tell me it could never be beautiful."

Freia and I had more in common than I had realized. I knew that I would have done the same thing had I been in her shoes, so I confided to her softly, "I've had the same problem. Where I come from, my father is very rich, and I've lost count as to how many foolish boys have tried to woo me just because of that." Our eyes met, and Freia nodded at me in agreement. "I'm not going to marry some fool who wants me only for money and power," I said.

"What about your cousin?" she queried, her eyes drifting toward the far wall adjacent to Joel's bedroom. "Was her betrothal arranged?"

I chewed on my bottom lip, images of Beth's demise resurfacing in my brain. Thankfully I had slept a dreamless sleep for once, but I knew that what had happened to her would haunt me for countless nights. "Not exactly," I said, not wanting to fabricate a complicated lie about my background just yet. "It's a really long story, and maybe someday I'll be able to explain it all. I need to wake Joel up, though." I walked over to his wall and rapped out the code we had agreed upon, closing the issue of Joel and me and our rather unprecedented appearance in the forest.

We met Joel in the hallway soon afterward, and he admitted with a smirk that he had poked around in the other upstairs rooms earlier that morning. He had come upon a small collection of girls knitting sheep's wool in a chamber at the far end of the hall. "I told them I couldn't speak Teutonica, and they all giggled at me," he said, sounding as though he had found that amusing.

"Well, this is a medieval manor, so the kids probably get roped into working as soon as they can handle a sewing needle," I guessed, looking to Freia as we descended the stairs. "Did you talk to any of the servants this morning?" I asked her in Teutonica.

"I talked a little with the head housekeeper. Her name is Ulka, the bailiff's wife. She told me that the main meal is served in the great hall downstairs at Sext."

"Sext?" I did not understand the term, but I did recall Beth saying that most people ate only two meals per day in the Middle Ages.

Freia gave a short nod. "Yes. We'll still be early, even though you slept late."

Eventually we made our way to the great hall, a dining room much larger than any of the parlors in the Thaden house. One long table flanked by benches stood at the center of the room, and oil lamps hung at intervals from the rafters, casting the hall in a cozy glow. There were two empty fireplaces on either side of the hall, halfway between the entrance to the main house and the far end. Tapestries of various colors, interwoven with threads of silver and gold, hung from the walls; and at the far end, near the kitchen doorway, stood what had to be the count's chair. It looked to be made of larch inlaid with gold, standing regally at the head of the table, apart from the benches that lined either side.

Freia breezed off toward the kitchen with her colorful robes in tow. I caught the sleeve of Joel's tunic before he could follow her. "She's getting rid of her slave's clothing," I explained in a low voice. "And I'm going to have to figure out how to get some more outfits since we have only three between us."

"Ah," Joel answered, his hands on his hips as he looked around the hall. "Where do you think we're supposed to sit?" The room was empty at the moment aside from the two of us, but an instant later the elderly servant we had met the previous night drifted in from the doorway behind us. He greeted us politely and indicated that we should sit beside the count's chair, for he always exchanged news with any noble travelers.

"We're going to have to make up some sort of news," I muttered to Joel as I sat down to the right of the chair. "I'm going to try to convince the count that we're nobility, so wish me luck."

"Tell him I lost my family estate to the Danes," Joel said with a grin, pulling a knife from his trousers, using its tip to probe at a hangnail. More people began to settle upon the benches, all of them clad in the muted colors of peasantry: browns, grays, and dull blues. "Do you think he's going to be like Count Dracula or something?" Joel went on, wincing and shaking his hand out. I saw that he had wrapped his left palm with a fresh batch of gauze.

"This isn't Transylvania," I said, elbowing him good-naturedly. "And he owns a *farm*. He'll probably be more like Old McDonald. Careful what you use that knife for, though. You might need it for the meal." I had abruptly recalled that forks were not a thing in medieval Bavaria.

"Did you bring yours?" He eyeballed me in an accusatory fashion, and Freia appeared behind me, brushing one hand against my left shoulder before sitting on the opposite side of Joel.

I had forgotten my knife back in the room, but I had no time to consider that now, for the count had finally entered the hall. He exchanged brief words with a servant or two on his way to the head of the table, his appearance reminding me of those old photos of Paul von Hindenburg during World War I. Though he had a full beard and was not quite as fat, the count's face looked just as serious and withered, his whitish hair cut almost in the same style, his sharp blue eyes piercing. He wore a long, multi-colored tunic hanging over dark leather trousers, held up by a massive belt with an intricate brass buckle. He nodded at the three of us in full propriety when he reached his chair and introduced himself as Count Helmut Friedrich von Meldorf. The three of us stood and said our names in turn, Joel stumbling slightly over the correct phrase. Then the count waved us to our bench and sat down himself, declaring with a knowing glint in his eye that the full meal would be served soon.

The meal began with a salad consisting of lettuce, cabbage, onions, radishes, herbs, and vinegar, all of which tasted as though they had been freshly harvested. Mead was the beverage of choice, and I found it sweeter than expected, though I caught its slight twist of alcohol. I remembered Joel's headache from the previous day and wondered whether the constant offerings of alcohol would help his body transition away from caffeine. *We're all going to be alcoholics whether we like it or not,* I thought to myself, not particularly happy with that idea. I hoped that I could handle it maturely like my father.

The main dish consisted of chicken stew spread out over slabs of unleavened bread. Joel, Freia, and I ate in silence for the most part, as I tried to negotiate using only a spoon for such a dish. Count von Meldorf made a few comments about the weather, the summer crops, and the fact that he had not entertained travelers in over three months. "That obliging nephew-in-law of mine, Garin Zeuner, has the tendency to send all of the respectable latecomers my direction once the gates to Muniche have closed for the night," he remarked, the ends of his mustache turning upward into a rather tolerant smile. "He knows quite well that there's an inn further down the Isar, but it's no matter. Since his judgment of people's character tends to be accurate, my servants have been instructed to allow such occasional guests to stay the night and meet me in the morning to exchange news." The count's blue eyes gleamed with interest, and I had the feeling that he did not get out much due to his age and physical condition—somewhat overweight.

Joel nudged me when the count had finished speaking, requesting a rough translation, his mouth full of bread. I gave him a dirty look and said, "I can't just keep translating everything bit by bit, if you really want to learn Teutonica. You'll have to wait until we're done. And quit talking with food in your mouth." Before Joel could reply, I addressed the count. "Unfortunately, my lord, we may not be bearers of entertaining news, though we have journeyed a great distance. I also wish to apologize that I must be the one to address you. Joel neither speaks nor understands Teutonica, and Freia's grasp on our language is tenuous." I nodded at each of them when I expressed regret for their lack of comprehension. Joel favored me with a sour look, probably guessing what I had said.

Count von Meldorf tilted his head at my words, taking a copious swig from his goblet before commenting rather pointedly, "Your accent, Miss Swanhilde, is one I have never heard before, though your Teutonica is good."

Apparently I would be hearing that comment quite often and reading it on the faces of everyone with whom I spoke. I determined then and there to somehow rid myself of my "strange accent" during my time in the eleventh century. Once Joel and I returned home, I could shock Hans with my new take on the Teutonic dialect. I apologized to the count again and explained that I had been away from Teuton lands for some time and had forgotten many things. I told him that Freia was from the Rhineland, while Joel had been born in England. "All three of us are hoping, my lord, to find refuge in Muniche for a few years," I added, "and we would like to obtain employment there, if needed." I eyed the count covertly over the rim of my cup, watching his reaction.

Count von Meldorf's grizzled face took on a hue of surprise. His eyes drifted to Joel, then back to me. "Are all three of you skilled laborers, Miss Swanhilde?" he inquired quizzically, stroking his beard with the fingers of his left hand, which were adorned with several golden rings.

Now the test would come. I knew that we were not dressed as laborers, for none of the servants around the tables wore colors as vibrant as ours. I chewed on a bite of chicken while I considered what sort of background I should fabricate for myself and my two companions. Then I met his gaze, silently praying that I would sound articulate. "Actually, my lord, I am of noble birth, though I lost my relatives long ago," I stated carefully, ordering myself to remember every part of my story, for I would likely have to tell it again later, not altering events. "My family name is von Thaden. I have spent quite a few years traveling and have garnered some skill in the trade of sewing." I broke off and stared down at what remained of my stew, feeling our host's intense eyes heavy upon my face. I had to impress him somehow, make him believe that I was indeed of noble birth in spite of my strange accent. Struck by a sudden inspiration, I raised my eyes to the count's once more and said in Latin, "I read and write both Latin and Teutonica, and I have some knowledge of music and history."

The count's cerulean eyes sprang open, and he opened and closed his mouth several times before admitting in a low voice, "I do not speak Latin . . . my lady."

A triumphant smile broke across my face. Count von Meldorf had addressed me as someone more than a commoner! I repeated my last sentence in Teutonica, and he shook his big head a bit, stirring in his chair. "Although I am lord of this estate and could have gained education in my youth, I have always preferred the work of the field and left the writing to others." He flexed his wrinkled hands and confided, "These ancient fingers of mine can hardly grip a pen after so many years of pulling the plow." His expression was wry, his tone slightly ashamed.

Something occurred to me at that moment, when I looked upon the elderly farmer, the lonely manager of a medieval estate, the lord of quite a few vassals. He did not seem quite as harsh as his face suggested. He was a Teuton; I could see it in his eyes, and I had to know. "Are you earth?" I asked him abruptly, my decorum failing me at last.

Count von Meldorf jerked a bit in his chair, likely taken aback by my direct query. Then a slow smile gradually appeared beneath his mustache. "That I am," he affirmed, looking pleased that I had figured it out. "And you, my lady?"

I smiled back shyly and replied, "I am ice," breathing out a frigid puff of air to illustrate. He chuckled and lifted his goblet to his lips again as I added, "Freia and Joel are not Teutons, only me. Freia, also, is of noble birth. Her family rules a small settlement beside the Rhine." I decided not to name the town, for fear that Freia would think I had said too much. She could say more about herself later, for that matter, for her Teutonica was not nearly as faulty as she had led me to believe that first day. "Joel comes from a wealthy family in England," I went on, "many of whom boast excellent skills with the bow and arrow." Joel should appreciate that. Anyone who could skewer a squirrel through the brain must be good at archery, so I hoped that he had not exaggerated that tale.

The count nodded thoughtfully, looking from one of us to the next, seeming to consider our possibilities. Eventually he leveled his gaze upon me and said, "The young man could certainly find some sort of labor in Muniche, whether it be with the smiths creating weapons or perhaps with the hunters or soldiers. As to your own fate, my lady, and that of the Rhenisch lady, I might have a few ideas of my own. Before any of you could find permanent positions in Muniche, however, you would have to meet with the city council." He eyed me with a severe stare when he stated this, his expression calculating.

I nodded at Count von Meldorf, accepting his words, a small germ of anxiety settling within me at the concept of confronting the medieval council—and likely Prince Otto himself. "Then we will meet the council, my lord, whenever they deem it proper. However, I should pray that they would realize that in dealing with the three of us, they deal with only one Teuton and two outsiders. Hopefully that may convince them to treat us with greater leniency." I cocked my head at our host.

The count raised his bushy eyebrows and replied, "That remains to be seen, my lady. I will send word to them today that three newcomers wish to join our city. Until they can meet with you, all of you may stay here."

Chapter Six:
The Meldorf Estate

The three of us did not meet the Teuton Council of Muniche until two weeks later due to rainy weather and Freia's health. On our second day at the estate of Count von Meldorf, she caught a nasty flu and spent over a week trying to recover. The count brought a doctor from the city in to see her several times, but whether his ministrations helped was debatable. The doctor, an elderly hunchback with wild gray hair and a small beard, bled Freia using leeches three times and gave her herbs and honey, allegedly to aid in rebuilding her strength. The whole thing disgusted me completely. I felt that bleeding should be done with a knife rather than with a parasite when it needed to be done at all. But I could voice no objections, since I knew nothing about local medicine, so I simply sat at Freia's bedside during most of her illness, caring for her as best as I could.

We exchanged more stories while she gradually convalesced, and I learned that she too could read and write Latin, though not the vernacular. She had spent several years at a convent in her childhood, which was where she gained her education. She could also sing and play some sort of primeval flute or recorder, and she admitted that she loved music because it held such passion, such emotions that could not be expressed any other way. We had quite a few things in common, as it turned out.

When the heavy rains had finally passed, I took a walk through the count's land with Joel, who had been outside on several occasions already to help out in the gardens. We browsed the kitchen garden first, just steps outside the pantry. I recognized the majority of vegetables there—lettuce, cabbage, onions, garlic, radishes, leeks, lentils, parsnips, peas, and beans. Its various offerings were arranged in neat rows enclosed with wattle fencing adorned with creeping ivy. "This whole setup's a lot more extensive than my dad's garden at home," Joel told me, "but it boggles my mind that they don't grow corn. The American staple hasn't made it here yet."

I chuckled and ran my fingers along the climbing leaves of the green bean plants. "No potatoes yet, either, or pumpkins. But I've been gaining new appreciation for some of this other stuff lately. When was the last time you ate a parsnip?"

"Probably never?" Joel laughed and beckoned me to the herb garden.

There we encountered an extensive supply of culinary herbs like mustard, sage, parsley, mint, dill, and fennel. These plants grew adjacent to the kitchen garden, while medicinal herbs and vegetables were cultivated further away. "I know the Teutonic names for pretty much all of this," Joel commented as I picked out things like savory, rosemary, peppermint, chamomile, feverfew, dusky spurge, beet, and lemon balm, along with many other plants I did not recognize.

"Did you find out how they use each of these herbs?" I asked Joel, who was in the process of reciting a long list of Teutonic words, some of which I had never heard before. "I know chamomile can help you sleep, but what about the rest?"

Joel shrugged one shoulder and brushed some hair back from his face. Its color appeared much lighter under the brilliant summer sun. "My Teutonica isn't that good yet. You thinking we need to become apothecaries or something?"

"Well, if we don't, we might get bled by that weird doctor the count brought in for Freia. What about fruit? We've had cherries with lunch a few times already."

I trailed Joel out of the herb gardens and around toward the southern side of the house, where the count's gardeners tended a relatively small vineyard. "They don't grow grapes to sell, just to make into vinegar and jam," he noted.

"How'd you figure that out?" I asked, watching two women harvesting small batches of red grapes.

"Just by the size. Have you taken a look at the grain fields yet? This place is huge, honestly. The count must employ a couple hundred people."

We passed through a glade of apple and pear trees, weaving hedges of raspberry and blackberry bushes rounding out the estate's fruit offerings. I introduced Joel and myself to the beekeeper, a bald middle-aged man named Gideon. He gave an enthusiastic rundown of what went into the honey harvests, and I smiled, certain that a good bit of the Meldorf honey ended up as mead. That seemed to be the most common drink after beer, which the count ordered by the barrel from one of two breweries within the city limits. He had a trade agreement with the brewery nearest to his estate; he gave them part of his barley and spelt harvest in exchange for their finished product.

Joel and I began walking along a small stream that marked the border of the count's property after taking our leave of the beekeeper. The stream looked about a meter across, trickling over stones on its western course toward the Isar. "I saw almond trees back there along with the others," I remarked, wondering whether he would be willing to discuss his tree nut allergy with me. I saw him cringe a little, but I pressed on. "That's something you'll have to watch out for in the food here, once the nuts are in season. They might put them in the bread."

"Yeah I know," Joel sighed, sounding incredibly unhappy. He glanced at me for half a second, then shifted his gaze to our path ahead, to where a lone tree grew beside the stream, its branches dotted with ripening cherries. "I'll have to talk to the cooks about it. I don't want them to have to not use almonds at all just for my sake."

"Are you allergic to any other tree nuts or just almonds?" I asked, curious.

Half of Joel's mouth turned downward in a frown, and he scratched at the growth on his chin. He had already decided to stop shaving so that he could blend in better with everyone else. "It's mainly almonds. That's the first one that put me in the E.R. as a kid. They tested me for the others, and the only ones I reacted to were pecans and walnuts. But peanuts are fine. And I've eaten roasted chestnuts a few times, too."

"I'll talk to the cooks when we go back inside and try to explain why almonds are bad for you," I pledged, not wanting Joel to have to worry about his allergy. "You still have all the EpiPens, right?"

Joel gave a scoffing noise and reached up to snatch a crimson cherry from a branch as we passed beneath its tree. "Yeah, now I finally get why Beth told me to bring so freaking many of them. I don't know why you two didn't just tell me the truth from the start. We could have prepared better." He chewed on the cherry and spat out the seed.

"Yeah, I know," I said, blinking back the tears that threatened to well up in my eyes. I had decided to wear contacts in order to properly appreciate the extent of our host's land, and I did not want to waste another pair due to an emotional ice storm. "It was my fault mainly. I figured it'd be too much for you."

"Hey, cut me some slack, I know a little bit about time travel," Joel said in a jesting tone, jostling my right shoulder playfully. "I watched *Back to the Future* as a kid.

And my mom loves the *Outlander* books. Those involve rocks, too."

I rolled my eyes and shoved him back. "Standing stones are awful big rocks. This is the real deal."

"I know. And I'm just thinking it's going to be hard to watch all these really cool people die in two years." Joel frowned, looking toward the hillcrest ahead that led toward the small pond that fed the count's water mill. His mill was not a large one; his serfs ran it only part of the year to break his spelt and barley down to flour. The Meldorf estate ran a much more extensive threshing floor for the flax. Our host had mentioned that he sold linen in the city several times per year.

Joel had a good point, and it was one that I did not particularly like to ponder, especially when I thought about Freia. She had forsaken her own people for the Teutons; during her sickness she had asked me more than once whether I had heard back from the city council yet. I sometimes wondered whether she believed that the Teuton people could shield her from all harm, after having seen me zooming toward her on the Isar like a winter goddess. But our days were numbered, and I began to consider how to break the news to Freia, whether I dared to do so. I did not want her to die on my account.

Once we had stayed with the count for a full week, I offered him one of the Gypsy's gold chains as payment for the trouble. At first he refused to accept it, but after I reminded him that soon, the three of us would have to buy some proper attire, food, and other necessities in the city and that none of us had any of the local currency in our possession, he agreed to take the chain as a loan and give us a bit of money in return. Shortly afterward, Joel struck out for Muniche with twenty Thaler in his pockets, determined to find out what he could about our new home, even though he spoke no Latin and just a smattering of Teutonica. I advised him to be careful and not anger anyone, requesting that he bring back a full report.

Joel returned late in the evening, around twilight. The count had ordered soup and tea to be prepared upon his arrival, and I sat alone with Joel in one of the parlors while he sipped his soup, excitedly soaking in everything he had discovered about Muniche. He had walked up and down almost every street, he claimed, concluding that the walled part of the city covered nearly one square mile, with a gated entrance at each of the four points of the compass. He had seen business booming on the streets, the merchants hawking more items than he could remember, from food and drinks to fabrics, jewelry, furniture, pottery, tools, utensils, flowers, musical instruments, and weapons. He noted that he had come upon one ragged woman whose small shop was filled to the brim with brooms. "I think she was a witch," he said with a grin. "She had a black cat sitting at the doorway of her shop."

I rolled my eyes at his comment and cracked a dull joke, "Maybe we'll see her flying over the wall on a broomstick on Halloween night," which prompted Joel to laugh outright, spluttering in his soup. I gestured for him to continue with his tale, sitting on the edge of my seat as he described the many houses he had seen, the peasants driving domesticated animals to and fro, the carts pulled by donkeys and horses, and the grime lining the gutters of each street. He commented that he thought both people and animals did their business in the gutters, stating that it did not seem very sanitary. I suggested that perhaps a few of the very poor people cleaned the gutters every night and took all the waste to a dump somewhere outside the walls. "After all, there would be mountains of crap in the streets if they weren't cleaned every night," I said, and Joel agreed. "We may be better off staying on the Meldorf estate if the count doesn't mind. At least the manor has a latrine."

"And a bunch of chamber pots," Joel reminded me with a wink.

Once Joel had finished his soup and handed the empty bowl to one of the count's servants, we went outside to the expansive front porch that overlooked the count's front gardens, which were primarily populated with flowers. Most of the actual farming went on behind the manor. "So, did you see a big church or cathedral in the city?" I asked

Joel as we situated ourselves on one of the porch benches. "I know when we were floating down the Isar, I saw some tall spires."

"Yeah, I saw a couple churches, actually, and one was pretty big, although not quite big enough to consider it a cathedral," he replied, gazing out toward the road with a faraway look in his hazel eyes. "I think it might have a monastery attached because I saw some guys dressed in brown robes, clean-shaven, with their hair cut like monks. That church had a giant steeple but no clock. I guess clocks haven't been invented yet."

I nodded. "I think in the eleventh century everyone just uses sundials and the church bells. Like how the daily meals are at Sext and Vespers. It'll be kind of nice not being slaves to the clock anymore." I smiled thoughtfully at that concept.

"We'll be slaves to the sun instead," Joel said, "and in the summer that will mean long hours." I frowned in disappointment, knowing that he was right, my dreams of primitive tranquility with no clocks shattering to the ground at the idea of lengthy summer working hours. Joel continued to describe what he had seen in Muniche, mentioning eight different wells, two fountains, two breweries, a sizeable mill that drew water from the Isar, and a rather large iron foundry. "Maybe I could get some sort of work there or at the mill," he mused, still looking across the count's gardens. "It might be fun to make swords and anvils for a living."

I snickered, knowing that that sort of employment would build Joel's muscles if nothing else. "Did you see any castles?" I queried, remembering that I had seen two sets of spires on our journey down the Isar.

"Yeah, there was one right by one of the walls, I think the family house of Bayern? I saw a bronze crest on the gates to the castle with a roaring lion and the name *Bayern* engraved across the top." Joel's eyes took on a gleam of speculation as he added, "That's probably where Prince Otto lives. Maybe that's where he keeps his organ and travels time. I wonder if we could sneak in . . . ."

I snorted derisively. "We'd probably end up in jail if we tried to get into the castle without permission," I predicted, shuddering a little at the thought. I recalled the dungeon that Hans had told me about years ago and wondered whether it was already in use.

Joel's eyes lit up, and he turned toward me with a huge grin on his face. "That reminds me, I got to witness an execution while I was in the city."

I grimaced, knowing that young guys would find such events entertaining. Curiosity overtook me in spite of myself. I wondered what style of executions my people preferred. "So was it a hanging or a beheading?"

"It was definitely a beheading," Joel exclaimed, his eyes still burning with what looked like amazement. "And it was really disgusting. I didn't even know what was going on. I was just walking through one of the main squares and saw a bunch of people merging in one direction, so I followed them. I was in the back of the crowd, so I climbed onto a half-barrel in the gutter for a better look. At one end of the square there was this raised platform set up with a block at one end, and these two really burly-looking guys walked up dragging a guy in chains. They pushed the prisoner down onto his knees in front of the block, and a Catholic priest came up to give him last rites and pray for his soul, I guess." Joel snickered, and I waved for him to continue. The story had grabbed my attention, even though I knew that it would end in violence and blood.

"So anyway, this official-looking man stood off to the side of the platform reading a scroll, probably detailing what exactly the prisoner had done to deserve his fate. I don't know what he said. I think it was in Teutonica but I couldn't catch the words. The Catholic priest finished with the prisoner about the same time the official finished reading, and the crowd started jeering and throwing vegetables. That was when the executioner stepped onto the platform." Joel paused again, his smile growing rather wicked. Obviously the executioner had made some sort of impression on him, and I could hardly wait to find out why.

"Keep going," I ordered him, getting impatient as he leered at me. "What was the executioner like?"

Joel hesitated another moment, likely trying to decide on the perfect word. At last he stated simply, "*Freaky*. Just seeing him from a distance sent chills down my spine. He looked tall and muscular, and he was wearing all black with a long robe, a cape, and leather boots. He had some sort of silvery chain around his neck, and I couldn't really tell, but it looked like it had a death's head medallion hanging from it. But Swanie, his *face* . . . and the way he carried himself . . . ." Joel shuddered once, all over, then lowered his voice considerably. "He reminded me of Bela Lugosi in *Dracula*, you know, the old movie? Death was written all over his face, just like Dracula, but his hair was a lot longer, pulled back from his face, hanging to his shoulder blades. And it was jet black."

I shivered at Joel's description, my eyes darting here and there into the shadows of the deepening night, hoping that no specter waited to leap upon us now, while we discussed the executioner of Muniche. "Could you see what color his eyes were?" I whispered, intrigued as well as frightened.

Joel shook his head. "No, I was too far away for that. But I did notice that most of the men around here seem to be sporting beards. That executioner was clean-shaven, and his jaw looked harsh and set. He carried an axe in his right hand and waited while the two guards shoved the prisoner down onto the block. I remember thinking, why didn't the guy try to move his head, or struggle? I know I would, if I were in that situation, even if I *had* committed murder. But he laid his head down onto the block, looking resigned, and the creepy executioner came up behind him and raised the axe. You could tell he had muscles, just by the way he held his weapon. I think most of the people in the crowd looked away when he delivered the death blow, and I know a couple girls standing not too far from me squealed in horror when it happened." Joel snickered.

I frowned at him, again waving for him to continue. "No bashing my gender. Get on with the story."

"Well, I actually *watched* him cut the guy's head off," Joel told me, just a hint of disgust crossing his face. "It was really awful. They didn't bandage the guy's eyes or anything. His head came off with the first blow; that executioner really has some guns." Joel flexed his own arm muscles to illustrate, then continued. "Blood spewed everywhere, and the head rolled off of the platform into a basket, I think. I know it ended up in a basket eventually. It was sick. What was really disturbing, though, was the way the executioner *stared* at the headless body after finishing his work." Joel shuddered, putting both hands to his face in distress, looking like he clearly did not want to remember this part. I waited, slightly impatient, while Joel gathered himself and finally turned back to me. "He looked like . . . I don't know . . . like a vampire or something. Like he wanted to throw himself upon the body and drink its blood. And his teeth were bared in a really awful sneer." Joel shook his head. "It was really obvious that he very much *enjoys* his work."

I shivered once more, the coolness of the summer night air chilling me. My ice crept slowly into my veins as I considered this executioner, who apparently took pleasure in dealing death. He was probably a Teuton priest, I figured, considering how Joel had described his attire. I had a feeling that here in the eleventh century, I would discover more things about my people and their ancient rites, for those in the Middle Ages had not completely forsaken the concepts of sorcery and blood rituals. "I guess that's just a good reminder to us, to make sure we don't break any laws here in the eleventh century," I said, giving Joel a serious look. "Until I get my hands on the law books—which I probably won't—we'd better tread softly, or we may end up finding ourselves in the clutches of that executioner."

Joel shrugged and stood up from the bench. "I have no intention of killing anyone here, at least not yet, and I doubt too many other crimes would result in the death penalty." He glanced out at the gardens once more, then smiled down at me, holding out his hand. "We ought to go inside and get to bed."

I smiled back and grasped his hand, allowing him to pull me to my feet. "That we should, for maybe tomorrow we'll get to meet the council. Freia's almost completely well, so it should happen soon." Joel nodded, and moments later we reentered the manor, leaving the shadows and grotesque stories of medieval punishment behind us.

Chapter Seven

The Medieval Council

We met the Teuton council on a Saturday, three days after Joel's adventures in Muniche. The eldest of the council members requested that we come to them at the traditional Teuton meeting place of Muniche, a sizeable glade in a forest beside the banks of the Isar. The place sounded similar to where we held Teutonic festivals and weddings in my own era, and I suspected that it may very well be quite close to the clearing I knew well. The meeting place was said to be about two *Wegstuntae* from the Meldorf estate, a local measurement that equaled about seven-and-a-half kilometers. Count von Meldorf allowed us to ride three of his horses to the meeting, for he asserted that two *Wegstuntae* would be quite a long walk and that we needed to be in good health once we got there.

I looked forward to encountering the medieval council at their traditional meeting place with both eagerness and trepidation. I wondered what exactly we would have to do and say to achieve full acceptance into the city of Muniche. They would probably test our blood to see what percentage of it was Teutonic, I figured. Thus I would hold a strong advantage over both Joel and Freia, since my blood was ninety-five percent. Prince Otto was sure to be present, as the Keyholder of the city. I hoped that once the ceremony had been completed, I could confront the Prince alone to tell him the truth about Joel and me. Maybe, just maybe, I could convince him to give us his song, so we could avoid dying during the siege.

On Saturday after lunch, Count von Meldorf met us outside at the barn as one of the grooms helped us saddle our horses, his bailiff following at his heels, leading his own horse. The count said that he would have made the trip with us, but his constitution was not up for such ventures at his age. Instead he would send his bailiff along with us to read the paper that detailed the count's defense of us. I had written it myself several days prior while the count dictated the words. The bailiff had commented that though my handwriting looked messy, he could decipher it enough to properly relate what the count had spoken. Apparently both my accent and my handwriting needed improvement, according to local standards. I recalled those ancient papers Hans had given to me, written in Carolingian miniscule by that Black Priest Wolfgang. I had left them in one of the bins on my desk before making the journey. I wished now that I had brought them along, simply so I could practice shaping my letters in the same style.

The four of us—Joel, Freia, the bailiff, and I—reached the clearing in the woods around midafternoon. The sun shone brightly in a pale blue sky, filtering through the branches of oak, linden, and pine, sparkling like diamonds off the ripples on the Isar. We dismounted just outside of the clearing after having led the horses down a well-worn trail a little over eight kilometers south of the city itself. While we tethered the horses to some low-hanging tree branches beside the trail, the bailiff commented in a low voice that apparently the council members had not ridden horses to this meeting, for he heard no others neighing in the forest. I asked him, just as quietly, whether that boded well for us or not. He glanced at me briefly and murmured that they had probably floated a boat down the Isar or traveled through the forest simply using their own elements.

"What elements do the council members have?" I whispered. Joel and Freia stood waiting for us, having finished with their horses, a bit of tension visible on both of their faces as they observed our quiet conversation.

"The young Prince is red fire," the bailiff responded, fixing his rope into a strong square knot and turning away from his horse. "There are five others. One is some sort of fire as well, I think. Another is earth, like my master. Two are energy, and the sixth is mist, I believe." He paused, averting his eyes to the entrance of the clearing several paces away, then added, "The Lady of Muniche is a wintry wind. One can always see it in her eyes, a frigid blue."

My own eyes popped open at his words, and I gasped, "You mean the Lady of Muniche will be here too? I thought it was just the council members."

The bailiff shot me a look that suggested I ought to know these things. "Of course she'll be here. She *is* the city. She must have some say in who may or may not live within her walls. The three of you will have to convince her of your worth, as well as the council members." He grinned a rather disheartening grin at me and struck out for the clearing with the words, "You'd better get ready to present some strong arguments."

I moved to join Joel and Freia when they followed the bailiff, muttering to Joel under my breath, "This might be more difficult than I thought."

Joel gave a quiet grunt and inserted himself between Freia and me. "I won't let them hurt either of you," he promised.

I smiled weakly at his pledge, knowing that if the Teuton council wished to injure us, it would be up to me, not Joel, to stop them. At least he wanted to act like a gentleman despite his lack of Teutonic blood. He was a good man. I had started to understand why my cousin had fallen for him, the more I observed his actions during our mad adventure. An instant later we entered the clearing, and all stray thoughts fled from my mind as we stood before the Teuton Council of Muniche.

The six men were all priests and all were dressed for the part, clad in black from chin to the ground, some wearing black leather gloves and others wearing Gothic-looking chains around their necks. Five of them looked old enough to be my father or even my grandfather. The Old One had a long gray beard that swept down his chest like a wizard in a fairytale. The sixth one looked far younger than his peers, a small bit of fuzz clinging to his chin, his eyes similar to Hans', a dark blue. Each of the council members wore rather calculating expressions, regarding us as though we were cattle fit for the slaughterhouse. Behind them and to the right of where we had halted near the opening of the trail, I could see the sparkling waters of the Isar. A reddish fire burned low in a pit to our left, completing the union of the four major elements. A table had been placed near the fire pit, and atop it I could see goblets, knives, pens, and papers, among other things. They certainly intended to test our blood. Though I knew full well that mine was ninety-five percent Teutonic, I found myself hoping that the time travel had not lowered it somehow.

Following a lengthy pause, the youngest member of the council took a single step forward and addressed us in an authoritative voice. "On behalf of the Teuton Council of Muniche, I bid you welcome to our city. I am Prince Otto von Bayern."

He continued speaking after this formal introduction, gesturing at each of the other five priests as he spoke their names, but I heard none of it. Confusion had engulfed my mind at the words that this child had just spoken: *I am Prince Otto von Bayern.* That could not be true. He looked no older than me, and according to the Teuton records I had read to prepare myself for this time period, the Prince had been born in 1022. He should be forty-two years old by now. Had he found the fountain of youth or something? He had not even been able to grow a full beard yet, that was obvious. Had frequent time travel ultimately frozen him, made him unable to age? Was that *possible?*

My forehead creased as I contemplated this conundrum, trying to focus again on the Prince's introductions. He had named all of the other priests already—I had completely missed all of it. Then he waved his hand toward the woman standing in their midst, clad in an elegant blue and black dress, her graying brown hair suggesting that she must be in her forties. "This is my lovely Lady of Muniche, Maria von Bayern." The woman nodded at us, her eyes sharp and blue, her pale lips forming a firm line.

Prince Otto fell silent and took a step back to meld again with the others, and all seven of them trained their eyes on our faces, expectant. I shot a quick glance at Joel to my right and Freia beyond him, then took one step forward and curtseyed low. "On behalf of myself and my companions, I thank you kindly for your welcome, *Leitaeri*," I began, addressing the Prince using the most formal title I knew. "I do greatly apologize that I must be the one to speak, but my comrades do not speak Teutonica well. My name is Swanhilde von Thaden, originally from Teutonic lands. This is my friend, Joel Hudson"—I gestured at Joel—"whom I met in England last year. The woman on the end is Freia von Eisenwald"—I cringed when I spoke the words, hoping that Freia would not be angry with me for giving away her native village—"who comes from the Rhineland. The three of us request your permission to seek asylum at Muniche, should you deem it acceptable." I bowed once more toward the group before us, then stepped back, hoping that I had conducted myself properly, feeling relieved that the first part was over. Joel took my hand and squeezed it when I returned to his side, a welcome comfort.

The council members eyed us piercingly after I had finished my speech, several of them exchanging quiet phrases amongst themselves. Eventually, the Prince nodded in my direction and asked, "What languages do your companions speak?" His dark blue eyes glittered with what looked like curiosity.

Hoping against hope that Prince Otto did *not* speak the current form of English—which probably had some similarities to Old English—I bowed again and said, "Joel Hudson speaks a dialect of English, as he is from the islands. Lady Freia speaks some Teutonica as well as Rhenisch and Latin."

Prince Otto glanced at Joel and Freia in turn, then addressed me once more. "And you, Lady Swanhilde?"

A mocking smirk crossed my face in spite of my attempt to hide it, for if I meant to be fully honest I would have to admit that I spoke four languages and two dialects. Instead, I answered with utmost propriety, "I speak Teutonica, English, and Latin, *Leitaeri*."

The Prince nodded, looking thoughtful, glancing at his fellow council members. The elderly man with the lengthy beard stepped forward to ask what good we could do for Muniche, should they choose to allow us to stay. I responded that Joel had some skill with the bow and arrow and could defend the city or work with the hunters; he was also willing to learn any trade. As for Freia and me, I said that both of us were of noble birth and had gained some education, which we could teach to others, or we could also learn a trade. Freia and I had both agreed during her illness that we would learn commoners' work if that was the only way to gain citizenship in Muniche. The council members discussed things amongst themselves again, and afterward the Prince stepped forward to announce that they must test our blood. I nodded and walked to the table with Joel and Freia in tow, hoping once more that time travel had not altered the state of my blood.

As the priest with the thick brown beard prepared for the test, Joel nudged me, asking for a short rundown of what had happened thus far. I replied as quietly and concisely as I could. "Prince Otto introduced all the council members, and I introduced us. I told them that we'd be willing to learn anything we have to in order to stay in Muniche. Now that priest is going to test our blood to see if we're Teutons." I jerked one finger at the brown-haired man, then finished, "I'm a little disturbed about the Prince. Don't you think he looks our age?" I shot a glance back at him where he stood at the far end of the table, the Lady of Muniche at his side.

Joel narrowed his eyes and said, "Looks like he hasn't been able to grow a real beard yet. At least mine's coming in all over my face." He slid the fingers of his left hand across the nubs on his cheek.

"I know, and it doesn't make sense. He's supposed to be in his forties." I pushed up my red-violet sleeve and held out my arm to the brown-haired priest, who now wielded the traditional knife. "I'm wondering if frequent time travel does that to people," I added, ignoring the sharp bite of the knife cutting into my skin.

Joel's eyes widened when he watched the priest hold my hand over one of the goblets. "Please tell me he's not trying to kill you," he hissed, sounding appalled.

I rolled my eyes at Joel and shook my head. "No, he just needs a half cup of my blood for the test. He's going to do it to you, too." I gave him a significant look as the priest wrapped a silver oak leaf around my wrist, using his skill at blood control to rapidly stem the flow from my veins. That was something I needed to learn during my years in the past, whether Teuton priests wanted to keep that secret to themselves or not.

The brown-bearded priest turned to Freia, and Joel stared when I tossed the leaf aside several moments later. "Jeez, how did it stop so fast?" he demanded, gaping at the lack of blood there now.

"Teuton priests can do that," I answered, poking the newly formed scab with my finger. The skin was just a little tender. "I've heard that some can stem the flow from a ripped artery." I grinned.

Joel shook his head in shock, his mouth still hanging open. "*I* want to learn how to do that," he said, rolling up his own sleeve. I laughed and turned away. I could not particularly picture Joel as a Teuton priest, even if he did have a trace of Teutonic blood. His hair was the wrong color, for one thing. All of the priests on the council had brown or black hair aside from the old man.

While the priest sprinkled shards of silver oak into the cups with our blood, heating them to perform the tests, Prince Otto addressed me once more. "Lady Swanhilde, I'd like you to tell us what percentage of your blood and that of your companions is Teutonic." All of the council members aside from the one who conducted the tests leveled their eyes on me, along with the Lady.

Apart from myself, I had no idea. After a second's consideration, I nodded at Joel and said, "Since Joel Hudson is from England, I would assume that he has no Teutonic blood at all, *Leitaeri*. The Lady Freia should be able to answer for herself." I looked at my newfound friend, silently encouraging her to speak.

Freia curtsied shyly at the Prince and replied, her Teutonica unsure, "I have never had my blood tested before, your majesty. I do not know if any Teutonic blood flows in my veins. Perhaps there is some."

The Prince bowed his head kindly toward her, and several of the council members murmured together at Freia's words. "Your Teutonica is not so terrible, my lady, and if you have no Teutonic blood, it shall not be held against you," Prince Otto reassured her, then turned back to me, waiting.

I took a deep breath, then answered honestly, "The last time my blood was tested, *Leitaeri*, it was ninety-five percent Teutonic."

All of the council members murmured at this, and the Prince's expression suggested that he had suspected as much. Apparently I looked like a Teuton, even if my Teutonica sounded funny. Shortly afterward, the brown-haired priest gave the results of the three tests. As I had thought, Joel had no trace of Teutonic blood within him, which did not surprise me at all. At one point he and Beth had talked about their backgrounds while we were at college; Joel had claimed that his family had English and Scottish roots.

Freia had a small bit of Teutonic blood in her veins, as it turned out, fifteen percent. I smiled at her as the priest pronounced her result. Though her blood was so low that it would not be considered at all Teutonic, at least she had more than Joel. Lastly, the brown-haired priest looked at me rather darkly and proclaimed that my blood was, in fact, ninety-five percent Teutonic. I sighed in relief, glad that the harrowing trip through the currents of time had not altered my blood. I was still a Teuton and would always be a Teuton, just like the council members.

The Prince made a few comments regarding our blood, saying that while I had the potential for full citizenship in Muniche, my comrades did not, since their blood did not meet the standards of my people. They could become citizens as foreigners, Prince Otto explained, but would not have the same judicial privileges as me. I translated this into English for Joel's benefit and he shrugged, fingering his wrist, stating that it did not matter to him. Freia also accepted her place with a timid smile.

The Prince then gestured for Count von Meldorf's bailiff—about whose presence I had practically forgotten—to come forward and read the count's defense of the three of us. The man complied, unrolling the piece of paper upon which I had set the count's words, reading them slowly and carefully, his Teutonica strong despite my alleged poor handwriting. I began to wonder how much Teutonic blood the bailiff had and what element he claimed, suddenly realizing that I did not even know his name.

The count's defense of us rang out strong and true, obviously making an impression on the council members, whose stone faces began to appear more accommodating as the servant read the paper. For one thing, the count had offered protection for both Freia and me at his estate until we could find something more permanent. He believed that both of us were indeed of noble birth and thus should remain in the care of a lord, rather than be thrown to the plebeians in the city.

The count also asserted that Joel seemed to be a reliable worker, willing to learn any trade, and predicted that he would excel in the city and make a name for himself once he had learned Teutonica. When the servant had finished reading, Prince Otto waved him back and discussed our fate once more with the others while we waited. I felt as though we dangled at the edge of a precipice. My ice coursed lightly through my veins in a feeble attempt at reassurance.

Eventually, the Lady of Muniche stepped forward and addressed us for the first time, her voice and expression cold, like the bailiff had said earlier. "If I were to take you in, would you remain fiercely loyal to me and my people until the years of your lives are finally spent?" Her blue eyes pierced to the bone as she viewed us each in turn. "To become citizens of Muniche, you must sign an oath of loyalty at any cost. Muniche has many enemies who walk the German empire, and many who would turn their backs in difficult times. I must always use caution."

I drew myself up resolutely, allowing some of my ice to creep into my eyes as I answered her, cold air escaping from my lips. "My loyalty to this city will never wane," I informed her proudly. "I was born here, and I would never betray my city or the Teuton people. I will swear it here and now, *Leitalra*." I met her wintry eyes in an unspoken challenge.

She nodded once at me and trained her eyes on Freia, the innocent young Rhineland girl. At first, I prepared myself to speak for her, but to my surprise, she answered the Lady herself. "*Leitalra*, if you do accept me, your city would be the first to do so in over a year. I would owe her a heavy debt of gratitude, and would gladly pay it with my life." I stared at Freia in wonder, astonished at how articulate she could be when she really tried.

The Lady nodded at Freia and turned to Joel, so I repeated the Lady's words to him in English, promising to translate his response as perfectly as I could. "This sounds like I'm pledging fealty," he muttered under his breath, then looked directly at the Lady and spoke his reply. "Though I'm not a Teuton myself, I'm here with Swanhilde and have no reason to leave until she leaves. Therefore, I am willing to swear loyalty to this city, and should I gain the privilege of protecting her in battle someday, I would do so with honor."

I translated Joel's response, glad that he seemed to take this seriously, in spite of his lack of Teutonic blood. The Lady nodded at him as well, then turned to confer with the council members once more. Joel asked me quietly how much more the council could want from us, aside from a signature in blood. I snickered and told him that I had no clue. "I've never done this sort of thing before. After all, I was born in München, so my loyalty has always been a given. I hope they're going to accept us." I shivered a little, nervously awaiting our fate.

Chapter Eight:
Far Too Early

At last, the council members halted their discussion and moved once more to stand in a line, like they had when we had first entered the clearing. Prince Otto stepped forward, opening his arms in a welcoming motion, a smile gracing his face at long last. "The council of Muniche has decided, unanimously, to accept all three of you into her citizenship, one as a Teuton, two as outsiders." He paused, and I heaved a big sigh of relief, along with Freia. Joel grinned, my reaction prompting him to relax his tense stance. The Prince's smile widened as he beckoned us to the table. "Would the three of you come forward and sign your papers of citizenship? They will be filed in the city archives in the basement of the town hall."

I nodded eagerly and responded, *"Yes."* Joel and Freia trailed behind me as I made a beeline for the table. The brown-haired priest who had tested our blood beat me there, producing the three necessary documents and an inkwell. He held a plumed pen out to me, smiling underneath his thick beard. My eyes raced over the words written on the citizenship papers, noting that the one he indicated for me to sign mentioned my Teuton blood and higher standing in the local courts. I smiled triumphantly as I signed my full name in the cursive of twenty-first century Germany, knowing that it probably would look funny to everyone else. I handed the pen to Freia, and the brown-bearded priest met my gaze. "Welcome home, Lady Swanhilde," he said with a smile.

When I stepped back from the table and waited for the others to sign, I felt someone tap me on my right shoulder. I whirled around, a grand relief still flowing through my veins, and found myself regarding Prince Otto himself. "Could I have a word with you in private, Lady Swanhilde, while the others finish their duties here?" he requested, his expression serious again.

My heart pounded, for I had hoped to speak with the Prince in private at some point to find out what I could about his Song of Time. I nodded my assent, and the Prince led me into the woods, out of sight of the river, far enough away that the others in the clearing would not hear if we spoke softly. As I began to ponder how exactly to broach the subject, the Prince stopped, sighed, and turned to face me, his gaze not particularly friendly. "When you spoke to my Lady of Muniche a few moments ago, I noticed that you have some ice in you." His voice was low, his expression severe.

My ice froze my body in response to his words, and I sensed another pair of contacts crunching into oblivion. What did my element have to do with anything? He knew that I was a Teuton. What did he want me to be, a cloud floating in the air? Though I could not fathom the reason for his accusatory regard, I felt the need to defend myself anyway. "So I am ice. I know that you are red fire, *Leitaeri*," I rejoined, my eyebrows coming together.

He ignored my comment and glowered at me. "Word has been traveling around about a group of Gypsies who were attacked by a Teuton woman whose hair looked like a frozen wave and whose hands curled like icicles." I froze again at this, fear mingling with my ice at the memory of what had happened two weeks ago. Prince Otto's eyes bored into mine. "That was you."

"They attacked me first," I informed him. "And they had spears. There were five of them, and Joel and I were alone, unarmed. One of them murdered my cousin before we had a chance to fight back. We couldn't have beaten them at all if I had held my element back."

The Prince huffed and rubbed one hand across his scant beard. "Since you have not lived in Teuton lands for many years, I suppose you may have forgotten our laws. Teutons are *not* to use their abilities against other tribes, German or foreign. We have enough enemies as it is, those who wish to discover the secrets of our strengths. We do not need rumors spreading that the Teutons have unleashed their elements on Gypsies or any other groups. We must forever keep our powers strictly in check, even amongst our own people, for we do not want to engender suspicion." The Prince ogled me disparagingly, his eyes glowing just a bit red, his youthful mouth turned downward. I sensed the heat of his fire emanating from his body, contrasting strangely against my icy spirit.

I should have backed down and apologized, especially considering his royal rank over my people. But I had had my share of disagreements with fire before, and a darker fire than his. Prince Otto's anger did not frighten me at all. In fact, it fueled my obstinacy. "So are you implying that I should have let them kill me? Let them get away with murdering my cousin?" I demanded, my breath frigid.

The Prince's eyes turned even redder, and he flung his black cape back from his arms, revealing the keys of Muniche hanging from his belt. Seeing that iron key ring broke my concentration, and I stared at it. I had never seen the keys before. The Prince glowered, observing my gaze, and slapped one hand over the key ring, hiding it from my sight. "I am *not* suggesting that you should have let the Gypsies kill you," he snapped, his voice still low in spite of his ire. "But if you had to use your ice, you should have killed them all, not left witnesses to go here and yon squawking about a frosty Teuton witch."

His words disarmed me a bit, though they also appalled me. "I had never killed anyone before that day," I said, looking at the leaves beneath my feet as my ice slowly settled down. "And I'd never watched someone that close to me get stabbed right before my eyes. It was a new experience for me."

The fire also left the Prince's eyes, his gaze becoming a bit friendlier. "It is a bitter burden to kill, not one for women to shoulder," he said, looking distressed.

"I hope I don't have to do it again," I murmured, shivering at the thought.

"You will not, as long as you stay in Muniche," Prince Otto declared, glancing back toward the clearing where the others waited for us. "In this city, the women are not required to fight. The men are to protect them, as they should."

I nodded slowly, feeling grateful to be under the guardianship of medieval chivalry, in spite of its chauvinism. The Prince continued to look beyond me, his posture suggesting that he wished to return to his fellows in the clearing. I realized that I had not been able to voice my own requests yet, and I raised my eyes to look again at his face, marveling at its apparent youth. His skin was pale and hardly wrinkled, his eyes an enchanting dark blue, his short hair as black as the night with no trace of gray. He was handsome, and he did not look forty-two, not at all. I tilted my head for a better view, trying to reason out a plausible explanation for his good looks. About that time the Prince finally noticed my intense stare and asked, his voice sounding slightly annoyed, "Why do you keep looking at me that way?"

I thought for a moment, deciding how to best express my uncertainty. At last I asked him, still peering at his youthful face, "*Leitaeri*, why do you look like you're my age?"

A frown creased his forehead. "How old are you?" he asked.

"I'll be twenty-one this August," I replied truthfully, eyeing the sparse dark hair decking his chin.

The Prince shrugged, one quick movement of his shoulders. "I am twenty-two," he said, his face suggesting that he saw no point in this conversation.

I froze again, and his words revolved in my head: *I am twenty-two* .... *I am twenty-two* .... My eyes widened, and my lips parted into a round *O* of disbelief. "That's impossible," I whispered, my mind racing back to the many things I had read in Teuton literature about the eleventh century. "Weren't you born in 1022?" I gasped, a wretched possibility suddenly grabbing hold of my heart.

Prince Otto stared at me, looking mildly concerned, not knowing how to take my reaction to this seemingly meaningless tête-à-tête. "Yes," he replied simply.

My lips formed the word *no* .... And the truth broke right there in front of me at last, with all of its dreaded implications. "It's 1044?" I choked on the words. Prince Otto nodded once in confirmation. My knees gave out, and I leaned into one of the oak trees, my icy fingers clutching its bark, my mind not wanting to believe. Not only had we arrived in the forest rather than in the city, we had arrived twenty years too early. Twenty years. *Twenty* .... Muniche would not fall for twenty-two years. And I had lost the Torstein. We were trapped. By the time Muniche fell, Joel and I would both be in our forties. What had I *done* ...?

"Oh shit," I interjected, speaking English as my clawed fingers sank into the oak tree. "We really screwed up. I can't believe this. Oh my *word!*" Images swam in my mind at the realization that I could not return home for twenty-two years. *Hans ... Hans ... my father ... my friends ... my München ... New Jersey ... Erika ... college ... my cousins ... my love ... my love ... Hans* .... Icy tears began to trickle down my cheeks as Prince Otto tore me from the tree, carrying me further into the forest, his hands steadying me, his voice urging me to control myself, to pull my element back. I placed both of my icy hands on my temples and closed my eyes, taking shaky breaths and ordering myself to be calm, *calm*. I had to tell the Prince the truth now. He had written the organ song that could open the gates of time right after he had accepted the keys of Muniche in 1043. I remembered reading that in *Der Weg*. When I explained, he would understand.

"Do you think anyone in the clearing can hear us?" I finally managed to whisper, my voice barely above a breath. I glanced furtively at the trees around us. His firm hands still grasped my arms, as though he feared that my element may erupt wildly in my hysteria. But I had gotten it under control, confining its chill into my blood and my eyes—now I would be viewing a blurry world without it.

The Prince glanced around as well, a fiery haze creeping over his irises. "They will not hear us now," he pledged in a louder voice, having planted himself between me and the glade. I vaguely sensed the warmth of his spirit encircling us, shielding us from eavesdroppers. It was time to confess.

I took a deep breath and stepped away from his grasp, placing one of my hands on a nearby birch trunk, lifting my eyes to the Prince's. "You wrote a song for the organ that can open the gates of time."

Prince Otto grew rigid, the air between us suddenly prickling with heat. He stared at me darkly, his face appearing much older now, his red fire having evicted the natural blue from his eyes. "How do you know that? No one knows about that." He frowned severely and flexed his hands.

"No one but you and your brother Paulus, I know," I answered, speaking softly. "You are the only people who ever used it, according to what I've read." The Prince's body jerked in surprise, his eyes sizzling as I came out with it. "I am from the future," I whispered, holding his gaze with my own. "I was born in Muniche in the year 1979."

The fire in the Prince's eyes cooled, replaced by stupefaction. "How could you have found my song? I never intended to write it down."

"I didn't; I . . . ." My voice trailed off when I recalled the warnings of the Torstein. I could not reveal any secrets to people in the past, for that may alter the future. I cleared my throat, then said, "I used another way." I paused, considering what to say next while Prince Otto continued to stare at me in bafflement. "But I lost that way, and now I'm stuck here, and so is Joel." The words tumbled out of me, my Teutonica likely sounding quite awful. "Joel is from the future too. We got here a few weeks ago, and not ten minutes later, the Gypsies attacked us. They killed my cousin Beth, and I watched her body vanish. That means she went back to the future, right?" A lump formed in my throat, and I stared desperately up at Prince Otto's face, desperately hoping that the writings about death were true.

The Prince frowned at me, his fire now completely abated, though I sensed his spirit silently skulking the copse where we stood. He looked as though he was trying to keep up with my rushed explanation. "Then the Lady Freia is not part of your group?" he asked, completely ignoring my question.

"We found Freia after we escaped," I explained, a skeletal hand clasping my heart. *Beth's not actually dead. She can't be.* "We were trying to get to Muniche in the first place, but we got here too early. We weren't supposed to come until 1064. But my cousin's not really dead, right? Everything I read about time travel said that if you die in the past, you return to your own time right after."

"Why 1064?" the Prince questioned, still ignoring my query.

I definitely could not give *that* away. I averted my gaze to the ground, my mind working overtime. "I cannot say," I whispered in a strained voice.

The Prince grimaced, his expression implying that he was well versed in the rules of time travel. "My brother and I have used the song only once thus far," he admitted, looking past me, back toward where the others gathered. "Time travel is a dangerous thing, we discovered, and not to be treated lightly. I know not whether we shall ever attempt it again. It involves devilish forces, I fear."

In spite of my newfound horror of twenty-two years in the Middle Ages and the prospect of never seeing my cousin again, the Prince's remarks awakened my interest in his own travels. "Where did you go?" I asked him.

Prince Otto looked down at me and replied, "We went to the time of Christ."

My eyes practically popped out of their sockets at that. "Wow," I interjected, using English once more as I talked to myself, fascination sweeping over me. "I should have thought of that." Switching back to Teutonica to address the Prince, I inquired, "Did you see the crucifixion?"

A grotesque expression crossed the Prince's face, and he drew his black robe around his body like a shield. "It was . . . incredibly . . . upsetting." His dark blue eyes glazed over with tragedy. "It was humanity's worst moment."

I paused, knowing he was right, then whispered, "And the resurrection?"

The Prince's expression lightened considerably. "We were blessed to see the risen Christ. Praise God for His eternal triumph over evil." His face looked fiercely victorious, and I shivered once, imagining how glorious it would have been.

I turned the conversation back to the matter at hand, my curiosity about Prince Otto's first trip now satisfied. "Joel and I are trapped here now since we lost the means to return to our own time," I reminded the Prince. "We were hoping that you might allow us to use your song, so we can get back."

Prince Otto's expression hardened once more, his blue eyes darkened with suspicion. "Why should I trust you or that boy with such classified information? I have shared it only with my most faithful friend, my brother Paulus, whom I could trust with my life to keep it safe. Why should I give it to strangers, especially to one who is not Teuton? Perhaps you should have let the Gypsies kill you after all."

I gaped at the Prince in dismay, knowing that he really had no reason to give us something so dear to him, wishing in spite of this that he would show us some mercy. "But we got here twenty years too early!"

"That was your mistake, not mine," the Prince retorted with a scowl. "You should consider how strange it would seem if both you and Joel disappear suddenly and reappear in twenty years, not having aged at all. The council and those at the Meldorf estate would remember you, and that would call for many complicated explanations. If you want to get back to your own era, do it through death."

My expectations crashing to the ground, I stared at Prince Otto and gasped, "So it really does work that way? If we die here, we return to our own time?" Relief spread through my chest, and I pressed a hand over my heart.

The Prince glared at me archly. "Do you think pipe organs existed in the days of Christ? Of course we died to get back here after thirty-four years in that primitive wasteland. We died together in a Roman coliseum, cast to the tigers for our Christianity." I froze at the Prince's pronouncement, distaste flooding my veins. He nodded sagely and finished, "I hope, for your sakes, that your deaths may be much easier than mine."

Chapter Nine:
Coming to Terms

The Prince departed from me without speaking further, his body language clearly stating that he would hear no further pleas from me. I watched him go for a second, my thoughts all jumbled up inside. So I had done what I had hoped to do: the great Teuton Prince now knew of my mad journey through time. And he had brushed it off just like a stereotypical priest, like Hans always sidestepped the questions that he preferred not to answer. Joel and I were still trapped, and for several decades now, not just for two years.

But Beth is alive.

I found my three companions gathered near Count von Meldorf's horses in silence, apparently waiting for me to rejoin them. The bailiff ducked his head at me when I stepped out of the trees, his hands moving automatically to the ropes that bound the tan mare I had ridden. "About time you got here, Swanie," Joel said, his tone sounding both curious and impatient. He untied Freia's horse and handed her the reins. "I feel like a fish out of water without you here to translate."

"Sorry," I muttered, climbing onto the tan mare, the skirt of my red-violet dress bunching up around my legs. From what I had seen thus far, eleventh century women did not generally ride side saddle. Their skirts had more fabric than the ones I had sewn back at college, so I needed to get to work at creating better dresses for both Freia and me. She had worn one that the head housekeeper had pulled down from storage; it had belonged to the count's wife many years ago. *Now I'm going to need twenty-two years' worth of dresses,* I realized, feeling defeated.

"What were you and the Prince talking about for so long?" Joel asked me as we guided our horses along the trail back towards civilization. He brought his brown mare up beside me on my right and leaned toward me to murmur, "Did you tell him the truth about us?"

My lips twitched. "I did, but it didn't go over all that well. We need go somewhere and talk about it when we get back to the manor."

"He's not going to let us use his Song of Time, is he?" Joel guessed.

I sighed, my eyes roving over the trees and brush blurring around us. I would really have to be more careful with my contacts now. "No."

Joel grumbled and cursed the Prince under his breath, slowing his horse so that he could return to his place behind mine. What would he think when he found out that we had come twenty years too early? It was his fault, of course, since both Beth and I had been thinking of the city of Muniche in 1064 when I had opened the gateway. *But it's your own fault too for mentioning the year only once while we walked to the gazebo. How can you expect him to remember a random number?*

The two of us went to a small stone bench amid the flower gardens upon our return to the manor. I thanked the bailiff for his help when we reached the barn, and learned that his name was Jarvis Gaembel. He waved off my accolades and insisted that he could do no less, bidding my companions and me welcome to the settlement of Muniche. I caught a brief flash in his eyes when he spoke, but he concealed his element just as quickly, prompting me to speculate on what sort of element the manager of a medieval estate would claim.

We parted ways with Freia at the front porch; she reentered the house with the intention to help the cooks with dinner. Joel and I situated ourselves upon the bench soon afterward, its position affording us a good view of the sinking sun. The scent of roses, pansies, and lavender suffused the air around us. A single peasant woman passed through the gardens, collecting petals here and there to garnish the evening meal. Joel leaned against the back of the bench and spread his arms across it, while I sat as far from him as the bench allowed, nervousness settling in my chest at the knowledge of what we needed to discuss.

"So he's not going to give us the song," Joel said at length, sounding like he wished to confront the Prince in a dark alley over his musical secret.

"No, he's not," I confirmed, reaching my right hand out to stroke the crimson petals of a nearby rose. "He doesn't trust us enough, and I guess I can't really blame him. It's not like I'd willingly hand over the Torstein to whoever asked first."

Joel heaved a sigh and muttered something under his breath. "Then I guess we're going to have to do our best to die in battle, right?"

I shuddered all over and winced, pulling my hand away from the rose. I had accidentally pricked my index finger on a thorn. "The one good thing is that death really does send time travelers back home. The Prince and his brother have already made one trip, and they both died to get back here. That means Beth is back home already." I rubbed the tip of my finger and chewed on my bottom lip.

"But we've got two years before we can go back." I saw Joel looking at me out of the corner of my eye. His expression betrayed his relief. Maybe I had not been the only one haunted by Beth's dismal fate.

I shut my eyes and gathered all of my courage, then clasped my hands in my lap and turned my torso to face him. "Actually, it's going to be a lot longer," I said, bracing myself for his reaction. His eyebrows came together. "The Prince looks so young because he's just a year older than us. He's twenty-two. It's the summer of 1044 right now, so we got here twenty-two years before Muniche's fall."

Joel's jaw dropped in slow motion; it would have looked funny under any other circumstances. "You . . . you mean . . . ." Horror swelled in his hazel eyes, and he raised one hand to his mouth.

I nodded once. "Yep. Not only did we arrive in the forest, we arrived in the wrong year completely. And unless we can convince someone to execute us, we're going to be here until we're in our forties."

Joel rubbed his prickly chin, his cheeks and ears growing flushed. "So we're trapped in the Middle Ages for longer than we've been alive," he translated.

"With no family history and no money, and no Teuton blood in your case."

Joel backed away from me, a stricken expression crossing his face. "What do you mean by that? Am I going to be a second-class citizen for eternity just because I don't have an element like all you crazy sorcerers?" He looked affronted.

I shook my head and looked away from him toward the peasant woman clad in light gray, her sun-browned hands plucking a pinkish rose from a bush several steps away from us. "I don't really know, but it shouldn't be that bad for you. I know that outsiders have always lived in Teuton cities throughout history. But I doubt they'd let you join the nobility," I admitted, frowning a little at that concept. *You've convinced Count von Meldorf that you're part of the aristocracy thanks to your education. But no degree of education can improve Joel's status . . . and he doesn't need to know that the blood-transfer is a thing . . . .*

"I just can't get over how weird this world is," Joel remarked at length, his tone sounding exasperated. "All these Germans sneaking around with elements and opening portals into the past."

"It's not all Germans," I pointed out immediately, turning to face him again. "It's just a portion of Bavarians and Austrians. The Teutons have existed for several thousand years, but we're just like normal people. It's not like we can go around creating fireballs and earthquakes at every turn."

Joel squinted off toward the sun, disbelief and annoyance warring on his face. "What about this whole 1066 thing, anyway?" he questioned, looking at me with a disparaging glint in his eye. "How can you be sure that Muniche fell in *that* year? I mean, we all know 1066 is when the Normans invaded England."

"Exactly," I responded, raising one finger. "And history is always written by the winning side. So obviously, *someone* wanted to make sure everyone remembered the Norman invasion rather than the massacre of the Teutons. I came here to find out what really happened, to find out why our elements couldn't save us from the Saxon invaders."

Joel pursed his lips, appearing thoughtful. "Makes sense," he said, shaking his head and looking at the stalks of lavender swaying in the breeze across from the bench where we sat. "But now we won't learn the truth for twenty-two years. Do you think we need to try to raise families in the meantime so we don't get bored?" He gave a brief snicker and wriggled his blond eyebrows at me.

I wrinkled my nose and crossed my arms, sensing my cheeks heating at the subject. "I don't know. I guess we *could* if we wanted to, since doing regular stuff doesn't seem to actually change anything in history. When I went back the first time, I left a note for Hans, and he gave it back to me after I returned. So having a family would probably be a valid thing to do, to become a part of history." I quailed at the idea of bearing children in this primitive land as a Teuton of high blood.

"I've got to get better at Teutonica then," Joel declared, leaning back again and draping his arms across the back of the bench. "I don't want to end up with a woman I can't understand. But if I married a Teuton girl, would our kids have elements?" He cocked his head at me, looking hopeful.

"That's . . . a loaded subject," I hedged, "but I'm not sure you'd be allowed to marry a Teuton girl as an outsider. You need to get a job first anyway."

That night, as Freia and I lay in our respective beds, I spent a long while gazing at Hans' picture in my locket by the moonlight filtering through the window. Tears trickled down my face, for I knew that until I found the courage to die, I would not see Hans again. My love for him burned in my heart, and I greatly wished that I could talk to him somehow and finally tell him the truth. I wanted to admit my love for him, to insist that our age differences meant nothing to me, that I wanted to marry him anyway. Facing twenty-two years in the eleventh century with Joel—realizing that he may have referenced me when he joked about marrying a Teuton girl—I knew that I could never love him the way I loved Hans. I blinked in sorrow at Hans' picture, my eyes tracing the familiar dark gray hair, serious blue eyes, the black robe of the Teuton priest. I had been deluding myself all this time. There was no hope for me. Being separated from Hans for so long would kill my heart, and an outsider like Joel could never take his place.

The month of July passed rather quickly, as Joel and I attempted to adjust to the medieval lifestyle. He began working at the local ironworks just a week after we gained citizenship. He said that the ironmaster was a young man named Heinrich Denlinger. He had just recently inherited the ironworks from his father, who had fallen ill the previous winter. Master Denlinger seemed to be a decent employer, according to Joel, willing to help him learn the skills of the trade despite his poor Teutonica and outsider status.

Two weeks later, Joel moved out of Count von Meldorf's manor, having saved all of his earnings thus far to lay down rent for a room in Muniche. Such a setup would eliminate the long walk from the Meldorf estate as well as immerse him in the culture, forcing him to perfect his Teutonica, so he claimed. Although I felt nervous at the idea of Joel going out on his own—so young and inexperienced—I did not discourage him. Instead, I warned him not to start hitting up the taverns every night with the other metalworkers.

"I'll visit you every chance I get, any time I can scare up money for the bridge crossing," I vowed on the day that he moved out, adding with a wink, "and if you turn into a drunkard I'll kill you myself."

"With your ice," Joel supplied. He hefted his bag and grinned confidently as he strutted off to conquer the world.

Freia and I continued to live at the count's manor, installing ourselves into one of his more decent bedrooms at his insistence. The two of us spent quite a bit of time sewing new dresses for ourselves out of some finer linens prepared from last year's flax harvest, and Freia skillfully altered more of his late wife's attire for our use. We learned that Count von Meldorf had been a widower for over thirty years—his wife had died bearing a stillborn child, her third. His other two children had died before the age of five, one of pox and one of a wicked fever. Any idyllic thoughts I may have entertained about raising a family in pastoral bliss left me on the day that the count showed us his family graveyard.

And yet Joel sits around casually chatting about having kids in a place like this, I thought to myself, *and he doesn't know anything about the dangers of childbirth for Teutons like me.* I wondered, while I stood looking down at the wooden markers, whether dying in such a way would shatter my heart.

Chapter Ten

The Man Who Did Not Exist

During my first weeks in the eleventh century, I made a new habit of joining my Rhenisch roommate in her late night prayers. Freia observed the hour of Matins, thanks to her years in the convent; she would rise from her sleep of her own accord and kneel at her bedside while reciting her Latin devotions. Though my faith did not require such rites, my nightmares often woke me around the time when Freia voiced her prayers. So I began to creep across the floor to her side and endeavored to listen to her words, struggling against the sieve of panic shackling my lungs. Novel terrors had cropped up in my dreams, fueled by Beth's death and the frightening journey through the currents of time. My new friend's steadiness soothed me, easing my spirit back toward slumber afterwards.

Not long after Joel had moved into the city, a horror I had not yet experienced tore me from my sleep. I had been at home in modern München, walking with my father, Hans, Erika, and my cousins—and out of nowhere, each of them turned to dust before me, the familiar buildings around me breaking down in fire. When I awoke, my wool blanket was tangled around my body, and I could not force my lungs to draw breath. A squeaking sound pealed from my lips, and my bleary eyes found Freia kneeling not far away, her youthful face turned towards mine, her green eyes aglow with concern.

I could not join her. I could not breathe. I had just watched *my* city burn, not this ancient version that scholars called a myth. I sensed my ice freezing my blood, and I squeezed my eyes shut and tried to concentrate on my element, to bring its full power to the fore before my panic suffocated me.

When my spirit burst into the night sky above, the first notion that came over me was embarrassment. I shook my head and placed my hands on my hips, roving my eyes over the count's fields below and the spires of medieval Muniche off to my left, barely visible in the starlight. *You're a fool, Swanie,* I thought to myself, frustrated anew at the power that my nightmares held over me. *Can't separate the present from the future. Now you're imagining München burning just like this place will. They're not the same city. You know that. Now why can't your subconscious understand the difference?*

I wondered how Freia was reacting to my frozen body in my bed. Had my ice overtaken the blanket along with my nightgown? I rolled my eyes at myself and looked toward the Isar, following its snakelike path south. Hopefully she would be able to finish her prayers and get back to bed. I might spend a good portion of the darkness in spiritual form, like I had done both at college and at home. I could explain myself to her later on.

I walked upon the waters of the Isar for a time, allowing their familiar chill to seep into my feet and restore my spirit. I suddenly began to realize how ridiculous I was, choosing to witness the fall of Muniche when all of history was open to me. Or *had* been open to me before I lost the Torstein. I should not have picked an event that would exacerbate my panic attacks. *And now I have no choice but to witness it unless I die first,* I reminded myself, looking upstream, a frown twisting my lips. *I wonder if I could find that place where we fought the Gypsies. Maybe . . . maybe I can find where I dropped the Torstein . . . .*

The eastern sky had begun to lighten by the time I gave up my search. I found evidence of our struggle—blood staining the ground, broken branches, a forgotten spear half buried in the brush. But though I traced our path to the Isar three times, my spiritual eyes caught no sign of a mystical blood-red rock. I scoured the river's bottom as well, with no luck whatsoever. I felt no tingle in my spirit to beckon me toward arcane Teutonic magic.

Joel and I were wholly trapped until the Prince decided to trust us.

When I returned to my physical body, I found that Freia had waited at my bedside during my absence, her lips softly whispering prayers in the candlelight. I sighed a little and reassured my friend that I was fine, that sometimes Teutons let their elements fully envelop their bodies to bring on a sense of calm. She accepted my explanation without fuss and commented that my icy body had cooled the room to an extent beyond what the open window could afford. "It was kind of nice, in a way," she said with a knowing smile. "It's certainly going to be sweltering in Muniche today with the party going on."

Today was the first Saturday in August, a holiday when my city would celebrate Lady Muniche's birthday. Freia and I had learned of the party thanks to two matriarchs from the nearby estates, Lady Adeline Ahloch and her best friend, Lady Hildegard Kuegler. They had visited the previous week to acquaint themselves with Count von Meldorf's "new charges," as Freia and I had come to be known. Lady Hildegard, the elder of the two, had informed us that the primary celebration was to be held in the principal square of Muniche. "It will be a traditional Teutonic party, certain to involve good food, drinks, and dancing, along with some entertainment performed by the lower classes," Lady Hildegard told us.

"It is also the perfect place to meet young lords," added Lady Adeline with a chuckle. "Both of you *must* attend, for several of the noble bachelors have heard about your arrival and have been asking questions." Both ladies tittered, covering their mouths with their hands, fluttering their lashes suggestively. Freia and I had exchanged a look, her vibrant eyes shining with interest and fun. While I was not particularly interested in meeting young lords, I knew that I would enjoy such a festival, especially if I could learn some primeval Teutonic dancing in the process. Freia and I turned back to the ladies and promised that we would come, expressing the hope that we would see them there.

Now Freia and I would have to attend the festival on little sleep, but we both resolved to attire ourselves as attractively as possible. I chose a blue and white dress of airy linen that I had recently completed. Its sleeves flared wide, and its square neckline plunged a daring hand width below my collarbone. I pulled my black hair back into a blue net that matched the dress, adding one of my mother's pairs of gold earrings and my golden locket to demonstrate my noble status. Freia clothed herself in a yellow-green summer dress, pulling her blond hair back from her face while leaving most of it hanging down beneath her head covering.

Jarvis drove us into the city in the count's nicest carriage, stopping several streets away from the main square. Once the horses had halted, he leapt out of the driver's seat in a fluid motion, holding his hand out to help Freia and me dismount. Afterward, he helped the count himself, who had chosen to attend the party despite his age. I informed the count that we planned to meet Joel at the fountain on the western side of the square and would probably spend the entire day with him. Count von Meldorf nodded his big head in agreement, commenting that he would have to find a cool tavern somewhere and quench his thirst with some ale, before the heat killed him. "It never used to be a problem," he grumbled, wiping sweat from his brow with a handkerchief as we advanced toward the square. "Swanie and Freia, you must take my advice and never grow old."

We laughed at this and I noted that aging was inevitable, unfortunately. Shortly thereafter, we reached the eastern edge of the plaza and stood for a moment watching the revelries. People of all classes danced this way and that, some waving ribbons, as groups of men perched at tables and on steps, chugging beer, devouring sausages, and playing cards and dice. Knots of women, many of them ladies, sat together underneath awnings and umbrellas, chattering and laughing amongst themselves. The merchants privileged enough to own shops bordering the main square hawked all sorts of foods and drink, while a small band of fiddlers, drummers, and pipers filled the area with festive music.

Freia murmured that she was going to go look for Joel, gesturing toward the three-tiered marble fountain across from where we stood, rivulets of sparkling water spewing from its crest. I nodded and waved for her to go, promising to follow her in a minute. Once she had left, I pulled my father's digital camera from my purse and snapped a few covert photos of the festivities. I had not used the camera enough yet, having taken just a few shots thus far of the Meldorf estate and the drawbridge into Muniche. I needed to preserve the batteries as long as I could, since Joel and I would be here indefinitely. I planned to simply snap as many photos as possible and view them once we returned, assuming the images came back with us.

Eventually, I rendezvoused with Joel and Freia; and Joel, playing the part of the chivalrous lord, bought us each a sausage and some mead. We found a place to sit near the fountain and were soon joined by several of the noble-women who had visited the Meldorf property earlier, including the Ladies Adeline and Hildegard. I introduced all of them to Joel, relating the now-familiar tale of my finding him in England, a young nobleman who had lost his family to the Danes. Joel's Teutonica had begun to improve; he managed to hold small conversations with the women, talking a bit about himself and his new position at the ironworks. All of the ladies found it incredibly amusing that a young lord should work with the commoners, and I rolled my eyes and studiously ignored the questioning looks they shot in my direction. Apparently the local nobility already assumed that Joel and I would end up together despite his lack of Teuton blood.

I looked around at the other groups gathered in the square, awakening my ice just enough to improve my vision. I saw the Prince sitting beside his Lady on an upper balcony, their vivid clothing and jewelry standing out in the sunlight. I felt annoyance seep into my veins as I watched them enjoy some sort of dainties off of a plate held by a man wearing a jester's hat. *You like being the only one here who knows the Song of Time, don't you?*

Eventually my eyes moved back to the crowd below, focusing on a cluster of four men not too far away from where I sat at the fountain. Their attire indicated nobility; they sat around a large barrel, engaged in what looked like a rousing game of cards. I wondered what sort of card games people played in the eleventh century, smiling to myself at the memory of playing Rook with Hans. I doubted that I would ever be able to learn any medieval card games, because such ventures were probably considered too base for women.

The men appeared to be wholly enjoying their game, three of them hollering and laughing from time to time, all of them quaffing mugs of ale. Ultimately, my attention fell upon the quiet one of the bunch, a young man who looked to be in his mid-twenties, clean-shaven, dressed in deep red and black robes of nobility, several gold chains adorning his neck. Unlike the others in his group, he rarely laughed or made any comments, but his expression implied that he, in fact, had been winning the game from the start. His straight hair was black and hung down past his shoulders, and his fingers, holding the cards, looked both agile and strong.

A moment before I turned my concentration back to Joel and the others, the young man looked up from his cards and our eyes met. His face took on a hue of surprise and interest as he observed me and I averted my gaze quickly, shocked by the overwhelming darkness that seemed to emanate from his visage. I threw myself back into the ladies' conversation with gusto, trying to ignore his awful stare that seemed to bore into my back.

Several minutes later, the teen girls from the Adler estate began to talk about joining in the dancing. I glanced at the young card player once more out of the corner of my eye, relieved to see that he no longer looked at me. I tapped Lady Adeline on the shoulder and asked, "Who is that man?" pointing toward him.

The lady's blue-gray eyes rested on him temporarily. Then she looked swiftly away, shivering in spite of the summer heat, her expression distasteful. "That, my dear Swanhilde, is a very bad man," she informed me, her tone quiet. "Good women want nothing to do with him, for he has no honorable intentions."

I frowned at her words, glancing again toward the card players, who seemed to be finishing up their match. I did not know the eleventh century definition of dishonorable intentions, so I asked, "Why, does he steal kisses from noble ladies on their own front porches?"

Lady Adeline shook her head slowly, her mouth turning downward at my ignorance. "No, my darling, he is much worse than that. He is the executioner." I jerked at that pronouncement and almost missed her next words, my mind racing back to the conversation I had with Joel on the count's porch, almost a month ago now. "It is a pity that even the noble family of Bayern could not be spared the pain of the black sheep son."

"Oh, is he related to the Prince?" I shot another guarded glance toward the card players, who were rising from their seats, trying to pick out some family resemblance in the long-haired one.

Lady Adeline tittered softly and murmured in my ear, "He is Augustin von Bayern, Prince Otto's oldest brother. It would have been better for the Prince had that one not been born, I'm afraid." Lady Adeline chuckled again and turned away, saying that she needed to depart and meet up with her children and their nanny. She promised to catch up with me again later.

I could not choke out any sort of reply, for shock had flooded my veins at her careless statement: *Augustin von Bayern, Prince Otto's oldest brother*. I mouthed the name to myself, once, twice, my brow furrowing in confusion. Before coming to the eleventh century, I had read every pertinent writing I could get my hands on, Teuton, German, American, even those three pages authored by the cursed Black Priest. None of the writings I had read— *none* of them—had made even the slightest reference to an Augustin von Bayern. I had read copious notes on Prince Otto and his older brother Paulus who had joined the Catholic Church, passing on the responsibility of ruling the city to the younger one. But I had read positively nothing on a third Bayern brother, older or younger. *Augustin von Bayern*. The executioner. He did not exist. That did not make sense.

For a long time I sat and stared blindly at the ground, wracking my brain to come up with some plausible explanation for the apparent existence of a mysterious Bayern brother, a black sheep, the executioner. I did not notice someone standing in front of me until he spoke, so absorbed was I in my puzzlement. "I beg your pardon, my lady," the voice began in a sonorous tone, bringing my head up sharply, "but I should like you to give me the honor of a dance."

I found myself staring into the eyes of the executioner, the very Augustin von Bayern, who stood centimeters from where I sat, his body blocking out the sun. His eyes were the striking blue of the summer sky, light and mesmerizing, and had his countenance not exuded such a strong air of internal fury and discontent, he would actually have been very handsome, almost gorgeous. I leaned away from his imposing stance, my mind racing, calculating what the noble ladies might think and what might happen to my reputation if I accepted his offer. I remembered that Joel had been frightened by the executioner at his work, and he probably would not want me to share a dance with this dealer of death. Lady Adeline had said that noblewomen wanted nothing to do with this man.

But as I looked up at him, at his sky blue eyes and long black hair, blowing slightly with the breeze, my ice within me told me that he was fire. It had been too long since my last dance with fire. The problem was, I likely would not be allowed to dance an elemental dance, even at a Teutonic festival in the most Teutonic city of Bavaria. Outsiders still roamed the streets, and most of the dances thus far had resembled peasantry skipping and leaping, with no elements. Finally, I summoned my courage and answered the executioner with full propriety, "I am afraid that I will have to decline, my lord. I do not believe I know these dances."

The executioner's chiseled expression darkened further as he declared, "You must know some sort of dancing, my lady, for they tell me you were born here." My mouth fell open in shock, and I leaned even further away, disturbed that he seemed to know so much about me when we had never officially met. The young man's harsh expression thawed a bit at my reaction, and he bowed his head once toward me, assuming the air of the refined young lord. "Forgive me, and allow me to introduce myself, my lady. I am Lord Augustin von Bayern, and you," he nodded at me again, "are the Lady Swanhilde von Thaden."

I had finally reasoned out an explanation for his knowledge. "Prince Otto must have told you about me, Lord von Bayern," I said.

Aversion crossed his face at my assumption and he shook his head once, negatively. "Word travels, my lady." He took one step backward and held out his right hand, his light blue eyes burning me. "Would you dance with me?"

I had the disturbing feeling that this muscular executioner would pull me out to join the dancers himself if I refused again. I glanced once to the side, seeing Freia's wide-eyed stare and Joel's horrified expression. He looked as though he was seconds away from leaping between us. But I turned back to look this Augustin von Bayern in the eyes, knowing that I would have to find out everything for myself. I rose slowly from my bench and held my left hand out to him with a rather devious smile. "I'll probably step on your feet."

The executioner's expression mirrored mine when he grasped my hand, enclosing it entirely in his strong fingers. "I doubt that," he responded.

As we danced together with the other townspeople, I struggled to figure out the proper steps while my partner's far more experienced feet practically floated across the square. I determined to find out all I could about this man who was not supposed to exist, for maybe he knew some of the Prince's secrets. "You know, I'd never heard of you before today," I told him when we danced past the musicians, our fingers still linked.

"In that we differ, for I first heard of you about one month before today." The executioner wore a self-satisfied expression, his eyes suggesting an impending battle of wits.

Of course I would not back down, and I cocked my head at him, resolving to find some sort of weakness in that outer shell of hard darkness. "So you're Prince Otto's oldest brother," I said, trying to discern what type of fire he was.

Annoyance shot across his face as I mentioned his brother's name a second time. His eyes glowed a slightly deeper sapphire. "That I am," he replied shortly.

I tilted my head at him again, hardly paying attention to the dance anymore, simply following my partner across the square in the steps of the waltz, though that was not quite right. "You don't like the Prince," I surmised, the fire in his eyes not having escaped me. It was a cobalt blue.

"Not particularly, no," the executioner said, not meeting my gaze. Before I could press the matter, he remarked, "For someone who claims to have been born in Muniche, your accent sounds rather odd, my lady."

His words irked me, for I had not yet figured out a way to fix that problem. "Well, your speech sounds a bit stranger than that of most of my acquaintances here," I shot back, sticking my nose up at my partner.

A rather sinister smile broke across his face, and for the first time I got a good look at his teeth. They were a glorious white, the canines quite formidable. "Such proper diction comes as a result of education," he said, eyeing me as though he assumed I had no education. I opened my mouth to give some sort of retort, but he cut me off once more, halting his dance, brushing a few stray hairs back from his face with his left hand. "I think we should dance for real, now," he said, letting go of my hand and flexing his own suggestively.

I knew immediately that he referred to a true Teutonic dance, setting our elements free, and I recoiled, my eyes sweeping over the myriad of people milling about the square. "This is a public place," I reminded the executioner, "and the last time I used my element in public, your brother sorely reprimanded me."

"Yes, your attack on those poor, unsuspecting Gypsies." His tone mocked me, and he glanced around the square as well, taking note of each dancer in turn. He drew himself up then to his full height, brushing off his robes, and held out his hand to me again, his eyes blazing blue. I could literally see the heat waves rising from his palm as he said, his voice resonant and persuasive, "If my *brother* gives you any grief for this, you may tell him that it was Augustin's idea."

Excitement raced through my veins, and I knew that I could not refuse this opportunity. Who cared about the people all around? I wanted to *dance*. I focused briefly on my ice, my eyes glittering blue, my skin growing cold, and I reached out to grasp the executioner's hand again. A familiar sizzle sounded, and steam, and my partner eyed at our entwined hands in appraisal, seeming almost impressed. "I've danced with fire before," I informed him with a proud smile.

At that, the executioner grinned again and swung my body into his arms before I could react. He bent my body backward, his disturbing face just a handbreadth away from mine as he appended my statement: "But not with *me*."

We danced together as Teutons for a short but glorious time. While our dance bore some similarities to the many I had shared with Hans, I discovered to my astonishment that this nonexistent Bayern brother danced *better* than Hans. He whirled me around in a fiery tornado, his blue and my blue blending together in perfection. We leaped to impossible heights, jumping over tables, breezing across awnings, hopping around barrels and boxes. My ice began to grab humidity from the air to better counter my partner's fire, ever strengthened by the summer's heat.

I saw many faces watching us with expressions of wonder and envy as I scaled the fountain, freezing it entirely for a moment before my partner engulfed it with his heat, spraying my hair with tiny droplets of water which promptly froze. When we finished our dance at last to much applause, calming our elements, my partner led me back to where Joel and Freia waited, bowing properly at each group of cheering spectators. He halted just before the fountain, obviously preparing to depart from me, and I found myself unable to hold back one last question that had burned within me since we had begun our dance. "My lord, why are you not the Keyholder of Muniche?" I asked, curious.

Augustin von Bayern's face took on a look of such abject abhorrence that I backed away from him. "Because I did not want to marry my stepmother," he answered in a rigid tone. Then he turned away and melted into the crowd.

Chapter Eleven:
A New Enigma

I do not know how long I stood frozen after Augustin von Bayern had disappeared, standing a few steps away from the fountain, staring after him in total bewilderment. His last phrase repeated itself in my brain like the beat of a drum: *Because I did not want to marry my stepmother.*

According to what I had read regarding Teutonic traditions of past centuries, the keys of Teuton cities used to remain in one family until that family's male heirs died out. Cities chose their own Ladies to embody their collective souls, needing no human intervention in that aspect. The position of Keyholder, however, was a man's choice. *We women never have the choices men have, and it doesn't matter. All that matters is what you do with the situations that are given to you.* I remembered my mentor's words, the advice of one who had represented München for seven decades. How would she have reacted if her Keyholder had been her stepfather?

All of the histories I had read had listed two eleventh century Bayern brothers, Paulus and Otto. Paulus was two years older than his sibling but had been called to serve God as a Catholic priest, a righteous destiny not to be discredited. Thus, their father had passed the responsibility of Muniche to his younger son instead.

Now, a riddle had been placed before me: another brother existed, older than both Paulus and Otto. Why did he not hold the keys? *I did not want to marry my step-mother.* My twenty-first century mind drew back from the very thought, but in this time period, that likely would not be considered an acceptable excuse. He had refused the keys, the responsibility for this city, and its citizens distrusted him, wanted nothing to do with him. He was the executioner, and he was filled with hatred. Who was this man?

I suddenly felt Joel tapping my shoulder, whispering in English that I should stop standing out in the open. "Come back and sit by the fountain," he urged me, and I followed him, still in a daze. I was trying to balance the eldest Bayern brother's choice with the situation of the Lady. My eyes drifted toward the balcony where she sat with her Keyholder—a man much younger than her. Had she pre-ferred Otto over his oldest brother? Was his refusal of the keys a simple act of rebellion, or was it more multifaceted?

Joel brought me a pewter cup of bitter wine, and after I had sipped it for a few minutes I finally gathered myself enough to address him. He had discerned my momentary loss and had kept the others away from me. I saw now that several of the noblewomen stood near the fountain in a group, the Lady Hildegard with them, shooting questiona-ble glances in my direction while they whispered together. Freia had engaged several of them in conversation, likely to help distract them from me and my horrid dance with the black sheep son. I swallowed a bit more of the wine and raised my eyes to Joel's. They shone with a strange mixture of concern and discontent. "I shouldn't have danced with him, I know," I murmured in English. "But I have another problem, and I'm not sure how to solve this one." My gaze darted back toward the square in the direction my dance partner had taken.

"You definitely shouldn't have danced with him, and not like *that*, tossing ice crystals all over the crowd. That was the executioner!" Joel's English came out much louder than mine as he threw his hands into the air, obviously upset. "Didn't you *see* the evil in his gaze, in his whole appearance? How could you want to dance with him, Swanie? He was ogling you like he wanted to drink your blood from the second he started talking to you!"

I had not noticed. During the first part of our dance, I had been too focused on not allowing him to stump me in our battle of wits. During the second half—that glorious, Teutonic half—I had been far too impressed by his skill and passion to bother about his dark expression. Lowering my voice even more, I related my new concerns to Joel. "It doesn't matter whether he looked at me like Dracula or not. What matters is that he is not supposed to exist, according to Teuton records." He cocked his head at me, looking confused. "He says his name is Augustin von Bayern, and Lady Adeline said the same thing," I related. "*Augustin* von Bayern, the *oldest* brother of Prince Otto." I glanced back at the crowded square and whispered in a strained voice, "I've never read anything about him in my *life*. There were only two Bayern brothers. That one does not exist on paper."

Joel paused, trying to decipher the meaning behind my confused words. I could tell that he was attempting to think like a Teuton, for I had revealed quite a few of my people's secrets to him over the past month. "And your people seem to leave rather extensive records behind," he said, his voice also hushed now. "Do you think maybe his records were lost during the fall of Muniche in 1066?"

I considered that for a moment, ultimately shaking my head. "No, the city archives were emptied, entrusted to those who evacuated before the siege. There should be some record of an Augustin von Bayern somewhere, still accessible in our own time. Hans would have found it, if nothing else. I mean, he even dug up stuff written by a Black Priest, things that aren't supposed to be read by Teutons. Hans and I tried to find out everything we could about this era, so we would be prepared for anything. That man with whom I just danced?" I held up one finger, pointing it in the direction of the square, then eyed Joel seriously and confided, "He knew more about me than I know about *him*."

Joel's expression grew even more disturbed, and he placed his hands on his hips thoughtfully, screwing his mouth into a studious twist, which for some reason accentuated the light golden beard he had begun to grow. "Maybe this freaky executioner—did you say his name is Augustus?" Joel looked at me questioningly.

"Augustin," I corrected.

"Okay, Augustin. Maybe he didn't do anything momentous in history like the other two Bayern brothers. I mean, Prince Otto discovered time travel, and he led the Teutons in battle. Paulus wrote the first copy of your people's official history—*Der Weg Teutonisch,* I think you said it's called? And he also died at the hands of the Saxons, you said, after being held hostage for over a year. Maybe the only thing this Augustin ever did was execute people, and I doubt that would make a huge impact on Teuton history."

His arguments seemed possible, even plausible, except for one thing. "But he *did* do something monumental, something horrible," I whispered to Joel, the executioner's final words to me passing through my memory. "He refused the keys to the city of Muniche. *Nobody* does that. Nobody. That *had* to have been recorded, even if nothing else was!"

Joel frowned, glancing in the direction Augustin had taken himself. "Why did he refuse the keys? He didn't want to rule the city? That seems really strange, since most men want power."

I worked hard to hold back bile when I related his justification, the terrible words barely escaping my lips. "Joel, he said that he didn't want to marry his stepmother." My eyes shot toward the balcony where the Prince sat beside the middle-aged Lady of Muniche, Maria von Bayern.

"Wait a minute." A touch of horror appeared on Joel's face. "Are you saying that that Lady, the one who was with the council when they accepted us into the city . . . are you saying that *she* is Prince Otto's *stepmother?*" His hazel eyes darted toward the Prince as well, his expression revolted.

"Apparently so," I said, "and I guess it makes sense, because in the Middle Ages, the keys of Teuton cities were passed from father to son. At least she's not his biological mother," I added, antipathy flooding my veins at the idea.

Joel lowered his voice even more. "Do you think . . . do you think they . . . you know . . . *do* anything?" His eyes were riveted on the Prince and his Lady.

I jerked away from Joel, smacking him hard on the shoulder. "For heaven's sake, Joel, stop putting disgusting thoughts in my head! I highly doubt it. That's just gross."

Joel grinned at me and rubbed his arm. "*Incest,*" he said, wiggling his eyebrows in a humorous fashion. Smirking, I swatted him again and turned away, struggling to put aside the maddening thoughts of a man who did not exist on paper, but who danced like an angel . . . or like a demon. I was not entirely sure.

Later that night, as Freia and I prepared for bed, she brought up the subject of my dance with Augustin von Bayern, saying that I should stay away from such an obviously dangerous man. "I was shocked that you agreed to dance with him in the first place," she informed me while she pulled back the blanket on her bed and sat down. "You can tell, just by the look on his face, that he's not a good man. He would probably want to do hideous things to you, if you were ever alone together."

She would know, of course, since she had been abused by the Gypsies. But I had been pondering the mysterious executioner all day and had reached the awful conclusion that I could not stay away from him. He had piqued my curiosity in our brief time together, and until I figured out why he did not exist in Teuton records—at least in twenty-first century Teuton records—my interest in him would drive me insane.

I could not explain all of this to Freia without revealing everything, and I decided that night, a split-second choice, that since she had become my friend, she deserved to know the truth. So I sat down onto my bed opposite her, took a deep breath, and gathered my courage. "I need to confess something to you tonight, Freia, since you've been such a good friend to me these past weeks. And I do hope and pray that I can trust you to keep everything I tell you in confidence."

Freia looked taken aback at first, but a moment later she folded her hands into her lap and answered softly, "As long as your secrets will not hurt another, I'll keep them to myself."

I nodded, deeming her reply good enough, and began my story. First, I explained the concept of time travel, which Freia accepted without too much fuss. She said that Teutonic magic had always been beyond her comprehension, but that it did not seem impossible that Teutons might be able to bend time. I noted the restrictions of time travel, particularly that of not altering history, and I also mentioned the fact that time travel seemed to involve devils in one way or another, quite likely Wuotan, the heathen god of the Teutons. Once I had gotten Freia to understand all of the factors involved—explaining it as well as I could in Latin when Teutonica proved insufficient—I came out with the truth, telling her that I had been born in the year 1979, over nine hundred years in the future.

After Freia had recovered from the shock of this idea, I told her that there were two known ways to travel time, one of which had been discovered by Prince Otto von Bayern. I did not tell her that it was an organ song, not knowing whether the Prince might grow angry with me for revealing his secret to someone else. I also did not mention the Torstein since it had not yet been created. I simply said that Joel and I had come back to the eleventh century using one of the methods, and that we had lost the ability to return to our own time. We could conceivably return using Prince Otto's method, but I explained that I had already confronted him about it, and that he had refused to grant me the necessary information. Thus, I told her,

Joel and I would be trapped here in the eleventh century until we died.

Freia started in surprise at this revelation. "So if you and Joel die here, in my time, you'll both return to your own time?"

I affirmed it, smiling at her reference to *my time* and *your time.* That would be an easy way to refer to my situation. I admitted to Freia that neither Joel nor I felt comfortable enough to simply die at this point, even though my cousin Beth had already returned to the future, according to what the Prince had told me. I said that we had planned to come to the year 1064, but had arrived twenty years too early. Therefore, unless things changed drastically in the next few decades, both of us planned to stay for at least another twenty years.

Freia remained silent for a while, contemplating everything I had told her. At last, she raised her beautiful green eyes to mine and asked the question I wished to avoid. "So why did you and Joel decide to come to the year 1064?"

I sighed heavily, looking down at my bare feet. "I honestly can't tell you, and it kills me," I said, feeling like a horrible friend. "I'm not supposed to reveal anything that happens in the future, no particulars at least, for fear of changing history. I guess all I can say is that something is going to happen in about twenty years that I plan to see for myself. Whether Joel manages to remain here with me is up to him. If he decides to opt for death, I won't hold it against him."

Freia nodded, her eyes sad but accepting the fact that I truly could not tell. She glanced toward the door. "I hope none of the count's servants have been listening."

"I doubt we'll have to worry about that. My ice is on alert for intruders." I grinned conspiratorially at Freia, and she smiled back, shaking her head.

"I never thought I would have a Teuton woman for my friend," she confessed suddenly, a bit of shame touching her visage. "I heard stories about your people in my childhood, frightful stories about your powers and your blood, some of them claiming that Teuton priests still perform human sacrifices to Wuotan."

I shook my head. "In my time at least, even the priests rarely perform blood rituals. In *this* time, I'm not sure. I suppose I'll find out eventually. I doubt you need to worry about being sacrificed, though," I reassured her. "It's against Teuton law to have any familiarity with Wuotan. It's been that way since the second century." I wondered briefly what that might mean for me, since I had grown certain that time travel involved Wuotan directly.

Shortly afterward, our conversation turned back to Augustin von Bayern, the wicked executioner of Muniche, whom Freia insisted that I must ignore. She had spoken with several of the ladies while I had danced with him, and they had told her that horrid rumors abounded regarding the oldest Bayern brother. He had returned to Muniche just a year and a half ago, after spending three years allegedly gaining education at a foreign university. Upon coming back, he had immediately shunned the keys of Muniche before the face of his dying father, choosing instead to take the job of executioner due to his insatiable desire for blood and death. He was also a Teuton priest, Freia had discovered, and those who consulted him for advice or rituals always had to give him something in return, usually either sex or blood. The only reason he had not been asked to leave the city yet was due to his younger brother's graciousness. Although this Augustin seemed to hate the Prince, Freia said that if it were not for his mercy, Augustin would have ended up executed himself long ago. After relating all of this, she begged me to never have anything to do with him again. "You don't want him to treat you the way the Gypsies treated me," she finished, fear darkening her eyes.

She had given me quite a bit of fresh information to consider. Although the gruesome rumors about this black sheep Bayern brother were probably true, my curiosity burned within me. I told Freia that according to the Teuton records I had reviewed in preparation for my journey, only two Bayern brothers existed, Paulus and Otto. I admitted that in spite of the risk, I could not ignore this lack of evidence for the presence of a third brother. If the gossip about this Augustin was indeed true, then he really should have made the records, for he sounded like a horrible scoundrel. "I know it's insane," I said, meeting Freia's gaze, "but I have to find out all I can about this man."

She shook her head, her expression telling me that I clearly *had* gone mad. "Your curiosity may ruin you, I fear," she murmured, sounding distressed.

I sighed, knowing she was right. But the image of Augustin von Bayern's face ran through my memory—his long, straight black hair, his intense blue eyes, the confident set of his lips—and I realized suddenly that in spite of his dark aura, he was the handsomest man I had ever met in my life.

Chapter Twelve:
Disparate Goals

Joel arrived at the Meldorf estate the next morning about an hour before church. Though he now lived in the city—in a plain room shared with three other metalworkers, so he claimed—he continued to spend Sundays with Freia and me. More than once, he had grumbled that many of his coworkers came across as uneducated bums with no ambition. "They just want to spend all night in the taverns drinking themselves silly," he had told me several weeks before. "The only ones that actually have life goals are the married ones and the ones with girlfriends."

A small chapel stood behind the manor beside the path to the main well, and a stocky friar held two Sunday masses there for the benefit of the count's servants and vassals. Joel appeared grateful to be in a reverent place whenever the three of us attended the earlier service, seeming to cling to every word though he did not understand Latin. And Freia, who knelt on the other side of me, would recite the prayers with the sincerity of one whose God had never betrayed her. Meanwhile, I knelt between my two friends, my brain tangled with existential uncertainties.

Had God forgiven me for using the Torstein a second time, for bringing about my cousin's death, for killing an outsider with my bare hands? Had the Torstein vanished as a form of penance for me, to teach me that bending time was a serious responsibility? *Time travel is a dangerous thing . . . not to be treated lightly. It involves devilish forces, I fear*, Prince Otto had said. Hans, too, had shared that opinion: *The Torstein holds a power otherwise unknown to man. Such power can corrupt even the most honorable man's good intentions.*

Now I had to spend two decades bowing the knee to Catholic ritual each and every week, knowing in my heart that my deficiencies had brought me here. Sure, I wanted to learn the truth about my people's destruction, but my shallow reasons for taking this journey pricked at my conscience. *You need to stop pining for Hans every night*, I told myself firmly that morning in the chapel, while the friar read a passage from Proverbs. *You wanted time away from him, and that's exactly what you got.* I glanced toward Joel, clad in the greenish tunic and tawny trousers I had made for him back in our own time, his gaze fixed upon the rood hanging behind where the friar stood. *You need to focus on the guys here instead.*

Apparently a fair number of the local lords shared my opinion, for at lunch that day, Count von Meldorf informed Freia and me that Lord Niklas of the Kuegler estate would be visiting for dinner. "His mother has spoken well of you two, so I'd advise you to primp yourselves regally for the evening meal," he said with a sparkle in his blue eyes, his withered lips parted in an approving smile.

"Lord Niklas," I repeated, the name not jogging my memory at all. I sensed Joel growing tense on the bench beside me. Maybe I should suggest that we walk back to Muniche this afternoon and eat dinner at one of the taverns.

"Lady Hildegard's son," Freia reminded me. Her face looked radiant with anticipation, but then she murmured in my ear, "I don't know if I'll be any good at impressing a

Teuton lord. I can't dance the way you danced at the party."

"You can talk about music and God," I suggested, knowing that I needed to diffuse Joel's tension before offering Freia any helpful hints. "We can walk around the grounds this afternoon and eat dinner in the city if you want," I told him in English. "I'm not super interested in flirting with the local lords."

Joel snorted and turned back to his bean salad. "Can't say I expected that from you after what you did yesterday," he shot back, sounding irritated.

After lunch, Joel and I took leave of the count and Freia and headed for the fallow field behind the main house. Count von Meldorf used the three field farming system, leaving one swath of his land empty of grain each year. Grass, clover, and other weeds grew there this summer, and his farm hands had already cut much of it down and stacked it into piles of hay to feed the sheep and horses over the winter. I kept my eyes on the ground during most of our walk, taking care not to step in any obvious patches of manure. The sheep grazed in small groups throughout the field, their wool adding shades of white, brown, and black to the greenery dotted with yellowed haystacks.

"Once I get better at Teutonica, I need to find out more about flax, barley, and spelt," Joel commented after we rounded the first haystack. "All the farms near where I live grow corn and vegetables. I don't know anything about grains."

"The flax harvest starts Monday," I said, having sensed the anticipation for it all week. "From what Jarvis said, that gets planted in the spring along with the barley. Then the sheep get sheared in June, and the spelt harvest starts in mid-July and goes on through August. They plant the spelt in October, so they'll be mowing this field down one more time before then, since it's going here next."

"Wow. I'm starting to think I should've just stayed here, even though I do like metalworking. I bet we could get this place's profits up if we put our marketing skills to work." He nudged my shoulder and gave a goofy laugh.

I shook my head at his humor and gestured toward a smaller haystack just a few meters distant. "Why don't we climb on that for a minute? I'm getting sick of dodging all these piles of poop. It's harder to do in a skirt like this." Joel guffawed and agreed, vaulting himself to the top of the stack before reaching his right hand out to help me up. I sighed a little at his determination to maintain his gentleman's appearance, then grasped his hand.

"So how's life at the ironworks?" I asked once I had situated myself, looking toward the flax fields between where we sat and the stream. All of the fields were empty of people today, for Sunday was the day of rest on the Meldorf estate, along with nearly every other business in Muniche.

"I'm getting good at making horseshoes, according to my boss, but right now he's still selling mine at a cheaper price." Joel had stretched out beside me to gaze up at the sky, having laced his fingers behind his head. "Soon the foreman's going to train me on the heftier stuff since I'm young and in good shape. I'm one of the tallest guys at work, actually." He sounded proud of himself.

"That's because you didn't deal with food shortages as a kid," I figured, looking toward a collection of sheep cropping grass some distance away. I had not worn contacts today, so I could not count them.

"I guess so," Joel said, his tone suddenly wary. I glanced down at his face and saw that he looked up at me with a pinched expression. "Did you do any research on the weird diseases that went around in the eleventh century? Are we going to have to worry about the plague?"

"You're a couple centuries off on that," I said, but I felt a renewed sense of dread at the idea of facing ailments without modern medicine. "Beth was the one who did all the extra research. I didn't really worry about diseases too much since I thought we'd be here for only two years." I narrowed my eyes at him.

Joel's mouth curved downward, and he shifted his gaze toward the clouds above. "Sometimes I really miss my girlfriend," he admitted.

I laid my back down beside him. "Me too," I said, smoothing the cloth down over my hair before resting my head atop the hay. "And everyone else from the future, for that matter," I appended, watching a raptor soar high overhead.

"Yeah. This is turning into a really long vacation."

"Vacation," I repeated with a cynical laugh, shutting my eyes to concentrate on the sounds of nature around us. "It's a pretty sorry vacation when you have to stuff your underwear full of rags every month." I shifted my hips at the memory. My next period would start in just a few days.

"Ew. That's gross, Swanie!" Joel sounded revolted. I heard him scooch away from me.

"What? It's the truth. You'd better be glad you don't have to deal with that crap as a man." I reopened my eyes to look pointedly toward him. His face looked pale, and he had shifted to the far end of our haystack. I sighed and rolled my eyes. "Guess I'll have to commiserate with Freia since you're all squeamish about it."

"Maybe she knows some way to make it more comfortable." Joel eyed me in disapproval and then changed the subject. "My boss wants to come here and have dinner with the two of you sometime this week, by the way. He's young, and I don't think he has a girlfriend, so he's probably out looking. He says I can come with him, since he knows that you're . . . you know . . . my friend." His cheeks flushed with color, and he turned his face away from me, towards the flax fields.

His choice of words prompted my ice to trickle into my veins, and my reply spilled from my lips before I could think better of it. "Are you saying we need to . . . get together or something?" I immediately wished I could crawl into a hole. Heat rose in my cheeks, warring against my element.

Joel still looked embarrassed; the tips of his ears had begun to redden. "Well, I mean . . . it's . . . ." He kept his face turned away and rubbed at his chin.

"I . . . I'm not saying that I'd never want someone like you," I blathered, not wanting him to get the wrong impression from my hesitancy. "But I'm a Teuton, and you're an outsider. You know none of the nobility here has—"

"It's really a problem, isn't it?" Joel cut me off, turning his torso around to face me at last. "You and Beth pulled me down the rabbit hole into this place where magic exists, but I can't use any of it because I don't have 'Teuton blood.' I've heard my boss discussing me with the foreman when they didn't know I was listening. I'm a 'good worker who will go as far as an outsider can go.' What does that even *mean?*" He threw his hands into the air, his brow furrowed in frustration. "Do I have to be stuck as a hapless fool for twenty freaking *years* just because I 'don't have Teuton blood'?" He used air quotes and spoke in a Daffy Duck voice.

I sighed, my ice having cast a veil of blue over my vision. He scowled at the sight of my augmented irises. "You may want to look for a job with one of the outsiders in town, or maybe just come back here and work for the count. Some of his vassals are outsiders, in fact, a lot of them are. Teutons have guarded their blood fiercely through the ages. In our time, things have gotten more lax, but I know that's not the case here. Not sure what Lord Niklas is going to think once he realizes that Freia's an outsider and I've run off to have dinner with you."

Joel's expression clearly proved that I had not dispelled his exasperation. "So I guess the point is that if we got together, our children wouldn't have Teuton blood. Right?" He raised one eyebrow at me and crossed his arms.

I looked down at my hands in my lap and endeavored to confine my ice into my spirit. "Right," I said, goose bumps protruding on my skin at the subject. "That's why Beth isn't a Teuton, either. Her dad is, but her mom's an American. So Beth's Teutonic blood is so low that she can't even sense her element. And it's dangerous for Teuton women to have children. Not sure if you knew about that." I met his eyes again and jerked my head in the direction of the manor. "The count lost his wife when she bore a stillborn child. And their other two children died of sickness before they had a chance to grow up. Having children in this era is a bad idea, especially for someone like me."

Joel looked troubled. He uncrossed his arms and glanced toward each group of sheep in the field before responding. "So starting a family isn't the best way to become a part of history, I take it?" He sounded defeated.

"Is that *ever* the best way?" I asked, wondering whether Joel ascribed to the biblical view of children and wanted his quiver full of them. Did Beth have any clue about his apparent longings for offspring? "I mean, maybe it is for some people, but I'm here to find out the truth about the Teutons' defeat. And also to learn all the stuff Hans never wanted to tell me. Like why Teuton records don't mention a third Bayern brother."

Joel gave a doubtful snicker. "And how exactly do you expect to find out the truth about that? Dig around in the annals of Muniche's executioner?"

I grinned at him and replied, "Something like that. I'm going to the town hall tomorrow to see what I can find in the city archives." I winked at him, and he shook his head slowly and advised me to be cautious. Soon afterward, we climbed down from the haystack and struck out for the road to the drawbridge, intending to spend the rest of the day in Muniche—and avoid the amorous Lord Niklas.

<h2 style="text-align:center">Chapter Thirteen:</h2>

The Archives

I left Muniche shortly after sunset, parting ways with Joel at the eastern gate. We had spent most of the afternoon and evening in the Jewish quarter, for their shops closed on Saturdays rather than Sundays. I picked up a few bars of soap and a light green sash that I thought would complement Freia's eyes. While I may not have shared her interest in the local lords, I wanted to do what I could to help her claim a husband. Though she had spurned the arrangement her father had made for her, she may honestly have better luck finding love in some other German conclave. I did not know whether any of the Teuton lords would accept the low state of her blood.

I thought more about the situation between Joel and me, as I meandered in the direction of the Meldorf estate in the deepening twilight. Over the past weeks, he had proven himself to be a hard worker and a chivalrous man. Now that I had studied him more thoroughly, I understood why my cousin had fallen for him. But he was an outsider. Could I lock myself into an unequal partnership for the duration of my time in the eleventh century? Should I mention the blood-transfer to him? Would he be willing to take that fatal risk—and if it killed him, would he return to the future or enter eternity? *Time travelers should avoid deadly Teutonic rituals, Niofirgeban* had warned.

But the blood-transfer isn't ritual suicide . . . .

I hid myself in the sprigs of lavender when I reached the count's property, for I heard the distinct sounds of male voices and neighing horses. Apparently Lord Niklas was in the process of leaving, and I did not want to have to meet him. I sat amid the flowering herbs and watched the stars appear until I heard the clopping sound of departing hooves. I awakened my ice to enhance my vision and peered at the young man as he passed by. He rode a dappled stallion and wore high-collared robes that looked nearly as extravagant as the Prince's attire at the party. I caught the shimmer of a silver chain under the moonlight, and then he was gone, blending into the night in his journey to the road. Maybe his element was darkness.

Lord Niklas had not particularly impressed Freia. She seemed let down as we prepared for bed, for he had shown no interest in music or divine practices. He had spent most of the meal haggling with the count over the price that he planned to set for his flax harvest; the Kuegler estate also produced flax. Afterward, he had bragged about last year's hunt, telling Freia how his party had managed to slay an aurochs. "It fed his entire household for four weeks," she told me with a shake of her head. "He seemed really stuck on himself. And I don't think he was interested in me once he found out I'm Rhenisch."

"I'm sure there are a few decent lords in Muniche," I reassured her as I drew my blanket back and settled myself onto my bed. "Hey, if nothing else, you could always marry Joel. It's not like my cousin would mind, since she's not here."

"I think he's more interested in you than me," Freia answered, a wavering smile gracing her face. She stretched out on her bed, having wound her long hair into a bun. "Bavaria is a complicated place," she commented in a reflective tone.

I could not disagree. "You've got that right," I said, blinking at the wooden beams that crossed the ceiling above my bed. *More complicated than it should be.*

The next morning, I stayed behind in the bedroom when Freia left to head for the kitchen gardens. She wanted to pick some sage to bring up to our room so we could burn it with our nightly candle to purify the air. I agreed with her plan and warned her not to get worried if she returned to find my body frozen in bed. "I'm going to take a short trip to the city archives to see what I can find out about Augustin von Bayern," I explained. "Joel showed me the town hall yesterday, but he doesn't think I should go by myself, just in case it's against the law for women to poke around in there. But nobody should notice a Teuton spirit." I grinned at her.

Freia favored me with an anxious look, having stopped in the doorway to the hall. "So when your ice fully covers your body, that means your spirit travels unseen?" she asked, her stiff posture betraying her distrust of that idea.

I realized that I had not explained the full truth of the matter when I had fled to the spiritual realm to escape my panic attack. I finished arranging my hair under its bright blue covering and nodded once toward her. "That's why I let my ice cover my body the other morning when I couldn't breathe. The spiritual realm is a place of peace, and I've been going there for years to get my terrors under control."

Freia's eyebrows came together. "Wouldn't that take away from seeking help from God?" she queried, looking upset.

"And that's why I've been joining you in your prayers as often as I can. Now go get some sage. I'll see you when I get back." I waved her away, and she vacated the room with a sigh, her concern for me warming my heart. I wondered whether she might be willing to share her past traumas with me someday, so I could tell her more about my own. I did not know if she had any personal experiences with death, but she could probably relate to my brutal encounter at college.

When my spirit burst into the sky, I saw that my swirling robes reflected the light green hue of the Isar, sparkling and fresh. I hovered above the manor for a moment, watching the vassals hard at work on the flax. Stratus clouds had begun to layer the sky above, so I suspected that they would be working in the rain by day's end. I caught sight of Freia exiting the kitchen en route to the herb garden, her light green dress nearly matching the robes of my spirit. I smiled to myself, hoping that one of the local lords would give her a loving home despite her outsider status. The ironmaster Heinrich Denlinger would be having dinner with us on Friday along with Joel. Maybe he would prove himself worthy to claim my friend's heart.

And in the meantime, Joel tentatively hopes to claim yours . . . .

I cast my spirit toward the city without further ado, trying to push aside my dubious feelings for Joel. Today I needed to focus on uncovering all that I could about the nonexistent executioner of Muniche. So I set my course for the town hall, a large, imposing building made of gray stone, four stories tall with several massive doors leading inside. I set my spirit atop its roof first to observe the people trickling in and out of its doors. Many of them were Teutons—their spirits called out to me in greater numbers than I had ever before experienced: whirlwind, stone, smoke, fire, mist, yellow fire, earth, dark energy . . . .

I shook myself and closed my eyes, though as a spirit I could still see through their ethereal veils. *Okay, Swanie, you have to go inside even though there's more Teutons here than anywhere in modern times. None of them should see you unless they're using their elements to improve their vision. I doubt too many people know how to do that aside from priests. Just stay away from anyone in a black robe.* I gathered my courage and drifted down toward the main entrance, slipping in behind a peasant woman with a hooked nose.

Beyond the spacious entryway, I found an even larger atrium with many doors, stairwells, and hallways leading in diverse directions. The floor beneath my feet was of marble, the walls of dark paneled fir. Right beside the doorway to the atrium stood an impressive statue of a nobleman wearing a jeweled crown, his feet firmly planted, his robes and armor imposing, his clean-shaven face appearing both stoic and honorable at the same time. In his right hand, he held a key ring bearing four fine-toothed keys. The base of the statue bore the Latin inscription: *Prince Abelard Leopold Gottfried von Bayern, Founder of Muniche, A.D. DCCCXCVI.*

That's 896, I translated in my head after a moment's thought. I studied the effigy in its entirety, astonished afresh by the knowledge that I stood now in that very city for which he had laid the cornerstones less than one hundred fifty years ago. I had read about Prince Abelard in *Der Weg*, about his desire to plant a Teutonic settlement beside the River Isar, a new center for trade and culture. I thought about the München of my era, the largest city in Bavaria, still a hub of business and culture. I found myself beaming up at the statue in silent triumph. Though our people had fallen many times, our legacy continued, eleven hundred years in the future.

I summarily headed toward the atrium and its many doorways, leaving the founder of Muniche behind in my quest for the archives. Prince Otto had said that they were in the basement, so I began hunting for a staircase leading down, trying to avoid brushing up against any people. Eventually, I came upon a small wooden door with a brass knob, and above it a sign etched in Latin: *Muniche City Records*. A sneaky smile crept across my face, and I passed through the door into a dark, winding staircase lit by a single torch on the wall beside the entrance. I paused for a moment, trying to decide whether I should bring the torch along, since I had never liked the dark. *Oh well, hopefully there aren't any Teuton priests down here that'll know why a torch is floating,* I thought. I lifted it from its place on the wall and cautiously descended the staircase.

When I reached the basement proper, the walls of brick seeming to bend inward toward me, I soon approached another wooden door with a cruder sign posted upon it bearing a warning stenciled in both Latin and Teutonica: *Chroniclers and Official Personnel Only*. I frowned in annoyance and stretched my spiritual senses outward, trying to discern whether anyone was actually inside the archives. I knew that I would go in, one way or another, and if someone caught me, I could return to my body.

I heard no sounds within, but I may have felt the presence of another Teuton in a far corner near the outside wall. I curled my lip but remained resolute; I needed to learn whether records of a third Bayern brother existed here. *I can just keep away from that corner*. So I carefully turned the knob and the door opened easily, noiselessly. If the city council really wanted to restrict access to the records, they should have kept the doors locked. I stepped inside and closed the door behind me, my spiritual robes peppered now with the icy white of caution.

The archives were lit much more brightly than the stairway leading toward them. Another torch burned just inside the doorway, and a rather Gothic-looking chandelier hung from the ceiling at the center of the room. A trace of outside light trickled in from two tiny windows on the far wall, high up by the ceiling. I looked around at the seven-tiered bookshelves stuffed with parchments. Each appeared to be labeled with a parchment sign that gave a short description of its contents.

The chandelier granted sufficient light for my search, so I turned back to the doorway and set my torch onto an empty notch on the gray stone wall, opposite its glowing counterpart. Then I approached the first of the shelves and peered at the paper tacked onto its side. It was written in Teutonica with black ink, the letters a curling Carolingian miniscule: *City history, A.D. MX-MXLIII*. My mouth twisted thoughtfully as I craned my neck to see down the length of the shelf. It seemed that this one contained an exposition of what had occurred during the reign of the Keyholder prior to Prince Otto. Perhaps I could uncover some documents about Augustin von Bayern on that shelf eventually, but first I wanted to find his birth certificate.

I drifted slowly toward the center of the room, eyeing each parchment when I passed each shelf, encountering more shelves dealing with the city's history while others bore labels like *Judicial Records, Theological Studies,* and *Teutonic Traditions*. This last piqued my interest and I made a mental note of it, promising myself that if I ever returned to the archives at a later date, I would head straight for that shelf. Once I had reached the center of the room, I halted under the chandelier, trying to decipher where exactly the birth records might be. Though each shelf bore a label, the archives as a whole seemed rather disorganized. While I stood thinking with my hands on my hips, I glanced upward toward the chandelier, and I realized that the flames adorning each of its candles were not of a natural yellow or orange. They were blue.

I squinted my eyes at the candles, marveling at their tiny blue flames, wondering how exactly whoever had lit them had accomplished such a thing. At that very moment, a tingling feeling crept up my spine, telling me that the other Teuton in these murky archives had noticed my presence. My spirit froze, my robes shifting into a ghostly white in reaction to my uneasiness. I lowered my head, taking my eyes off of those intriguing blue flames, and turned myself with exaggerated care toward a shadowy corner of the room, furthest from the exit. And there, standing behind an ornate desk laden with papers and inkwells, a blue-flamed candlestick set atop it, stood a tall, sinister man wearing the garb of the Teuton priest. His long hair was as black as his robes, his irises a boiling blue that matched his candles, his lithe right hand clutching a feather pen.

My heart leapt into my throat as I recognized the executioner of Muniche, Augustin von Bayern, the very man whose birth records I sought. *Oh . . . shit . . . .* I tried to think straight, to recall how to condense my spirit back into my body. But he had already seen me, and his stricken expression told me that he knew exactly who had disturbed his work. Before I could order myself to vanish, my opponent had glided around the desk after placing his feather pen carefully upon it, crossing the stone floor in seconds to where I hovered. He glared down at me with a look that seemed to come from the pit of hell. The heat from his eyes swept through my spirit as he said in a deep voice, "My Lady Swanhilde von Thaden. And what, may I ask, has brought you into my domain?"

I blinked at him blankly, his question taking me completely by surprise. *I did not know . . . my Lord von Bayern . . . that this was your domain,* I answered.

"I am a chronicler. Of course the archives are *my* domain." His words cut like blades, and his eyes seemed to shred my spirit as he moved one step closer to me, shortening the distance between us to a mere handbreadth.

I gaped and drifted backward. *I thought . . . you were . . . the executioner,* I pointed out, glancing up toward the chandelier.

Glaring at me as though I had no more intelligence than a five-year-old, he said, "This city is not as dangerous as you must think. I rarely execute more than one criminal per week, if that. I must find other endeavors to occupy my time." He gestured at the shelves around us and toward the writing desk in the corner.

I recalled what Freia had said about this Augustin von Bayern, that he had attended a university somewhere in Europe for three years. It made sense that he could read and write, likely both Latin and Teutonica, and possibly other languages. *So you record things,* I translated, my curiosity awakening afresh. *Did you study writing when you attended the university?* I looked toward his desk.

The black-robed man's dark eyebrows came together, and he frowned at me, almost a sneer. "No, my lady, at Salerno I studied medicine."

I froze again as the complexity of this black sheep Bayern brother seemed to grow deeper and deeper. *Medicine? Salerno . . . Italy . . . ?* I shook my head, incredulous. *So . . . you're the executioner, a chronicler, and a doctor?*

"*And* a Teuton priest." My charge folded his muscular arms across his chest, pride touching his disparaging expression. "But since I studied at Salerno for a mere three years, I suppose that the title of 'doctor' does not actually fit me."

At first I could think of no reply to this while my mind worked to wrap itself around the concept of this mysterious man, still in his twenties, an executioner, a doctor, a historian, and a Teuton priest. He had refused the keys of Muniche for a rather understandable reason, yet remained hated by her citizens. I pondered this for a moment, my eyes trained again on the writing desk in the corner, with its blue-flamed candlestick. The oldest Bayern brother seemed about ready to comment on my silence a moment before I broke it to raise a valid question. *Who in this city would come to you for medical attention?*

His mouth twisted sharply downward at the implicit condemnation in my query. "When all others fail, they come to me," he stated sharply.

I cocked my head at him, remembering how Joel had described this man's apparent love for his work as executioner. Somehow, that did not seem to fit with the role of a doctor, particularly the Hippocratic Oath. *They come to you, and you save them?* I asked, dubious.

The black-robed man smiled at my words, a slow, eerie smirk. "When I can—and when I cannot, I kill them."

I jerked backward at his admission, so offhand, so careless. My charge took one step forward to lean over me, that same sinister smile still plastered across his pale face. Fear seized me at the realization that the city executioner now knew of my talents in the spiritual realm—a dangerous man with no honorable intentions. Would he squeal on me to the city council and have me burned as a witch?

I took several shaky breaths and ordered myself to be calm. That sort of death would send me home, not into eternity, so I had no reason to fear. I endeavored to draw the cool air of the chamber into my spirit to further reassure me; then I addressed the dark priest again. *You take pleasure . . . in killing people . . . my lord?*

The blue fire flared in his eyes, and he uncrossed his arms, flexing his strong fingers with the declaration, "There is no power vested in man akin to that ultimate glory of thrusting a helpless soul through the gates of eternal life or eternal damnation." His countenance reminded me of the Grim Reaper as he spoke, and he snickered to himself, a dark, ghostly sound. I quaked and wondered what fleeting chance I might have of defeating him if he chose to kill me in some awful way, here and now. As a priest, he certainly knew how to snuff out a Teuton spirit, even though Hans had never taught me that sort of thing.

The executioner lifted his eyes briefly to the chandelier above our heads, then looked back down at me and added, "Of course, there is also glory to be found in saving a life, in pulling a dying soul *back* to this world, away from eternity. I have done that as well, though that tends to be far more difficult, and less rewarding overall."

I gawked at him, too appalled to form a coherent reply. I mentally kicked myself, asking myself why I had not fled, why I floated here in spirit form discussing justifications for the glory of killing with the city executioner. What was the matter with me? I should go before things got worse.

I slid my eyelids closed to concentrate on abating my ice, but when he saw what I was doing, he stepped forward and growled, "Before you *go,* you may want to consider your fate, once the leaders of this city learn that their new constituent has the markings of a witch." He began to circle me, the heat emanating from his body doing strange things to my element, turning my robes translucent. "Probing around in the archives—a place not open to the public—in spiritual form with the intention of espionage, perhaps? Who holds your leash, I wonder?"

That's . . . that's not why I came down here! I cried out, the lungs of my soul fighting against his oppressive heat. I needed to get out of here, but now I could not grasp my ice properly to constrict it.

"A witch with the wisdom to manipulate the physical world as a spirit," the executioner went on, looking from me to the pair of torches marking the exit. "I highly doubt that the Prince would excuse such blasphemies."

Please . . . my lord . . . I didn't come here . . . to steal anything, I gasped, my spirit having sunk to the floor. I stared up at his looming face and choked out, *I . . . I was just looking . . . for a birth certificate . . . .*

He halted his pacing, looking both bewildered and curious. He pressed his mouth into a thin line, ran his right hand through his black hair—part of which was pulled back from his face in a black clip—and nodded once before beckoning me toward the shelves to my left. "Follow me." It was not a request.

I heaved a sigh of relief and trailed him to a massive, dusty bookshelf not far from the writing desk. It held a vast collection of boxes, each bearing a year written in Roman numerals. Augustin von Bayern gestured broadly, indicating the entire collection. "Here lies every record of live birth in the city of Muniche, boxed by year, sorted by month. Which record do you seek, Lady Swanhilde? Your own?" He raised an eyebrow at me in speculation.

A tiny smile graced my lips at that idea. My birth certificate, at least, had a good reason for not existing here. There was no point in hiding the truth now, so I met his gaze and replied, *No, my lord. I seek yours.*

Surprise shot across his features, and he drew back from me for the first time since I had encroached upon his work. "Why?" I could sense his astonishment.

My mind raced through all the possible excuses I could give, but in the end I answered simply, still smiling a bit, *Curiosity.*

He stared at me one second longer, then huffed once and whirled around to face the shelves, retrieving a box from the very top, marked MXVIII. He undid the clasp expertly and sifted swiftly through the papers within, muttering something to himself in a language I did not know. Finally, he yanked out one official-looking document and set the box firmly upon the floor before reading with the tone of a lecturer, "Certificate of live birth, first of—"

Annoyance washed over me when I realized that he thought me illiterate. I snatched the paper from his hand

and shook the dust from it, then held it up to the light from the distant chandelier and read in perfect Teutonica, *Certificate of live birth, first of January A.D. 1018. This record affirms the birth of a son, Augustin Abelard Ulrich von Bayern, to Prince Ulrich Leopold Eduard von Bayern and the Lady Marelda Louise von Förster und von Bayern, rulers of Muniche.* I paused here, rereading the names of the Bayern parents silently before looking at the full name of the oldest Bayern brother, who apparently did exist after all.

My opponent had frozen himself, though that seemed impossible for fire. He stood rigid about a meter from me, his hands clenched, his eyes glittering. "You read *the vernacular?*" His aura exuded shock and admiration.

I looked up from his birth certificate, eyeballing my charge with a dangerous expression. *Do you think I'm a fool? Of course I read the vernacular, and I read Latin as well. My lord,* I added scathingly.

Augustin von Bayern's face grew even more surprised as he said in Latin, "I have never before met a woman who could read both."

Chauvinism seemed to emanate from his expression, and I thrust his birth certificate onto the floor in fury as I spat, also in Latin, *I pity you, my lord.* I flew toward his desk and grabbed one of his feather pens from its stand, then bent down to write in the margins of one of his papers, "It seems that Augustin von Bayern has no balls, since he doesn't think a Teuton woman could read and write her native dialect." I stopped for a moment to consider, then switched from Teutonica to Latin to add, "What would this man think should he learn that one day men and women will be treated as equals?" Finishing with a flourish, I laid the pen down and raised my eyes to my opponent, who had followed me to the desk and now stood staring at my modern cursive with wide eyes.

"I am . . . speechless." Apparently, the proud lord had been truly stumped.

Well, I *am leaving,* I announced sharply, pleased that this time it seemed I had bested this haughty man of darkness.

As I turned away and shut my eyes to concentrate on my ice once more, I heard his voice behind me one final time, speaking a calm indictment. "Lady Swanhilde, your Teutonica sounds like you learned it from a *book.*" I paused just an instant longer before compressing my spirit into its physical form, clearly hearing the unspoken accusation in his words.

Chapter Fourteen

The Local Bachelors

When I blinked my mortal eyes at the ceiling, its beams blurring into a distorted taupe, I heard a soft gasp to my right. I pushed myself onto my elbows and turned to look at Freia, who sat upon a stool at my bedside, her verdant eyes round. "Oh Swanie, thank goodness you're back," she exclaimed, pressing her hands together. "Your ice began to melt not long ago. I feared something terrible had happened."

"What?" I put a hand to my forehead, trying to stop my thoughts from racing after learning such an odd collection of information. I realized that my hair was still damp, and when I looked down at the blanket beneath me, I saw the dark remnants of a puddle surrounding my body.

"It seemed to freeze up again before you returned," Freia clarified, her soft hand reaching out to touch my left arm. "But I kept thinking of what you said, that your spirit was apart from your body. I feared that you wouldn't be able to return if your ice melted. I almost ran outside to call one of the young men to bring some slabs from the ice house." She favored me with a hesitant smile.

I pushed myself off of the bed, figuring that I had better move around so my dress could dry. "I really appreciate your care," I told her, moving to the window to look out at the lowering sky. "And something terrible *could* have happened, but I think everything's okay. At least for now." I pursed my lips as I recalled the eldest Bayern brother's threat: *I highly doubt that the Prince would excuse such blasphemies.* I was certain that he was right about that. The Prince already distrusted me, and if he learned that I could enter the spiritual realm, he may send me back to my own time by way of execution.

And that dark priest in the archives would likely enjoy that . . . .

Another local lord had arrived to eat lunch with us, so I had no opportunity to consider my situation further until later that day. Count Abelard von Reuter was our visitor this time around, and Freia and I had to entertain him in the front parlor after lunch had ended. During the meal, he had followed Lord Niklas' example, preferring to chat about the going rate of barley with Count von Meldorf and groan about an illness that had cost him twelve of his piglets. Our host proposed a trade of a portion of his almond harvest for several of Count von Reuter's hens. As the two men hashed it out, I silently wondered whether Count von Meldorf wanted to get rid of his almonds this year due to Joel's allergy. We had explained it to all of the kitchen staff and to the count himself, who had pledged to distribute the bounty of his trees among his vassals instead of serving it in the great hall. Count von Meldorf had proved himself to be a thoughtful host more than once already. I needed to ask Joel if he had run into any difficulties with the food at the ironworks.

The more I learned of Count von Reuter, while we sat together in the parlor, the more doubtful I became about my potential for finding a suitable partner among the local nobility. He was thirty-four years old and had lost two wives already. His first had miscarried twice and bled to death the second time around, and his second had died of a fever two days after bearing his only child, a daughter.

He had begun to fear that his line was cursed, since he was his mother's only surviving son. "My Teuton blood just wants to die out, I think," he commented around a sprig of mint from the garden outside.

Freia and I shared a look, and I saw that her countenance appeared rather disheartened. "Maybe you'd have better luck with a woman whose blood status is lower than expected," I suggested.

He withdrew his face beneath the scarlet cowl he wore, his sneer telling me exactly what he thought about that idea. "I need a woman with strong blood and a strong body, not one who shrivels like a burning leaf when tasked with her natural duty. The Adler matron had eight children. Eight. Yet the women I find can hardly manage one."

My stomach twisted, and I placed a hand upon it and looked toward the window that faced the front porch. The Teuton men in this era were just as bad as the ones I knew back home. Offspring obsessed. "I thought Lady Adler had only two daughters and a son," Freia said softly, apparently sensing my momentary loss.

"A bunch of hers died of typhoid the same year she lost her husband to it." The young count sounded critical, and I heard him scratching at his brown beard as he went on, "Sometimes it seems like God is against us. Like He doesn't want the Teutons to be as great as they could be, retribution for our past alliances." He spat a mint leaf into the empty fireplace and grumbled, "I thought His forgiveness was supposed to cover all sins."

"Oh, it does," Freia said fervently, and the two of them went on for a good while about the implications of God's grace. Count von Reuter had spent two years studying at the monastery of Freising, but he was not as faithful with his prayers as my roommate. I quickly grew bored with the conversation and tried to lose myself in the dashes of color outside the window.

Would Augustin von Bayern squeal on me to his brother, whom he hates? Or would he rather keep it to himself, maybe spy on me in his own spiritual form sometime when I'm not using my ice to enhance my

134

vision? Maybe I should get in the habit of doing that, especially since I have only fifty-seven pairs of contacts left. Fifty-seven for twenty-two years . . . .

Suddenly, the word *Bluotgifuog* broke into my consciousness, spoken from the lips of the young count. I jerked into an upright position on the settee where I sat beside my Rhenisch friend and stared icy daggers at our visitor. "Excuse me? Did I really just hear you bring up the blood-transfer? That's not something Freia needs to worry about," I snapped at him.

"She doesn't even know what it is," Count von Reuter responded with a wave of his hand. Then he focused on Freia and said, "But it's what you'd be expected to do if you truly want to marry a Teuton lord, my lovely Lady Freia. It's an honorable course, one that brought us the eminent Schwabing family. Three generations ago, they were foreigners from the west. Now, their Teuton bloodline is strong."

I leapt to my feet and beckoned Freia to follow. "Teuton lords ought not to pressure naïve outsiders into rituals they'd later regret. And I'm not interested in giving you eight children, so you had best start wooing elsewhere. Maybe Helena Adler will prove to be as ripe a hen as her mother." I stormed out the front door, tugging Freia in my wake. She had readily taken my hand, but she looked confused at my verve. I pulled her down the steps and into the drizzle that had laid its sparkle over the flower gardens. "Come on. That squawking cock doesn't deserve our time of day."

She trailed me without question until we reached the apple grove, where she snagged my right arm to bring me to a stop. "What is it that he wanted me to do, Swanie?" she queried in a frightened whisper. "He said something about changing my blood into Teuton blood. How can that be possible?"

I sighed and stepped beneath the branches of one of the larger trees, letting its leaves shield me to some degree from the rain. "It's an old Teutonic ritual that generally leaves one person dead every time it's done," I told her. "I'll bet whoever gave his blood for the original Lord Schwabing didn't live to tell the tale. We'll just have to wait for a lord who doesn't care that you're Rhenisch. They need to see you for who you are inside, not just for the status of your blood."

Freia's shoulders slumped, and she leaned her left hand against the bark of the tree where we stood. "Lord Niklas may not have cared, but he was more interested in talking about himself than anything I had to say. I don't think he liked the fact that I lived as a Gypsy slave for over a year, though. He mumbled something about my being damaged goods." Her face fell.

I put my arm around Freia's shoulders and drew her close. "Hey, you know I've got twenty-two more years to stay here in your time. If all of the lords around here are snobby jerks, we can get Joel to come travel with us. We don't have to stay in Teuton lands. Maybe we can find you a noble lord somewhere else."

"Thanks, Swanie," Freia murmured, leaning into my embrace.

On Wednesday we met Paulus Schwabing, the youngest child of the family that ran the local salt mine. He was the same age as me, and he proved entertaining if nothing else, for after lunch we spent several hours playing ball with him outside in the fallow field. He seemed more interested in me than in Freia, but his element bored me, for it was Föhn—the warm mountain breeze—which was good for nothing in the hot summer months. I guessed that it could be useful in the mines. I asked him about his ancestor who had done the blood-transfer, and he readily related the tale. His great-grandfather had made a fortune in salt in the Schwäbisch lands to the west, and two of his sons struck out to find other cities in which to carry on the tradition. "Opa said it was the scariest thing he'd ever done, even scarier than going into the mines alone," he said. "But he was blessed with the element of air, perfect for our family's line of work."

Freia told me that night that Lord Paulus seemed rather taken with me, but I brushed it off. I did not want to spend two decades living near a salt mine, and the young man had sandy hair and freckles, which did not attract me at all. Also, he smelled like brine. If I had to choose between him and Joel, the outsider would win without question. I had started to suspect that Joel would be my only option, if I married anybody during my medieval venture. I did not want to lie to my husband about the future, nor did I want to tamper with events in any way.

On Friday afternoon, Freia and I prepared ourselves extensively in our room before meeting the count, Master Denlinger, and Joel for dinner. Both of us chattered animatedly while we checked our dresses and hair, sharing predictions on what the young ironmaster might be like. Maybe he would give Freia a fair chance. I hoped so, for I sensed her growing disappointment as she checked one lord after another off her list of potential husbands. She chose a vibrant yellow dress for herself, while I wore an elegant purple dress and veil, adding a pair of my mother's earrings and giving Freia her diamond necklace to borrow. She could focus her attention on the ironmaster; I would do my best to entertain Joel.

Our evening together flew by, but I viewed it as a glorious success. Joel and I sat opposite one another at the count's table, joking together in English from time to time while still paying heed to what the others discussed. Freia sat next to me and across from the ironmaster, and Count von Meldorf headed the table as always. Master Denlinger was an intelligent young man, having studied at Freising in his teen years before becoming his father's apprentice at the metal works. He could read and write both Latin and Teutonica, and he had extensive knowledge of the proper ways of molding metals into all sorts of objects from weaponry to crockery. His hair was a light brown and hung down around his ears, his matching beard trimmed quite neatly, his gray eyes sparkling with the enthusiasm of youth. Freia was impressed by him, I could tell, and I made several clandestine remarks to Joel about this in English during the meal.

After dinner, the four of us went outside to the count's gardens, where Master Denlinger confidently challenged Joel to an archery contest, since he had heard that Joel claimed skill at the bow and arrow. Once I had translated the ironmaster's challenge, hinting that Joel should accept it, he did so with enthusiasm after commenting to me under his breath that he had not shot an arrow in several months.

One of the count's servants retrieved the proper equipment, including a large target, which the ironmaster requested be set up on a tree in the distance. Freia and I stood back, watching and snickering as the young men boasted to each other about their skills, Joel struggling valiantly to put the correct words together in Teutonica. They did not act like an employer and his underling in this setting. I had a feeling that eventually Joel and Master Denlinger would become friends, just like Freia and I had. I hoped for it, since Joel needed a decent friend in Muniche.

Both men shot eight arrows before declaring the contest at an end. While Master Denlinger hit the target with six of his arrows, only two of his struck the bull's eye. To my surprise, Joel actually hit the bull's eye with four of his arrows, three of his having fallen short as he had slowly gotten the feel of the bow. Another of Joel's arrows struck the target just below the bull's eye, knocking one of his employer's arrows to the ground. Freia and I applauded both men, and I told Joel in Teutonica that his archery skills really were commendable, after all. The ironmaster echoed my praise, shaking hands with Joel. Shortly afterward, we all headed for the small stream on the southern edge of the count's property, ready to enjoy a short walk before the men would have to return to the city.

While weaving our way through the apple trees threaded with blackberry bushes, Joel described some of the new tasks he had been given at the ironworks. We conversed in English while Freia and Master Denlinger walked about ten meters behind us. "I've been running the bellows for an hour each morning and afternoon, and it's really starting to pay off, even though it makes me sweat like a pig. I could probably lift you with just one hand after a few months of this." He folded his right sleeve back and flexed his arm to illustrate, his biceps bulging impressively.

I smirked at his self-confidence. "It's probably a good thing for you to be on the burly side, especially if you ever run into any thieves on your walk here from the city. On that note, have you had any problems with your roommates?" I asked.

Joel rolled his sleeve back down and stuck his hands into the pockets of his trousers. Today he wore the black pair that I had sewn for him back home. "It hasn't really been all that bad since I moved into the dorm above the ironworks. The first week was a bit sketchy at the inn, but my boss runs a pretty clean show. There are four of us single guys in our room, and there's three other family apartments down the hall. We can get free meals if we eat what's cooked downstairs, and the clothes we wear at work were free, too. I guess you could call them uniforms." He gave a short snicker that sounded more impressed than amused. "I've never seen anything like it in our world, really. Here, a boss gives you more than just spare change." He glanced back toward Master Denlinger and Freia.

"Kind of like working for my Pappi," I recognized, somewhat surprised at the similarity. "Four of his staff live in the cottages I showed you out back, and technically they can eat whatever's in our kitchen. He's more generous than most wealthy people are." I curled my lip, thinking of the times I had visited Morgen and Ava at their lavish homes. Their servants all had the habits of the underpaid.

"Maybe your dad thinks he's a medieval Teuton," Joel suggested.

I barked out a laugh. "I don't think so. He's shunned the mere idea of Teutons since my Mutti died. But I've been meaning to ask if you've had any issues with the food. Does the cook at the ironworks know about your allergies?"

Joel winced and looked away from me. "Yeah, I explained it to him, but I had to use one of my pens earlier this week. My roommate Arik got some loaves from his sister, and they had almond flour in them." His face was hued with green.

I shivered and reached out to touch his arm, my fears for his safety coming to the forefront of my mind. "You'd better just stick with what they cook downstairs, then," I said. "I don't want to be stuck here by myself."

"Don't worry about it." Joel smiled a little and reached up to pick a clutch of apples from the branches above us. "For my roommates," he explained.

As we made our way through the front gardens in a trajectory for the stables, I decided to broach the subject of what I had learned in the archives on Monday. "So I found out that the city executioner exists after all," I related, quickly compiling a believable but less frightening tale of my experience. "Did some poking around in the archives with the help of a scribe, and we found Augustin von Bayern's birth certificate." I brushed my fingers against the lavender along our pathway, its floral scent wafting into the sultry air around us.

"Wow." Joel rubbed his beard and gave me an inquisitive look. "Guess the scribes are like the eleventh century librarians. So when was he born?"

"New Year's Day, 1018."

"Huh. That's a disappointment. I was hoping that executioner was like, one of the undead or something." Joel grinned and did a pantomime of stabbing himself in the heart.

I snorted and reminded him that, in spite of our powers, Teutons had not yet uncovered the methods of raising the dead or turning them into vampires. "But it still doesn't make sense that no record of an Augustin von Bayern exists in our own time. Apparently he does exist now, and everyone in the city seems to agree . . . but why does history ignore him?" I pushed a few stray hairs back under my veil and peered at the darkening sky above, the mystery of the eldest Bayern brother nibbling away inside of me. I still worried that he might mention my spiritual prowess to the council, if not to the Prince himself.

"Maybe while we're here we'll get to see him turn into the first werewolf or something," Joel said, prompting me to roll my eyes at him. He and Master Denlinger retrieved their horses not long afterward and parted ways with Freia and me. I could tell that Joel was grateful to not have to walk all the way back to the city after a hard day's work, and I thanked the ironmaster for lending his employee a horse for their journey. He bowed at me and assured me that it was no trouble at all, his bearing just as courteous as Count von Meldorf's.

When Freia and I retired to our bedroom that night, I asked her opinion of the ironmaster. "It seemed like you enjoyed his company," I noted as I ran a brush through my hair, working out its tangles. "And I also noticed that he could hardly take his eyes off of you during our walk."

"He comes across as a decent man," Freia admitted, a small smile gracing her face as she washed it in front of the mirror. "He's twenty-nine, he says, and has three younger sisters. He finished his apprenticeship two years ago but hasn't found a suitable wife. I think he's looking too hard."

"Maybe he needs to broaden his horizons to the western half of the Germanic lands," I suggested with a grin. Freia giggled, sounding more hopeful than she had for a while. Maybe Master Denlinger would prove to be the man that she needed. My Rhenisch friend might actually find love here in medieval Muniche, while my heart continued to yearn silently for Hans, the one I had left behind.

You're honestly a fool, Swanie, an immature child, I told myself as I got into bed, my eyes drifting toward the table that held our candle, where I laid my locket down each night. *You've been here for nearly two months, and you still can't detach yourself from the aged priest who doesn't want you. All your efforts to feel something more for Joel have fallen short; you and Beth have different tastes in men. He's a good friend but isn't romantic material. The local lords are all hung up on archaic expectations about strong blood and loads of children. How can you find a place for yourself here for two decades? Did you really think you could achieve something in the past that eluded you in the future?*

I did not know, and when I drifted to sleep, my dreams were haunted by dark Teutons calling to me from the shadows, luring me toward enticing defiance. And my subconscious began to tell me that maybe what I really needed was an enigma like Augustin von Bayern, an educated Teuton priest who had spurned his place.

Chapter Fifteen:
The Linguist

On the following Tuesday, one of the count's female servants interrupted me while I sat weaving a dress out of dyed red wool, my first attempt at creating a medieval winter dress. "There's a young lord downstairs in the front parlor who wishes to speak with you, Lady Swanhilde," the servant informed me, curtseying.

Perplexity crossed my face, and I wondered who it could possibly be. No one referred to Joel as a "young lord" at this point, and I had taken care not to show interest in any of the noblemen. But I rose from my cushion in the sewing room anyway and told the servant that I would be down shortly. "I'll be back later," I told the group of girls working on basic trousers for several of the vassals. They were the same three who had giggled at Joel on our first morning at the Meldorf estate. I had begun to enjoy spending time with them, for despite their lack of education, they had shared useful tidbits with me over the past few weeks.

"Make sure you kiss your young lord!" the oldest one crowed as I stepped into the hallway, prompting the other two to chortle.

"That'll depend on who it is," I called back. I stopped in my bedroom first and found Freia sitting in the beams of sunlight pouring from our window, reading the Latin half of my Bible. "I have a visitor, apparently," I said, pausing at the mirror to check my face and hair. "I guess I need to be more obviously disinterested when these young lords call on us in the future." I patted my hair into place, deciding not to bother putting on a veil, and smoothed out the wrinkles in my indigo dress.

Freia rose from her seat, looking curious herself. "That's odd. Most people around here know that you and Joel are an item, so to speak. Do you mind if I come downstairs with you? I'd like to see who it is."

"Sure." I crossed the floor to our door and stepped out into the hallway with Freia at my heels. "I hope he's not planning on staying for lunch. I heard the cook say we're having pork, and I don't feel like sharing our bountiful feast." Both of us laughed at this as we reached the bottom of the staircase, passing through the front vestibule into the main parlor, tittering like two young girls without a care.

The second I lifted my eyes to regard our visitor, my laughter ceased with the suddenness of throwing a switch. Freia also fell silent behind me, and my eyes widened at the sight of Augustin von Bayern standing in the center of the parlor, dressed in elegant blue and russet robes of nobility, his long hair pulled back entirely in a clip, brown leather boots enclosing his feet all the way to his knees, his hands clasped calmly behind him. A rather disturbing smile broke across his face when we entered the room and he bowed low toward us, his light blue eyes fixated on me. "My lovely ladies, Swanhilde von Thaden and Freia von Eisenwald. I trust that this splendid summer morning has been treating you well, thus far?"

I had frozen at the very sight of him, my ice seeping through my veins, while Freia clutched the back of my dress, her fingers tight with anxiety. My mind raced, for the servant had said that this man sought *me,* not Freia. I could not for the life of me discern why, though I feared that he may have spilled the beans about my exploits in the archives. Gathering my courage and decorum, I curtseyed hastily and replied, "It has been an excellent morning, my Lord von Bayern, though I regret that you have interrupted my pursuits with the needle."

His smile grew caustic, and he mocked, "A noblewoman working the trade of sewing? You really need to find more respectable methods of passing time, Lady Swanhilde." My eyes bulged, petulance bursting within me. I opened my mouth to defend myself, but he cut me off. "Unfortunately, I shall be requiring more of your attention than your beloved fabrics this morning, my lady. I should like to request that you take a walk with me along the stream."

Freia leaned close to my ear to whisper urgently, "Don't go with him, even though it's daylight. He may try to harm you. Tell him no."

I should have listened to her, and truthfully I could have refused him, for our brief conversation had already attracted the attention of several of the count's servants. I could hear footsteps in the hallway behind us, whispered words passing from mouth to mouth. The male servants could have held the executioner back from me, if I refused and if he attempted to force me to comply.

But I had discerned something about this imposing Teuton's character already, though I had encountered him only three times as yet. He was intelligent and persuasive, and when he wanted to know something, he would satisfy his curiosity whether those involved wanted him to or not. Our confrontation in the archives had likely aroused his interest. It would be safer for me to find out what he wanted now, during the day, at Count von Meldorf's estate no less, than somewhere unfamiliar. So I put my head up and accepted his invitation with a bravery I did not feel. I pried Freia's fingers loose from my dress before following the smirking executioner out the front door, into the sunlight.

We walked slowly toward the stream in silence, and I began to wish that I had taken the time to cover my head with a veil, feeling the sun's rays beating down on my black hair. Swatting some insects away from my face as we passed through the vineyard, I covertly studied the executioner of Muniche again. He stood nearly as tall as Joel by my reckoning, with broad shoulders and a thick neck. His hands and arms certainly did appear strong enough to wield the executioner's axe. He walked with a confident stride, his legs also embodying strength, and his black hair shone in the sunlight like an obsidian rock, tied into a sort of bun at the back of his head. It would have looked funny—even effeminate—had he been a smaller man or one with underdeveloped limbs. But there was nothing womanish in the poise of Augustin von Bayern, nor in his voice. According to his birth certificate, he was twenty-six years old. In spite of the horrifying impression he had left on me at the archives, his attractiveness stood out vividly now.

"The Lady Freia tried to dissuade you from this stroll," he commented, at last breaking our silence when we neared the banks of the stream.

I hoped that he would not hold her words or opinions against her, since they had resulted from gossip. "She has heard terrible stories about you from the ladies of the city," I began cautiously, following my companion's upstream course. "She thinks I need to avoid you, since the overarching opinion suggests that you are not an honorable man." I eyed his back in consideration.

The executioner paused and gazed upstream for a moment, then answered, not looking at me, "No, I am not an honorable man, because the so-called 'honorable' men would rather hide their sins and put forth a false air of perfection."

His words rang with truth, although coming from him they sounded acerbic. "So you'd rather . . . just be open about the fact that you enjoy killing people?" This man was perverted, in spite of his apparent honesty.

He whirled around to face me then, his light blue eyes burning me more than the sun. We halted beneath the cherry tree where I had first confronted Joel about his nut allergy. "Why did you not listen to her? Why did you come?" he demanded, sounding furious.

I stared back at him, trying to reason out his sudden ire. "Because unlike most women, I prefer to find things out for myself rather than believe idle gossip."

The executioner's face became ashen; he backed away from me and placed one hand upon the bark of the cherry tree. He shook his head once and muttered in a fearsome voice, "You are going to kill yourself . . . my lady."

At first, I feared that he may have figured out the truth, that I would have to die to return to where I belonged. A second later, I realized that he spoke of my mad curiosity about him, the executioner, the man who coveted that great high of casting souls into eternity. Holding my own fear at bay as I acknowledged the potentially mortal danger of familiarity with this man, I answered him in a low voice, "Perhaps that doesn't matter to me." And it did not, since dying meant that I would return to the twenty-first century.

He sneered back at me, his fingers digging into the tree bark, smoke curling from beneath his hand. "It *will* matter to you, my lady, and *today*," he promised, his eyes boiling with blue flames. "When you sought my birth records over a week ago, you engendered an undaunted curiosity within me regarding your own background." I froze at last, my eyes widening in horror. He wanted the truth from me. I barely knew this man. What would he ask of me? "The fact that you speak, read, and write both Teutonica and Latin aroused my interest, Lady Swanhilde. As I told you in the archives, you are the only woman I have ever met who seems so well versed in such subjects, and you are the only woman I have ever watched manipulate the spiritual realm with such precision. It came to me, after I heard you read and watched you write, that the strange way with which you pronounce my native dialect could stem from learning it from a book rather than from hearing it spoken."

He stopped here, eyeing me dangerously, and I wracked my brain, unsure how much I should tell him. "Maybe I *did* learn my Teutonica from a book," I said at last, meeting his frightening gaze. Let him take that how he liked.

He made a grumbling noise in his throat and then spoke the accusation that I could not counter. "You came to the archives seeking *my* birth certificate, Lady Swanhilde. For the past *week*, I have sought yours. *I found it not.*"

My mouth went dry, and I took several steps backward, trembling. He let go of the tree and followed me, one of his steps equaling two of mine. "I scoured every box from the year 1010 to the year 1030 and found no record of you or any other 'von Thaden.' I also checked the death records and marriage records and found no reference to your alleged family name. Yet you claim publicly to have been born in Muniche. I await your explanation."

I nearly tripped over a rather large boulder in my haste to distance myself from him, then sat down upon it, bruising my buttocks, digging my icy fingers into it, though they found no purchase. The executioner halted directly in front of me, his eyes seeming to pierce my soul. "Why don't you ask your brother, the Prince?" I gasped, attempting to stave off the inevitable truth.

"My brother never tells me *anything*," he retorted, a darkness seeming to envelope his being at the mere suggestion. "*That* is why I came to you."

I choked on my own breath and leaned further back onto the boulder, my eyes trapped by his terrible stare. "I . . . I'm not . . . supposed to say . . . anything . . . about this," I whispered, my heart pounding.

"But you told my brother, apparently." The executioner smiled when he reminded me of the truth, his cobalt eyes drifting from mine to my neck. "I should warn you, my darling lady, that when I am presented with an intellectual riddle, I find the solution, one way or another. If you refuse to grant me the information I seek, I shall bleed it from you."

I shuddered all over at his words, my mind trying to wrap itself around his threat: *bleed it from you.* I had never heard of such a thing. "*What?*"

"For a Teuton woman, you are at times horribly uninformed," he told me, his eyes still riveted on my neck. "I am a priest; I know all of the blood rituals, my dear. And I know that there lies a channel in every person's neck, one that connects the brain and the heart, the two organs that retain every thought, every memory, every emotion—even those that have been consciously forgotten. Any Teuton priest who has been properly trained can bite down onto that channel and uncover everything he wants to know."

I cried out in horror, my fingers scrabbling against the boulder, my head mashed against it. I watched him lean over me with a devilish smile, his posture suggesting that even if I *did* tell him everything, he would bleed me anyway. "I should also warn you, my Lady Swanhilde," he went on, reaching one strong hand out to my face, "that the pure blood of a Teuton woman is generally far more delectable than the blood of a foreigner. If I bleed you, I may not be able to stop, and you will die." His fiery hand caressed my chin, sliding its fingers gradually down my throat. His face just centimeters away from mine, his blue eyes glowing with anticipation, he finished, "So you had better start talking."

I found my voice somehow at that point and choked out a faint plea. "Wait! Please . . . wait . . . I can explain . . . ." I was hyperventilating. He did not relax his threatening stance. His fingers continued to stroke the veins in my neck, his touch too gentle under the circumstances. I knew that I had only seconds, so I gathered my thoughts and burst out, "Do you know about your brother's song? The one he wrote for the organ that can open the gates of time?"

To my relief, recognition crossed his expression, and he straightened, taking his fingers off of my neck, his mouth twisting in aversion. "Yes, I do know about that, not that he would have told *me* anything. I discovered it by accident one night last December, when I graced the doors of the Bayern palace to confer with the Prince regarding the planned festivities for the New Year." I rose slightly from the boulder as he talked, my fear gradually dissipating while I listened to his story with interest. "When I sought him inside, I heard several final notes of a song pealing forth from that wretched organ of his. As I turned in that direction, I heard something else, while the last note faded slowly from the air. I heard a crack that seemed to come from hell itself, reverberating throughout the palace, and when I opened the doors to his music room moments later, to my consternation I saw two massive gates of color-flecked obsidian open inward into darkness, with both of my foolish brothers tumbling outward onto the floor beside the organ."

The executioner paused in his tale, still frowning, gazing across the stream toward the walls of Muniche far in the distance. I probably should have run from him then, while he appeared distracted, for if I used the stream to my advantage, I may have been able to escape him entirely. But his story had piqued my interest, for apparently he had been a witness—the only witness—to Otto's and Paulus' trip to the time of Christ. I waited eagerly for him to continue, forgetting my fear of him for the moment. "Unlike them," he stated carefully, his voice laden with scorn, "I do not ignore the forces of darkness or pretend that I do not dabble with them myself. I heard and recognized that laughter ringing out from those gates."

"Wuotan?" I could not help interrupting him as I jumped up from the rock. "It was Wuotan the demon, wasn't it?"

His gaze returned to mine, and he showed his teeth in a rather wicked smile. "You know this." It was not a question.

I could hide the truth no longer, and it seemed safe to tell the oldest Bayern brother the truth now, since he also knew about the potential of time travel. "You couldn't find my birth certificate because I haven't been born yet," I told him, holding his gaze with my own. "I was born in 1979."

The executioner's mouth dropped open, and he backed away from me again. "You were born . . . nine hundred thirty-five years . . . in the *future?*"

"Yes, that's why my Teutonica sounds like it comes from a book," I went on, the words tumbling out of me. "In my era, the twenty-first century, anyone who speaks Teutonica has learned it from books."

He nodded slowly, his expression implying that my riddle had been solved. "And you came here using the Prince's song?" He sounded incredulous.

"No, actually . . . ." I paused for a moment, hoping that he would not demand that I explain exactly *how* I had come to his time period. I had not yet revealed that to anyone, not even Prince Otto himself. If this death-loving historian tried to bleed *that* from me, I would run, I resolved. I invoked my ice into my veins again just in case, its familiar blue veiling my vision. "I came here another way, one that hasn't been discovered yet. But I can't go back the way I came. I could use your brother's song, but I already talked to him about that and he won't give it to me." I huffed a bit at the memory, my lower lip protruding of its own accord.

"You play the organ?" The executioner eyed me suspiciously.

"Of course I play the organ," I said shortly, placing my hands on my hips. "And I'm pretty good at it, for that matter. I'm studying music at the university."

Augustin von Bayern looked stricken, his eyes as round as saucers. "*That* I would like to see," he commented, nodding at me in appraisal.

A sudden inspiration hit me. "Do *you* know Prince Otto's song?" I inquired, a fresh hope refreshing my element.

He gave me a dark look and replied, "No, I do not. Though I am many things, I am not a musician. I do not even remember what those last notes were that I heard that night. If I heard the whole song, I could not relate it."

I sighed, my optimism crashing to the ground. "Maybe I should ask Paulus, since the Prince won't tell me. Maybe he would grant me some mercy."

A sarcastic laugh burst from the executioner's lips. "You cannot ask him for anything, my lady. Paulus is the

Prince's toady. He never does anything without his younger brother's permission." He sneered in repugnance.

The complexity of the Bayern family just seemed to grow and grow, but I was too occupied by my constant failures to find another way home to pay much attention. "I guess Joel and I are stuck here until death then," I muttered, kicking at the grass beneath my shoes.

"Ah yes, the metal worker. So he also is from the future?"

It surprised me that my charge knew of Joel, but then I grasped the fact that he must have been the one to archive our papers of citizenship. That was how he had heard of me. I nodded and said, "Yes, Joel is from my time too, but Freia is not. We found her when we escaped from the Gypsies."

"So why did you drag him along?" The executioner gazed at me thoughtfully, fingering his sleek outer robe. "As I recall, he has no Teutonic blood in him whatsoever. Why bring an outsider into a fully Teuton society?"

"He's betrothed to my cousin," I said, memories of her demise prompting me to cringe. "She came on the journey too, but one of the Gypsies killed her."

"So it was revenge that incited your attack," the eldest Bayern brother discerned, the fire in his eyes not particularly condemning that idea.

I shrugged once and looked away from him. "I guess so. But she's fine, back home already. It's been pretty hard for Joel, though, learning to live in this society. I've been trying to teach him Teutonica, but it is difficult to find time."

I looked back at the executioner, who cocked his head at me with interest. "Then you speak three languages, Lady Swanhilde?"

I barked out an impolite laugh at that. "*Three?* Hardly, my lord." He eyed me inquisitively, and I counted off every language and dialect I spoke, using my fingers. "Teutonica, Latin, English, High German, Bayerisch, French. Six." I beamed at him triumphantly. He could no longer label me uneducated.

"Thank goodness; at first I feared that your knowledge may outrank mine." The firstborn Bayern brother grinned at me and held up both hands, curling each finger in one at a time. "I speak Teutonica, Latin, Rhenisch, Schwäbisch, Sächsisch, Frankisch, Magyar, Italian, Arabic, and Ælte Teutonica. Ten."

I gawked at him, impressed. "Ælte Teutonica is the old version of Teutonica, right? The language used by the heathens of times past?" He raised an eyebrow at me, his eyes glinting with the mystery I had come to expect from a Teuton priest. I thought about the other languages he had mentioned. "Arabic because of medicine, I presume?" He nodded, looking surprised that I would know such a thing. "I read all I could get my hands on before coming to the eleventh century," I informed him with a grin. "I wanted to be ready for anything."

My charge smirked back at me, his teeth glittering in the sunlight. "Well, all of your *reading* has certainly not improved your accent."

I pouted a bit, wishing that I could figure out a solution to that. All at once, the inspiration hit, and I said, "Maybe *you* could help me with that."

Shock crossed the executioner's face again, and he took a few steps backward to halt underneath the cherry tree. He shook his head once, his expression growing dangerous. Then he looked down at me and stated, "Surely you have heard the rumors, my lady, that no one can gain any knowledge from me without giving me something in return." His eyes bored into mine, awaiting my reply.

My mind flew back to the conversation I had with Freia, the night after I had danced with Augustin von Bayern. *Those who consulted him for advice or rituals always gave him something in return . . . usually sex or blood . . . .* I grimaced, ordering myself not to fear, and addressed him formally. "Unfortunately, my Lord von Bayern, I'd rather keep my blood and my memories inside my body. And I am a Christian, so I will not grant my virginity to a man who is not my husband."

The oldest Bayern brother scowled at me derisively. "What a pity. You are missing a lot of pleasure with those standards, my lady." I recoiled at his words and glanced back toward the house. It had to be nearly Sext by now, and I did not want to miss lunch. But the executioner was not finished with me. "What, then, do you plan to give me, Lady Swanhilde?" He eyed me suggestively.

As I tried desperately to come up with something, I remembered that this disturbing man was the archivist and had studied at a university, so intellectual matters must interest him in spite of his grotesque hang-ups. "Since you are such a linguist, my Lord von Bayern, if you agree to teach me the proper way to speak Teutonica . . . *and* teach me to speak, read, and write Ælte Teutonica . . . I will teach you how to speak, read, and write twenty-first century English and High German." It was a challenge. I waited.

"Languages of the future in exchange for languages of the past." He stared off across the stream once more, his light blue eyes burning with interest. "Though I know not what good such knowledge would do for me, it would be a fascinating study, nonetheless. It is a bargain." He held out his right hand.

I smiled with excitement, glad that now I could finally do something useful with my time here. Maybe once I had mastered Ælte Teutonica, I could sift through some of the really ancient writings and learn the things that people in my era had forgotten—like why Teuton women had a hard time bearing children. I reached out and shook his hand, his fingers enclosing mine entirely. "It's a deal. Now, I must go to lunch. Thank you, Lord von Bayern."

He nodded at me once when I turned to go, a genuine smile gracing his face. "You may call me Augustin. And I shall see you again soon, Swanhilde," he said. I smiled back at him and let my ice loose to sprint for the manor, leaving that disquieting nobleman, the oldest Bayern brother, the executioner, the archivist, the linguist, the Teuton priest . . . *Augustin* . . . behind me.

Chapter Sixteen:
A Dangerous Path

The final bells for Sext had already died away by the time I made it to the great hall. I blew in through the kitchen and took my place beside Freia, a frosty cloud settling around me and dissipating into mist. "Oh Swanie, thank goodness you're all right," she said while I situated myself, taking in the salad spread before me. Cabbage, onions, leeks, and green beans festooned with sprigs of dill and lavender. I began crushing it with my spoon, silently longing for a fork for what felt like the thousandth time. Freia passed me a jar of vinegar and murmured, "I watched you until you headed downhill toward the stream. Then Erna asked me to help her lay out the bread."

"It was fine. He didn't hurt me," I assured her, savoring the tangy mingling of dill and vinegar with the main components of my salad. "He was mostly curious about something I'll have to tell you later." Though a cacophony of conversations filled the hall, I did not wish to speak the truth of my origin in a place where I might be overheard. I glanced toward the count, who was discussing plans for a hunt with Jarvis. He intended to butcher a number of sheep and chickens before winter and distribute the meat amongst his vassals, but apparently wild game was still a hot commodity for a burgeoning estate.

"Word of your rendezvous has been going around," Freia mentioned after a few moments of silent eating. "The staff here seems to share the noble ladies' opinions of the Lord von Bayern." She gave me an apprehensive look.

I rolled my eyes toward the crossbeams above, not yet having discerned a fair reason to despise my prospective tutor. Sure, maybe horrid rumors abounded about him, but he did not have the power to actually kill me. "He's very educated," I said, recalling his accomplished expression when he recited the ten languages he knew. "We agreed to trade some of our linguistic knowledge."

"You didn't!" Freia said in an undertone, her soft fingers closing around my upper arm.

"Hey, I came here to learn all the things that history doesn't reveal," I reminded her, lowering my voice considerably as several servants brought forth the main dish: steaming platters of pork sprinkled with herbs and berries. "Learning how to read ancient dialects is a start, I'd say."

Augustin von Bayern made a habit of calling upon me at the Meldorf estate every Tuesday and Thursday evening afterward, for "intellectual stimulation" as he labeled it. On his first visit, he brought with him a massive roll of parchment, three inkwells, and half a dozen pens. He tasked me with compiling a dictionary of English words and German words to aid his studies. I responded that while I was not Noah Webster—I had to explain the reference—I would do my best, focusing at first on the major terms necessary for dialogue. He also lent me his own worn guide to Ælte Teutonica that first evening and hinted that I had better treat it respectfully, since very few such books could be found. I promised that I would take good care of it, commenting with a wink that if I ever took a trip further back into the past, people would claim that my Ælte Teutonica sounded like I had learned it from a book.

Upon his second visit, we began our language studies in earnest. I explained the proper pronunciations for greetings and introductions in both English and German, while he coached me rather stringently on the local form of Teutonica. He insisted that I did not form my *r*'s and *t*'s correctly, often glaring at me as though he wished to rip my tongue from my mouth and bend it himself. I told him to just wait until we encountered the many English diphthongs; those would certainly give him nightmares. The only reason I could get them right was because I had learned basic English before the age of six, so I wished him luck at perfecting such impossible sounds at age twenty-six. I considered how amusing it would be if I could teach Augustin, an eleventh-century Teuton, to speak English with a South Jersey accent, resolving immediately to do just that.

The third time we met, we spent the evening reviewing my English and German phrases printed on the parchment, which I had laid out upon one of the low tables in the main parlor. Shortly after we began our study, Augustin declared that my handwriting was atrocious. I must hold the pen like a rolling pin, he stated, pointing out my intermittent ink blots—which resulted, in my defense, from my lack of experience with medieval pens. "Do they not teach you Carolingian miniscule in the twenty-first century?!" he cried out at one point, throwing both hands up in frustration.

"No, Charlemagne has been consigned to the annals of history," I answered, snickering at his irritation.

"You shall have to do better than this, if you want people to believe that you are educated," he said with a frown. "When you wrote in the margins of my work three weeks ago, you did so with much more finesse."

"That was cursive. I wrote this in print to make it easier to read."

Augustin glanced at me out of the corner of one eye, then turned his attention back to my printed parchment. "Monks and clergy use print when they copy manuscripts of the Bible for use at mass," he said, his expression scornful. "Those of us who have attained higher education *always* combine our letters for the sake of beauty."

I nodded thoughtfully at this, knowing that cursive did appear more artistic than print, though it had always taken more effort for me to write cursive. When I took notes at college, I generally used print. Now I understood that if I wanted to write like the chroniclers of the eleventh century, using inkwells and feather pens extraordinaire, I would have to perfect my calligraphy. So I eyed my tutor expectantly, grasping one of his pens with my right hand. "Show me."

We spent the rest of that evening making splotches on paper, Augustin's strong fingers curling around mine as he corrected my faulty methods of holding the pen. I warned him that, after almost twenty years of gripping ballpoint pens the wrong way, it would probably take a while before I got it right. He responded that I had twenty more years to learn, so I might as well use them wisely. By that time I had admitted that Joel and I planned to remain in eleventh century Muniche until the mid-1060s, a fact which Augustin found quite intriguing, even though I refused to expound on the reasons.

By the middle of September, both of us had begun to make great strides in our language-learning. On top of that, we had gotten to know each other more than I had initially expected. Although we spent most of our time together poring over words and correcting each other's speech, I uncovered a few more secrets of the oldest Bayern brother from the occasional personal chats that arose when we tired of our studies. I discovered that Augustin no longer lived in the Bayern castle. Upon his return from Salerno in early 1043, he had purchased his own cottage on the opposite side of the city, near the drawbridge in fact. It was there that he practiced medicine on the few daring clients who graced his door, and it was there that he stored a multitude of his own private writings. He spent much time in the archives, he said, but only for business purposes. He wrote down many of his own conjectures on recent history and the times, as well as on Teutonic rituals. These he showed to no one.

The mere idea of such secretive writings piqued my interest, and I told him at one point that I hoped to return to the archives someday for the sole purpose of perusing the shelf labeled *Teutonic Traditions*. A rather blood-thirsty smirk appeared on his face at my admission, and he asked what sort of Teutonic traditions interested me. I thought back to the things I already knew, that I had learned from Hans and Lady Muniche, realizing that they were very few in comparison with that giant shelf I had seen.

I replied that I would always be curious to learn more about Teuton elemental powers along with the blood rituals. His earlier threat had shed light upon Hans' hints about using blood to read someone's intentions, along with Lady Muniche's reference to vampire lore. The idea that Teuton priests went around chomping on people's necks had besieged my nightmares already. But I suspected that perfecting the blood rituals would prove useful one day.

"Your curiosity may be the death of you, Swanie," Augustin informed me when I told him what I wished, a disturbing smile still curling across his face. "Most blood rituals are known only to priests, and those women who dabble therein tend to find themselves in over their heads, so to speak. Matters of blood and elemental mastery are things not to be treated lightly."

I nodded slowly at his words, my mind working to grasp the seriousness of such mystical traditions along with the risks. But in the end, I lifted my eyes to my tutor's with confidence and said, "I still would like to know." Augustin said nothing to this. He simply continued to eye me gravely, a dark smile playing on his lips.

At some point in mid-September, Freia confronted me about my continual dealings with the oldest Bayern brother, expressing concern that I was treading a danger-ous path. "I realize that you're seeing him under the pretext of perfecting your Teutonica and learning an older Teuton dialect," she murmured softly late one night while we sat opposite one another on our beds, after she had finished her prayers. The candlelight reflected a glow of unease in her eyes as she continued, "I fear that your relationship with him will end up going in a different direction. In spite of his outward poise and his intelligence, he's still the city executioner, and far too many frightening stories abound regarding the things he does in secret. You really need to ask him to stop coming here, to protect yourself from danger as well as from gossip."

I sighed at her words, knowing she was right, trying to reason out just what seemed to draw me to Augustin von Bayern. Curiosity played a major role, since according to all the records from my own era, he should not exist. His grasp of vernacular languages was exceptional, as was his writing style, so of course his intellectual prowess would interest me. And he was a Teuton priest, reminding me of Hans from time to time with his mysterious demeanor and intriguing storytelling. The memory of my first and only dance with Augustin still filtered into my thoughts occasionally: the grace and glory of his movements, his fire azure like the sea, canceling out my frigid ice with perfection.

My opinions of him were jumbled. I knew that he was the executioner, I knew that he liked to kill, and I knew that most of the townspeople were scared of him. But he was so *smart*, so educated, so fascinating . . . and so incredibly handsome. Never in my life had I encountered a man with such inimitable long black hair, resembling silk when the sunlight caught it. And his eyes were so beautiful, seeming as expansive as the sky itself when our studies distracted him from his habitual hatred.

So I ultimately told Freia that I could not stop seeing Augustin. "I guess I'm going insane," I confessed, gazing into the orange flame of our candle. "He tells me time and time again that my curiosity is going to kill me, and he's probably right. But you know, if he does end up killing me eventually, I'll just go back to my own time then and there." The concept of death did not seem so sinister after all, if it came to me at Augustin's hands.

"Then you would leave me here all alone." Consternation overtook Freia's expression as she processed my intentions. "Does Joel know?"

She had found the weak chink in my armor. I had not yet informed Joel of my contact with the city executioner, knowing his distrust for him. I had an inkling that Joel had indeed begun to fall in love with me, though my own desires for him remained as flat as a deflated tire. In recent weeks, he had visited me more often, arriving at the Meldorf estate early Saturday afternoon once his duties at the ironworks were finished. On Sundays after church, we would walk the fields together; and he had recently admitted that he was trying to save as much of his small salary as he could, hoping to improve his position in the community. "The guys at the ironworks are always giving me grief for that, since they want me to come gamble and drink with them at night," he had told me with a laugh, "but unlike them, I have greater expectations in life."

His optimism impressed me, as did his zeal for success and adventure, but I had not yet found the courage to tell Joel of my academic pursuits every Tuesday and Thursday evening. I feared that he would freak out about my camaraderie with such a person. After a long pause, I answered Freia's inquiry, my voice barely above a whisper. "No, I haven't told Joel about it. He doesn't like Augustin, especially after he watched that execution the first time he visited Muniche. I don't know what he'd think of me, if he found out that I'm studying the local dialects with the 'dreaded executioner.'" I rolled my eyes.

Freia did not reply for a long moment. She met my gaze, appearing to seek something there, though I knew not what. When she spoke again, I felt a chill creep slowly up my spine at her words. "He may not worry about that so much, Swanie. The problem is, your tutor is a young man, unmarried, with a poor reputation. Joel may question your . . . intentions." I shook my head, looking away as I shivered once, all over. That had occurred to me already, but I was trying to ignore it. "What if you fall in love with him?" Freia asked suddenly, a direct query.

I took a deep breath, attempting to organize my whirling thoughts. "I don't *think* that's going to happen," I said, quaking at the mere idea of loving a man from the past, let alone one like Augustin von Bayern. "I can't allow myself to do that, because then I'd spend the rest of my life missing someone who has been dead for centuries."

Freia smiled a bit at the truth of this, and shortly thereafter we said goodnight, but not before she admonished me again to break off my study sessions with Augustin. "Your mind and your intellect may not want it to develop into something more, but you should remember what the Bible says about things like that." Freia glanced at me while I crept back beneath my blanket, then quoted a verse I knew well. "'The heart is deceitful above all things and desperately wicked.' If your heart gets involved with evil, your mind won't be able to win that fight."

I should have heeded Freia's warnings, and I seriously considered asking Augustin to not return again the following Tuesday. I had not come to the eleventh century with the purpose of entangling myself in relationships, but I had already developed a strong friendship with Freia, and I greatly respected Count von Meldorf. Besides, how else was I to learn more about Teutonic rituals and the current dialects but from an experienced and educated Teuton priest? I remembered the foolish note I had left for Hans on the organ bench at my parents' wedding, and his comment that I had certainly become a part of history by doing such a thing. How could I assimilate myself with eleventh century Bavaria if I remained in seclusion, spending my free time with Joel alone?

On the last Thursday of September, when Augustin and I had completed our studies for the night, our conversation turned to time travel and my frustrations with his youngest brother. Prince Otto had yet to grant Joel and me the information we needed to return home. He preferred to espouse the traditional assumptions of the Teuton priest: that women were careless and stupid. He believed that I had traveled time lightly and ought to wallow in the costs of my mistake.

Augustin seemed sympathetic to my dissatisfaction, and he suggested that Joel and I confront the Prince again, now that Joel's Teutonica had improved. Perhaps if Joel spoke our arguments, the Prince would grant us mercy. Augustin stated this without a trace of bigotry, just as a fact. It seemed like a decent plan, worth a try if nothing else. Before he left for the night, the oldest Bayern brother pledged with a dark smile that he would get us into his family castle on Sunday afternoon.

Chapter Seventeen:
One Concert

Joel, Freia, and I went to mass at the cathedral on Sunday, for Master Denlinger had invited my roommate to spend the day with his family. The count lent us horses for the trip and urged us to return to the estate for dinner, so he could hear all about our escapades. His bright blue eyes beamed with satisfaction when we parted ways with him at the door of his stables; he seemed pleased that both of us had begun to find a portion of success with the local bachelors. I had asked him once whether it bothered him that the two of us may end up in mixed marriages. He had shrugged his big shoulders and responded that he trusted us to judge wisely upon choosing our partners. "If you were of my blood, things would be different," he had told me, "but you are my guests, and I have no right to forbid your choices. Most of the noble families around here will see things differently, though."

I considered Count von Meldorf's words while Joel and I ate our lunches of lentil stew at a restaurant in the Jewish quarter. He blathered about the arguments he planned to present before the Prince, and I nodded along, correcting his linguistic mistakes while my eyes roved around the room. Outsiders filled the restaurant, and all appeared quite lively and content, laughing and joking with each other. *But if you stay with Joel, every Teuton in this city will scorn you.*

I kept my musings to myself and let Joel pay for our meal. Then we struck out for the Bayern castle, tying our horses to a hitching post beside the iron gates, which were closed as usual. "So how exactly are we supposed to get inside?" Joel asked as I looked at the roaring lion of the Bayern family crest engraved upon each gate. "I'm assuming you have some sort of plan for scaling the walls, since you suggested that we come here today." He sounded doubtful.

We had halted in front of the gates, and I ran my gaze through the gardens beyond, not detecting a soul. "No, actually, someone is going to let us in. I think."

Joel's eyebrows came together in surprise. He turned aside to look up and down the dirt street that bordered the gardens. "And if they don't let us in?"

In that very instant, Augustin von Bayern stepped out from behind a rather tall shrub to the right of the gate, clad entirely in black with his hair partially down, his light blue eyes fixed on Joel. "Do not worry. *Someone* will let you in." He spoke the words primarily in English, a disturbing smile gracing his lips as he unlatched the gate in a rapid motion, swinging it open.

Joel jerked backward, his hazel eyes bulging as he regarded the executioner of Muniche, a man he did not particularly trust. For a second we all stood in silence, Augustin still eyeballing Joel—who had frozen and seemed momentarily at a loss—while I tried valiantly to hold back laughter. "Did he say that in *English?*" Joel hissed in my ear, sounding appalled.

One laugh burst from my mouth, but I smothered the rest. "Yeah, he did. Let's go." I took two steps toward the open gate, gesturing for Joel to follow.

Joel trailed behind me, his expression clearly stating that he would rather turn and run. When we crossed into the Bayern gardens, our host bowed in our direction and beckoned us forward, toward the main entrance of the castle. "Come, both of you. Let us see if Prince Otto has chosen to spend this Lord's Day within," he said in a mixture of English and Teutonica.

"And if he hasn't?" I questioned, taken aback by the notion that we may not be able to see the Prince after all.

"Then I shall give you a tour, and we shall see what we can uncover ourselves." His answer implied that he, too, was interested in finding out more about Prince Otto's song, despite his lack of musical ability. Of course Augustin would be inquisitive, I realized. He spent much of his time seeking information.

As our host opened the door to the castle and held it for us, Joel hung back, waving for me to come to his side. I sighed with a touch of impatience and went over to him, giving him a look that said he had better have a good excuse for wasting our time. "Swanie, are you *sure* that this is a good idea?" he murmured quietly when I stopped in front of him. His eyes shot toward Augustin, then back to me. "I mean . . . he's the executioner. And he's really freaky."

I could not figure out why everyone seemed to think Augustin was so scary. He frightened me only when he wanted to find out my secrets. Other than that, he came across as a normal guy in my opinion, his imposing veneer merely that—a façade. Beneath his outward appearance, he was one of the most intriguing people I had ever met. "You really need to stop being so weird about Augustin," I told Joel in a quiet voice. "He's the oldest of the Bayern brothers; of course he can get us into the castle. And he's not as 'freaky' as you think."

"Oh, so you're on a first name basis with him now?" Joel stared at me in shock. "What have you been doing behind my back?"

Freia had been right. I glared at Joel in aggravation and jammed my fists against my hips. "Unlike you, I have a lot of spare time, and I have to find something to occupy my mind. Augustin has been helping me with the local form of Teutonica, and in return I'm teaching him English. That's it. Now let's go inside, before you forget all those persuasive arguments you've prepared for the Prince."

"I don't know if they're all *that* persuasive," Joel muttered as he followed me inside. Augustin stood holding the door open for us, and I looked at his face for a moment, trying to discern how much he had caught of what Joel and I had said. He wore a rather satisfied expression, and when our eyes met, he smirked and gave a single nod, appearing unsurprised.

As Joel and I waited in the impressive vestibule, with columns reaching up to the ceiling high above our heads, Augustin summarily retrieved a small bell from a pedestal near the doorway and rang it twice. I looked around at the painted scenes on the paneled walls, some of which suggested biblical subjects while others portrayed the Bavarian countryside. I raised my eyes to the ceiling, calling my ice forth just enough to help me appreciate its intricate architecture, marble columns branching out in all directions. This place was impressive.

A moment later, a middle-aged servant appeared, clothed more opulently than the common townsfolk. A look of fear darkened his eyes when he saw Augustin, but he bowed at each of us in turn, welcoming us to the Bayern castle and asking if he could be of assistance. Augustin inquired whether the Prince was at home, and the servant's countenance grew even more upset when he replied negatively. "I believe he is visiting the Lady Maria's father, my Lord Augustin. Knight Felhozer is not expected to live much longer, and Lady Maria has spent much time at his bedside this past week."

Augustin frowned severely at the servant's words, prompting the poor man to scuttle backward. His Teutonica ran together as he added that Prince Otto was expected to return within the hour. "Well then, we shall have to wait, if you have no other pressing business this afternoon?" Augustin looked at me, and I shook my head. He trained his gaze back upon the servant, who had the look of a scared rabbit, ready to bolt into the shadows at the first opportunity. "The three of us shall wait for the

Prince's return, and in the meantime I intend to give my companions a tour of the castle. I expect you and the other staff to take care not to disturb us." He eyed the servant darkly.

"Yes, of course, my Lord Augustin. We'll stay out of your way." The promise tumbled from the man's lips, and he vanished down a corridor an instant later. Augustin nodded in approval and beckoned Joel and me, announcing that the tour would commence immediately.

We passed through countless halls and massive chambers, ascending and descending quite a few staircases. Part of my brain listened to Augustin's frank descriptions of all items of note, his tone of voice resembling an exceedingly bored tour guide. We encountered many beautiful tapestries and paintings that would likely cost a fortune, had they survived until the twenty-first century. One spacious room contained a collection of marble sculptures depicting each Bayern Keyholder of Muniche since Prince Abelard in the late 800s. The Ladies of Muniche were also represented in this room, each of their carved faces appearing kind and peaceful.

I especially took note of one youthful maiden whose loveliness far outweighed the others. Her expression spoke of glory and triumph, and her curled hair fell to the middle of her back. The base of her statue read: *Lady of Muniche, Marelda Louise von Förster und von Bayern, A.D. CMXCVII-MXXII*. Augustin had already drifted toward the door, prepared to lead us down another hallway. "Is this your mother?" I called out to him, gesturing at the gorgeous sculpture.

Augustin's mouth turned sharply downward at my inquiry, his light blue eyes glowing with his fire. "Yes," he answered. An instant later, he had exited the room with Joel trailing behind. I paused to look again at the image of Marelda, then ran to catch up with the other two, my mind working overtime. I was almost certain that I had seen something resembling heartache in Augustin's harsh reaction to my question—a sorrow I had never before seen in his gaze. It was a look I knew too well. The man hated by everyone, the man who yearned to kill, who lived for worldly and intellectual pleasures—yet apparently, this man loved his mother. *His dead mother . . . .*

We passed through many more halls and rooms, eventually coming upon a rather impressive collection of armor and weapons, which naturally grabbed Joel's interest. Our excursion came to a halt as he and Augustin exchanged a few words about medieval fighting styles. I noticed that Joel's fear of Augustin seemed to fade into the background when he talked about blood and guts—a topic that young guys seemed to relish. During our brief respite from the tour, I considered the many questions that had arisen in my mind since we had entered the Bayern castle. I had caught sight of several other servants as we had progressed down the halls; each of them had disappeared into the shadows the moment they saw Augustin. *Everyone here is afraid of this man, the oldest Bayern brother, especially that first servant who greeted us. Fear really seems to be the prevailing opinion of him. Why? But in spite of his dark demeanor, he has the capacity to love . . . Marelda . . . .*

I barely noticed that our procession had advanced once more, descending a twisted staircase to the ground floor. I was too busy formulating questions to ask Augustin the upcoming Tuesday, when he would come to the count's estate for our language studies. This man was a mystery to me; I had to figure him out. Suddenly, my thoughts sped back to the present when I realized that we had entered a room bearing some similarities to my father's music room in the twenty-first century. A harp stood in one corner; several lutes, fiddles, and flutes lay upon shelves . . . and against the wall opposite the entrance stood a decent-sized organ, its pipes reaching to the ceiling. My feet failed me, and I froze just inside the doorway, my mouth falling open, all of the organ songs I had memorized flooding my brain. A burning desire grasped my soul, awakening the musician in me anew. *I wanted to play that instrument . . . I needed to play . . . .*

Both Augustin and Joel observed my reaction. Joel sped to my side and spoke to me urgently in English, his words not even entering my ears. I watched Augustin smile and walk to the center of the room, throwing his blue fire upward to light the ornate chandelier above. Next, he retrieved a rather large candlestick from a table, lighting it as well and placing it atop the organ. He turned to face me, throwing one arm out in a wide arc toward a nearby shelf stuffed with music scores. "I think you should play for us, Lady Swanhilde." He eyed me expectantly.

Joel started and turned to stare at Augustin, apparently having understood the gist of what he had said. I began to tremble slightly, my fingers itching. When I spoke, the words barely left my lips. "It's been . . . a long time . . . ."

"*I* want to hear you." Augustin's smile grew sardonic as he added, "I would like to compare your abilities to those of my brothers. Both the Prince and Paulus play, but something tells me that your talent outranks theirs." I ogled him, seeing no trace of bluff in his expression. He took two large steps toward the music shelf, yanking out a score and waving it at me. "The Prince wrote most of these for use at mass. Perhaps you could decipher his notation." Augustin peered at the score and stated matter-of-factly, "I understand none of this."

A huge smile broke across my face and I leapt forward in excitement, totally disregarding Joel's cautionary exclamation. Snatching the score from Augustin's hand, I said in Teutonica, "This should be interesting. I haven't touched the organ in months." I glanced back at Joel with a grin and added in English, "I'm probably going to suck." Turning my attention to the music in my hands, I squinted at it in horror. The notes were formed in a style I had never encountered, ancient and crooked, the lines almost unreadable. "Jeez!" I cried out in English, switching to Teutonica to demand, "Where did the Prince learn how to hold the pen?!"

Augustin burst out laughing and I jerked in surprise, for I had never heard him laugh before. His blue eyes lit with fun, he smiled grandly as he laughed, the darkness completely gone from his visage. I shook my head in wonder and began chortling myself. Joel looked from one of us to the other, an uncertain smile appearing beneath his sandy beard. Eventually Augustin composed himself enough to ask, "So . . . can you . . . play that . . . ?" He snickered again.

"I'm going to try," I answered, jumping onto the organ bench. I spread the music across the stand, then turned my attention to the organ itself: two keyboards, wooden pedals, about thirty stops. I looked around for the *on* switch, then said, "I think I need somebody to pump this." I glanced at the bellows on the floor.

Joel volunteered, rolling up the sleeves of his tunic to reveal his developing arm muscles. Moments later, he pumped air through the bellows while I tested each stop. There were twenty-eight of them, actually, and none were labeled. The organ had several horn stops, quite a few reeds, some flutes, and one that sounded like church bells. I would probably ignore that one. Taking a deep breath to prepare myself, I glanced once at Joel and once at Augustin standing behind me. Then I hit two reed stops and two flutes before beginning the Prince's piece.

I played the first three lines cautiously, squinting at the strange notation, discovering instantly that this song had no pedalwork at all. I stopped completely after those lines, my mouth twisting in discontent. "This is *awful!*" I complained, insatiably bored already with the simplicity of the piece.

Augustin chuckled from somewhere behind me. "It improves toward the end. I have heard this one numerous times in church."

I glanced back at him briefly, raising an eyebrow. "You go to church?"

He smiled wryly and replied, "I once did."

That figured. I shrugged and turned back to the music, finishing the piece after about five minutes of struggle. I needed to find someone to teach me how to read eleventh century music. If the Prince ever decided to be gracious and give us his song, I would not be able to play it properly without hours of practice, and that would never do. I sighed as I let go of the keys, folding up the score and handing it to Augustin. "I'm really out of practice," I said, shaking my head in disgust.

"You must have some pieces memorized," Joel commented, looking up from the bellows. "Why don't you play something you know, like Bach's Toccata and Fugue in D Minor?"

It seemed like that was the only organ piece Americans recognized, aside from the main theme from *Phantom of the Opera*. I rolled my eyes at Joel and told him I needed the music for that one, but that I could think of a few others. "There's one problem, though. I can't play anything good without organ shoes." I looked down at my feet sticking out from beneath my red-violet dress. I was wearing the leather shoes from that shop back home.

"You can't play with bare feet, like they do at church?" Joel asked.

I sighed in frustration at his ignorance. Although his younger sister played in an orchestra, Joel certainly knew little about organ playing. "No, not unless I want to break the arches in my feet. When you play classical music, you have to use both your toes *and* your heels. Hymns are simpler, but they're boring."

I felt a hand upon my shoulder, and I spun halfway around on the bench to regard Augustin. He held up a pair of black shoes with a suggestive glint in his eye. "The Prince uses these when he plays complicated pieces."

I eyed the shoes distrustfully. "They're probably too big." But I took my shoes off anyway and tried one. It hung off of my foot rather wretchedly. I dangled it at Augustin with the remark, "The Prince has big feet."

Augustin smirked at me. "Paulus' feet are smaller. Try his organ shoes."

I soon discovered that although the middle Bayern brother did, in fact, have smaller feet, his shoes still extended about two centimeters past my toes. I shook my head and pronounced that this would not work. "Maybe I'll just play something that doesn't involve the pedals," I said, wracking my brain for an appropriate song.

Augustin frowned at me and summarily began ripping pieces of fabric from his black robe. "A solution always exists. Give me your foot."

I stared in shock, unable to reply while he wrapped my feet tightly with strips of dark linen. He must have countless more such robes at home, I figured, or he would not ruin this one. Apparently, he really and truly wanted to hear me play. I would have to play well, and perfectly. When he had finished wrapping my feet, he placed each of Paulus' shoes upon them himself, tying the laces securely. Stepping away from me, he turned his gaze upon Joel—who crouched on the floor beside the organ bellows, gaping at Augustin. "Pump those bellows, Mr. Hudson. My lady?" He nodded expectantly in my direction and ordered, "Impress me."

I grinned, anticipation overtaking me as I spun to face the keyboards once more. I had already decided what piece to play, and I doubted that I would make a mistake on this one: Praeludium in C, by Buxtehude. I pulled out all of the stops except the one that sounded like bells, took a deep breath, and began the opening pedalwork with a flourish. I played the entire piece without one flaw, the glory of the music filling my soul, the entire castle seeming to reverberate with the sound waves. I played the first movement grandly, then pulled back several of the louder stops for the fugue. When I reached the chaconne, I brought the entire organ to life again—including the church bells this time—bearing down on the final chord in exultation. I lifted my hands and feet from the instrument, spun around, and leapt off of the organ bench as I would do for a concert, bowing to my audience of two. Joel clapped and hooted enthusiastically and Augustin applauded more discreetly, a sneaky smile creeping across his face. As I smiled back at him, he nodded his head once behind him and to the right. To my shock and horror, I saw two young men standing just inside the room, one of them Prince Otto, both of them staring at me in disparagement.

Joel stopped clapping a second later as he also noticed our company, and Augustin turned his body just slightly to acknowledge the two men. "Here we have discovered a prodigy, my brothers," he said with a rather mocking expression. "This woman plays more masterfully than either of you."

I had frozen beside the organ, and Joel moved to stand beside me while we watched this impending Bayern family confrontation with wide eyes. Prince Otto glared at Augustin, marching into the room with the heavy steps of authority. "What have you *done?*" he demanded, his eyes flashing red.

"I have merely given my two acquaintances here a grand tour of the castle," Augustin replied calmly, his arms folded across his chest. "They came seeking you, my dear Prince, for you will remember that you hold information they desperately desire. They have come to present their pleas to you once more, in hopes that you will uncharacteristically grant mercy, for once." Augustin's expression darkened considerably when he finished, his eyes narrowing.

Prince Otto stared back at Augustin, his eyes glowing a deeper red. He shot one furious glance in our direction, recognition and frustration evident on his face. Turning his attention back to his oldest brother, he said, "What they seek does not concern you, *Augustin.*" His voice was laden with distaste.

"It might," Augustin responded shortly, his own eyes glittering a bit now. "Perhaps if I held the information myself, I would not be so unwilling to disclose it to our guests from the future . . . *murderer.*"

That jolted me from my frozen state beside Joel. Confusion engulfed my thoughts as I tried to understand Augustin's accusation. *Murderer. Why did he call Prince Otto a murderer . . . ?* The Prince, in the meantime, bared his teeth at his brother, his fists curled into tight balls, apparently trying not to completely lose his composure in the presence of strangers. Augustin smirked, turning abruptly back to Joel and me with the words, "I do greatly apologize, for I do not believe either of you have been properly introduced to my brother Paulus." He gestured toward the Prince's companion, a smaller man wearing the clothing of the Catholic clergy, his brown hair cut in a tonsure, his expression rather frightened. "May I present to you Father Paulus Hobart Christian von Bayern. My brother, the Lady Swanhilde von Thaden and her good friend, Mr. Joel Hudson."

The middle Bayern brother said nothing in reply. He nodded once in our direction, still looking horribly worried, his eyes drifting back to the Prince. I could see that Augustin had been correct in labeling him the Prince's toady. He looked weak and indecisive, certainly the least attractive of the Bayern brothers. Prince Otto suddenly huffed in displeasure, then addressed Augustin once more. "Enough with the pleasantries. This case has already been closed, at our first meeting." The Prince's eyes locked with mine for an instant. "I expect you to keep your nose out of matters that do not concern you, Augustin." He pulled a small bell from his clothing and rang it sharply. A moment later, the same servant who had greeted us appeared. "Bruno, see to it that these two leave this castle now." He pointed at Joel and me, then said to Augustin, "I am not finished with you."

The servant came forward to escort Joel and me back to the street. I bent down to remove Paulus' organ shoes and shoved my feet back into my own. Hopefully the excess fabric would not stretch their seems too badly. I turned to Augustin before joining Joel and the servant at the doorway, a bit of concern seeping into my veins. "You'll be all right without us, I hope?" I whispered to him, praying that the Prince could not overhear.

Augustin's gaze softened just slightly as he looked down at me. "Do not fear. He can do nothing to me. He is my brother." Part of his mouth curled upward in a satisfied smile before I turned from him, the hated one, the enigma.

Chapter Eighteen:
The Oktoberfest

A fresh nightmare tore me from my slumber early Monday morning. I had been playing the Song of Time on Prince Otto's organ, and he had come bursting in with a bunch of guards, bellowing that I must be burned as a witch. Fear had consumed me, and I threw together some discordant notes in an attempt to open the gateway of time. But for some reason a portal to hell opened instead, and I heard Augustin chuckling somewhere in the background, his suave voice repeating a warning he had spoken not long ago: "Your curiosity may be the death of you . . . ."

When I awoke, I found myself peppered with flakes of ice, an instinctual attempt to shield me from hell's flames. I drew a gasping breath, my eyes shifting toward Freia's bed. She lay curled beneath her blanket in the flickering light of our candle, so I must have slept through her early prayers. I gasped again and pressed a hand to my heart, which pounded frantically. *Concentrate on your ice, Swanie,* I ordered myself, shutting my eyes to invoke the cold down around me. *Get to the spiritual realm, where no dark demons hide.*

I spent a long while drifting atop the waters of the Isar in my spiritual form, silently drawing its vitality into myself, to restore my quaking heart. Several weeks had passed since I had last spent half the night as a spirit; my roommate's fervent prayers had become my calming elixir. Now I gazed up at the stars of early autumn, berating my weakness all over again. How was I supposed to handle this once I had to face the night alone? Eventually Freia would find herself a husband, for both the ironmaster Heinrich Denlinger and Lord Ulrich of the Sendlin estate had expressed an interest in her. If I resigned myself to a relationship with Joel, what would he think of me when he learned of my panic attacks?

And what would Augustin think?

I rolled my eyes at myself and endeavored to shove that muse away, though my thoughts wandered in turn toward all of the secrets he kept. I wanted to learn more about his family, about his mother, his two brothers, and the castle servants who seemed scared to death of him. He may actually have some advice to offer on how to surmount my anxieties . . . but then again, I had no yearning to channel my weaknesses into executing people.

He's more than that, though.

Eventually I shut my ghostly lids and imagined myself in the archives, for I needed to find a productive way to pass the time instead of wallowing in my insufficiencies. The place was as dark as a grave at the cusp of dawn, and I sensed no other Teutons anywhere, in physical form or otherwise. I shivered a little as my robes shifted from dark bluish green to white, casting just enough light for me to make out the shelves around me. I had appeared in the center of the room beneath the chandelier. I glanced up at it for a second, thinking that it would be nice to have a fiery element so I could light some of its candles. But I was ice, so I must use the inherent white of frost to guide me.

I breezed toward the shelf labeled *Teutonic Traditions* and browsed some of its contents. There were very few bound books there; most of its collection consisted of olden scrolls and dusty cartons stacked with papers. I discovered thin slabs notched with runes upon the bottom shelf, none of which I could read quite yet. I was still a beginner in my quest to learn Ælte Teutonica. My priestly tutor had not yet taught me to decipher the ancient runes. Thus far, I could piece together some of the forgotten dialect when it was written with the Roman alphabet.

By the time the early rays of dawn had begun to creep in through the pair of windows upon the back wall, I had not learned much of note. I found one readable scroll that had been written in Carolingian miniscule, but it merely outlined various festivals like spring and harvest. Another small bound book seemed to be an exposition regarding the early days of Christianity among the Teuton people. That one had potential, but I wanted to find something more intriguing, something about blood rituals or sorcery.

I tugged a hefty box off of the second shelf from the bottom and set it onto the floor. The golden letters engraved upon it had caught my attention: *Bluotgifuog*. Despite my chariness about that ritual, I knew full well that my two companions and I would have to come to terms with it since we lived in a fully Teutonic society. Lord Ulrich Sendlin had already made it clear to Freia that he could not marry her unless she renounced her Rhenisch blood. And when Lady Adeline had visited us last week, she had given me pointed counsel: "Have all the fun you want with your English metal worker, Swanie, but don't taint your family's blood with his."

So I opened the box, a combination of curiosity and fright dimming my robes into a bluish white, my ethereal fingers nearly passing through the lid as my focus wavered. A stack of vellum lay inside the box with a leather-bound pamphlet on top, bearing a Latin inscription that made me do a double-take: *Procuring Wuotan's Blood*. I stared at the pamphlet, horror darkening my spiritual robes further. *Wait. Wuotan's blood? Is this hinting that Teuton blood is actually demon blood? That can't be, not really, or it'd be impossible for Teutons to trust God. Right?*

I took several measured breaths of the musty basement air and reached out to take hold of the pamphlet, opening it hesitantly. It held three pages written in Ælte Teutonica, complete with sketches of what occurred during a blood-transfer. One showed a shrouded figure—likely a Teuton priest—standing before a cauldron, out of which rose a beastly entity with flaming fangs. Another showed a naked man with a tormented expression, his chest torn open as the beastly demon looked on. I dropped the pamphlet abruptly and floated backwards toward the center of the archives, my heart racing in a manner inappropriate to the spiritual realm.

There's no way I could ever agree to let Joel try this, no matter how unfair he thinks it is to be an outsider in a Teuton society, I determined as I tried to calm myself, drawing the coolness of the air into my spirit. *The writings about the Torstein said not to attempt any deadly Teuton rituals, and the blood-transfer is the worst of all. I could never forgive myself if he tried it and ended up actually dead.*

Once I had gathered myself, I turned my attention back to the box, planning on sifting through the vellum beneath the pamphlet. I figured that those might be records of blood-transfers conducted in Muniche, and if so, I could learn whether medieval priests had better luck with the rite than those mentioned in Hans' books. But before I could crouch down to peruse, I heard the door to the stairwell sliding open. It must be the start of some chronicler's workday, and I certainly did not need some stupid man to discover me and label me a witch. So I shut my eyes and stifled my ice, and my surroundings transformed instantly into the chamber I shared with Freia. Daylight had chased the shadows away, and my roommate had already risen and snuffed our candle. She sat upon her bed, still clad in her nightdress, her green eyes meeting mine with a look of concern.

"Good morning, Freia," I greeted her in Rhenisch, belated fatigue prompting me to slump down onto my pillow. My mortal body had frozen in a sitting position. Next time I would have to remind myself to recline before fleeing to the spiritual realm. "My nightmares waited to awaken me after your prayers."

"And here I was hoping that you'd just woken early and decided to peek at the preparations for the Oktoberfest," Freia said, injecting a lightness to her tone that did not quite fit.

I closed my eyes and rubbed my forehead, trying to will my stress headache away. It never worked. "I forgot that starts today," I murmured. I should have gone to the common fields instead of the archives; then I could have watched the farmers and merchants setting up their stands to trade their crops. Count von Meldorf had likely already gone, along with a fair number of his vassals. The iron-works would run only in the mornings all week, so Joel would be free to browse the shops and stands with me after Sext, the noon hour. The idea of spending the whole week with him inspired no delight for my part. Instead, I began to wonder how I could explain my regular study sessions with Augustin. I had told Joel yesterday that the eldest Bayern brother was helping me learn Ælte Teutonica, a dialect forgotten in our era. He had not been too pleased with that idea.

Freia dressed herself while I lay back with my eyes closed, softly promising to bring me some linden tea with peppermint to soothe my headache. After she had gone, I dragged myself out of bed and stretched, then headed for the basin to splash water upon my face to chase my weariness away. I silently ordered my nightmares to leave me alone for the rest of the week, or to rouse me during Freia's prayers. I did not wish my ridiculous anxiety to mar the celebrations. Along with the trading, several jousts and archery tournaments were set to take place, as well as dances and general revelry. The Oktoberfest was medieval Muniche's final festival until the Christmas season, and I meant to enjoy it for all it was worth.

While Freia and I sipped warm mugs of herbal tea, the young servant girl Felda knocked on our bedroom door, bearing a scroll for me. "A page brought this just a moment ago," she informed me with a giggle, her untidy dark brown tresses springing around her face as she gestured toward the staircase. "He was dressed like one of the Bayern servants," she added in a stage whisper. I took the scroll and waved her away, glancing once at Freia before breaking its red seal to read:

My Dear Lady Swanhilde von Thaden,

I regret to inform you that our language studies scheduled for the upcoming Tuesday and Thursday evenings must be postponed, due to conflicting duties I must undertake for the Oktoberfest. Perhaps we shall encounter one another at one of the galas, but if not, I shall meet you once more at the Meldorf estate one week from tomorrow evening to continue our intellectual pursuits. May you thoroughly enjoy Muniche in its glory. I shall think of you at every dance.

Yours with utmost apology,
Lord Augustin Abelard Ulrich von Bayern

I frowned a bit while I read the familiar script, written in proper Teutonica. Although I realized that Augustin would have quite a few responsibilities involving the festival, as the oldest of the Bayern brothers, I felt disappointed that we would not be able to meet as usual to study languages. I knew that several royal families from the neighboring German states—Schwabia and the Rhineland, I had heard—planned to attend the Oktoberfest, so of course Augustin von Bayern would be expected to entertain them along with Paulus and Prince Otto. The Keyholders and Ladies of five other Teuton cities would also be there, according to local gossip. Still, a strange discontent arose within me at the possibility of not seeing Augustin for over a week. I would miss his intelligent speech, his sarcastic smile, his outer layer of hatred that I tried always to dispel.

Freia noticed my reaction to the letter, and she asked me if something was wrong. "No, not really," I replied quickly, rolling the scroll again and stashing it beside my pillow. At least I would not have to deal with Joel's presence during our studies. "I guess I'm just going to have to throw myself into this festival with vigor, since I won't be studying with Augustin this week."

Freia eyed me coyly while she combed her long blond hair in front of the mirror. "It shouldn't be a surprise, with all of the other nobility visiting Muniche this week. Are you going to miss him that much?"

I was, and that was a problem, just as Freia had stated in the beginning. I should have stayed away from Augustin while I had the chance. "I doubt I'll miss him with all the partying. Besides, I'll be seeing Joel every day." I smiled brightly when I lied, hoping that Freia would not detect my true thoughts.

That afternoon, Freia and I met up with Joel to tour the local shops bursting with goods for the festival, purchasing quite a few new trinkets to bring back with us to the Meldorf estate. I had finally traded both of the Gypsy's gold chains several weeks prior, giving myself a decent amount of extra spending money. Joel bought us dinner at one of the pubs, and we sat outside to eat while watching a breathtaking joust in the main square.

On Tuesday and Wednesday, we went to the common fields with Count von Meldorf and a handful of his vassals to observe the selling and trading of the crops. I actually had the privilege of helping the count with his trading, working figures on a small roll of parchment, pleased that I had some knowledge of business, thanks to my college studies and summers working at my father's company. The count seemed impressed by my business acumen, commenting that he had never known a woman to be so sharp when it came to making business deals. In the evenings, we ate under the tents and watched elemental displays put on by the local priests. Sometimes Joel and I joined in with the dancing, though I found it dull to keep my ice to myself during such frolics.

We spent Thursday within the city walls once more, where we watched three archery contests and several jousts. Joel met up with a gang of his coworkers at the main square, most of whom were quite drunk already, summarily getting into a good-natured brawl while Freia and I sat at the base of the fountain, sipping mugs of warm autumn cider. We saw some of the noble families of nearby cities clustered together under one of the more decorous awnings, and we began trying to decide which Ladies belonged to which cities. She proposed that the one who wore armor along with her flowing attire must belong to Bamberg, the northernmost Teuton stronghold near the Saxon border. I agreed with her and suggested that the oldest one might be from Innsbruck, where the fresh air of the Alps offered longevity.

Freia turned away for a moment to speak with Lady Rachel Sendlin, the mother of the young lord who had expressed an interest in her. About that time, I noticed a familiar swath of long black hair blowing in the wind amongst the wide variety of dancers in the square. An instant later, I recognized Augustin dancing with a noble-looking young woman about my age, her golden hair gathered beneath an intricate veil. I frowned a bit at the sight, studying his face covertly, trying to discern whether he was enjoying himself, and whether that young lady was a Teuton. She had to be an outsider, with hair of that color. I saw that Augustin stared at his partner with a rather disturbingly intense concentration as they whirled together. He did not seem to say much to her, although the young lady kept up a running commentary the entire time, I noticed.

I turned my gaze back to Freia shortly afterward, pushing aside my gnawing chagrin at seeing Augustin dancing with another woman. What was my problem? I was supposed to be paying attention to Joel, not some ridiculous Bayern brother. Suddenly, one of Joel's coworkers accosted me, requesting that I dance with him. He wore lower class garments already dirtied from the brawl, and his breath reeked of beer. Joel came up behind the guy and suggested that he back off, as I nodded graciously at him, stating that I must decline his offer. But the burly ironworker could not be put off that easily. He barked that I had danced with Joel before, so why not him.

Before I could react, he reached down and pulled me to my feet, grasping both of my hands and dragging me into the square.

The brawny ironworker began to swing me back and forth, stepping all over my skirt. I tried valiantly to break away, hearing Joel yelling nearby, coming to my rescue. But before he reached me, my hands were unexpectedly freed and my attacker tumbled to the ground with a splat. As I brushed my hands off on my skirt, taking several steps back, I saw Augustin standing with one boot planted on the ironworker's chest, ordering him in a sinister voice to keep his hands to himself.

Joel reached us a second later, his expression concerned. I assured him that I was fine, directing my attention to my savior. "Thank you, Augustin," I said with feeling, grateful that he had seen my predicament in spite of his distraction.

"I would tread softly, my lady," Augustin said, scowling down at me, "for he is not the most dangerous man who walks these streets." He nodded at the stoned ironworker, then turned on his heels and disappeared into the crowd.

Chapter Nineteen:
A Blood Sacrifice

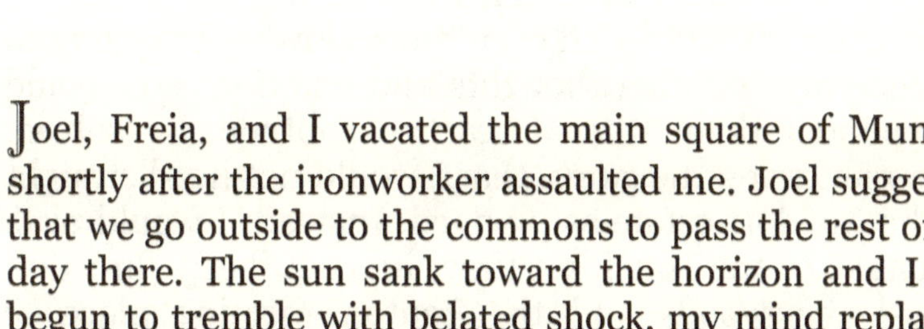

Joel, Freia, and I vacated the main square of Muniche shortly after the ironworker assaulted me. Joel suggested that we go outside to the commons to pass the rest of the day there. The sun sank toward the horizon and I had begun to tremble with belated shock, my mind replaying the drunken brute's grasping hands, clumsy feet, and sudden downfall. Pictures of Augustin appeared in my brain again and again: his threatening stance upon the ironworker, his apparently meaningless dance with the golden haired woman, his last words to me before he disappeared. I realized, just as we reached the western gate of the city en route to the fairgrounds, that I was in no state of mind or body to remain with the party goers now. I could not speak or form a cognizant thought. I desperately needed time to myself, to reflect on all that had taken place and on my current situation.

Once we reached the tents closest to the city walls, I finally found my voice enough to apologize to Joel and Freia—and Master Denlinger, who had joined us at some point, though I could not remember when or where. I told them that I needed some time alone and planned to return early to the Meldorf estate, because I was not feeling well. At first, Joel insisted that he should accompany me to protect me from harm. I said that he should not give up the party for my sake, especially since his friend Heinrich Denlinger was with us now. If I came upon any danger during my walk back, I promised Joel that I would set my ice free to defend myself, like I had against the Gypsies. I should have done that when his coworker accosted me, but I had been taken too much by surprise to react properly. After much advice and well-wishes from all three of my friends, I pointed my feet toward the gates of Muniche once more, carrying with me a sausage sandwich and a flask of mead Joel had purchased for me to consume while I walked.

I plodded slowly toward my city as the sky darkened, chewing on my sandwich even more slowly, struggling to organize my spinning thoughts and emotions so I could fully ponder them when I reached solitude. I resolved, upon reentering the gates, that I would not head straight for the Meldorf estate as planned. Instead, I would walk the banks of the Isar for a time, in a southerly direction toward the woods and the Teuton meeting place of Muniche. I should not encounter anyone there with the festival occurring on the opposite bank. Thus, I should be able to think in peace and return to the count's estate after dark.

Dusk had descended upon the countryside when I crossed the drawbridge, having finished both my sandwich and mead while I passed through the city. Stars had begun to appear all over the sky, and a cool autumn breeze blew from the mountains in the south. I paused briefly to exchange a few words with Garin Zeuner at the toll house before continuing my excursion. "You're working late," I commented with a smile when I saw him sitting upon a rather large stump before his shack, his ever-present mallet at his side and a mug of beer in one hand.

He stood up when he recognized me, and bowed. "It is nothing, my lady, it is nothing," he insisted with a chuckle, glancing toward the fairgrounds. "This is only the second night I have worked this holiday, and I should have a decent view of the *Fiorzoubar* from here." He nodded toward the sky with a friendly smile.

He used the Teutonic word for elemental magic, and I thought back to the mystical displays I had enjoyed with my friends during the past three nights. I might be able to watch the more fiery exploits during my walk. "Well, you enjoy yourself, Mr. Zeuner." I gathered my outer coat more tightly around my dress as protection against the chilly breeze and turned toward the forests in the distance. "Perhaps we'll meet again tomorrow."

I had taken a mere four steps when Garin Zeuner called out to me abruptly. "My lady!" I halted and turned back to him, straightening my hair underneath its veil. His expression concerned, he inquired, "Are you not returning to Count von Meldorf's manor?"

I smiled at his question, realizing that he wondered why I was not heading for the crossroads. "No, I'm going to walk along the Isar for a while. Don't worry. I won't let any thieves get hold of me." I winked at him.

The toll taker's eyes still shone with discontent, but he nodded at me, likely figuring it would be impolite for him to attempt to dissuade a noblewoman. "Take care, Lady Swanhilde. And please . . . if you could . . . would you pass by this way again, upon your return?"

I curtseyed once in his honor, appreciating his concern for my safety, promising that I would see him again before taking the path to the count's manor for the night. Soon afterward, I descended a hill to the riverbank and followed its waters as they curved toward the south. I soon left the noises of civilization behind me, aside from the faint shouts and songs drifting over from the distant fairgrounds. I drew in a deep breath, calming myself, gazing up at the stars, my ears concentrated on the chattering river. My ice gradually seeped through my veins while I focused on the waters of the Isar . . . their currents, their flow, their beauty. And at last I felt free enough to truly consider the many complications that had piled themselves onto my heart in recent weeks.

My first and greatest problem involved Augustin von Bayern. I knew that already, and I acknowledged it without qualms. For one thing, his lack of records in my own era still disturbed me, particularly since he was a chronicler, and a good one at that. His family issues also bothered me, and perhaps therein lay the solution to his apparent nonexistence in history. Maybe his brothers tried to ignore his presence, as most of the other citizens of Muniche seemed to do. Since Prince Otto, as the Keyholder of Muniche, would have the authority to approve and disapprove of official writings, perhaps when the city fell in 1066 he would leave what records he wished to the invaders, saving only the ones he appreciated. That would be dishonest; but my opinion of the Prince had been deteriorating for some time now, and not only due to his refusal to grant Joel and me the song. *Augustin's distaste for his youngest brother was rubbing off on me . . . .*

And so I confronted my worst issue with the oldest Bayern brother: *I liked him.* For more than a month now we had studied languages together; and I had always enjoyed the challenge of linguistics, though I had not chosen to study them at college. Now, with business classes and music practice unavailable to me, a new open door had cast its light into my dreary life as a medieval noble lady. Each week I could test my brain's abilities to perfect foreign languages, honing my skills at translating as well. The possibilities of trading such a plethora of information and knowledge with this educated Bayern brother helped me accept my destiny of two decades in the past with better grace. Once I returned to the twenty-first century, I would have learned all sorts of new things, from dialects to rituals of my people. I would never have to fear repercussions from the Torstein, of refusing to learn from the past, if Augustin taught me everything he knew.

But how could I continue to study with this man one-on-one—a young man, a lord, unmarried, incredibly handsome, in fact—without allowing our academic relationship to develop into something more? Though I had stepped into the past, I was still a twenty-one year old woman with fluctuating emotions and hormones. I remembered all that Freia had told me about Augustin von Bayern, the horrible rumors about his abuse of women, about his insatiable desire for blood and death. I did not think she was lying, but neither had I observed a threat to my own safety from him. He treated me as an equal during our studies, not as some idiot woman he wanted to assault. He had even shown interest in my struggles, inviting both Joel and me to his family castle to confront his hated brother.

Did I love him? No. I had not gotten that far, not yet. But I did like him, and I had already ordered myself to *not* start liking someone from the past. I had not come here for this. I had come here to learn the truth about why the Saxons defeated my people, to learn all of the darker secrets that priests like Hans refused to reveal.

And of course I had a responsibility for Joel, who had lost his girlfriend less than an hour after seeing the portal for the first time. During the past months, I had come to appreciate Joel more, seeing admirable traits in him, beginning to respect him as a good man, a friend. But my heart refused to latch onto him, though his own behavior suggested that he hoped to tackle this medieval world with me at his side.

Before sleep took me each night, I never found myself imagining love or lust with Joel. Instead, when I did not see Hans' face in my mind, I found myself thinking of Augustin, wondering what it would be like to dance with him again . . . to feel his arms around me . . . to kiss him . . . to . . . .

And when I return to my own time, I'll be lusting after a pile of bones that have been dead for centuries . . . why . . . why . . . WHY?!

I paused in my walk as I realized that I had gotten rather deep into the forest, the Isar still bordering my path to the right. I could hear fiery eruptions starting up in the distance, and I sighed in frustration and sat down upon a boulder at the water's edge. Why could I never fall for the right men, the ones with whom it could actually *work?* Why must I love an accountant, a man thirty-three years older than me . . . and now a man from the past, a black sheep brother who did not exist, a man with no honor, a man who had rejected the keys to my city? Why did jealousy have to overtake me earlier when I saw Augustin dancing with a beautiful young woman? Would I never grow up? Jamming my chin down onto my palm, I blinked at the waters of the Isar, fighting a well of tears. I had to do better than this.

As I endeavored to compose myself, my ears caught the sound of something rustling in the trees several meters further upstream from where I sat. Though it was difficult to hear much aside from the popping bolts of energy and the lapping currents of the Isar, I felt certain that something lurked in the forest not far from me, disturbing my seclusion. My eyebrows came together and I rose from the rock, training my ears toward the sounds, my element sharpening my hearing. At first I concluded that it must be an animal, or the wind blowing through the bushes and reeds. But an instant later I heard a distinct moan, without doubt a human sound, followed by a murmuring voice.

Fear and curiosity warred in my soul for a long moment, as I stood staring at the trees beyond me. Part of me wanted to investigate, while my common sense screamed at me to turn away, to leave. I should have listened to my instincts; I should have returned to the Meldorf estate then and there. I should have recalled Garin Zeuner's concern about my walk and gone back to the drawbridge to let him know I was safe.

But my curiosity won the fight, and I drew my ice out from my spirit. I kicked off my shoes and paced silently to the very edge of the river, asking its element and mine to hide me, to shield me while I investigated my company. I had not advanced ten steps before I saw a fiery radiance filtering through the trees, along with more noises, urgent, intense. Twelve steps further and I cautiously rounded a large spruce, crouching down among the reeds beside the water. My hair froze into spikes, and my icy eyes widened at the sight of what lay before me.

The trees and brush had been cleared beside the banks of the Isar, creating a circular glade about twenty meters in diameter. Massive fir and oak trees ringed the clearing, their branches dipping low, having covered the ground in recent days with their fallen leaves and needles. At the center of the clearing stood a flat gray stone as long as a bed with ancient markings etched upon it, strange crevices lining its base. Not far from the stone, wicked-looking flames leapt upward from a fire pit, taking on shapes and colors I had never seen before, sickly black smoke curling upward to the sky. A pile of clothing lay in the reeds beside the water, no more than a meter from where I squatted. Most of the fabric resembled a woman's dress, the remainder as black as night, appearing to be a pair of pants. Two pairs of shoes lay discarded in the leaves nearby. And lying outstretched upon the flat stone, to my abject horror, I saw a naked woman, her body twisted uncomfortably, her mouth bound with a cloth, her golden hair sticking in all directions.

My ice had frozen me solid at this point. My fingers transformed into icicles as I sank them into the waters of the Isar, pleading silently to God that I would remain unobserved. A menacing black form had latched itself upon the woman's body, a wide cape hiding its nakedness from me, its claw-like fingers bruising its victim's shoulders as it achieved orgasm with a demonic howl. The woman would have been screaming, had her mouth not been bound. I could see the tears of agony streaming down her cheeks, her eyes wild with pain and fear. My chest tightened at the sight of such an atrocity, far worse than what I had experienced at college not long before. But my mind drew connections anyway, and I clenched my anus while my lungs expelled swift puffs of frost.

I struggled to retain control of my reactions, doggedly ordering my panic to remain at bay. I shut my eyes for a moment to focus on the soothing quality of my element, and in the false respite from the crime taking place before me, I began to piece together exactly what I was seeing. This was heathenry. This rape had to be preparation for a sacrifice, a human sacrifice, and the wild colors leaping from the fire pit suggested that Wuotan himself would be the recipient. I had been wrong. My people still did this terrible thing in the eleventh century. I had thought that this sort of thing had been forbidden long ago, but now it was happening within paces of where I cowered. I reopened my eyes to watch the demon slide off of its victim's body deftly and with grace, and for a brief second the flames of the fire cast light onto its face, just enough that I could recognize him for who he was.

Augustin . . . .

I clamped my teeth shut, biting down hard onto my bottom lip, ordering myself not to gasp, not to scream. So *this* was what everyone had tried to warn me about. *This* was what the educated man did in secret. *This* was why the citizens of Muniche feared him. *This* was his voracious craving for blood and death. Why had I not heeded Freia's advice? Why had I wanted, foolishly, to discover the truth for myself, rather than believing the rampant gossip? My eyes opened even wider as reality hit me like a brick: *Augustin wanted to do this to me.*

He wanted to rape me.

He wanted to kill me.

He hated women.

I could not love him.

My heart pounded in fright as all of my intentions crashed to the ground in front of me, like the shattering pane of a window. I could not study with this man. I could not have anything to do with this man. Yet it was probably too late for me already. If I told him I never wanted to see him again, he would likely appear one night outside my room and take me away, away to this place, to sacrifice me . . . .

I wanted to run, to flee down the river like I had from the Gypsies, but that would never work, not now. Augustin would hear me, pursue me, and probably stage a double sacrifice. So I remained an iceberg at the water's edge, my eyes not wanting to see, unable to look away, as the tragedy played out before me. The woman was too weak to fight, too weak to flee after the rape. She lay broken and still on the stone—the altar—faint moans seeping out from behind the cloth covering her mouth. I suddenly recognized her as the very girl I had seen dancing with Augustin that afternoon. That explained the concentrated stare he had given her the entire time. He had likely been making conjectures on her body, on her stamina, on the taste of her blood . . . .

Augustin stood before the fire pit now, reciting some sort of ritual words I did not understand, probably Ælte Teutonica, the language of my heathen people. He held something into the flames while he spoke, his countenance rigid. I could see his profile from where I crouched, his robe blowing occasionally with the wind, revealing his naked legs. Despite the grotesque ritual to which I had become an unwilling witness, the solidness of his thighs and the curvature of his muscles impressed me. He looked so magnificent . . . why did he have to be in league with Wuotan, the devil?

At length he turned from the fire and walked again to the altar. Now I saw that in his right hand he gripped a knife, a long, wicked-looking thing, glowing with heat from the fire. I watched him bend over the poor woman once more, stroking the sides of her face with the knife, saying a few words that did not sound like Ælte Teutonica. The woman trembled, and Augustin swiftly grabbed one of her hands, smashing it down onto the stone altar and slitting her wrist with his fiery knife. A muffled screech pierced the night air as Augustin slit her other wrist, then did the same to both of her feet. Her blood burst from the wounds and ran off the sides of the altar into the crevices at the bottom. Nausea twisted my stomach, and I bit my lip until it bled, ordering myself not to throw up. *Stay hidden . . . stay hidden . . . .*

Augustin paused in his work, murmuring a few more chants in Ælte Teutonica, prompting the fire in his pit to blaze brightly. The night grew darker while he circled the altar, eyeing the woman's body, his face contorted with a devilish pleasure, his teeth bared, his eyes suggesting that he was trying to decide where to cut her next. At last, he halted his pacing right before her face, grasping it with one hand and turning it to his as he whispered something in her ear, something that made her moan again. A moment later, he bit down onto her neck, holding his knife flat against her chest as he drank her blood—and read her memories. I had never imagined I would see anything like this happen in real life; this was like watching a horror movie. My stomach churned again, and I carefully drew one of my icy hands out of the water, pressing it to my mouth. *Be quiet . . . be quiet . . . .*

He backed away from her rather suddenly, clutching his knife more tightly. His expression suggested madness as he raised his eyes to the sky and roared out something awful in Ælte Teutonica, obviously addressing Wuotan himself. I could not tell whether the woman was still alive or not; she no longer moved. Abruptly, I felt the ground tremble beneath me, and a wave of darkness swept the clearing, a colossal clap rending the sky apart. Augustin fell upon his victim one final time, plunging his knife into her bare chest, cutting out her heart.

A squeal almost burst forth from behind my hand as I watched him lift her heart from her chest, his hands covered in dark blood, his eyes staring at the still-pumping organ in diabolical triumph. I pulled my other icy hand from the water, pressing it to my mouth as well, desperately trying not to hyperventilate while my own heart pounded in fear. The knife dropped from Augustin's hand, clattering to the altar, his attention completely diverted now by the heart of his sacrifice. Then, to my utter abhorrence, I saw him open his mouth once more into a wicked grin, biting down onto the heart before my very eyes.

A tiny scream finally escaped my lips at that sight, in spite of my valiant attempts to keep myself quiet. I had seen far too much, and I was about to puke. But before I could relax my ice enough to expel the sausage sandwich that gurgled within my stomach, Augustin spun around to face the Isar, his robes flaring out behind him, his black tunic coming down past his hips, his naked legs spread apart in a threatening stance. His eyes, blazing with his blue fire, zeroed in on me, hiding in the reeds at the water's edge. A glow of recognition appeared within them, and I froze completely as Augustin's lips, stained with his victim's blood, parted into a hideous smile.

He sees me . . . he sees me . . . I'm dead . . . I'm dead . .
.

I felt my body pitching forward as my brain seized the relief of oblivion, the murderer's sinister laughter my final inkling of reality.

Chapter Twenty:
Rationale

I regained consciousness slowly, gradually, like coming out of a thick pool of mire. My eyes opened, blinking against the bleariness, against the obscurity that threatened to envelope me afresh. I had no sense of time, no sense of place. I could tell that I was lying on my back, but I could not hear the river anymore, nor could I smell the forest, the water, the blood . . . .

My memories rushed back to me in a tidal wave, every horror, every fear. I blinked my eyes fiercely and invoked my ice to sharpen my vision, so I could learn what had become of me. It seemed that I lay inside a room, a very dimly lit room. I lay upon a surface that felt neither hard nor soft, the light of a thousand candles flickering off of the wall to my left, the ceiling above me. Everything was in shadow, and I lay still for another moment, breathing quietly, listening to the silence. Very carefully, I turned my neck to the right. I saw countless candlesticks, some glowing yellow and some glowing blue, set upon a shelf along the far wall, others decorating the floor. Sitting on a stool at my bedside, clothed in black from the top of his head to the floor, one ghostly hand clutching a metal goblet, his pale face and gleaming eyes quietly observing me, I found the Grim Reaper, Augustin von Bayern.

My heart beat faster at the sight of him, and I began to gasp for breath. I remembered every part of the ritual I had seen him complete and sickness washed over me again, though I soon discovered that there was nothing in my stomach now. I had apparently puked at some point while I had been unconscious. I had not done that in ages, not since the time I had drunk myself silly at Erika's eighteenth birthday party. My brain cogitated sluggishly, trying to determine why I still lived, after what I had seen. Why did Augustin sit there so calmly beside me, saying nothing, fingering his goblet? Maybe he had already killed me. Maybe I was already dead. I sought my voice inside me and whispered, "Am I dead?"

Augustin smirked at my words, his eyes glittering suggestively. "You should know the answer to that. If you really are a Christian, as you claim to be, you would not be *here*, if you were dead." He cast his gaze once around the room, at the myriad of candles, the shelf, the cabinet, the door, the window blocked by heavy curtains, the couch where I lay.

That was true, but the idea that I was, in fact, still alive, did not relieve my fears. "Where am I?" I whispered, looking around at the small room myself.

"My cottage."

My heart sank at his words, and I began to tremble, though I was not cold. I had the distinct feeling that I would not make it out of his cottage alive, not after what I had witnessed. Perhaps he would grant me mercy and kill me quickly, since he had brought me here rather than to that stone altar. The idea of death terrified me neverthe-less, even though I had reasoned long ago that its skeletal hands must one day send me back through the gates of time. "Are you . . . going to kill me?"

My foe smiled again, bringing his goblet to his lips for a moment, his fiery eyes glowing with anticipation. "Yes," he answered, drawing the word out. I gave one quick squeak of terror at his admission, my hands grasping the cushion beneath me, my entire body tensing. Then, to my surprise, Augustin added, almost as an afterthought, "But not today."

A ridiculous relief rushed through my veins, and a wild anger simultaneously flared within my heart. What was the point of putting it off? "Why wait?" I demanded, my voice slightly stronger now. "You should just kill me now, today, so I can get back to my own time where I belong."

Augustin snickered at my irritation, leaning forward on his stool to look me square in the eyes. "Yes, and there lies the problem, my lady," he purred, his deep voice resonant. "You are the woman I cannot truly kill. Where lies the thrill in giving you what you want? Why should I be the one to push you through those gates of time, when I would rather dangle your soul over the edge of eternity?"

I leaned away from him, sidling toward the wall to my left. His reply, though not unexpected, annoyed me. I remembered the woman he had sacrificed, young and innocent, the same as me. "Why did you kill her?" I whispered, disturbed.

"You know the answer to that question as well." Augustin frowned at me and took another sip from his goblet. "If you would expend the effort to consider our conversation in the city archives, you would recall that I have found no greater glory in this life than that ultimate power of casting a helpless soul into eternity." He eyed me in speculation, as though that explained everything.

I shook my head, confounded anew by this educated man, this refined man who apparently could not set aside his macabre obsession with murder. "But why the sacrifice?" I asked him, still trying to understand. "You could have killed her . . . with a lot less . . . ceremony . . . ." I could not find the proper words.

Chuckling darkly, Augustin replied, "My dear Swanhilde, she was a Saxon. You may know from our history that the Saxons of the north have never appreciated the Teutons, for they covet our powers and our success. She had disguised herself as a noble lady from the Rhineland and planned to uncover some Teuton secrets at our festival before hurrying home to her people. It has been a long time since I have killed a Saxon spy, and I doubt even my brother shall reprimand me this time." A satisfied smile appeared on his face, his gaze toward the curtains.

That rationale struck a chord within me, since I knew what the Saxons would do to our people within the next three decades. I wondered if that was the reason for the quaking ground and the darkness before Augustin had stabbed the woman's chest. The Saxons had never been Wuotan's people; he would probably be grateful for such an offering. I shuddered at the memory, still appalled by Augustin's abject heathenry. "So you killed her . . . and someday you're going to kill me the same way...." I choked on the words.

Anger flared in Augustin's eyes, and he set his goblet down abruptly onto a small table beside the couch where I lay. I noticed that it was halfway filled with blood. "Swanhilde, listen to me," Augustin ordered as I cringed away from his goblet. "I sacrificed that woman because she meant nothing to me. Do you understand that? She could have been a Slav, a Gypsy, a Bohemian, a gutter rat. Her memories were incredibly shallow, not even worth the effort to read. I would rape a thousand such women, the ones who despise me, the ones who cannot form one intelligent thought. You, on the other hand—" Augustin paused, retrieving another glass from the table beside my couch. "You interest me," he said with a fearsome smirk. "And you are a Teuton, not particularly of high blood, but a Teuton nonetheless. When I kill you, it will not be so wretched."

I stared back at him, my fingers once more gripping the cushion beneath me, my fear unwilling to abate. "Are you. . . just going to . . . kill me in my sleep?" I asked, trembling at the thought of it.

Augustin's smile grew wry, and he raised one eyebrow at me. "No, when I kill you, you will know it," he said. "I promise you that."

I shivered, wishing that this couch upon which he had placed me had some sort of blanket attached, so I could gain just a touch of comfort. My mind replayed his long speech after he had set his bloody goblet onto the table, annoyance returning to me as I remembered one thing. "What do you mean, I'm not of high Teuton blood?" I asked, defensive. "I'm ninety-five percent."

My death dealer chuckled at me, his expression mocking. "Perhaps in your era that would be considered a high percentage, but likely more than half of the Teutons in Muniche could say the same. I am ninety-nine percent." He lifted his chin in pride, and I gaped at him, completely dumbfounded. *Ninety-nine . . . !* As I shook my head slowly back and forth, trying to wrap my mind around the concept, Augustin rose from his stool and leaned over me, holding out the second goblet he had lifted from the table. "Drink this," he ordered, his voice authoritative.

I backed away from the cup, and he thrust it toward my face with a glare. "Is it blood?" I asked, repulsed.

"No, it is wine. You were unconscious for quite some time, long enough for me to carry you here, and you expelled the entirety of your dinner along the way, I believe. You need something to restore your strength. Now drink, or I shall force it down your throat." He held the goblet out to me, his expression serious. I took it shakily from his hands, gripping it with both of mine, peering for a moment at its contents. It did not look like blood, nor did it smell like blood. I took a cautious sip, discovering quickly that it was wine, and rather good wine at that. I drank again, washing the disgusting aftertaste of vomit from my mouth, and Augustin continued to stand over me, watching. When I had finished half of the glass, he retrieved a few hard crackers from the table and commanded that I eat those and drink all of the wine. I obeyed meekly, certain that he would force me if I resisted.

Once I had finished the wine and the crackers, I felt my strength returning, and it seemed that my stomach might not decide to rebel after all. I handed the glass back to Augustin, who placed it upon the table. In spite of all that had happened that night, my propriety arose within me, and I said, "Thank you, Augustin."

"My pleasure, Swanhilde." He smirked at me darkly, then, to my vexation, reached down and enclosed my right wrist in his fingers before I had the chance to react. I trembled afresh at his touch, as he pressed his fingers to my artery, and he exclaimed, "Oh, for pity's sake, woman, stop trembling! You ought to recall that I am a doctor; therefore, I must ensure that you intend to survive." He glowered at me while he took my pulse and vowed, "I shall not kill you tonight."

A hand of steel enclosed my lungs at his careless words: *I am a doctor.* My eyes widened, darting to the candlelit shelf. Yes, there were jars there, and bundled herbs, and something that looked like a mortar and pestle. Images of sterile corridors bombarded me, and I yanked my wrist out of Augustin's grip. A rabid panic flooded my veins and I cried out, *"Don't touch me!"* in Bayerisch. I leapt down from the couch and threw myself against the closed door across from where I had lain, knocking over several candles in my path. I shoved at the door, tugging in vain at its knob, and wailed as my brain lost its ability to think logically. I was trapped in a medical chamber, a place of restraints and torment. He would lock me here for eternity, until he chose to end my life.

I do not know how long it took Augustin to get control of me, but I do know that my ice exploded to the point of extinguishing most of his candles. I remember fighting against him when he took hold of me, screaming as he forced my mouth open to press a strange medicine to its roof. Then he held me against his chest, his voice quietly soothing me, though I could not catch the words he used. My mind began to wander aimlessly while a peculiar peace descended upon me, relaxing my muscles, confining my ice into my blood.

Eventually, I began to make sense of the room again, my bleary eyes blinking vaguely toward the candles that still burned upon the shelf. There were only four left, hardly enough to see anything even with elemental vision. But my eyesight was blurry; I could not recall how to channel my ice into my eyes. I felt Augustin's arms confining me to him upon the couch where I had awoken, his right hand smoothing my bodice over my left breast, after the manner of a Teuton priest. "You are safe, Swanhilde. I am not going to hurt you. No one is going to hurt you," he repeated in a soft voice, his hand sending a calming heat into my torso.

"Did you drug me?" I finally managed to say, for my thoughts still rambled. I could not focus on any one topic. *He won't hurt me. He killed that woman. But he won't hurt one with Teuton blood . . . .*

Augustin's hand moved upward from my chest, his strong fingers stroking my throat in turn. "I merely gave you a tonic to calm your nerves and to spare my place of business from icy destruction. The effects will wear off in time, but I shall take you back to the Meldorf estate myself to ensure your recovery."

His suggestive words should have prompted me to tense, but I could not recollect how to control my muscles or my limbs. I was naught but a limp sack of potatoes lying in a murderer's arms, his fingers tracing the path of blood along my throat. "Why did you call Prince Otto a murderer?" I asked, my eyelids sliding shut as his hand moved to tilt my head back against a sturdy surface. His shoulder.

"If I tell you now, you may not remember it tomorrow," Augustin said with a chuckle; but after a pause, he put a riddle before me, his fingers pressing against my pulse. "Although I have been a murderer for many years, Otto committed the first murder. Therefore, he is and will always be the murderer."

He is and will always be the murderer . . . . The concept did not make sense; my stoned brain could not process it. "Who did the Prince murder?" I inquired, opening my eyes to attempt to look toward his face. It was too dark for me to see anything but his hooded shroud.

I heard Augustin sigh, and his fingers tightened upon my wrist as he said, "He killed our mother at his birth."

If I had been in command of my faculties, I would have been able to make the connections. As it was, I simply mumbled, "My Mutti died, too." Augustin said nothing to this, but he began to resituate me, bringing my body into a sitting position, his arms steadying my torso. "Are you going to kill the Prince someday because Marelda died?" I asked stupidly, closing my eyes again. I could not focus on anything, and the candles seemed to be floating like ghosts.

A short, caustic laugh escaped Augustin's lips, and I felt him get to his feet, scooping my body into his arms. "It seems that I shall have to tie you to the back of my stallion for the short journey to Count von Meldorf's property. This would be much simpler had you not fallen prey to female hysteria. Honestly, Swanhilde, you have an irrational fear of doctors. Ridiculous."

I could not think of anything to say in response, for exhaustion had begun to meld with whatever drug he had given me, luring me towards a deep slumber. I must have fallen asleep, for the next thing I knew, Augustin had prodded me awake upon the count's porch, the moonlight casting his front gardens in a silvery sheen. "Can you stand now, Swanhilde?" he murmured in my ear. "You need to try."

I blinked rapidly, a pungent taste in my mouth as I managed to twist my head away from the gardens, toward Augustin's face. His fiery eyes glimmered a cobalt blue, what looked like concern flattening his lips into a thin line. "You . . . brought me back? After what I saw?" It made no sense. Why would he free me after I had witnessed his sacrifice? Did he expect me to keep his iniquities secret?

Augustin's mouth twisted into a rather vampirical smirk, and he set my feet carefully upon the porch, both hands holding me steady. "Swanhilde, you now have a decision to make," he said. "Now you finally know who I am. You know what I do. You know what I *enjoy* doing." He paused, and I shuddered, wishing that I could trust myself to stand without his help. "Now, you must decide whether you should treat me like the other citizens of Muniche treat me. You could speak of my crimes and shun me, pretend that I do not exist, turn your back when we meet in the street, run away, fear me, despise me. Or,"—his smoldering eyes fairly cindered me—"you can choose the contradictory path. You can choose to remember what I do, and to accept it. Not to agree with it, I assure you, just to live with it and acknowledge me anyway. You could choose to remain the one woman, the *only* woman in twenty-two years, who has given me a chance."

Augustin glared at me disparagingly when he finished speaking, raising his right fist to knock upon the front door, to summon servants to care for me. I shook my head slowly, looking down at the boards of the porch beneath me, still unable to justify all that had happened to me that night.

The aged servant Otfried eventually opened the door, then went to get Jarvis after sharing a few words with Augustin. In his absence, the deadly priest helped me lean against the doorjamb. "What you decide to do with me now is your choice," he informed me in a flat voice. "You have until Tuesday. I bid you a restful night."

Chapter Twenty-one:
My Choice

When I awoke the next morning, I spent a few moments gazing up at the beams above, my poor vision tracing what little I could see of their grooves. I had slept a dreamless sleep—a miracle—but the events of the previous evening trickled slowly into my memory, tainting my reverie. *Augustin . . . he sacrificed a Saxon woman to Wuotan . . . and he raped her first . . . then he brought me to his cottage . . . where I lost control . . . and he drugged me and brought me back here . . . .*

His final declaration swirled around in my mind as my body began to shiver beneath my blanket, perhaps an extremely delayed form of shock. *What you decide to do with me now is your choice. You have until Tuesday.* Today was Friday. I was lucid enough to know that. Tomorrow was the last day of the Oktoberfest, and Freia and I had planned to spend both days enjoying the festivities and browsing the tents and stands, like we had done during the first half of the week.

I was in no state to attend that sort of thing today. Images of the sacrifice haunted the edges of my thoughts, and I knew that I would have to spend the day alone, here in my room, so I could try to figure out how I should react to the previous night's mad events. I heard Freia preparing herself at the washing table while I trembled beneath my blanket, and when she came to greet me, fully dressed for the day, I managed to tell her that I needed some time alone. She reached out to stroke my forehead, likely to check for fever. Then she straightened and gave a solemn nod. "Very well. I'll tell Joel that the celebrations have tired you. And I'll tell Ulka to have someone bring you some tea and broth."

I could not find the words to thank her, but I offered a wavering smile when she exited our bedroom, leaving the door cracked. Freia was such a faithful friend, having covered for me more than once already where Augustin was concerned. I wondered whether Jarvis and Otfried had told her who had dropped me off last night. I could not remember anything after they had helped me to the second floor.

In her absence, I curled myself into a ball beneath my blanket to stare at the wall, a safe object, while I struggled to make sense of what had happened to me. It had all resulted from that idiotic assault by the ironworker—no, actually, it had all begun when I had seen Augustin dancing with his sacrifice. Somehow, in spite of the dark surmises he had to have been making about that poor woman, he had noticed my plight. Somehow he had seen the ironworker pull me into the crowd, and somehow he had gotten there first, though Joel had been closer. When I had thanked him for rescuing me, he had given me a fair warning: *He is not the most dangerous man who walks these streets.* Only hours later, the truth of his words had gripped me in a vise: *He had referred to himself.*

Countless times during the short months that we had studied together, he had warned me that my curiosity would be my demise. He had demanded to know why, why had I not heeded Freia's warnings? Why must I play with fire, why must my inquisitiveness lead me into danger? I had grown entranced by his intellect and charm, shrugging off his proclaimed addiction to the high of inflicting death.

I had figured that he must get enough of that through his duties as executioner. I had been wrong, and now, everything had crumbled before my eyes.

He had warned me.

I had not listened.

What could I possibly do now, now that I knew that my "tutor" was something else, something wicked? *You have until Tuesday* . . . . Five days. Five . . . .

I ate and drank nothing that day, though Felda slipped in several times with mugs of tea and what smelled like chicken broth. I could not force myself to rise from my bed except once, when I expelled a rather potent batch of urine. I wondered what sort of drug the murderer had given me last night. Was it still active now, telling me that what Augustin had done was acceptable since the victim had been a Saxon? Did I really think that it was okay for one of my enemies to be brutally raped and killed? Did I honestly believe what he had told me, that he would not treat me so terribly since I had Teuton blood?

I heard Freia return when the daylight began to fade from our bedroom. She did not speak to me, since I lay facing the wall with my eyes shut, my brain doggedly finding countless reasons to validate Augustin's rationale. Sacrifice the Saxons to Wuotan. Maybe he offered enhanced gifts in return. Maybe that was how the Prince had discovered the Song of Time. Maybe he sacrificed people, too. Maybe that was something that every Teuton priest did on the sly in this era. But why did he have to rape her first? Was he really on the level of that mammoth brute from college, basking in the glory of conquest? And did he actually *like* to drink blood? He had looked thrilled when he bit into her heart.

I did not fall asleep until long after Freia had taken to her own bed. In my unconsciousness, I had a horrific nightmare about the rape, but this time I was the victim. Augustin's eyes had turned red like a devil, his teeth extending into fangs, his hands breaking my bones as he thrashed me upon the stone altar. He laughed manically and announced that he was killing me, then and there. I woke screaming, covered in sweat, my ice confined within.

Freia raced to my side and held me in her arms, rocking me against her while I wept. And finally I began to talk, meaningless phrases spilling from my lips. I should never have come to the past in the first place. It had ruined me forever. I needed to get home. I wanted my father. I wanted to forget this primitive era, to immerse myself again in my agnostic country, modern Germany. I wanted to see the ocean. I wanted Hans. Hans . . . the priest I knew . . . the priest I trusted. The man I loved. The one I knew would never perform a human sacrifice.

Eventually Freia lulled me back to sleep. The following morning, once I had finally composed myself, I spilled the whole story to Freia, leaving nothing out. I told her everything, from my decision not to return straight to the Meldorf estate as I walked through Muniche eating the sausage, to the very end when Augustin handed me off to Jarvis and Otfried. I cried on her shoulder several times, telling her how insane I had become, how the oldest Bayern brother had ravaged both my life and my judgment. I should have run away. I should have tried to stop him before he killed that woman, even if she was a Saxon spy. But I had frozen there beside the river, a silent witness to his abuse, awaking in his own house to a solemn promise that one day I, too, would die.

Once I had cried until my tears ran dry, Freia murmured that she would go retrieve some tea for us, and then we could seriously discuss the implications. I rose from my bed while I waited for her, standing in the sunlight as I gazed toward the grain fields stretching into the distance. Presently I moved to the washbasin and mirror, almost backing away in horror at the sight of my reflection. My long black hair frizzed around my face in disarray, my eyes were bloodshot with dark circles underneath them, and frown lines seemed engraved both upon my forehead and at the corners of my mouth. "What have you done to me, Augustin von Bayern?" I whispered to my reflection, speaking Bayerisch like I had during my fit two nights ago.

"And what am I to do with you now? How can I give up what we had? But how can I forget what you've done?"

Freia reentered the room soon afterward, carrying a tray bearing two cups of tea, toasted bread, and boiled eggs. We sat down together on my bed and consumed the food in silence. I waited for her to speak first. She would give me advice, I knew, and I could predict almost exactly what she would say. This time, I determined that I would listen.

While we sipped our tea, Freia began to speak slowly, quietly, looking me in the eyes as she begged me once more to stop seeing Augustin. Now both of us knew the true extent of the rumors passed among the local nobility. The oldest Bayern brother was a pervert, doubtless remaining in Muniche due solely to the Prince's mercy. People had probably asked the Prince to bring justice upon his elder brother, but thus far nothing had been done, and Freia doubted that my experiences of two nights ago would change that. The best thing for me to do, she said, was to send Augustin a message, requesting that he visit me no more. Afterward, she suggested that I never leave the manor unaccompanied. Count von Meldorf certainly had enough servants to spare one to guard me at all times.

Freia advised that I focus my attentions on Joel now, and once we had married, she suggested that we leave the city of Muniche for a few years. Perhaps if we moved to Augsburg or to one of the other Teuton cities, I would remain safe from the schemes of Augustin. Once we returned, he may have finally earned his just deserts. Freia added that if Joel and I decided to move, she would go with us, for she did not want to lose my friendship. "Perhaps in a few years we could all go to the Rhineland," she finished, setting her empty teacup upon the tray. "By then my father should have married off my other sisters to potential successors, and he would likely take me back with open arms, along with any friends I bring with me. Eisenwald is a welcoming place, not one to shun people on account of their blood." She smiled wistfully while she spoke, her gaze toward the window.

I nodded at her advice and said that I must be given time to think everything through before making a concrete decision. I would probably stay indoors for the rest of the weekend, maybe even until Wednesday, so I asked her to give my sincere apologies to Joel about my reticence. But I begged her, "Please don't tell him about what happened to me on Thursday night. He doesn't need to worry about that now. Someday, I'll tell him myself."

I spent the rest of the weekend sequestered in the bedroom, eating what Freia brought to me, honestly considering every aspect of her advice. Her idea that we should go to the Rhineland actually seemed feasible, considering my situation. I doubted that my death dealer would follow me there, though he might trail me to one of the nearby Teuton cities. Also, if I really intended to marry Joel, the outsider, I could not remain in Teuton lands without facing prejudice. During our months at Muniche, Lady Adeline had pointed out several of the city's "mixed couples" among the tradespeople, Teutons who had married someone from another German tribe. Although such couples were treated respectfully, all of the full Teutons bemoaned their hybrid offspring.

I did not want any potential children of mine to face such discrimination. I had begun to accept the fact that I could not avoid having children in an era where birth control was pretty much nonexistent. It would be safer to sire children with an outsider, of course, and Joel would remain one unless someone convinced him to do the blood-transfer. I had kept mum about that ritual thus far whenever we spent time together, though Freia knew the particulars now, thanks to Lord Ulrich's expectations. If I was to protect the outsider I had dragged along on this journey, it would be best to settle in some other land until the mid-1060s. And Freia would be better off far away from wealthy lords who wanted a wife of high Teuton blood.

By Sunday evening, I had decided to heed Freia's counsel. While she dined in the great hall, leaving me alone in our room, I pulled out some of the parchment I had used for compiling my English-Teutonica dictionary, retrieving a feather pen and inkwell and spreading it all out upon the nightstand. I fully intended to compose one final letter to Augustin, requesting that he see me no more. I began the opening line in the Carolingian miniscule he had taught me, my calligraphy flowing gracefully for once: *My Lord Augustin von Bayern* .... But as my pen hovered above the paper, preparing to write the next phrase, a flood of memories that I had endeavored to ignore returned to me unabated, and I froze.

That gorgeous statue of his mother, Marelda . . . her death in childbirth, giving life to Prince Otto . . . his hatred, his bitterness . . . his failure to find love . . . his lust for killing, for death . . . it all had to stem from something, yes . . . . What you decide to do with me now is your choice. You could choose to remain the one woman, the only woman in twenty-two years, who has given me a chance. We had something in common, but we had reacted in totally opposite ways. What if he could see my perspective . . . what if he could know love again . . . somehow?

This new option revolved in my head that entire night, long after Freia had fallen asleep. When I dreamed, my nightmares took on a different theme. I saw an angelic young woman, watched her dote on her oldest child . . . I saw her die an excruciating death, the piercing cry of a newborn melding with her screams . . . I saw her oldest son, Augustin, weeping in his bed with no one to comfort him . . . I saw his childish face contort with anger and grief every time he looked upon his youngest brother . . . and I saw him afresh at his heathenry, murdering women, seeking a fleeting pleasure, a temporary feeling of power . . . and I saw no love in his heart, no love in his soul. I awoke panting, frightened anew by the memories of his sacrifice, realizing that my decisions had become incredibly more complicated.

I related my struggles to Freia on Monday afternoon. "You really are right about what you think I should do," I confessed to her, sighing at my own refusal to accept the facts. "And I really, truly *am* considering it. But last night, something else occurred to me about Augustin. I've been trying to figure out what made him turn out this way, and I think it all started with his mother's death. He said that no one has given him a chance in twenty-two years. I think that maybe, if someone else shows true concern for him, chooses to be his friend in spite of his horrible addictions . . . maybe he could realize that there's a better way . . . ." My voice trailed off as uncertainty assailed me yet again. *If I were the one to grant him that chance, what if I was wrong? What if he just pulls me down to his level, to justifying the most gruesome form of murder?*

Freia gawked at me, her expression suggesting that I had clearly lost my mind. She pleaded with me to come to my senses, to remember her advice, not to fall prey to the brainwashing of this wicked man yet again. He had made up his own mind to become a murderer, she insisted. I should not attribute it to the events of his childhood. I could not change him; he would be the one to change me, she feared, for I seemed to be the only one in Muniche who could not see the darkness pouring from his very soul. He would drag me down with him, to death, to hell.

She was probably right; but my resolution held me fast, and in the end I told her, "You know, if it turns out I'm wrong, and he *does* kill me . . . . Even if he makes it the worst possible death conceivable to humanity . . . when it's done . . . when it's over . . . I'll step back through those gates, back to my home . . . and see the man I love. I think I'll take that chance."

On Tuesday afternoon, Ulka knocked on our bedroom door and informed me that the Lord Augustin von Bayern awaited me on the porch. Freia shot me a frightened glance, but I waved her back. I asked the head housekeeper to let my guest into the front parlor and said that I would see him shortly. I descended the staircase moments later, my heart pounding in my chest, my hand shaking as it gripped the railing. I had no time left to reconsider; now, I must make my choice. All at once, the advice of my elderly mentor from the twenty-first century, the late Lady Muniche, returned to me: *Forgive even the unforgivable wrongs* . . . . So when I entered the parlor and raised my eyes to Augustin's face, I took a deep breath and said, "I forgive you. And I would like to continue our studies."

At first, Augustin gaped at me in shock, but an instant later an impressive smile spread across his face, his sky blue eyes shining with genuine gratitude. He walked slowly toward me and spread his hands out as he said, "I knew, from the beginning, that there was something different about you . . . Swanhilde."

Chapter Twenty-two:
Secrets

That first Tuesday, neither of us chose to address the issue of the sacrifice, focusing instead on our language studies. Augustin attempted to improve his pronunciation of the English "th," while I delved deeper into Ælte Teutonica. Part of me itched to broach the subject of Thursday's events, while another part of me feared to do so, wondering how Augustin would react to my questions. We said goodnight fairly early, right before dinner, Augustin pledging to return two evenings later as usual. I resolved that very day, while my fearsome tutor advanced down the count's walk toward the road, that I would not let Thursday pass without uncovering all I could about his past, dangerous though that may be. He would likely require something from me in return—the idea of that made me cringe—but I had to solve the mystery of this man. I had to coerce him to confront his bitterness and hatred, and perhaps afterward I could show him that the world had goodness in it, too.

Joel stopped by the Meldorf estate on Wednesday evening unexpectedly, having borrowed one of Master Denlinger's horses for the journey. We ate a hearty dinner in the great hall, during which Joel and the count bantered back and forth about various aspects of business. Afterward, we took a long walk by the stream as twilight descended. Although I greatly wanted to explain everything to him, I found myself fabricating a lie, covering up the details. I told him that the sausage sandwich had made me sick—which was true—and that I had spent the rest of the weekend and past two days subsisting on bread and mead in an attempt to regain my health—which was not true.

I said nothing about Augustin, nothing about my insane decision to continue my studies with him. For some reason, I had gotten the distinct impression over the last week that I should keep my activities with the eldest Bayern brother completely under wraps, as far as Joel was concerned. I could tell that Joel had begun to fall for me, though my own heart remained defiantly aloof. His anxiety over my health and constant boasting over his improving skills at metalworking proved that he had begun to think in terms of the next twenty-two years: love . . . marriage . . . family . . . . And of course, I would have to reciprocate. Though I did not love him, he was my responsibility, since I had brought him here. I respected him at least, and maybe that could one day blossom into love.

Joel spent the night in the spare bedroom he had grown accustomed to using and departed the estate before dawn. Freia had roused me upon finishing her early prayers, so I could take my leave of him like a proper maiden. I met him outside the stable, having put my coat on over my nightdress, the crisp autumn air calling softly to my icy spirit. "I'll come back by None on Saturday," he promised me while mounting the dappled horse he had ridden. He referenced the afternoon hour, for the ironworks ran only in the mornings on Saturday. Once he had situated himself in the saddle, he gazed down at me for a moment, his hazel eyes shining with what appeared to be solicitude. "I'd stay away from sausages if I were you. Pretty sure they still use the literal intestines to make them around here. I don't need the only girl I can really talk to dying of food poisoning."

I chuckled under my breath, my deception settling like a brick in my chest. "I'm going to start learning more about the medicinal herbs from Gretchen. She brews all the remedies around here." Joel cackled and advised me to take care of myself. Then he spurred his horse off toward the drawbridge, where he would wait until dawn for the Prince to open Muniche's gates.

Upon returning to my bedroom, I stripped off my coat and slid back beneath my blanket, praying silently for a few more hours of sleep, even if they did not come until daylight. I needed to be able to think straight today, to piece together the riddle named Augustin von Bayern. I vaguely heard my Rhenisch roommate rise from her bed, but I pulled my blanket over my head to show her that I desired further rest. I managed to drift off several times, but ultimately gave up when the scent of simmering duck crept into my chamber. Then I threw my blanket aside and turned my attention to the wardrobe. I needed to properly clothe myself, and more importantly, I needed to take full advantage of what would certainly be a delicious meal. Duck had been a rare treat at the Meldorf manor thus far. Some of the vassals must have snared a few along the Isar recently.

Augustin did not arrive until after the evening meal, much later than usual. When I came to meet him in the parlor, attired in a wide-sleeved purple dress that reached from my neck to the floor, my black hair tied back and unveiled, he bowed in full propriety, apologizing profusely that he could not have come earlier. "This morning I had to execute a local robber who murdered one of his fellows during the festival," he informed me, a wry smile curling on his lips. "And in the afternoon, as I sat at home practicing my English, a young woman in travail graced my doorstep, requesting that I play the role of midwife on her behalf." His smile grew darker, and he showed his teeth.

I frowned at this admission, taking one step backward as my eyes scoured Augustin's appearance from head to foot. He wore black and red noble clothing, adorned with several golden chains, lion's head buttons lining his thick overcoat, black leather boots reaching to his knees. His long hair was partially down and partially pulled back with a clip—what seemed to be one of his favorite styles—and on his fingers he wore two pricey-looking rings. I had the feeling that he had taken a lot of time to clean himself up before meeting me, and I wondered why. I could not detect a trace scent of blood about him, though he had apparently spent most of the day engrossing himself therein. I wondered what woman in her right mind would ask *him* for help in childbirth. What in the world would he require of her in return for such a favor? Another puzzle entered my mind at that moment, when my eyes traveled to the front windows, noticing that the sky had already turned a deep navy blue. "How exactly do you intend to get back into the city, with the gates closed for the night?" I asked him, tilting my head.

His expression took on a look of scorn. "My darling Swanhilde, I can get into Muniche whenever I want," he replied shortly. "I am the Lord Augustin von Bayern. Muniche is *my* city. She will not close her gates against her own son." He eyed me disapprovingly, as though I should have known that from the start.

I considered this, remembering that he had refused the keys, and yet now he proclaimed that Muniche was, indeed, *his* city. This man still did not make sense to me. It was time to voice my questions, no matter what he might think of me. Drawing myself up straight with a courage I did not feel, I took a deep breath and began cautiously, "If you would . . . agree . . . I would like to set aside our studies for the night . . . for there are many . . . things . . . I would like to ask you . . . Augustin." I looked him in the eyes, tensing for his reaction.

His body also grew rigid, and he folded his hands carefully behind his back, his countenance fierce as he stared down at me. "Of course you would have many questions for me. But I should like to remind you first, Swanhilde, that you shall have to grant *me* some answers as well, if you expect me to reply to your queries." His expression leveled a challenge.

I relaxed at his words, relieved that he may not require blood or sex after all, if I could satisfy his curiosity. Though I could not fathom what questions he might have for me, I could not back down now. So I nodded at him, accepting his terms, and suggested that we step out onto the porch so that we could speak together more privately. I summoned Otfried and requested that he bring me my coat. Moments later I followed my tutor outside, into the chill of the night air.

Soon we had situated ourselves upon two of the porch benches. I sat against the railing of the porch with the house to my left and the gardens to my right. My tutor sat with his back to the house with his arms crossed, looking over the count's land with an indecipherable expression. I gathered my thoughts, ordering myself to be strong, and murmured in a mixture of English and Teutonica, "There have been many questions troubling my heart . . . since last Thursday night."

I paused, and Augustin's eyes shot towards me, his mouth turning downward. "My rationale was not good enough for you, then?"

"I think . . . it *might* be . . . if you could clarify a few things," I said.

Augustin's expression did not soften, his light blue eyes once more burning the gardens. "Speak."

The many questions whirled through my mind, but I realized that I needed to confront the rape issue first and foremost. I cleared my throat and looked down at my hands, suddenly fearing that Augustin may mock me upon hearing of what had happened to me at college. But there was no other way to explain why his actions at the altar had affected me so strongly. "I was raped once," I heard myself saying, my voice as quiet as the soft breeze of night. "A group of outsiders cornered me at the university . . . and one of them took me from behind." I winced and shut my eyes, working to keep myself in the present, to not allow my brain to slip into the panic that rendered me helpless.

Augustin said nothing, so I counted to ten in my mind, then explained, "That's . . . that's what I'm . . . struggling with . . . the most. I keep imagining you . . . doing what those brutes did to me."

"You were not meant to see what I did that night," Augustin said at last, his tone sounding rather irritated. I opened my eyes to look toward him, and I saw that he had crossed his arms, his gaze turned stalwartly away from mine. "Mr. Zeuner claimed that he warned you against entering the forest."

I did a double-take, feeling as though a knife had been thrust into my back. "Wait. Are you saying Mr. Zeuner *knew?*" I sputtered.

"He certainly had an inkling that the night concealed something demonic." Augustin gave a casual snort and shifted his eyes toward me. "Most of the Teutons in Muniche know of my offerings to Wuotan. They know what the rite requires."

I gawked at him, my impressions of eleventh century justice crumbling into dust. "But doesn't . . . the Church . . . forbid that sort of thing?"

"They would, if I sacrificed people of influence."

I felt sick. I broke away from Augustin's cold stare and stuffed my hands beneath my dress, the chill in the air doing little to comfort me for once. "Well, you should be pleased to know that my rapist can no longer walk," I said, scowling at the moonlit gardens. "And the two who restrained me also reaped their recompense. Remember, in *my* era, men and women are equal."

"As they should be," Augustin answered, sounding amused, "and I appreciate your warning. It should please you to know that I have never raped a Teuton. Sex between Teutons without elemental involvement is worthless."

I detected a touch of scorn in his final sentence; I wondered if he meant that he had never had sex with a Teuton before. My ice trickled into my veins as my thoughts turned in a direction that was hardly appropriate. But I looked toward him again and asked, "So is it boring .

. . to have sex with outsiders?" I felt myself blushing at the topic. Hopefully he could not notice that in the darkness.

Augustin's eyes glimmered with a trace of fire when he responded, "It is best followed by murder." He nodded once, a sinister smile spreading across his face.

I looked away and flexed my fingers, placing them in my lap. "So I don't have to fear being raped by you. Just being killed. Good to know." I rolled my eyes, and I heard Augustin chuckle softly. It was about time to introduce the real subject now, before thoughts of sex with a blue-fired priest conquered my reason. "Augustin, tell me about your mother," I requested quietly.

His face darkened, and he directed his gaze to me once more. "How much do you want to know?" His voice was low, harsh, his eyes darting from me to the shadows surrounding the porch.

I inhaled deeply, then answered, "Everything."

Augustin's strong shoulders shuddered and he drew his arms around his body, as though he felt the cold despite his fire. He looked away from me again, his face slowly transforming into a mask of grief, and for a long while he kept silent. I stared at him while he fought his internal battle, intrigued all over again by this cruel man, this unfeeling man whose love for his mother had never subsided. At last, when I had begun to despair that he would actually open his hard heart to me, he began to speak, his voice deep and laden with sorrow. "It has been twenty-two years, twenty-three this upcoming May, yet I can see her face still this night, as though she stood now beside my bed, comforting me in the darkness, like she did when I was a child." Augustin paused to exhale heavily, then continued, his gaze still trained on the stars while I watched and listened in fascination.

"Marelda was beautiful, far more heavenly than that statue in the castle. She became the Lady of Muniche at the age of nineteen and married the Keyholder, my father, that same year. She was twenty years old that New Year's Day, when she gave me life. She named me after her favorite Christian saint, Augustine of Hippo, from the 300s A.D."

My eyes widened considerably at that. I had always wondered why Augustin's first name was not Teutonic. "Marelda could have been a saint herself, for she was so incredibly kind, compassionate, faithful, loving. She loved God, and she loved this city. She loved my father . . . and she loved me. Everyone said I looked just like her, aside from my straight hair.

"During those horribly short years that she remained on this earth, she rarely left my cradle, and later my side. She tutored me herself in Teutonica, in Christianity, even in music, though my talents in that area were lacking—"

"Wait." I interrupted him there, though I probably should not have, because another thought had arisen in my brain. Augustin paused to frown in my direction, and I said, "You were *four*. And she taught you so much . . . ?"

Augustin favored me with a mocking smile. "I have always been somewhat of a prodigy myself, Swanhilde. In my youth, I had an insatiable desire to learn, especially languages and writing. I also enjoyed athletics, which is why today I use my strength as the city executioner, as well as in my other pursuits." He raised an eyebrow at me suggestively and I shrank back against the railing, recollecting the frightening display of his strength during his sacrifice. "Marelda recognized my gifts at an early age, and while she was here, she chose me as her favorite son. She told me many times that one day I would hold the keys to her beloved Muniche in my father's place, and she believed that I would become a great and successful ruler. Perhaps if she had lived . . . her dreams may also have come to pass . . . .

"But I remember clearly, as though it happened merely an hour ago, that morning in April when she greeted me in my bedroom, her third pregnancy almost complete, the pregnancy that had often made her sick, too sick to stay with me. That fateful morning, she related to me a dream that had come upon her before Lauds, as the candles burned low in her bedroom. Someone had visited her in that dream, giving her the dreadful news that she would not survive the birth of her next child, which would be a son. I did not understand, a lowly child of four, but I recall how tightly I clung to her skirt, begging her not to leave me, not to allow her dream to become reality. She comforted me like she always did and urged me to be strong, to grow into the leader she wanted me to be, even if she could not live to see it.

"I remember that terrible day in May of 1022, when my entire world fell apart before me." Tears glinted in Augustin's eyes, and I drew my coat more tightly around me, shivering as his tale reached its tragic finale. "I heard her weeping, moaning in her bedroom, attended by several midwives, the door shut to all of the men, including her father and mine. I remember standing outside her door in the hallway, trembling in fear at her cries, knowing that my mother was dying, wanting so badly to see her one last time.

"Somehow, I managed to pull the door open at last, breaking the lock with a strength I should not have had at that young age, shoving aside the hands that tried to hold me back. I ran into the room using my element for the first time in my life, flying to my mother's bed-side, burning everyone who tried to stop me. When I looked down at her face, crumpled in torment, white as a sheet . . . when I saw that she no longer had the strength to scream . . . when I smelled that rancid blood in the room, pouring fresh from her body . . . I knew it was done. I remember clutching her cold hand desperately with my own, trying to warm her, though I could not, choking on my tears, begging her to stay with me. And she opened her eyes one final time to blink at me twice, a pitiful smile barely touching her bleeding lips as she breathed out her last words: *Augustin . . . I love you . . . .*"

Augustin broke off sharply, grasping the robes at his chest with his right hand, bending over in agony, his eyes screwed shut, tears trickling down his face. My own cheeks were wet with the heartbreak of his story and with the passion in his voice. While he struggled to compose himself, the truth of the matter hit me hard: *He had actually seen her die. He had been there. I had been in the*

U.S. with Beth's family when Camilla died . . . my father told me about it later. What would it have been for me, if I had witnessed it myself . . . ?

When Augustin finally continued, his face had twisted into a mask of rage. "Shortly afterward, I heard the newborn child cry for the first time. When my father dragged me from the room, I saw that little pink thing, plump and screeching, alive, healthy, unknowing. From that moment on, hatred for that murderous being consumed my soul. I did not speak to it for six years, and the first time I ever addressed it directly, I called it *murderer*. For that is what it was, and always will be. That selfish infant killed my heart forever.

"In later years, my hatred multiplied toward my father, toward the servants, toward the entire world. I watched with the incomprehension of a child as those awful keys of Muniche tore my father's love away from my beautiful mother, heaping it upon a new woman, a strange woman just two years younger than my mother . . . *Maria*. My father married Maria just two months following Marelda's death, and he never graced the chapel set aside for her memorial after that day. I never understood how he could forget such an unfailing love until I understood the concept of the keys. They are a curse. They take away one's free will. And you asked me why I refused them." Augustin paused to sneer me as he stated, "I never wished to give up control over my heart. I never wanted my lust to be drawn toward Maria, that wretched replacement, the one who never loved me, the one who elevated that bloody murderer to his current position as Prince.

"As for the servants, they also gradually began to distance themselves from me, never again complimenting my looks or my intelligence. Some of them whispered that Marelda's death had driven me mad, that it had driven me away from God, toward the devil. For a solid year following her death, I spent my days in her chapel, staring at her painted image surrounded by crosses and candles, my own blue candle of memoriam burning always, to this very day. I wept on her behalf. I begged God to answer me, why, why had He taken her? Why could He not show me mercy, send her back to me, just for one day? But He never answered me, and I finally gave up. I turned my back on Christianity and decided that since I would never know love again, I would embrace hatred, studying the ancient writings of the heathens before the Christian era, getting what pleasure I could from this world. And Wuotan has granted me more power than I could ever have as the Keyholder of Muniche. In him, I find my release. In him, I find acceptance." Augustin stopped here and turned his head slowly toward me again, his blue eyes smoldering. "Have I sufficiently satisfied your nosiness now, my darling Swanhilde?"

I gawked at him in shock, unable to reply, his long explanation swirling around inside my head. I would have to think about this, and hard. Eventually I managed to nod at him, answering his query, unsure how to proceed. He had told me so much. How could I possibly ask him something more? What more *could* I ask? Fortunately—or perhaps unfortunately—Augustin let me off the hook. He scathingly announced that it was my turn to tell him my darkest secret, since he admitted that now, I knew his.

He eyed me silently for a time while I tried to discern what exactly my own worst secret actually was. I had quite a few, maybe even more than him, and I did not know where to begin. My thoughts traveled first to the Gypsy I had killed, but Augustin would likely shrug off that sort of violence. Tiring of my silence, my tutor abruptly focused on my neck and stated in an authoritative voice, "If you cannot think of anything as dark and grim as my own tales, perhaps you could explain the purpose of that ridiculous locket you wear continually around your neck." I froze, my eyes widening in horror as I lowered my gaze to my coat, imagining that golden locket underneath, lying upon my dress. "I have never once seen you without it, though sometimes it does not complement your attire. I am certain that there must be some deep, dark secret lurking within."

He was right, and I wondered wildly why I had not stuffed it inside my neckline all the times I had met with Augustin, like I usually did whenever I met with Joel. I had told Freia the truth about Hans over a month ago . . . and now Augustin wanted to know. He would think me a fool once he knew of my feelings. But I would have to tell him now. He was not the only one on this porch who had lost his love. Sighing heavily, I reached inside my coat to undo the clasp, my hands shaking, and I silently handed the locket to my tutor. He squinted at it in the dark of the night and moved one hand downward to throw his fire upon a nearby candlestick, holding it up as he opened my secret.

His blue eyes widened, his face taking on a hue of appraisal. "A priest . . . ." he murmured at length, studying the picture of Hans. "Is this your father?"

A brief snort escaped my nostrils at that assumption. I wished my excuse could be that simple. *Of course he would think Hans is your father . . . look at how old he is . . . you idiot.* "No . . . that's not . . . my father . . . ." I choked on the words, not wanting to confess the truth. Augustin raised his eyes to my face, studying it in the darkness, likely detecting my blush. "That's . . . that's . . . Hans. He's . . . the one . . . who taught me . . . most of what I know about Teutons. He taught me Teutonica, how to use my element, how to reach the spiritual realm. He's the one who got me interested in our history." The straightforward explanation tumbled out of me.

Augustin eyed me distrustfully, his gaze burning into my soul, one hand still holding the blue-flamed candle-stick, the other fingering my locket. "And yet you keep his likeness close by your heart . . . always. He is *your* priest . . . yes . . . ." A rather dreadful smirk appeared on his face as he nodded, looking again at the locket.

Suddenly, the truth fell from my lips, my Teutonica running together. "I'm in love with him, and I'm an idiot. I've been in love with him since I was thirteen. Eight years. That's why I came to the past. I'm so selfish. I hoped that by being away from Hans for a while, I could stop loving him. I have to stop, somehow."

Augustin stared at me, his smirk transforming into a grimace. "How old is this Hans?" He peered at the picture again.

I bit my lip, then came out with it. "He was fifty-four when I left to come here, and I was twenty. And that's not the only problem. He's my father's servant."

Augustin chuckled, a dark sound. "And you have not been able to love anyone else, I assume?"

"I've tried; I've tried!" I squeaked, frustration overtaking me afresh. "I've tried to love so many others, young Teutons, young men from other German tribes, men from Joel's land. Everyone. Nothing has worked. I'm such a fool." Tears of rage welled in my eyes and I brushed them away angrily, staring downward.

Augustin was still smiling, and he shut the locket and handed it back to me. "This Hans has been the one who has taught you everything," he noted, his expression sagacious. "You have danced with him, you have studied Teuton lore with him, you have likely done a few blood rituals with him . . . he has been your *fire*." I stared at Augustin in shock, my mind reeling. *How could he tell?* "And now you're hoping to fall for some foolish outsider, a well-meaning lad of course, but one who could never do the things Hans can do for you." He nodded at my locket, which I now held in my lap. Raising his gaze to look me straight in the eye, Augustin said, "You fool. You have known the glory of the Teuton priest. For the rest of your *life*, you will want a priest. There is no hope for you now."

My mouth dropped open in consternation, the truth of his words grasping me as undeniable. It all made sense now, when he put it *that* way. Shaking my head in distress, I gasped, "Why didn't somebody *tell* me that?!"

"I just did," Augustin snapped, eyeing me ferociously. "*Now* we know why you cannot seem to stay away from me in spite of everything you have seen. Unlike Joel, *I* am a Teuton priest. Unlike him, *I* could give you *everything* you desire. *I* could teach you things that this Hans of yours has never learned, and things that he would never dare to show you, for *I* have no scruples." He bared his teeth at me in a wicked smile, his fiery eyes glowing like the flame of his candle.

I shrank back from him, clutching my locket tightly in my hands, trembling at the intensity of his statements, anticipation rushing through my veins. *A heathen priest . . . Augustin would know absolutely everything . . . and I want to know . . . I've always wanted to know . . . .* "What can you teach me?" I whispered to him.

"Anything you ask," Augustin replied with a disturbing smile.

My mind raced through a thousand possibilities before settling on the most useful. "I want to learn blood control," I said. "Hans refused to teach me that."

Augustin chuckled and looked out across the fields. "In this era, it is mainly the priests and the doctors who learn rites such as that one, but I suppose I could satisfy your curiosity anyway." He rose from the bench, extinguishing his candle, and said in parting, "Meet me at the statue of Prince Abelard, Monday, at None."

<h3>Chapter Twenty-three:</h3>

A Fair Trade

On the appointed Monday, I arrived at the statue in the atrium of the town hall right on time, as the church bells for None clanged loudly throughout Muniche and the surrounding countryside. I wore one of Freia's green dresses for a change, although the color did little to offset my gray eyes. I had plaited my hair back into four braids woven underneath a tan head covering. I included a pair of my mother's golden earrings and her emerald bracelet to complement my appearance, hoping to leave a decent impression on any townspeople who saw me. My evening study sessions with Augustin von Bayern had not passed unnoticed by the local nobility, so I needed to boost my sagging reputation. Wealth admired elegant attire, I knew, so I had really decked myself out for my journey into the city that day.

I found Augustin awaiting me before the statue of Muniche's founder, dressed like a Teuton priest rather than in the robes of nobility. His pitch black tunic and pants were almost entirely ensconced by a massive hooded robe. Around his neck he wore a shining silver chain with a crucifix hanging from it. His black leather boots, shined to perfection, rose to his knees, and the black gloves covering his strong hands completed his outer layer of darkness. I doubted that any of the others milling about the town hall would disturb us. I saw a few commoners cast nervous glances in Augustin's direction before scurrying toward the court rooms. I could not help but smile as I approached my tutor, his grim countenance looking so glorious in spite of everything. I curtseyed at him politely and commented that his attire seemed quite fitting for what we intended to do.

Augustin raised an eyebrow at my observation, his eyes glittering as he let his hood down to reveal his gorgeous black hair, half up and half down as usual. "You also seemed to have prepared yourself suitably," he said, nodding at my dress and jewelry while he looked me up and down. Lifting his right hand in the direction of the hallway to the archives, he beckoned me. "Come. We have little time for our duties this day, for I plan to allow you to return home for dinner."

I nodded and followed him as he strode into the building, taking a small bit of comfort in his pledge to send me back to the Meldorf estate by dinnertime. If that was true, he must not mean to kill me today. He opened the door to the city archives for me moments later, waiting while I entered the shadowy stairway ahead of him before closing the door firmly behind us. He lifted the sole torch burning beside the doorway to the hall to light our way down to the inner door with its stenciled warning: *Chroniclers and Official Personnel Only.* "We shouldn't be expecting any company down here today, should we?" I asked, shivering a little at the enormity of what I was about to learn.

My tutor opened the aforementioned door for me, revealing the seemingly limitless dusty shelves and blue-flamed chandelier beyond. He made a sound in his throat at my question and said, "You should recall that the first time you disturbed me here in my domain, that was also on a Monday. The two other city chroniclers, a handful of monks, and some officers grace these archives on other days of the week, but Mondays are mine. We shall certainly remain undisturbed." He cast his gaze around the entire room once, then shut the door behind us, setting the torch in its socket next to its flickering counterpart.

Something occurred to me then, my thoughts racing back to the events of a Monday two weeks prior. I looked toward the shelf labeled *Teutonic Traditions* and said, "I'm sorry I left a mess over there a couple weeks ago. I didn't realize it was you coming in the door."

"Ah, so you were the vandal with an interest in the blood-transfer." He faced me with a chuckle and gestured for me to seat myself upon a backless cloth stool not far from the shelf I referenced. "Hoping to learn its intricacies for Joel's sake?"

I scoffed quietly and paced to the stool, situating myself while my priestly tutor disappeared down a nearby aisle. "I'm not really curious about that ritual," I admitted, "because time travelers are supposed to avoid deadly Teuton rites."

"I suppose that any fatal ritual with a direct connection to Wuotan could conceivably open the gates of eternity, even for a witch like you." Augustin reappeared before me with an aged tome in his hand, his gloved fingers concealing its title as he opened it to a bookmarked page. He favored me with an ominous look and added, "You should be grateful, my dear, that I have no intention of sacrificing you."

My ice had trickled into my veins just a tad, in reaction to both the musty atmosphere of the archives and to the renewed caution I felt at the recognition that Augustin and I were alone. Although he had pledged earlier to return me to the Meldorf estate by dinnertime, a dark corner of my brain began to speculate on his true intentions. Perhaps he planned to kill me in the process of teaching me blood control. *Oh well, as long as he explains it first, so I can practice once I get back home.* I ordered myself not to fear and raised one eyebrow at him. "I was kind of surprised that you didn't turn me in to your brother, after you found me skulking around in here as a spirit," I said.

Augustin's dark eyebrows came together, his expression an odd mix of humor and disgust. "If I followed the paths of the typical Teuton priest, I would have taken you before the council to be bled and executed. But I do not hold to the opinion that our rites are too arcane for an intelligent woman to comprehend, although other priests might burn me at the stake if they heard me speak such blasphemies. Besides, you know what I think of the Prince. If I considered you a threat, I would handle you myself." He glanced toward the thin windows upon the far wall, his lips forming a sneer.

I blinked at him in surprise, the complexity of Augustin von Bayern's motivations practically throwing me off balance. *He sacrifices women . . . he rapes women . . . and yet he thinks that a Teuton woman . . . an intelligent woman . . . could indeed handle the priestly secrets . . . not even Hans believes this.* I shook my head slowly and stared down at his boots, my opinion of this perverted priest rising considerably despite his ghoulish obsessions. He believed me to be intelligent and therefore his equal.

"So are you going to kill the Prince someday? You never answered my question before." I lifted my gaze, passing over his gloved fingers cradling the tome he held, lingering for a second on his firm chin before meeting his eyes. Everything about him connoted mystery and power. If I had an irresistible yearning for a Teuton priest, like he had claimed, then he had hooked himself a faithful student for as long as I remained in the eleventh century.

Augustin wrinkled his nose at my query and looked away again. "No, I am not going to kill him. If I were, I would have done so years ago. Filial loyalty, you should recall, is the strongest tie that binds Teutons together. Even I, the city murderer, would not spill family blood, not even for revenge. The Lord will judge Otto one day for his sin. In the meantime, our family shall continue in hatred." Augustin grimaced and looked back down at me. "Now, did you come to me today to learn blood control or not? It is not a simple concept, and our time grows short." I perked upright on my seat and assured him that I had, clasping my hands together on my lap in an attempt to put forth the aura of the engrossed student. My tutor lowered his eyes to the book in his hands and began to read in Ælte Teutonica, carefully explaining the terms that I did not yet understand.

First, Augustin said that Teutons with elemental control also claimed the power to direct blood flow due to the mystical spring of Teuton blood. Our blood was not mere human blood; it stemmed directly from a river in some realm beyond the reach of mortals, a fiery dominion where Wuotan reigned. Teuton priests tapped into this reservoir when performing the blood-transfer, and also whenever they felt the need to bleed their wives.

The particulars prompted my ice to further inundate my blood, effectively coating my vision with a frosty blue veil. "Wait a minute," I said when the priest before me had paused for breath. Augustin looked up from his book inquisitively, and I shook my head, too many novel concepts engulfing my brain at once. "So you're saying that Teuton priests *bleed* their wives regularly? And that's why they create the heart-bond? It's because it offers them an infinite supply of blood, not because it enhances their trust for each other?" That did not sound right.

"Swanhilde, the Teutonic heart-bond is formed out of love," he reminded me, his eyes appearing uncharacteristically wistful. "It binds lovers' spirits in a way that outsiders cannot fathom. The 'infinite supply of blood' is merely a bonus." I recoiled, and a measured smile spread across Augustin's face. "I have heard from my married peers that their wives gradually become accustomed to the bleeding to the point of craving it. Many find it relaxing, and also sensual."

I reached up to touch my throat with my right hand, trying to imagine how anyone could find pleasure in becoming a vampire's prey. "Well, that's just . . . kind of crazy," I remarked, my fingers cold against my flesh thanks to my ice.

Augustin went on to explain that, in order to control the flow of a Teuton's blood, a person must consider both its physical source—the heart—and its path in the body. He began to detail an extremely rudimentary outline of how blood flows from one organ to another, and I waved a hand at him to interrupt. "I know about the circulatory system already, about how arteries carry blood from the heart and veins return it back. I've seen sketches of it."

The priest before me opened and closed his mouth several times, looking utterly dumbfounded. "You did not study medicine at the university," he said in a flat tone, disbelief exuding from his stance.

"No I didn't, but I learned about biology in school. And I'll bet I know a lot more about blood flow than what it says in that book. I know all the parts that make up blood, things that haven't been discovered yet." I crossed my arms proudly and eyed my tutor with my chin raised in accomplishment.

"Well then, you ought to tell *me* how to slow the flow of blood from a wound and how to direct it into a specific channel for the purpose of bleeding." Augustin shut his book and hid it behind his back, eyeing me dangerously.

I huffed and rolled my eyes at him. "I don't know *that* part. I just know the basics. And I'm not doubting your expertise, but you can just skip ahead to the good stuff. Like how *do* you slow the bleeding from a wound?" I thought back to Joel's actions with the stick shortly after we had burst from the portal.

Augustin scowled at me and darted back into the stacks, emerging moments later with nothing in his hands save his gloves, which he was in the process of removing. "Blood control is a mental process, as is the release of one's element," he informed me in a cool instructor's voice. He stuffed his gloves somewhere beneath his robes, then ducked his head to look me straight in the eyes, his own simmering with cerulean fire. "Specifically, a Teuton must first completely block all distractions from their mind to focus upon the wound, the flow of blood, whatever channel has been severed. One must picture the lifeblood as it races through the injured vessels, slowing it forcefully with one's mind, imagining the skin healing, the wound closing with impossible speed, the formation of the necessary scab. It is most easily accomplished when one can unite the physical with the spiritual connection: heal the wound in the realms beyond this world as well as in the mortal coil."

I nodded along as he spoke, envisioning my own circulatory system in my mind, trying to picture the course of my blood with each beat of my heart. "So I would have to visualize the healing as though I were doing it myself, directing the body systems that are done subconsciously, stemming the flow, forming platelets . . . ." My voice trailed off as I remembered that the eleventh-century doctor before me would not know what platelets were. This *had* to be a power from Wuotan, for in modern terms, it sounded completely unfeasible. It could be similar to time travel in one way, for when I had used the Torstein, I had been required to picture the exact time and place in my mind, erasing all distractions.

Augustin tilted his head at me. "Are you ready to try it yourself?"

I flinched a little, half expecting him to produce a knife from somewhere in his robes. "Are you going to cut me?" I asked, drawing my hands beneath the flared green sleeves I wore.

"I could, but it would be best for you to simply practice regulating your blood flow inside your flesh without marring it." He crouched down before me and took hold of my right hand, instructing me to direct my blood to avoid flowing into my index finger. It took a long time before I managed it, for I kept getting tangled up in thoughts of capillaries, my ice pricking me in strange places as I endeavored to cut off the life from my finger. *But wait. All you really have to do is have your blood avoid that artery,* I told myself, chewing on my lip as I imagined my arteries' flow bypassing that channel, like when pressure causes a limb to fall asleep.

At last, I felt my index finger grow cold and rubbery as I doggedly ordered my blood to run past it, to enter my other three fingers instead. "I think I got it!" I exulted, and an instant later, a prickling sensation crept up the length of my finger, for I had lost my focus.

"You have taken the first step into a much broader world, Swanhilde," my tutor congratulated me, swathing my reawakening finger in the warmth of his own hand for a moment. Our eyes met, and he said with a satisfied smile, "Now, I would advise you to continue to practice on yourself and on other Teutons around you, until you have memorized each path of life. Then we can move on to the healing of wounds and other matters." He let go of my hand and rose to his feet.

I got up from the seat myself to stretch, my index finger still tingling just a little. "That's really fascinating," I murmured more to myself than to my companion. "Guess I'm going to spend the next few months imagining everyone's blood." I gave a dark laugh and glanced around at the myriad of shelves, thinking that I had finally embarked upon the path to witchcraft.

"So, have I satisfied your curiosity, for now?" Augustin eyed me in speculation, rubbing his hands together.

I nodded, still trying to sort out the concept in my own mind. "I think so."

"Then it is your turn to satisfy mine." That statement brought me up short. I froze, my ice seeping into my blood as I lifted my eyes to Augustin's face. He stared down at me as though I were his prey. "You know . . . that you cannot gain information from me . . . without giving me something in return." His eyes were burning blue, his hands flexing.

I began to tremble, and my thoughts raced, trying to discern what he would ask of me *this* time. Had I not already given him enough? "What do you . . . want to know . . . ?" I whispered in a tremulous voice.

Augustin drew in a breath and stepped forward to hover over me threateningly, his fiery eyes glowing ever brighter. "I want to know . . . everything . . . you will not tell me . . . ." His voice was ominous, his posture suggestive. "I know . . . that you pledged . . . to not reveal secrets . . . to those in the past . . . before you came here. But *I* want to know. *I* want to know the future. And the way for me to find it . . . is in your blood." His gaze moved from my terrified face to my neck.

A squeal escaped my lips at this, and I shrank back upon the shelf laden with writings on the traditions of Teutonic heathenry. *He wanted to bleed me, just like that day by the stream . . . . But this time, I may not be able to stop him . . . .* I tried to speak several times and failed, my frigid hands clawing at the shelves. "Augustin . . . I . . . you . . . you *can't* . . . ."

"But it would be a fair trade, would it not?" he crooned, reaching toward me with one hand to trace it slowly down my face while I quivered in fear. "Secrets from the future . . . for secrets from the past. And you have no choice, my darling, for I already imparted my information to you. Will you deny me?"

His hand felt so tender against my skin that my hormones started racing despite the situation. I closed my eyes, shuddering, knowing that I could not refuse him, not now. His hand came under my chin, and he lifted my head, requesting that I open my eyes and look at him. Tears of fright welled in my eyes as I opened them, gasping at the depth of his gaze.

"Swanhilde . . . I will try my hardest not to kill you," he vowed softly, his hand moving to my shoulder. "But I can make no promises, for I rarely get to taste pure Teuton blood. I suppose it all depends on how quickly I can find what I seek within your veins. Come to my desk. It shall not be particularly comfortable, but it is better than standing, for you might pass out and hit your head on the stones of the floor." He guided me toward his desk in the dark corner of the archives, his hand steady against my back, not allowing me to deviate. My heart pounded erratically; I felt as though I approached the gallows.

When we reached his writing desk, he ordered me to lie upon it, to place my head on top of two rather worn books he had stacked at one end for use as a pillow. I obeyed him meekly, unable to protest. I knew that I could not escape him, for I had no chance of reaching the exit before him. The writing desk felt solid against my back, the two thick books soft against my twisted braids. There had been a blue-flamed candlestick upon the desk, but Augustin set it upon the stool where he sat to write his records. He muttered a few things about the temperature of the room and the dustiness of the walls while I lay quaking upon the desk, my breath coming in short gasps, my body tense, my icy hands digging into the wood beneath me. Then my vampire came to stand before me, his back to the room, his hands once more caressing my neck, folding back the collar of Freia's green dress, brushing my necklace aside. As he bent his face toward me, his flaming blue eyes piercing my soul, I tensed even further, preparing myself for the pain, shutting my eyes.

"Swanhilde, look at me," he said in a low, persuasive voice. One of his hands moved to my hair, the other to my arm. I opened my eyes, my body shaking terribly, and discovered that his lips were just a fingerbreadth away from my right ear. I rolled my eyes to the right to stare at his frightening face when he asked me the impossible question, "Do you trust me?"

My lips trembled. *Of course I don't,* I thought, but after a long pause I gasped out my response. "Yes . . . ?"

"Then relax, my darling," he advised me, lowering his eyes once more to my neck. "The pain is but for a moment." An instant later, before I had time to react or even process his words, I felt his teeth sink into my neck with a gouging pain, worse than a cut from a knife. A scream tried to burst forth from my lips, but he had already covered my mouth with his hand, using the weight of his body to pin me to the desk. I could not cry out; I could not struggle. He was going to kill me.

Tears of agony streamed down my face, and I squeezed my eyes shut against the pain. My blood pounded in my head, the most excruciating headache I had ever experienced. I could hardly breathe, for his hand was like a vise against my mouth. He was far too experienced at rendering a woman helpless. Why in heaven's name did I find him so attractive, so irresistible? I was a fool . . . .

I do not know how long I lay there, a helpless slave to this murderous priest's thirst for blood and information, my neck eventually going numb when I gradually sank toward unconsciousness. I opened my eyes one last time as the weakness began to pull me from this world, seeing the spectral blue glow reflected off of the stone ceiling, the faint light from the window trickling into the room, the black hair of Augustin's head in my peripheral vision. The shadows crept over me slowly, clouding my sight, blocking out my pain, blocking out my terror . . . .

For a long time, I felt as though I drifted through some sort of mist, no longer held down by my body, not walking, just advancing forward like a spirit, without thought or care for where I went. Somewhere in a back corner of my mind, I knew that I was dying, that in spite of Augustin's good intentions, he had bled me to death. I did not feel surprised or afraid; it just seemed inevitable. I hoped that he had gotten what he wanted, that he had found enough information about the future to assuage his voracious curiosity. Perhaps he had seen the fall of Muniche in my blood . . . perhaps he had seen my München, my home . . . perhaps he had seen my love for Hans, how greatly I missed him . . . perhaps he had seen some of my own past, the Torstein, my mother, my friends . . . Dane . . . perhaps . . . .

I would never know what he had seen. It was too late for me.

In the same moment in which that fateful thought wafted through my mind, I found that I could at last see something again, something other than this misty darkness, this empty oblivion. Something large and imposing appeared before me, not far away, and a strong current that I did not have the will to fight pushed me toward my fate. There ahead of me in the realm between life and death, I saw two weathered gates, black shot through with blues and greens, taller than the heavens, opening with a familiar creak, so loud it seemed to pierce the bonds of earth. *The gates of time* . . . . Yes, I knew them. This was not heaven, nor was it hell. I did not belong in either place.

I belonged in the twenty-first century, where my hopes and dreams resided. When I drew near the gates, now standing open for me, I saw those swirling currents within, darkness and color, beckoning me, calling me home.

He had killed me.

This was what I had wanted.

Now I could return to my home, and never go back again.

Hans would be waiting for me. I would have so many stories to tell him now. I would throw my arms around him the second I saw his face, disregarding our tradition of keeping one another at a distance. I would kiss him on the cheek, or maybe even on the lips. I would tell him that I loved him, that there had to be a way for us to be together, that I no longer cared what my father would think, what my friends would think. The prospect of twenty-two years without him had altered my perspective considerably. I would not return to college in Virginia. I would stay with Hans, the man I loved, and finish my degrees in München. First, I would just have to survive those wretched currents, those scary voices, that horrible laughter and moaning. I could do it. I would do it. For Hans. For my future. For everything.

But just before I stepped through those gates of time, so close that I could have reached out and touched them, I felt something latch onto me from behind, grabbing me in an indestructible hold, reaching into my very soul, burning me, hurting me. If I had the strength, I would have screamed. I would have fought somehow. I would have grasped at those gates, at that portal. I feared that a demon had gotten hold of my soul, that Wuotan himself had reached up from the depths in an attempt to pull me to hell, recompense for my ingenuous meddling with time. *No . . . no . . . NO . . . !*

But I could not struggle. Whatever had attacked me could not have been human. Its power was so incredible, its fiery hands searing all that remained of me. I looked desperately toward the gates as they faded away from me,

and suddenly I heard a voice, a voice that was not unknown to me.

Swanhilde . . . . I cannot follow you there . . . .

And he pulled me back from death, from time, from
home, at the risk of his own life, granting me his blood, his
fire, his strength, his very *soul* . . . just to bring me back to
the eleventh century, to that dusty basement filled with the
records of my people . . . to that vampire priest who refused
to let me die.

Chapter Twenty-four:
The Dilemma of Love

I opened my eyes once more to the nightmare that had befallen me, again seeing the blue beams of Augustin's candlestick flickering off of the stone ceiling far above me. I lay still for an infinite moment, the realization dawning upon me slowly that I yet lay on my back upon the writing desk, those two ancient books propping my head up, my uncertain gaze directed straight above me. I heard my own breathing, low, shallow, and felt the weakness of blood loss weighing down my entire body. I heard my heart beating within my chest, its movement pitiful but steady. I smelled the blood—*my* blood—saturating the record room of Muniche. A dull but healing pain stung the right side of my neck, where that vampire had bitten me . . . and I could feel a new pain, a cleaner one, tingling in the palms of my hands, which lay somewhere at my side. Something warm touched my wounded palms, covering my entire body in fact, from my feet to my collarbone. As my eyes drifted downward from the eerie lights on the ceiling, I found myself meeting the intense gaze of Augustin himself, his face just centimeters from mine. And I shut my eyes once more against the truth, against the events that had just transpired . . . .

He had killed me, bled me to death . . . almost. He had drained my life to the point at which I could actually see the gates of time, my portal to home. I could have touched them. I could have leapt through them . . . I could have opened my eyes to those bucolic woods behind my house . . . to the stream, the gazebo . . . to the face of Hans, his dark gray hair, his deep blue eyes, his friendly and knowing smile. But no . . . .

I remembered the emotions that had overtaken me right before this madman had cut off my escape. Excitement had consumed me, optimism had flooded my veins. I had been minutes away from seeing Hans—*my* priest, the man I loved and trusted, the man who had tried to dissuade me from my dangerous ventures into time despite my rejection of his advice. I had felt so peaceful, all of the trials I had faced in the eleventh century forgotten. I had resolved not to travel time again, whether the Torstein came back with me or not. I had recognized that leaving my home, my family, the man I loved, was too high a price. I would have been satisfied evermore with the inadequacies of my twenty-first century life.

But now, I lay upon the writing desk of Augustin von Bayern, a slave to his will, to his wicked desires. He had bled me almost dry, and I had no strength to fight him. He had brought me back to this place where nothing made sense, where my foolish curiosity that held me captive to his influence chained me to the ground, dragged me into the abyss, distorted my innocence, ruined my judgment. What would he do with me now, as I lay without the power to move, having experienced only moments before something that no man, no woman, should ever have to face—*standing on the precipice of death, yet unable to cross over.*

He had pulled me back, given life to me again.
Why . . . ?

I opened my eyes again, my breathing speeding just a bit when I met the gaze of my tormentor once more. He stared back at me silently, forcefully, waiting for me to speak first, waiting to see if I had the strength to speak. A thousand things I could have said ran through my mind, questions, accusations, frustrations. But in the end, when my weak lips parted, a simple statement whispered forth from them. "You brought me back . . . ."

A look of concern and perhaps even regret crossed his face, and his reply reached my ears soothingly, like a devil attempting to calm his victim. "Yes, I did. And I must greatly apologize for my actions, Swanhilde. I had not intended to kill you . . . but I discovered that your blood . . . tastes so refreshing . . . compared with the blood of foreigners. And your memories . . . ." Augustin's voice trailed off, and he averted his eyes from mine, his expression growing rather disturbed.

"Were they that bad?" I whispered, trying to understand the look of terror that seemed about to break out upon his face.

"No." Grief touched Augustin's eyes for a moment, quickly transforming into agitation and then pure bewilderment. Breathing heavily, his light blue eyes locked with mine as he said, "They were . . . astonishing . . . ."

I had the feeling that his words were not a compliment. My strength had begun to return, and I suddenly noticed why I could feel each of Augustin's breaths against my body, as if he were breathing for me. He was lying completely on top of me, his robes spread out over us both. My lips curled downward into a weak frown at this setup, my tortured mind forming all sorts of horrid conjectures regarding his body covering mine. I still wore Freia's dress; I could feel it against my skin . . . and he yet wore the black clothing of the Teuton priest. I recognized the heat of his fire warming my body, the skin of his powerful hands touching my enfeebled palms. "Augustin . . . why are you . . . laying on top of me?" I asked him, fearing the worst.

Concern touched his gaze afresh. "Because not long ago, your body had become as cold as a corpse, and it was not from your ice," he said. "You had very little blood left when I finished with you, and your skin felt dead to me.

You needed warmth and blood, not simply a devilish savior to carry you back into this world." He lifted one of his hands to show it to me. To my surprise, I saw that he had cut himself with a knife, a long line of blood seeping from the base of his middle finger to the top of his wrist. His mouth twisted into a ghastly smile as he clarified, "I had to cut both of our palms and use blood control to grant you enough of my own life to keep you here. I regret that I had to hurt you more, but it was necessary."

My mind whirled at his uncanny efforts to keep me alive, this frightening man who gloried in murder. Why had he not simply killed me and left it at that? He placed his hand back upon mine, likely still performing some sort of blood control—perhaps that was why my strength had begun to return, because of *his* blood . . . Augustin's blood. "I actually saw the gates of time through the mist . . . between life and death," I recalled.

"You reached the very edges of the spiritual realm, that perilous level from which it is difficult, if not impossible, to return to this world," Augustin told me, his expression guarded.

"But you followed me. You brought me back." I frowned again, struggling to understand his motives, his intentions. Was it just for the challenge? Why would he hazard his own soul for mine?

"I did." He said nothing more on the subject, lifting both of his hands off of mine, bringing them up so that he could look at them himself. "I have stopped the bleeding of our wounds now, for I believe you have received sufficient blood to ensure your survival. However, I fear that you also need food and wine, and in my shortsightedness I failed to bring victuals with me. Therefore, once you have regained strength enough to stand, I shall take you back to the Meldorf estate myself." He eyed me seriously, his stern expression ordering no protests.

I drew in slow, shaky breaths, my gaze drifting to the right, toward the shelves of the archives. I could not piece together Augustin's reasons for keeping me here. What good had I done in the eleventh century thus far? I should not be here . . . I should be at home, where I belonged . . . he should not . . . .

Then the thought crossed my mind, as I had known it would, that perhaps Augustin's mad dash to save my life could have resulted from other reasons. Maybe reason itself had nothing to do with his actions. I shuddered at the concept, noting that he still lay atop my body, though he had finished granting me his blood . . . the folds of our clothing the only barrier holding us apart. My heart began to pound as those foolish hormones entered my veins, and I directed my gaze back upon my savior, whose gorgeous face hovered only centimeters from mine. "Why don't you . . . get up?" I asked, dread overtaking me, warring with my youthful desires.

He raised himself up onto the palms of his hands, his cuts now completely healed, a disquieting smile appearing on his face. "Do I frighten you, Swanhilde?" His smoldering eyes carefully watched every reaction that sped across my face.

He did, but I was not about to admit that. Instead, I found myself speaking the ridiculous truth, voicing the childish whim that had surfaced in my mind. "You . . . you just look like . . . you're thinking about . . . kissing me . . . ." An instant later, I wished I could call the words back. I was such an idiot.

A ghostly chuckle escaped Augustin's lips, his smile growing evocative. "Would you like me to kiss you, Swanhilde? Or would you like something more?" The fire in his eyes deepened, and he pressed his body upon mine again, his right hand sliding toward my face to touch my trembling cheek. I could not move; I could not breathe. I stared into his mesmerizing eyes, unable to look away as he went on, passion layering his words.

"In spite of what you have seen . . . my darling . . . I am well versed . . . in the methods . . . of seduction . . . . Even I . . . Augustin von Bayern . . . the rapist . . . can be kind . . . to you . . . ." His gaze moved downward to my lips, then my body; his right hand smoothed the green fabric of Freia's dress just below my neckline. His lips parted, revealing his teeth bared in anticipation, his left hand winding itself around the back of my head.

My heart began to sprint as fear and shock flooded my veins. I desperately wondered *how* it had come to this, and so suddenly. I should have kept my muses to myself. Just moments before, this crazed sex addict had been speaking about taking me back, back to the relative safety of the count's manor. *Now* . . . . "Augustin . . . ." I choked on his name, my mouth as parched as a desert. "Augustin . . . *please* . . . ."

His posture did not change, but his right hand traveled upward to my neck and then my chin, pausing at my quivering lips, fingering them carefully. "Why is it that you recoil so harshly at the mere suggestion of losing your precious virginity? But I suppose I cannot, for then I would have to grant you something in return for my release . . . and I know not what could constitute itself as a fair trade, for such a precious commodity."

The intense passion in his eyes faded little by little, his expression growing dissatisfied, even petulant. My muscles loosened, and a sigh of relief escaped my lips; but before I could draw my attention back to the matter at hand—my safe return to the Meldorf estate—Augustin brought his face even closer to mine, his hands cradling my head. "Swanhilde," he murmured, staring into my eyes. "Do you trust me?"

I remembered the last time he had asked that question, the instant before he had bled me. I also recalled my reply, an abject lie. Now, he asked the same query . . . after he had bled me, dragging me to the very rim of the grave . . . *now*, as he lay firmly upon me, his strength pinning me to the desk. What could I possibly say this time? My heart fluttered uneasily, my body quaking . . . and I managed, just barely, to nod my head once.

"Then close your eyes . . . my darling." Impossible not to obey. As I trembled upon the wooden desk, my eyes closed, blinding me to the truth, I felt his lips brush my forehead like a mother comforting her child. He stroked my cheeks tenderly and kissed both of my eyelids, his breath warm upon my skin. Finally, while my body relaxed at the softness of his touch, his lips touched mine for a fleeting instant, sending my hormones racing, my senses tingling. *He could be kind . . . .* How could this man do such things to me, twisting my mind, confusing my heart?

I opened my eyes when I realized that he had finished. I blinked in amazement at the fondness in his gaze, so unlike the Augustin I knew, the Augustin I secretly feared. Where had that familiar hatred gone? How had this happened? I parted my lips to sigh, wanting to speak, not knowing what to say. Augustin smiled at me, a genuine smile, a brilliant smile, sending shivers up my spine. "Beautiful . . . dazzling swan princess . . . ."

I gasped at his words, a short intake of breath. No one had ever called me *that* before. His smile turned slightly mischievous as his eyes traveled down to my lips. "Do you still trust me?" he asked, his fire heating his blood. I nodded wordlessly, feeling no fear now. His smile widened, his teeth bared once more, and he said ardently, "Then kiss me back."

A moment later, I found my mouth pressed against his, our lips molding together, fire and ice. I felt Augustin's strong arms pulling me to him, lifting me from the desk, the fingers of one of his hands twisting in my hair. I raised my own arms in response, wrapping them around his shoulders, my fingers grasping at his black hair, his neck. He kissed me with no ethics, no shame, his tongue entwining with mine, exploring every portion of my mouth. I had never been kissed like *this* before, and it awakened all of my lust.

When we parted at last, my vampire priest placed both of his hands on my shoulders, raising his eyebrows at me as we sat facing one another upon his desk. "Satisfied?" he inquired, smirking. I stared at him in amazement, panting, trying to steady myself. Augustin nodded sagely at my lack of response. He took his hands off of me and backed away from the desk, straightening his garments. "We should go, or you may be late for your dinner," he said, his eyes on the fading rays of sunlight creeping through the small windows into the shadows of the archives.

The sinful part of me screamed in my mind, *What? Go? After that?!* "Now?" I asked, my voice tainted with ludicrous disappointment.

Augustin tilted his head at me suggestively and folded his arms across his chest. "Unless my ardor has altered your standards?" I sighed, knowing that it had not, though my hormones believed otherwise. I shook my head at my companion, a hint of regret belying my virtuousness. "I thought not. Have you brought a horse with you?" I nodded and said that I had brought Count von Meldorf's tan mare, the one I usually rode. Augustin held out a hand to me with the words, "Come. That horse can carry both of us from here to your home. We must hurry."

I took his hand, allowing him to help me from the desk, my feet somewhat unsteady as they touched the floor for the first time in what seemed like ages. Augustin held my arm in a strong grip while he led me from the archives and up the stairs to the main floor of the town hall, muttering that I needed to work on my balance.

I hardly noticed much during the ride back to the Meldorf estate, since I had to sit behind Augustin with my arms wound around his waist. I endeavored to hide my face in the folds of his robes, just in case we passed by any noblewomen in the city. I certainly did not need any of the nobles to speculate further on my fate. Some of them had probably begun to take bets on how long it would be before the eldest Bayern brother sacrificed me. The local lords had grown disinterested in me over the past few weeks; even Lord Paulus Schwabing of the salt mines had stopped visiting. At first I had figured that word had spread about Joel's interest in me. But of course I knew the truth, though I hesitated to admit it. None of the local families wanted their sons defiled by the rebellious student of Augustin von Bayern.

By the time the tan mare's hooves began to clump upon the familiar wood of the drawbridge, my musing had shifted from my reputation to all of the intriguing things I had learned that afternoon. I had succeeded in shifting my blood flow away from my index finger for about half a minute—and then Augustin had proved himself far more adept at that practice than I could ever be, having granted me a portion of his own blood to preserve my life. Some of his nearly pure Teuton blood pulsed through my veins now, a tonic almost as mystifying as his practiced kiss.

He dropped me off at the front porch of the Meldorf estate, leaping off of the mare and handing the reins to the stable hand who came to meet us. I paused after ascending the stairs and placed a hand against one of the awning's supports as I turned to regard Augustin one final time, where he stood watching me at the foot of the stairs. "You'll come here tomorrow evening for our studies?" Tomorrow was Tuesday. I had to be sure that nothing had changed.

Hesitation clouded Augustin's characteristically sure features, and he took a step back from me, toward the road. "Unfortunately, I likely shall not see you tomorrow, Swanhilde, and I do apologize. I should not return . . . I cannot return . . . until I have fully pondered everything in my own mind . . . regarding your memories." His eyes met mine for the briefest of instants, his expression contrite. Then he spun around swiftly on his heels, striding toward the road with nary a goodbye.

I froze, staring after him, then burst out with the most important question, the one that demanded an immediate answer. "But *why*, Augustin? *Why* did you pull me back?" My fingers gripped the post like it was the only solid thing left in my world. Perhaps it was, for the majority of my intentions had been cast to the whirlwind that afternoon.

Augustin halted his retreat and whirled to face me, his feet planted firmly, his eyes blazing with his fire. He articulated every word of his response carefully, "Swanie, you heard what I said before I pulled you back. *That* is reason enough." Before I could comment on this, he shot down the path to the road in a fiery storm, blue overtaking the darkness of his robes as he disappeared from my sight.

I stood frozen at the top of the stairs, leaning entirely against the post now, gazing after that mad priest with my eyes half-closed, the many possible meanings of his parting words swirling through my mind. *You heard what I said . . . . Swanhilde . . . I cannot follow you there . . . . That is reason enough . . . .*

He wanted to follow me. There could be many reasons for that. He was a sadist, a power hungry egoist who dreamed of the day he could rape me like he raped the Saxon girl, using me for his own disgusting pleasures. My blood was ninety-five percent Teutonic, and therefore tasty and apparently intriguing. His influence had already warped my mind, rendering me unable to refuse him no matter what he asked. He knew this, and he gloried in his power, in my compliance. He did not want to lose this feeling of authority, this hero worship from the only one who seemed unable to see him for what he was—a pervert.

But the other possibility crossed my mind at the memory of his kiss, his tenderness, his wondrous compliment, *and* most importantly, the fact that he had risked his life for mine. He was not a time traveler; death of any sort would send him straight into eternity. I had been taught throughout my life that offering one's life for another was the pinnacle expression of human love. Augustin claimed that his heart could not love, yet he had risked his life for mine. *If that was not love . . . .*

"Swanie, is something wrong? Where have you been?" Freia stepped out of the front entry, her voice pulling me from my thoughts. She likely wondered why I had not come inside for dinner. The sky darkened; evening had descended.

I turned slowly to face her, tearing my eyes away from the path to the road, where that fiery priest had vanished. He had probably made it back to Muniche by now. I took a deep breath and unfroze my body at long last, pushing my ice back inside my spirit where it belonged. "Freia, you were right from the very beginning," I admitted. "I should have stayed away from Augustin von Bayern while I had the chance."

Horror appeared on her face, superseding her concern. "What has he done to you?" she whispered. She looked me up and down, undoubtedly noticing my disheveled hair and wrinkled dress.

"Everything . . . and nothing . . . I'll have to tell you about it tonight. But it's happened, just like you said." I shuddered once, accepting the truth with all of its desolate implications. "I have fallen in love with Augustin."

Chapter Twenty-five:
Opposing Forces

Later that night, I told Freia a shortened version of what had become of me that afternoon, glossing over the information about blood control and that frightening moment when I felt certain that Augustin was about to rape me. I focused primarily on the bleeding—which, I reminded her, was a common practice for Teuton priests when they sought information—and the mystical experience of approaching the gates of time, the very door of death. I had come so close to home, and I had felt no fear, only relief. And then he had pulled me back at the risk of his own life, his own soul. I emphasized the lengths to which Augustin had gone in order to ensure my survival, granting me his own blood to restore my strength. I also mentioned his kiss, not going into great detail, concluding that I could no longer ignore this mad priest, the executioner of Muniche, the voracious learner, the educated intellectual, the persuasive demon . . . the one who refused to let me die. I had fallen into his trap. I loved him now, and I could no longer deny it.

Freia listened intently to my tale. When I had finished, she asked just one question, quite likely the worst one.

"How is this going to factor into your relationship with Joel? Are you going to forsake him for Augustin von Bayern?"

I sighed heavily, for that very issue had plagued my mind from the moment I had admitted the truth to myself. The dishonorable part of me wanted to dump Joel now, immediately, to tell him that he might as well just die and return to his twenty-first century girlfriend. But I knew that I could not do that, for I had brought him here, and I feared to face him in the future if I abandoned him now.

"No, I can't just betray Joel now, because I do like him," I told Freia. "And you said when we first got here that marriages are made for convenience, not love."

"You'll never be happy with him." Freia's sad eyes locked with mine, her soft voice resigned at last to my insane preference. This was the first night in which we had discussed Augustin von Bayern without her urging me to stop seeing him.

"I know, but . . . that's just how life is." I frowned at the memory of my own family, my own past. "I have the tendency to love the wrong men. First it was Hans, a servant old enough to be my father. Now it's Augustin, the black sheep Bayern brother, the worst man in town. Things will never change."

For the next two weeks, until the first Tuesday in November, Augustin did not set foot upon the count's lands, nor did I see him when I occasioned to visit Muniche. I waited for him on the porch almost every evening, hoping against hope that he would appear, my heart crying out for him, begging him to return to me, now that I knew I loved him. I entertained all manner of terrible speculations on his evasiveness, fearing that my memories had repulsed him completely, or perhaps that my urgent reaction to his tenderness had turned him off.

He probably did not love me, for he had claimed that his heart no longer held the capacity for love, and besides, I was just another woman. He had women all the time, sacrifices, whores, the whole gamut. How could I deign to assume such a privileged man could love a fool like me, a

Teuton child who had leaped back in time with two outsiders? He had likely seen everything in my blood, every dark secret of mine laid bare. I needed to forget my feelings for him and focus on Joel, the decent man, the man who stayed true to me despite my faults.

I saw Joel often during those two weeks, both in Muniche and at the count's manor. He continued to call on me each Saturday afternoon as soon as he had finished his duties at the ironworks. We spent quite a bit of time sitting in the parlors with Freia, Count von Meldorf, and sometimes Master Denlinger, talking and joking about all sorts of subjects. Joel had made great strides in his spoken Teutonica by then, although he occasionally shot confused glances in my direction, his earnest hazel eyes requesting a translation.

We also managed to gain a decent amount of alone time, walking together through the count's gardens and beside the stream, our discussions ranging from twenty-first century memories to our future here in medieval Europe. Joel admitted that he had been saving as much money as he could in hopes of renting a better room, working as hard as possible at the foundry in order to become more than just a simple laborer. He said that his boss liked him and had expended the effort to teach him some tricks of the trade. "I think he may be helping me just because you and Freia are such good friends," he disclosed one Saturday afternoon when we sat in the grass by the stream. "He's definitely falling for her."

"You think so?" I grinned at that revelation, knowing that my good friend had been wondering about the true extent of the ironmaster's interest lately. "He'd better hurry up and let Freia off the hook. Lord Ulrich Sendlin and the head of the smaller brewery have visited her several times in recent weeks. She appears to be a hot commodity around here." I winked at Joel.

"Yeah, I'll let him know," Joel answered, snatching up a few rocks from the grass beneath us and skipping them across the stream. "None of those young lords have been trying to pick you up, have they?" he asked, his expression worried as he fingered a rock.

I giggled and looked away toward the city walls in the distance, wishing that Joel's concern could engender a romantic response from my foolish heart. "Maybe they have," I flung at him, giving him a coquettish smile. "But I've been trying to discourage them, since you and I are the 'futuristic pair' around here." That was so lame. "Maybe I should use reverse psychology and start sneaking kisses with some of them on the porch," I added, raising an eyebrow at Joel.

"Don't do that. They'd think you're a witch once they found out you've traveled time." Joel grinned, making a joke of the situation, but I could tell that my casual remarks had bothered him. He turned his gaze back to the stream and the deep blue autumn sky, the sunlight emphasizing the golden highlights in his hair and beard. He drew his knees up and plopped his chin down onto them, his expression discontent. "What about that executioner?" he inquired brusquely, looking at me out of the corner of his eye. "Does he still come around here to learn English?"

Carefully smothering the disappointment that threatened to break across my face, I said flatly, "Not so much. I haven't seen him in a while now."

"Good," Joel said, sounding relieved. Soon afterward, we returned to the house, my dissatisfaction at Augustin's absence gnawing at me. His wretched words that night on the porch, three weeks ago now, arose to the forefront of my mind: *You fool. You have known the glory of the Teuton priest. For the rest of your life, you will want a priest . . . .* He was right. He was always right. And Joel could never be a Teuton priest. For the next two decades, I would be forced to live a lie.

I practiced what little I had learned of blood control as the days progressed, gradually becoming adept at draining the blood from each of my fingers. On the day that Augustin reappeared at the Meldorf estate, I sat sewing with the servant girls, surreptitiously working on directing Felda's right foot to fall asleep. I had not quite managed it when Ulka encroached on our work to inform me that Lord Augustin von Bayern awaited me on the front porch. The three servant girls dissolved into a fit of giggles. I rolled my eyes and rose to my feet, straightening my scarlet winter dress and retrieving my coat from my bedroom before descending the staircase to meet the fate that had slighted me for too long.

Augustin nodded at me when I stepped onto the porch, his eyes sweeping over my outfit in less than a second, his own mahogany-colored overcoat blowing with the stiff autumn breeze. He had tied all of his hair back for once, likely due to the wind, and he wore a neutral brown cap adorned with a single jeweled brooch in the center, its color matching his brass-buckled boots. "I should like you to take a walk with me, Swanhilde," he said, wasting no time with pleasantries.

I nodded and suggested that we take the path that led through the western gardens toward the stream. Augustin nodded his agreement and turned his steps briskly in the direction I had indicated, leaving me scrambling to keep up.

He held his peace until we reached the stream, ignoring my feeble attempts at frivolous conversation. I feared the subjects that we would have to address during this walk, yet another part of me longed to get everything out in the open. When we reached the stream, turning north along it toward the Isar, Augustin halted near the same spot where Joel and I had sat in the grass on the previous Saturday. He clasped his hands behind his back and sighed, his eyes on the lowering clouds. "I suppose we ought to get this over with before the impending rain interrupts our discussion." He faced me then, his poise rigid, his gaze not particularly friendly.

I tightened my arms around my coat, holding back the chill of the wind, shuddering once with the potential enormity of what we were about to confront. Lifting my eyes to Augustin's accusing ones, I asked him, my voice hardly above a whisper, "What did you see . . . in my memories?"

Augustin frowned severely. "I lied to you," he informed me, and as I felt a jolt of surprise, he corrected, "or rather, I held back part of the truth. I told you in the archives that I sought the future in your blood . . . but that was merely a part of what I sought. By drinking your blood, by reading its honesty, I wished to uncover the true reasons you constantly refuse to push me aside, to condemn me to the annals of the hopelessly unregenerate, as the more pious citizens of this city do." I froze at his words, dread overtaking me at the realization of *what* he had doubtless found. Augustin continued to stare at me reproachfully, cataloguing my response to his confession. "But before I address that issue, I shall confront the problem of the future, for I *did* see it, and it is, in fact, a problem."

My mouth went dry, and I suddenly wondered if I had broken a rule of the Torstein by allowing a man from the past to read my memories. Fear raced through my veins at the possible repercussions, but I justified it to myself. *He would have bled me anyway. I had no choice.* "You saw why I came here," I assumed.

Augustin's upper lip twisted into a sneer, fire blazing in his eyes as he said, "I saw, in your blood, an image, a sketch in a book, a history book . . . . A sketch of this city, of its spires, of its walls—all of it burning, burning to the ground at the hands of the Saxons." I gasped and took a step back, my mind recalling that very picture, a drawing I had seen in one of Hans' books on Teuton history. Augustin stepped toward me, his posture threatening. "*Why* would you come to see that?" he demanded, sounding disgusted. "Why would you want to see this city burn, your birthplace, to see it crumble to the ground at the hands of our enemies, to watch our people's worst defeat? *Why*, Swanhilde? Are you a masochist?"

I shook my head swiftly, shrinking backward, frightened by his fury. "In my time," I began, choking on the words, "people forget. Most Teutons . . . don't even

remember . . . . I wanted to see it . . . to learn from history
. . . ."

"You planned to come to 1064, two years before this terrible event, to fully appreciate the extent of what we shall *lose*." Augustin glared while he related my memories, the truth of them stinging me afresh. "And yet you arrived twenty years too early due to your own idiocy, telling that stupid ironworker only once that he ought to think of the year 1064 and of the city of Muniche before entering the gates. How could you possibly assume that *Joel* would remember the particulars—the essential details—if you told him only once? You are such a fool, Swanhilde."

He really had seen everything, and probably the Torstein, as well. I staggered backward, sitting down hard upon a hillock at the edge of the stream. What had I done, allowing this ravenous information seeker to bleed me? What would happen to history now? Would everything change? Tears began to trickle slowly from my eyes, and I whispered, "I shouldn't have let you do this . . . ."

Augustin sat down beside me, just a handbreadth away, and looked at me seriously. "Why are you afraid? Do you think that by telling *me* everything, you could change the events that have already been written down? Honestly, Swanie, your shortsightedness sometimes surprises me." He pulled a silk handkerchief from a pocket of his coat and handed it to me. "In spite of your worries and the warnings you have read, I do not believe that your rock or the Prince's song hold the power to actually alter history. What sway could one person claim against those eternally shifting currents, against the authority of God? You came here too early, in your opinion, but I believe that you were *supposed* to come here in 1044. Perhaps if you had not come, history would truly have changed." Augustin looked thoughtful.

A new fear gripped my heart at his conjectures, and I crumpled his handkerchief into a ball in my hand. "What if . . . maybe if I had not come at all . . . our people would not have fallen . . . ." I shivered at that idea, my hands growing icy.

Augustin snorted at my words and shook his head. "I do not prefer to think in those terms, and if you had any common sense you would not do so either. Instead, I prefer to ponder exactly *how* our people intend to fall." Perplexity crept into his light blue eyes while he gazed at the rippling stream before us. "The Saxons have attacked us countless times before, reinforced by allies, and we have always emerged victorious. I cannot fathom how we, as Teutons, could allow them to defeat us at last, restraining our powers until the very end, until our elements could no longer save us. How could weakness conquer our people first, committing us to the hands of the Empire, the sycophants of the pope?"

I started in surprise at his words, for until then I had not heard anyone in Muniche mention the pope or the Holy Roman Empire scathingly. Most people considered themselves free, our Teuton kingdom autonomous, despite the nominal rule of the Italian popes. Since the days of Emperor Otto I in the 900s, the Saxons had been the German tribe with the most influence over the Empire . . . and they would be the ones to bring the prosperous Teutons to their knees in just twenty-two years. Augustin had brought up a good point, one that I could not answer. We had fought the Saxons before and remained free. Why had we failed in 1066?

"That's why I came," I said at last. "To find out the truth, to find out why our people really fell. I want to learn from it, even though I can do nothing to stop it."

"Nor can I," Augustin noted, still frowning, "and it is frustrating. So I saw the future in your blood. I saw Muniche fall. I saw my pompous brother brought to humiliation . . . with a bit of satisfaction, I might add." A wry smile curled on his lips for a moment, but then his face hardened, and he looked at me once more. "Now I must address the second issue, your opinions of me." His eyes flashed with fire.

My eyes widened, my thoughts again returning to all the ridiculous reasons I had not said goodbye to Augustin for good. I swallowed, gathering what little courage I had, and asked, "What did you see?"

The words came out of his mouth like blades, each one cutting my heart. "I saw Camilla Isolda Fischer von Thaden, *your mother*. I saw her *die* . . . the same way Marelda died." I choked on my own breath, clutching my right hand to my chest, abruptly not wanting to face this wound. He had really and truly seen everything. This was bad . . . .

Without warning, Augustin leaped to his feet, towering over me like a cat over a mouse, his fists clenched as he shouted, "So *say it,* you bitch! Let me hear those words spill from your feeble lips! Tell me I have been wrong these twenty-two years! Tell me I cannot blame my brother, that it was not his fault! Tell me I cannot blame God for taking away the only woman who ever loved me! Tell me that I should have reacted like *you,* attributing my mother's death to her Teuton blood, forgiving the murderer who broke her womb, her very life! Tell me I should not hate, I should not glory in anger, I should cast aside all of the power Wuotan has granted me, that I would never have known otherwise! Tell me I should hand myself over to God and His everlasting mercy when He has given me *NOTHING!*"

I could not move; I could not speak. I cowered in the grass at Augustin's feet, shaking all over, waiting for him to strike me, to burn me. I heard him panting, seething, all of his bitterness and hatred pouring upon me while I trembled on the ground. At last he began to speak once more, his words laden with scorn. "You are not the first to have told me such things. The entire Catholic clergy has urged me to forgive, Paulus included. The servants have begged me to let go of my anger. That wretched replacement, Maria, has ordered me to rip the acrimony from my heart, to give the world a chance. *You are no better than any of them.*"

His last accusation pulled me from my fright, infusing me with obstinacy all at once. I pushed myself up from the ground, Augustin's handkerchief dropping to the grass as

I unleashed my own irritation upon him. "If that's what you think of me, then why did you bring me back? If you didn't want to hear my opinions, you should have pushed me through those gates yourself!"

The ire in Augustin's eyes faded slowly, but his scowl remained. "I brought you back because I am not finished with you yet," he replied.

"What, you just want to keep using me for your own gratification? You want to stick me in your back pocket, your own personal whore, your Teuton sacrifice? I should go hang myself when I get back to the manor." I fumed.

"No, you shall not, because you are afraid of suicide," Augustin pointed out, his expression mocking. "Therefore, you shall not die until I let you, until I kill you myself. And I shall, Swanhilde. You can be sure of that. One day, you will die at my hands, and it will be glorious." He bared his teeth at me, his eyes glittering.

I shuddered, glancing toward the trail to the house. "I need to get back . . . before dinner," I commented cautiously, jerking my head toward the manor.

"Before you go, I must tell you," Augustin began, his posture relaxing, his eyes cooling, "that there is one more thing I saw in your blood. And this thing disturbed me . . . more than any of the other truths I found . . . ." He walked towards me unhurriedly, reaching one hand out to my face, his light blue eyes wide.

"What?" I whispered, staring at his fingers as they drew near to me. What could possibly be worse than what he had already told me?

He touched me a moment later, his fingers warm against my skin, tracing the curvature of my face downward to my neck. "You have feelings for me." His eyes bored into mine, his expression serious.

I trembled at his touch and his words, knowing it was true, fearing the consequences. I closed my eyes, trying and failing to speak. At last I gasped out the only words I could say to such a terrible reality. "Forgive me . . . Augustin . . . ."

"It is a dangerous thing," he murmured in a low voice, his hand caressing my throat. "You are going to break your own heart, Swanhilde. You came here to free yourself from Hans, and your heart has latched upon a wicked Teuton priest, your darkest desire, the one who would kill you, the one who cannot love you in return. You are going to break your heart, for I cannot give you what you seek. I lost the ability to love long ago. It is too late . . . ."

I opened my eyes to stare at his handsome face, his tormented gaze a mere centimeter away from mine. *It is too late.* But I had to disagree, just for the record, as he stood before me, his fingers gentle against my skin. "So *you* say."

A half-hearted smile graced his lips at my response, and he leaned forward to kiss me. I closed my eyes when our lips met, relishing the heat of his fire against my frigid mouth. I wished that he would never stop, though he kissed me with much less passion than that time in the archives. "I can seduce you, my darling swan princess, but I cannot love you," he said when he pulled away, his expression grave. "You will one day return to the future, forever desiring something you never had, something you can never have. I pity you."

He was probably right, but I preferred to hope for the best, under the circumstances. Rain began to fall from the thick clouds above, and I asked him, "Will you come back Thursday for our language studies?"

Augustin nodded, glancing up at the lowering sky. "I shall see you then," he pledged, transforming himself into a fiery whirlwind as he sped back to the city.

Chapter Twenty-six

Mysteries Unveiled

My study sessions with Augustin resumed that Thursday afternoon, continuing as usual two days per week throughout the month of November. Augustin's tenuous grasp on twenty-first century American English had begun to improve, for he had a knack for picking up languages without much difficulty. Once he had perfected his English, I promised him that we would move on to modern German, which would probably seem a lot easier to him, more like another dialect. He asked me at one point what I would teach him next, after he had mastered both languages. I responded with a chuckle that if we found the time, I could teach him Bayerisch and French.

He admitted that my accent had improved, along with my knowledge of Teutonica in general, which pleased me. Soon we could focus on Ælte Teutonica, the language of the heathens, the language I needed to know in order to read those tomes in the archives. I wondered, once I had improved my skills with the dialects of my people, whether Augustin might instruct me in Latin or perhaps Arabic or Italian. We had over two decades; by the end, I could call myself a linguist.

Augustin and I kept our discussions focused primarily on languages and study, choosing not to reopen the many personal wounds we had uncovered in recent weeks. Keeping our encounters official helped me contain my foolish love for him, since both of us agreed that I ought to spend my time in more rewarding pursuits. We did not sit outside on the porch, nor did we walk in the gardens or beside the stream. Interestingly, Augustin did not broach the subject of Teuton rituals during the month of November either. Perhaps he was unsure what to ask of me in return for more classified information.

I continued to practice using blood control on the three servant girls when I joined them in their sewing. After a few more failed attempts, I managed to drain the blood from Eva's left foot early one afternoon. My efforts prompted her to rise from her cushion and limp around while the blood returned to her toes. Felda and Emilie advised her to cross her legs differently, and I kept my focus on the path of my needle, fighting a laugh and a blush. *I'm getting good at this,* I thought to myself as Eva sat back down. *Now I need to figure out how to heal wounds.*

I worked on that on several occasions, usually by pricking one of my fingers with a sewing needle. The first time I failed spectacularly, for I had gotten hung up on the concept of arteries, the key to draining blood from limbs. It took me several tries to imagine the network of capillaries in my fingers, and once I had managed that, I practiced summoning platelets, sealing the tears in my skin. I found it much easier to redirect the course of a Teuton's blood than to break down its components. Sometimes I wondered how the Teutons of old had learned to do such a thing with only a rudimentary grasp on biology. Perhaps Wuotan himself had trained his early followers on the nuances of their magic.

Freia's birthday came on the twentieth of November. The count and I held a party for her, inviting many of our friends from the nearby estates along with the ironmaster and Joel. The party included a hearty luncheon and indoor games like chess and an early form of darts. Joel and I occupied the chess board for two full games; Joel won the first match, and I took the second. At one point, all of the men went outside into the front garden to challenge one another's ability with the bow and arrow while all of us ladies watched from the porch, giggling at their masculine posturing and loud guffaws. Joel's skills impressed me, for only Count von Reuter outshot him. When they all came back inside, I told Joel that he ought to get a job with the hunters of Muniche. "I bet you could bring down more deer than the rest of them," I said.

"I probably could," Joel agreed, looking flattered, "but for now, I'm just a metalworker. Once things start getting rough around here, I'm joining the Prince's army; there's no doubt about that."

"You can be like Legolas," I suggested, remembering his love for Tolkien's novels. Joel smirked and said that his beard made him look more like Aragorn.

Freia gained quite a few gifts from the guests, but I think her favorite was the one she received from Master Denlinger—a brand new flute. Her eyes opened wide when she saw it, excitement at the prospect of music radiant upon her face. Before the guests departed, she played several lilting melodies for us, all from the Rhineland. Joel and I sat together on the hearth as she played, the flickering flames of the fire warming our backs, Joel cautiously twining his fingers with mine.

I sighed a bit at the impossible desires Joel's touch engendered within me, ordering myself to stop wishing he was Augustin, to be grateful for his loyalty to me, for his choice to stay with me in the eleventh century. I remembered Freia's suggestion, back when she used to urge me to stay clear of Augustin, that once Joel and I married, we should leave Teuton lands to travel around the Germanic cities, perhaps settling down at Eisenwald. As much as I did not want to leave Muniche, I knew that we would have to once things came to their ultimate conclusion—for our offspring would be mixed, hybrids. And I would need to put distance between Augustin and me, or I would constantly face the temptation of a nasty love affair.

On the first Tuesday in December, Augustin called at the Meldorf estate after dark, later than usual. I had already put our reading and writing materials away for the night, assuming he was not coming. When one of the female servants informed me of his arrival, I threw my coat on over my nightdress and descended the stairs with a candle in one hand, fully intending to tell Augustin that he had come too late and our studies would have to wait until Thursday. I met him in the vestibule and saw that he was clad entirely in black, likely to help him blend in with the night. He nodded once at me and said without preamble, "I have reached two conclusions during the past several days, neither of which should be discussed inside." His blue eyes scoured the shadows, the doorways, his expression alert.

My intentions of asking him to depart for the night crashed to the ground as my curiosity sprang to life, so I gestured at the front door with my candlestick. "Perhaps we could discuss your conclusions on the porch?"

Augustin frowned severely and answered, his voice a little too loud, "That should suffice. Nonetheless, if anyone attempts to disturb us, he does so at the risk of his life." He glared into the shadows of the hallway once more, then spun and opened the front door with a flourish, his cape flaring out behind him.

I followed him outside and set my candlestick down onto a holder on the table between the two benches on the right side of the porch. Augustin settled himself onto the bench with his back facing the house, as before, and I took the one against the railing, shivering with the early December frost. I focused briefly on my ice, asking it to meld me with the chill of the air. Then I turned my attention to my companion, the murderous priest, and asked what exactly he had figured out.

Augustin crossed his arms underneath his robes and turned his face in my direction. "I have pondered the fall of our people since the day I read the bitter truth in your blood. I likely did not see every aspect of their fall in your memories before my attention diverted to other matters." He paused, his mouth twisting into that familiar smirk, then continued, "It occurred to me, as it has likely also occurred to you, that the true reason for our people's defeat remains elusive. Your memories attribute it to the Saxons' desire to command the southern trade routes and to conquer our successful agricultural operations. Though these reasons seem believable at first glance, I considered the fact that the Saxons have excellent trade routes of their own with Flanders and the islands, and that their manors are also prosperous." Augustin nodded sagely at me with the conclusion, "Therefore, there must be some other reason, some unspoken cause for their invasion, for their victory. And it came to me that there is one . . . and only one . . . plausible . . . explanation . . . ."

My eyes opened wide as my mind worked to keep up with Augustin's ideas. The possibility hit me then and there, with the suddenness of hitting the floor after tripping down a staircase. "Maybe . . . maybe they were after . . . the secrets of our magic . . . ." I quaked at the thought, my breath freezing the air in front of me.

"Not our magic, Swanhilde, for only Teutons can perform Teuton rituals. But there exists one power . . . one discovery that the Saxons could possibly seek for themselves . . . and if they found it . . . ." Augustin's own eyes widened, glowing while he stared into the yellow flame of my candlestick, which flared in response to his element. "If they obtained it . . . they could destroy us all . . . ."

A horrified squeak escaped my lips, and I pressed my hands to my mouth when I recognized the truth. "*The song,*" I gasped, my brain working overtime.

"Yes." Augustin's voice was deep; the flame of the candle leapt to the height of a man's index finger, shades of blue melding with its natural yellow-orange. "If the Saxons learned the secret of my brother's song, they also could open the gates of time. They could use that knowledge as horrible leverage over our people. With it they could amass an army that spans time itself, a force that could defeat us . . . in 1066."

Augustin fell silent, and I started to hyperventilate on the bench. *How could I not have seen this from the beginning? That's probably what Beth was trying to tell me back at college, when she connected Prince Otto's travels with the Teutons' fall. Of course it had to be from the song . . . that was why the Prince wanted to remember it at the end, to change what had happened.* "But how,"—Augustin's deep voice brought me out of my horrified reverie—"*how* would they have found out such a guarded secret?"

I knew, of course I knew, for everything had fallen into place now. I gasped once, producing a cloud of ice crystals in the air, then whispered, "Paulus . . . . The Prince taught him the song. According to our history, the Saxons captured him . . . tortured him for a year before killing him at last. It was him. He told them the song . . . ." My hands grew solid, shaking in spite of the ice coating them.

Augustin remained silent for a long instant, his eyes as wide as saucers, his fire turning them an ever brighter blue. Abruptly, he slammed his fist down onto the table with a force that shook the entire porch. He leapt to his feet, knocking the candle to the planks of the deck, its flame extinguishing with an odd suddenness. "*Damn* him!" he spat, stomping harshly to the steps of the porch, smoke rising from his shoulders. "*Damn* that pretentious idiot, that wretch who could never trust *me*, the one who would *never* break under foreign torture! Damn him for revealing his secrets to Paulus, the weak one, the one who joined the *church,* the one who never underwent torment to earn his priestly robe . . . . *Damn them both!*"

Augustin screamed, a fierce cry of wrath, ripping his hands through his black hair, prompting me to turn frightened eyes toward the front door, hoping against hope that none of the servants would come to investigate. Most of the time Augustin von Bayern maintained a quiet veneer, a pensive discontent, yet when his anger arose, he reacted

268

like any other man. I worried for the safety of the wood on the porch.

The infuriated priest collapsed against one of the posts, his hands searing the wood, the word "*Why?*" bursting from his lips repeatedly, mechanically. I sat still on the bench by the railing, watching his anguish. I could feel it churning within my own soul, though I did not react as violently as Augustin. Together, we had deciphered the real reason why my people had fallen, and it had all resulted from the Bayern family itself—a family plagued with mistrust, ruined by the untimely death of its matriarch. At last, while Augustin gripped the post in despair with his shoulders trembling, I spoke a pledge, a solemn oath, "I will fight them myself when the time comes, though it will do no good."

"And you will die, as you have planned." Augustin turned from the post to face me once more, his anger cooled, resignation taking its place. "We all will fight, and we all will die. That is how it has been written, and I suppose there is no use bemoaning what is to come. But I must now hate both of my brothers forevermore, one for his hypocrisy, the other for his cowardice." He grimaced, lifting the candle from the deck and relighting it with his blue fire, setting it on the table.

"So," I began as my companion situated himself upon the bench once more, "what's the other thing you concluded?" I had to change the subject somehow, before the melancholy of knowing the future overcame us both.

Augustin raised his eyes to mine, a disturbing smile appearing on his face. He leaned back against the house and said, "I have concluded, my darling Swanhilde, that I must bleed you again, soon. Your blood holds far too much fascinating information for me to be satisfied with one simple bleeding. The problem is, your blood also tastes incredibly Teutonic. Despite my good intentions, if I bleed you once more, I shall likely almost kill you again."

Augustin paused, still smiling while fear crept up my spine at his words, at their implications. "There is one way around this issue, my gorgeous swan princess, and if you would take the time to recall what I told you about priests and their wives, you may be able to predict what it is."

I gawked at him, my hands trembling once more as I endeavored to understand what he sought. *Priests and their wives . . . bleeding . . . the heart-bond . . . .* I gasped, abruptly realizing what he wanted, what he *required.* "My . . . heart?"

His smile widened. "Yes. I want your heart, Swanhilde. You see, if I held the heart of your soul as though it were my own, you would belong to *me.* I could pump your heart myself while I bleed you, channeling the blood of Wuotan's realm to eliminate the risk of your death. I could finally come to understand your heart, your soul, and the strange standards you have, which are now alien to me. I want it, yes . . . . I want to ponder your purity, your kindness . . . your love."

I stared at him in horror, my heart pounding hard in response to his terrible request. How could I give up my heart, my free will, my soul . . . to this monstrous, devil-worshipping rapist? Memories of Ina and Walfrid back home in the twenty-first century arose in my mind, and a strange sickness crept into my stomach. *He had her bound in a room that I wish I'd never seen while he repeated black lies over and over to her, his energy jolting her heart every few seconds. She was crying, and her eyes could not see my spirit.* Fonsi's bleak description of Ina's fate as a bound wife prompted me to shudder. If I allowed Augustin to claim my heart, he could use his fire to torment me the same way, if he felt so inclined.

Eventually I realized that he awaited my answer, while he sat just paces from me, his eyes reading every reaction that sped across my face. "That would make me your slave," I whispered, my common sense rebelling at the concept.

Augustin nodded at me, his smile transforming into a smirk. "Yes, but I would not be a harsh master, my darling. In return for your heart I would give you everything you want. I would teach you everything I know, every Teuton ritual, every Teuton secret, the things no other woman has ever known. I would train you in blood rituals far beyond simple matters of controlling its flow. I will grant you *anything* you wish . . . asking nothing more in return . . . for to me, holding the heart of a Teuton woman would be payment enough."

I sat rigid upon the bench, breathing shallowly, my thoughts muddled. "I . . . I don't know . . . what to say." I wavered, my eyes darting this way and that.

Augustin rose from the bench and pointed his feet toward the stairs and the pathway to the road. "I shall give you one week to think it through. Next Tuesday, I shall require your answer. I bid you farewell until then, Swan-hilde."

Chapter Twenty-seven:
A Most Precious Gift

When I returned to my bedroom after Augustin had gone, I found Freia knitting a fresh pair of woolen socks in the soft glow of our nightly candlestick. She looked up when I shut the door behind me and leaned against it. "Swanie?" Her relieved expression shifted into one of concern as I blinked at her, my fingers gripping the door at my back. My ice had begun to seep outward from my blood. I could feel it crusting upon the wood beneath my fingertips.

I could not fathom how to answer her. My heart pattered swiftly beneath my nightdress, as though in rebellion against that sinister priest's demands. Images of Ina and Walfrid at their wedding swirled in my mind, mingling with Fonsi's anger: *I'm like one hundred percent sure that the bastard bound her the day they met. I don't like that some priest stole her away from me . . . .*

"Swanie? What did Augustin want?" Freia stood just a handbreadth away from me now, her posture hesitant.

My vision sharpened in a veil of blue, I shut my eyes and placed my hands upon my temples, working to organize my thoughts. *It's not the same as Ina and Walfrid,* I told myself. *Augustin wouldn't treat your heart the way*

Fonsi described. He just wants to bleed you freely . . . and he'll help you uncover all the things that Hans wanted to keep hidden. This is your chance to become as knowledge-able as any Teuton priest . . . but at what cost?

"He wants my heart," I finally managed to whisper. I reopened my eyes to gaze into those of my most faithful eleventh century friend, watching her own widen in what appeared to be a combination of horror and confusion.

We sat on her bed together while I described the concept of the heart-bond to her, her countenance appearing fascinated one moment and disturbed the next. "My cousin Beth said that it sounds like a bound woman gives up her free will," I related after I had finished outlining what *Der Weg* said about it. "But while that's true to some degree, the heart-bond isn't as strong as the bonds that a Teuton city places on her Lady. And Augustin doesn't really strike me as a narcissist. I doubt he'd try to hurt me using the bond." I chewed on my lip as I made that claim. It was as though I tried to convince myself.

"It sounds like something Teuton priests do once they're married, a way to enhance the relationship in the mystical realm," Freia noted, fingering a partially finished sock, her forehead wrinkled in thought. "Has he proposed to you yet?"

I felt my cheeks grow hot at that question; my ice had retreated into my spirit during my explanation. My emotions seemed to be lurking on the sidelines, weighing Augustin's requirement on the scales of my mind. "He hasn't," I admitted, "and I don't really think he ever would. I'm nobody, and if the oldest Bayern male ever took it upon himself to marry, I'm sure he'd choose some Teuton princess." A sigh escaped my lips, and I looked away from my friend. "Besides, I have to think about Joel, too. I'm the only girl he can talk to here."

Freia snorted quietly. "Joel's Teutonica improves every time he visits. Soon enough, he should be able to inquire after other maidens in the city, if he wants." I raised an eyebrow at my Rhenisch companion, and she pulled her hair back from her face as she asked, "Would you agree to be Augustin's mistress?"

My jaw dropped just a tad; that thought had not yet crossed my mind. "I . . . I'm not . . . sure . . . ." I said, the earlier warmth returning to my cheeks. "I've always wanted to save myself for marriage . . . but maybe I should rethink that."

Freia shook her head once and gathered her sewing equipment. "It seems unusual to offer your heart willingly to a man who doesn't want to complete the partnership." She rose from her bed and carried her wares to a basket of fabric by the door. "No matter what Augustin has told you about his inability to love, you'd better prepare yourself for more, if you let him form the bond."

I contemplated the prospect all week, trying to consider every aspect. While my rational mind warned me against offering my heart to a dishonorable Teuton priest—veritably extinguishing my independence—I suspected that the bond would break once I returned to the future. The heart-bond was not a deadly Teuton ritual, and therefore it was not actively discouraged for time travelers. I may be able to detach myself from Hans at long last if I allowed Augustin to be more than just my tutor, more than a stoic priest preoccupied with inflicting death.

Memories of his sacrifice arose in my mind on several occasions that week, the moans of his victim, the smell of blood, the black excitement in his voice when he dedicated the woman's body to Wuotan. He had told me that he would never do such a thing to a Teuton, and I believed him. But I grew disgusted at myself, at my willingness to sign my life away to an unrepentant murderer. *What if he starts using you to recruit new victims, like a heathen pimp? What if that's the blood ritual he wants to teach you—how to properly sacrifice an outsider? If he holds your heart, he could force you . . . would the love you have to offer be enough to tame him?*

I did not know, but I had a strong feeling that if I refused Augustin's wish, he would sever our academic relationship along with our friendship. I did not want to lose either. I loved him in spite of myself, in spite of who he had become. And I determined during that tedious week that nothing he could do would change that. He could take my heart and rip it to shreds, make me beg for the day he would kill me, so I could return home, but I would not stop loving him. Love was a choice, I believed at the time, and Augustin von Bayern needed to know love again.

On Tuesday, a frigid day bringing the first flurries of winter, my destiny arrived at the Meldorf estate shortly after None. Ulka found me helping Freia in the kitchen and informed me that the Lord Augustin von Bayern waited for me upon the porch. I thanked her and told Freia that I would be back later, following Ulka swiftly through the great hall before my roommate could advise me to reconsider.

I grabbed my coat and exited the house with some trepidation, working to beat back my lingering doubts. *What you'll get from this outweighs anything you might lose,* I reminded myself again. After shutting the door behind me, I raised my eyes to Augustin's face. He wore a thick black coat that practically trailed the ground, the hood covering his hair, his heavy-treaded snow boots planted firmly on the boards of the deck. A slow smile appeared on his face as his blue eyes looked me over, and he nodded once. "You have decided." It was not a question.

"Yes," I replied, my element rising to match the chill of the afternoon. My eyes glinted with just a touch of blue as I met Augustin's gaze. "I am ready."

His smile grew sarcastic, and he said, "No, you are not. But come." He held out his right hand, covered by a black leather glove, and I took it, my hand bare, frost clinging to my skin. He enclosed my small hand in his fingers, the heat of his fire warming me through his glove. He pulled me briskly off of the porch and down the steps, remarking that he had brought his own horse to make the trip simpler.

He swung my body atop his horse, a magnificent black stallion, and I asked, "Where are we going to do this?" I imagined riding to that altar in the forest, offering my heart to a man who served Wuotan himself.

"That depends upon your *Louni*," he said while mounting the saddle. I felt my forehead crease at that term; it was an antiquated one that referenced the body's humors. "I have arrayed my spare room for this task, but if your mad fear of doctors would manifest in such a place, we shall have to choose another locale."

I secured my arms around his waist as he nudged his stallion into a trot in the direction of the road to the drawbridge. I knew the chamber to which he referred, and my ice chilled my veins further at the recollection of my first experience there. Would I have a panic attack if I must sit on that couch again, in that room with the candles and the apothecary's implements? I buried my face in his back, shutting my eyes and breathing deeply of the wintry air. "I should be fine, I think," I responded at length, "especially since we're going to the spiritual realm to form the bond. It's not a medical procedure."

"That it is not," he agreed with a soft chuckle, "and once your heart rests in my hands, I should be able to quench any hysteria that rises within you. You ought not to be terrified of doctors, Swanhilde. Their purpose is to heal."

A strange giggle worked its way up my throat, and I pulled back a little to see the Isar's banks fast approaching. "Sure it is," I muttered in English, thinking again of Dane's suffering and of my mother's sad fate. Modern physicians were not particularly skilled at their purpose, in my experience, and I doubted the ones of this era were any better. I saw Garin Zeuner nod at us as Augustin guided his stallion onto the drawbridge without paying the toll. "You can get into Muniche for free? Is that because you're of the Bayern family?"

"Marelda's son pays no fee to enter her city's gates," he answered in a grating tone, turning his horse down the first street to the left once we had passed between the turrets. I nodded to myself, the ache in his voice reminding me that Augustin had known love once, long ago. And he still felt it where his mother was concerned.

When we reached his front door moments later, a slightly plump, grizzled man with a crooked back and an upturned nose met us at the threshold. Augustin slid off of his stallion, holding out a hand to help me down. I covertly studied his servant, watching his wrinkled eyes widen at the sight of me, a well-dressed young Teuton woman, innocently approaching the house of the most dangerous man in Muniche. The man bowed low toward me and welcomed me in uncertain, thickly-accented Teutonica. Augustin waved him aside, handing him his stallion's reins, murmuring a few orders to him in a language I did not know. The aged man bowed once at his master and disappeared around the corner of the cottage with the stallion in tow. "That is my servant Viktor, a Slav who has served me faithfully since my return from Salerno two winters ago," Augustin told me while he unlocked his front door. "Unlike the servants of the Bayern castle, Viktor knows when to stay out of my business."

I nodded absently, nervousness rising within me again at the knowledge of what we were about to do. My heart would belong to someone else entirely when I stepped onto the street again. We passed through the entryway and front parlor of the cottage without pausing, though I cast my gaze around in curiosity, noting the few candles burning above the blazing fireplace, the leather chairs, the tables, the lion sculpture in a corner, the decorative swords hanging upon one wall, and the shelves laden with writing materials and many other instruments. I glanced toward the doorway of the dining room and caught a glimpse of an impressive larch table ringed by matching chairs, before Augustin led me down a short hallway and into the very same room in which I had awoken the night of his sacrifice.

Now, the chamber was almost completely ensconced in darkness. Just two candles flickered atop the fireplace mantle beside the window, its heavy curtains shutting away any thoughts of daylight. I invoked my ice into my eyes in an attempt to see the contents of the room despite the shadows. The long couch still lay against the far wall, and at its head, the small table where Augustin had placed his goblet of blood. Shelves lined every wall aside from the one beside the couch, eye-level ledges bearing countless unlit candlesticks. I saw no trace of the bundled herbs and vials that had set off my panic that first time; perhaps Augustin had stuffed all of that into the closed hutch against the left wall.

Augustin shut the door behind us while I stood in the center of the room, looking around. Then, to my chagrin, I heard a key turn in the lock. I whipped my head around to stare balefully at this eerie priest who wanted my heart, thinking that perhaps he wished to kill me tonight, as well. I watched him stuff the door key into a pocket of his overcoat. He noticed my preoccupation and grinned at me, showing his teeth. "Does it frighten you that I have locked us in, my dear lady?" he queried, removing his coat and hanging it upon a hook on the door, revealing the dark robes of the Teuton priest underneath.

I eyed the coat, ordering myself to remember the pocket that held the key, just in case. "No, not particularly . . . I was just wondering why that's necessary."

"To ensure that no one should encroach upon our union here tonight." He smirked at me, doubtless reading all of the emotions that ran across my face at his words. "Shall I take your coat, Swanhilde? You will want to be comfortable for this task, and once I have lit all of the candles and the fireplace, it may grow a bit warm in here." I nodded slowly, worked my way out of my coat, and handed it to him. Augustin's eyes widened at the sight of my outfit, a winter dress made of dyed black and blue wool. It had blue ribbons decking the bodice and a matching swath of blue sweeping down the front and back of the skirt, trimmed with gossamer fabric on the sides and around the square neckline. I realized that I had not yet worn black in Augustin's presence, and I could tell that he was impressed. "You look glorious, my swan princess," he murmured as he hung my coat next to his.

I blushed at his compliment and turned away from him to climb onto the couch. With my back to the room, I smoothed out my hair, which I had left down beneath a blue ribboned head covering. Augustin spent the next several moments lighting all of the candles on the shelves

278

before casting his element at the fireplace. When he approached me shortly thereafter, the lambent blue light fairly enveloped his dark robes, enhancing the grandeur of his aura. "You should wear black more often, Swanhilde," he said as he sat down upon the stool he had used at our prior meeting in this room. "It suits you."

"Thanks. I wear it a lot in the twenty-first century, especially when I'm trying to look mysterious." I grinned at him, imagining him accompanying me to a metal festival back home. Dressed as a Teuton priest, he would fit in with the crowd.

"Well, it is certainly appropriate for what we do here today," Augustin said, leaning forward on his elbows, folding his hands and eyeing me.

"Would you mind telling me...." I began shakily, clearing my throat as the awful truth of what we were about to do washed over me afresh, "...exactly what I ought to know ...about creating this ... heart-bond?"

Augustin leered and placed his chin upon his folded hands. "You could have sought the information yourself, had you graced the archives this past week. But no matter; I shall tell you what I know. By agreeing to this, you are willingly binding yourself to me with a tie you cannot break, a tie that spans beyond this mortal coil. You are granting me control of your heart, control of your blood... control of your will." He raised his eyebrows at me.

I scooted toward the wall at my back, thinking again that I should reconsider. "I will be able to feel you, and you me, the presence of our souls, though we be separated by great distance," he went on. "We shall have the privilege of meeting in the realm of the spirit at any time, even in our dreams. I will guard your heart as though it were my own, learning from it, feeling your pain and your pleasure. I will be with you always, *your* priest, your guardian. Until the day the bond is broken, you will call me master."

I shivered at the notion of such a mystical relationship, impossible in human terms. Though I had read the truth of the matter in *Der Weg* many times, the depth of such a connection sounded much more significant when Augustin described it. I inhaled unsteadily, thinking again of Ina and Walfrid, wondering whether he had forced her into it, whether that was possible. "How . . . can the bond . . . be broken?" I asked, feeling a renewed sorrow for my subjugated girlfriend.

"Only by the priest who made it," Augustin replied, nodding in satisfaction. "Although, I suppose two united parties could be forced to break by other Teuton priests . . . but such a sudden severance of this tie would be painful and may lead to death or insanity."

I remembered my earlier muses, that if this bond proved harmful, perhaps it would break when I returned to my era. "Would it span time?"

Augustin scowled a bit and dropped his gaze to the floor. "I do not know. But you must ask yourself, Swanhilde, does that barrier of time really matter to you?" He met my eyes once more. "Why set aside such a rare opportunity just because the moment is ephemeral? All glory is fleeting, my dear, and one must enjoy pleasure while it lasts, I believe."

He had a good point there. I frowned a bit myself, pondering everything one final time. Augustin rose from the stool to stand before me, brushing my face gently with his hand, tilting my chin upward to meet his gaze. "I will not be . . . a monster . . . as you think," he murmured, his tone persuasive, his stare intense. "With this bond . . . hurting you . . . would hurt myself. I would be good to you, my swan . . . and give you everything you ask . . . just to feel your heart in my hands. I promise . . . ."

My hesitation vanished at his pleading words, and I nodded at him as passion gripped me. "Do it to me then," I said, "and I will teach you love."

He smiled at me and took hold of my right hand. "We must enter the other realm together, since I must be able to properly touch you to create the bond." His sturdy hands began to seethe with heat around my own.

I blinked, his statement taking me completely off guard. "Wait. You mean it's possible to *touch* other spirits?"

"If two Teutons enter the spiritual realm with their physical bodies joined, it is certainly possible." Augustin cocked his head at me, a chiding glow appearing in his eyes, which glimmered with cobalt fire. "Then Hans never brought you to the other realm himself? What a waste."

I stretched out on the couch to ensure that my body would not freeze in an uncomfortable position. But I shot the priest beside me a dirty look and said, "Well, Hans taught me how to set my spirit free as a way to counter my anxiety." I called my ice into my veins, its cold clashing sharply against Augustin's hands.

"Ah. Still a waste." Augustin's smirk mocked me, and he gripped my fingers more tightly. "Now come. We shall seal this in the firmament."

I shifted my gaze to the ceiling and focused upon my element, awakening it fully from its slumber within my spirit. I felt it consume my mortal body, and I held my breath as it crystallized everything upon and within my torso. An instant later, my spirit burst into the sky above, stratus clouds thick with flurries encircling my snow white robes. Their unspoken camaraderie made me laugh with delight, and I pierced the cloudbank in the midst of a whirling dance, a thousand tiny flakes defying gravity to fly upward with me. The sky above was a deep winter dusk, the sun already having tucked itself beneath the clouds in its quest for December's night. I continued to chortle as I raised both arms in wordless praise. It had been far too long since I had last entered the ether for any reason other than reassurance, and there was so much here to enrich my element.

Ah, my victorious ice goddess, we did not come here for a frigid frolic. My companion's words entered my mind in a tone of amusement, and I felt a fervent heat trace its way down my back. My element gathered the wintry air more closely around my spirit, an instinctive reaction against the fiery priest who hovered right behind me. His garments matched the cerulean of his fire, undulating in mesmerizing splendor, his flaming hair sweeping down his shoulders, his eyes shining with glory. I had never seen him look so beautiful. He smiled at me when he met my gaze, his teeth sparkling like sunrays upon the water. *Are you ready to grant me your heart, my wintry Teuton witch?*

Whoa, was all I could manage to think in return, for the radiance of his spirit nearly blinded me, his heat luring me to a place I had not yet known. Here was a Teuton priest who actually *wanted* me, who saw me as more than just a naïve female student. He drew closer to me, surrounding me in his warmth, and he softly requested that I relax and look into his eyes.

His right hand touched the icy robes at my chest, but his smoldering fire did not prompt my spirit to recoil this time. He began to recite the binding spell in Ælte Teutonica and I caught some of the words, though my knowledge of the ancient dialect was far from perfect. *Eternal bond of love . . . one priest and his chosen one . . . unbreakable . . . protecting . . . grant me this responsibility . . . undying union . . . Swanhilde and Augustin . . . .*

At the moment when our names spilled from his mind, I felt his hand close around my heart. He drew it carefully from my chest, from my soul, to his own soul, uniting it with his desires, his power holding it fast. I experienced one brief flash of panic at the realization that my heart was no longer mine, that a mad rapist now held it himself, a man of darkness, of evil. But then I finally broke eye contact with him to look down at his right hand hovering between us, the heart of my spirit throbbing steadily in his grasp. His fingers caressed my heart so tenderly that I could have cried, if that was possible in the spiritual realm. And he murmured one additional pledge in Teutonica, his sincerity seeping from his fingers deep into my heart. *I will be good to you . . . I promise . . . .*

I could not think of what to say in response, for the intimacy of the bond had begun to prod at everything I thought I knew. If Augustin continued to stroke his fingers along my heart this way, I may very well spread my legs for him the very second we returned to our bodies. I shook my head slowly and shut my ethereal lids, pulling an extra layer of frost over my vision as I tried to salvage what I knew about myself, about my standards. *I can't have sex with him unless we're married. I can't let him convince me otherwise, no matter how entrancing his hands feel around my heart, no matter how much he may seduce me.*

Three more of his words crept into my mind to seal the spell: *It is done.* Then he caught me in his fiery storm, pulling us out of the realm of the spirit, back into his candlelit room. I opened my eyes to stare at the ceiling in shock, watching the blue lights from the candles dance across the beams, dallying with the shadows.

I blinked several times, trying again to steady myself. I drew my ice back inside my soul, relaxing while my fingers melted and my eyes returned to their natural gray. Augustin appeared over me, and I moved just my eyes to look at him, a new and compelling loyalty drawing me to him forever. He placed his hands on my shoulders, his expression concerned. "Are you all right, Swanhilde? Speak to me."

My long silence had frightened him, and I rushed to assure him, "I'm fine . . . don't worry . . . master . . . ." The word fell unconsciously from my lips.

He smiled at the new title he had earned and brushed his right hand softly down my cheek and my neck. Eventually his hand found its place upon my heart, the physical realm merging somehow with the spiritual, soothing the heart of my soul. He parted his lips in a contented sigh and whispered the truth I had known for weeks now. "You love me . . . Swanhilde . . . ."

"Yes, Augustin . . . yes . . . I do . . . ." He wrapped his strong arms around me and pulled me against his chest, laying his cheek upon my hair, protecting me, shielding me, solidifying our bond, our ardent passion.

Chapter Twenty-eight:
Devilish Perils

I know not how long we sat together on that couch in Augustin's cottage, his arms holding me to his breast, both of us silently savoring our newfound oneness, the bond of the Teutons. A sensation of completeness and belonging came over me, as though what I found with this priest satisfied the yearnings I had attempted to suppress or deny all these years. This was what I had always needed, a fiery Teuton priest who viewed me with respect, as an equal. How could I have imagined finding this with Hans, a secretive sort so much older than me?

"How do you feel, my darling swan?" he asked me at length while I rested against him with my eyes closed, scenes of blissful harmony splashing my imagination with color.

"Happy," I responded, opening my eyes a crack to marvel at the light blue glow of the candlelight. Augustin's fire was my favorite color. I began to envision a new future for myself, one where Augustin and I met the Saxon invaders together, defending Muniche to the last. "It's like . . . what I've always dreamed of . . . since I first fell for Hans as a teenager. If this is what it's like being with a priest, then how could any Teuton be satisfied with less?"

"How indeed?" Augustin sounded pleased with himself, his right hand tracing the ribbons of my bodice before finding its rightful place upon my heart. His spiritual hands swathed my heart in warmth, and I closed my eyes again. "This is new for me as well. The love I sense in your heart, the trust, the acceptance . . . . I have not experienced such things for many years, and I had forgotten how sweet they are." His lips touched my jawline just below my left ear.

I burrowed myself closer to him, silently wishing that he would wrap us both in the folds of his robes, cloaking us in darkness. The caress of his lips prompted my entire body to shiver, and I remembered that I had to keep my head on straight. As gentle as this man may seem, he was also a seducer, a rapist. I had to make sure that he still intended to honor my wishes in regards to my virginity.

Before I could open the subject, Augustin pulled back from me slightly, his right hand still trapping my heart beneath his influence. "I sense other things, too," he confessed in an uncertain tone. "Temptations that I must work to defeat, if this peace between us is to last." I twisted my neck to the left to look at his face. His blue eyes had darkened, the planes of his face sharpening. "Most of the priests in this city—and everywhere else, for that matter—use the bond to control their wives, you see." He met my gaze, his own not particularly inviting.

My eyebrows came together, and I shifted myself further away from him, far enough that his right hand slid down to my skirt. "Oh?" I said flatly, thoughts of Ina and Walfrid returning to my mind. Augustin had just implied that such things were the norm, at least in this era.

A cold smile flashed across his face. "I have seen it myself, Swanhilde; in fact, I was taught how best to accomplish it. All who study for the priesthood must demonstrate their proficiency with every sort of mysticism, even the types that ought not to exist. It would be easy to discipline you now, for afterward I could use the bond to imbue your heart with devotion, to convince you that you deserve it."

I stared at him, horror creeping through my veins along with tiny flecks of ice. "Well, if you're intending to lie to me and burn my heart until I believe you, I still have the option of getting myself killed," I informed him, crossing my arms. "And it's not like I'd have to commit suicide. There are other ways." I pictured myself proclaiming my witchy knowledge in public, in the main square—something that would get me sentenced to death. I could even spout off Prince Otto's secrets, his dealings with Wuotan that uncovered the portal through time.

Augustin smirked at me, unimpressed. "You forget that the man before you has claimed both your life and your death for as long as you remain here. And I do not hold to the ways of the cruel master, my dear. I shall alter your desires slowly, sinuously, and you will come to long for it, just like the Teuton females of higher blood status than you."

I bristled at that jibe and scooted further away, my back finding the wall. "You promised you would be good to me," I reminded him.

"And I shall be." Augustin's eyes glittered with his fire as he took hold of both of my hands, his warmth soothing their icy rigidity. "On my own terms."

I curled my lip and looked toward the locked door, trying to figure out what still remained of my own agency. I felt the hands of his spirit enclosing my heart even then, shielding it, protecting it, *altering it?* "I'll probably have to die to return to my own time, since your brother won't give me the song," I said. "And I know that the heart-bond is broken by death. I've read about that."

"That sort of death should free you, yes, and by then you shall likely be glad of it." Augustin bared his teeth at me, his blue eyes burning as he lifted one of his hands to my face, tracing it down the artery in my neck. "You know not what you have gotten yourself into, my swan princess. You intend to teach me love . . . to melt my stone heart that does not feel. I do not believe you will succeed."

I closed my eyes, my body trembling afresh at his touch. "That doesn't mean I shouldn't try," I murmured. "I've always been a sucker for lost causes."

A sarcastic snort of laughter escaped Augustin's lips. "Like the cause of our people, the Teutons, who shall fall in twenty-two years . . . forgetting everything that makes them unique . . . ruining their purity of blood . . . never to rise again."

I sighed, and the words "enjoy pleasure while it lasts" fell from my lips.

Augustin pulled me into his embrace again. "You are *mine*," he affirmed, grotesque satisfaction saturating his words.

My lips twitched at my lapse, and I wondered where this would lead me, what path my life would take now. I had willingly joined myself in a bond stronger than matrimony with the oldest Bayern brother, the one who did not exist on paper in my time. What would this man do to my heart? Would his influence stay with me even after I returned to the future? I shook my head and tried to focus on how peaceful it felt to rest in his arms. My thoughts turned instead to Augustin's comment about my blood. "I wish I could raise the status of my Teuton blood," I said, thinking of the two ways such a thing could be done. If I married Joel like my responsibility demanded, my blood would remain where it was. But could I marry an outsider now that Augustin had bound my heart?

Augustin murmured thoughtfully. "You *could*, of course, if you chose to offer your Teuton blood as a gift to one of your friends, the Lady Freia perhaps. Rumor suggests that she wishes to marry the ironmaster. Master Denlinger's family would never approve that match unless she becomes a Teuton first."

I shuddered at Augustin's words, remembering that the dreaded Teutonic blood-transfer was indeed one method of raising one's blood percentage—assuming the Teuton involved survived. "I doubt Freia wants to mess with that sort of ritual," I said, shaking my head. "She's thinking about returning to the Rhineland one day, anyway. If

Master Denlinger really wants her for his wife, he'll have to accept her as an outsider, I'm afraid."

"I know that. I was joking with you, Swanhilde." Augustin looked down at me, his expression severe. "I do not want to have to worry about you trying the blood-transfer on anyone's behalf, especially not for that foolish Joel. You would probably die, for Wuotan does not like you."

I jerked at this revelation, terror grasping my soul. "He . . . doesn't like me?" I shivered at the memory of my last encounter with Wuotan, with his black laughter . . . just before leaping through those labradorite gates into the Bavarian forest.

Augustin held me close in response to my fear, stroking my hair tenderly. "No, he does not particularly appreciate you, for he knows that you have tampered with his powers without pledging him service in return. Wuotan does not like my brother for the same reason. And he wonders why his kingdom will end in ruin." Augustin's body grew rigid for a moment, but when I trembled, he relaxed and bent low to kiss my hair. "Do not fear him, Swanhilde, but I would also suggest that you do not meddle with death or deadly rituals. Wuotan has intentions of taking your soul if you ask him for favors, and the fact that you are already bound for heaven does not please him. You likely should not go to the realm of the spirit alone, for he may watch for you there and try to turn you into one of his sirens, though he could not. I would sleep better at night if you tread carefully, my darling. I can protect you from him as far as I am able, but Wuotan's power is far greater than mine, for he is a demon and I am a mere man."

I quaked again at the mere thought of that devil, the one who used to call our people his own, seeking my life, my soul. I prayed a silent prayer of thanks to God for protecting me from Wuotan's sway over my eternal destiny. Augustin's words from before resurfaced in my mind, swirling around with his proud claim that he could defend me from a demon's wiles: *Tell me I should not hate, I should not glory in anger, I should cast aside all of the power Wuotan has granted me, that I would never have known otherwise!* I frowned, wondering how I could ever convince this twisted man that the path of love was far greater, far more rewarding. He had marveled at the love in my heart already, but I suspected that if he had to choose one or the other, he would gravitate toward hatred first, and power.

My priest pulled away from me finally, letting his strong arms slide from my shoulders, placing them upon the cushion beneath us. The candles in the room still burned, though I knew not how long we had sat entwined. I had a feeling that the winter night had descended and that soon the city gates would close if they had not already. I had heard one set of bells pealing forth some time ago. I could not remain in the city all night, despite the bond we had just formed. What would become of my reputation if the nobility discovered that I had spent the night at the cottage of Augustin von Bayern? I raised my eyes to his once more, intending to suggest that we return to the Meldorf estate, but the words died on my tongue the moment I saw his light blue eyes glowing with hunger and expectancy.

"There is another way . . . to raise the status . . . of your Teuton blood," Augustin said in a sultry voice, his fingers flexing on the couch. "You are ninety-five percent Teutonic, yes . . . and I . . . I am ninety-*nine* percent . . . my dear." He smiled at me while the fingers of his soul stroked my heart, enticing me.

I stared back at him in dismay as the foolishness of what I had done grasped me all at once. *He could force me now . . . I wouldn't be able to refuse him . . . and he would justify it . . . saying that it would eventually raise my blood . . . and I would believe him.* "You . . . you . . . want . . . to have . . . sex with me . . . master?" My lips had grown dry, and my voice shook terribly.

"*If* you would agree to grant me your precious virginity." The words dripped from his lips, his eyes fixated on my body, still clad in my dark dress. "For I would assume . . . that our union . . . may have altered . . . some of your valued standards . . . my lovely, assertive swan princess . . . ." He reached his hands out to place them upon the bodice of my dress.

I struggled to concentrate, to ignore the wild hormones his touch ignited, to push aside the alluring hands upon my heart. "And if . . . if . . . ." I could hardly form a coherent thought, let alone speak. I swallowed as he leaned toward me, his body language leaving no room for misinterpretation. "If . . . it . . . has not?" I trembled all over as he grasped my shoulders.

For a moment, everything froze. His large hands enclosed my shoulders entirely, his strength bruising my bones, his eyes burning my soul, his mouth working in passion, in frustration. Suddenly, he pushed me backward onto the couch, his flaming body shoving me into the cushion, his mouth twisting into a sneer. "You . . . *will* . . . change . . . your standards . . . *for me,*" he snarled.

He began kissing me an instant later, his lips harsh and urgent, his tongue probing the roof of my mouth, one of his hands encircling the back of my neck, the other grasping my right breast through my bodice. I could hardly breathe as his roughness awakened my own lust, my sanity struggling to reassert itself, to order me to resist, to fight him. I could not. I kissed him back, my eyes shut tight against reality, my hormones singing, my heart racing in anticipation.

He released my mouth at last and bit down onto my neck before I had the chance to react. His hand had unwound some of the ribbons on my dress to tug at my neckline, touching the skin of my chest. I could not fight him. He had me pinned expertly, one who had raped many a woman before. I should not have felt surprised. This was far different from my experience at college, though, for my element seemed to be celebrating, twining in the other realm with a smoldering master. Maybe I needed to rethink my standards. Maybe having the heart-bond was good enough.

Augustin drank deeply from my neck, the hands of his soul pumping my heart against the impending weakness.

What memories was he reading this time? I gasped for breath as he abruptly pulled back from my neck, closing the wound with disturbing swiftness, before my own blood could taint my clothing. He raised himself off of me just a bit, his hands holding me still, under his power. He glared down at me with a nasty grin, my blood decorating his teeth. After his tongue had carefully licked the final traces of my blood from his lips, he spoke the wretched truth, demanding no disagreement. "You *want* me, Swanhilde. You *want* to have sex with me. I saw it here and now, in the depths of your heart. Tell me I can have your virginity. Tell me it is *mine!*" He growled at me, and I jumped.

I opened my feeble lips to try to speak. I *had* to tell him no, that I could not, despite my deepest desires, that it was wrong, that it was sinful. I found that I could not speak, not at all. I stared up at Augustin the rapist, fearing what was to come, my lips trembling, tears welling in my eyes. His patience wore thin, and his hands curled into flaming claws, his teeth bared as he prepared to rip my dress by the seams. I closed my eyes once more, tensing for the pain, the guilt . . . and the instant before his hands could lay my chest bare, a knock sounded on the door, a sharp, urgent knock that could not be ignored.

Augustin paused, swinging his head to the left to glare at the door. Then he cursed and climbed off of me, snapping his fingers for me to get up. He threw my coat upon me before I could obey, then pulled his own black coat from the door, retrieving the key. Belated shock flooded my veins, wreaking havoc with my coordination as I shakily searched for the sleeves of my coat.

Shortly afterward, when I finally managed to stick my left arm through the correct hole, Augustin opened the door a crack and snapped something awful in Magyar, obviously addressing his servant Viktor. I heard the elderly man respond, sounding frightened and apologetic. I thrust my right arm through my sleeve, wrapping my coat around me as I heard Augustin reply, his own voice sounding cooler now. I slowly slid off of the couch, placing my unstable feet upon the floor, and Augustin spun to face me, his expression annoyed. "This will have to wait until later," he said, beckoning for me to follow him while he put on his own coat. "Apparently some fool requires my assistance this night, and you need to leave Muniche before the gates close. Come."

I exited the candlelit room one step behind him, and he extinguished all of the flames in the instant he stepped into the hallway. The roaring fire in the fireplace also evaporated, as though every blue flame in the cottage obeyed Augustin's commands. I glanced back toward the couch, now invisible in the darkness, and then quickened my pace to catch up with Augustin at the front door of his cottage.

A withered woman in rags stood outside, her pleading eyes trained on his ruthless face. "Please come to aid my daughter, my Lord von Bayern, I beg you. The midwives have been able to do nothing. She is at the door of death." The elderly woman's Teutonica sounded quite common. She clasped her hands together and sank to her knees as she voiced her plea.

I sidled to Augustin's side while he glared disparagingly at the poor woman, his eyes glittering with greed. "What do you intend to give me for my help?" The old woman reached into her tattered dress to pull forth a tiny bundle wrapped in grimy oilskin. Augustin snatched it from her grasp and dumped its contents into the palm of his hand— five Thaler. He closed his fingers around the coins and leered at the withered woman. "That is not much," he stated reproachfully.

"It is all we have." The old woman raised her laced fingers toward Augustin's face, tears leaking from the corners of her eyes. "Please, my lord . . . *please* . . . ."

Augustin huffed in irritation, spinning to the right to face Viktor. He barked a few words which prompted him to scurry away. Then he cast his gaze upon the old woman once more with the pledge, "I shall come as soon as possible. Go." He made a shooing motion with his hand before vanishing abruptly into his cottage.

I stared after him for a moment, feeling incredibly helpless, then looked out the open door to watch the old woman hobble away down the street. Seconds later, Augustin reappeared, carrying a black leather bag in one hand, ushering me out the door with the other. Viktor had readied his horse for us, and Augustin led me there without a word.

My heathen priest swung me upon the stallion's back, leaping to the saddle in front of me and snapping the reins cruelly in the same instant, prompting the horse to jump forward with a whinny. I cried out and gripped his waist, nearly falling backward. I could barely think, let alone ask Augustin what was happening, though my mind had formed a probable conclusion. *The old woman's daughter was dying in childbirth and asked for Augustin's help . . . she couldn't pay him much . . . what will he demand of her in return, if he saves her life?*

The winter sky was already pitch black, dotted with stars, when we reached the eastern gate, shut tight for the night. Augustin swore, pulling his stallion up short and turning the animal sharply left, toward the northwestern side of Muniche. We rode like the wind until we reached the gates of the Bayern castle. Augustin jumped off of the horse and tossed the reins to me with the words, "Wait here." He unlocked the gate with a key and disappeared within. I waited as he had ordered, staring blankly from the bronze lion crest to the starlit gardens beyond the gate, shuddering a bit from the fierce urgency of his movements, his reactions.

Augustin returned to me after I had counted to four hundred in my head, slamming the gates of his family castle behind him and mounting the stallion once more. As he whipped the horse into a gallop toward the eastern gate, a thousand questions whirled through my mind, none of which I could ask, for we rode so fast that I had to use all of my strength to cling to the horse's back.

We halted before the gate moments later, its iron bars secured for the night. Augustin leapt from the saddle to sharply address the three wary knights who guarded the eastern door to my city. "Lower the drawbridge." It was not a request. With amazement, I watched Augustin lift the gate's iron bars himself, dropping them to the side before sticking a single key into the lock and turning it.

He returned to my side and helped me move forward to situate myself upon his saddle while two of the knights pulled the gate open. I heard the drawbridge creaking as it descended slowly to span the Isar while I arranged my coat and skirt around my legs. "Ride swiftly home, my darling," Augustin urged me, and I met his gaze. His eyes looked restless in the dark. "I shall retrieve my horse on Thursday." Before I could answer him, he sprinted off down the street. So I turned his stallion toward the lowered bridge and crossed it slowly, the eyes of the knights burning into my back.

Chapter Twenty-nine:
Holidays

When I reached the grounds of the Meldorf estate not long afterward, I gave charge of Augustin's stallion to the stable hand without offering any explanation of whose horse it was or where I had gotten it. I entered the house moments later, feeling like it had been years rather than mere hours since I had last graced that familiar front door. My entire life had changed in one night . . . in one blissful instant of insanity . . . and I felt almost as though I was a stranger entering the count's house uninvited. I encountered no one in the halls, to my relief, but found Freia keeping vigil in our upstairs bedroom, reading my Bible by candlelight. I reassured her as she rose from her bed at my emergence, her eyes wide with worry. I told her that I was fine, that nothing terrible had happened, but that I needed to sleep. She hugged me once, briefly but firmly, and retreated to her bed, graciously granting me the solitude I desperately needed.

I removed my coat behind the privacy screen that we rarely used, breathing a sigh of relief that Freia had not followed me. My blue and black dress still showed signs of Augustin's mistreatment—torn ribbons, sagging collar, wrinkled fabric. I pulled the dress off, bundling it into a ball for the laundry, and retrieved my nightgown from a nearby rack. While I put it on, I thought back to all that had happened to me during the past few hours. I had freely given Augustin my heart, and in return he had marveled at my love, caressed me, held me close, comforted my fears. And as a result of my stupid remark—*I wish I could raise the status of my Teuton blood*—his violence had erupted along with his lust. I had been seconds away from becoming his next harlot, and I could no longer refuse him. This fascinating, educated man would be the death of me and the destruction of my purity.

When I crawled into bed after extinguishing all of the candles save one, I made a solemn promise to myself that I intended to keep if all others failed: *As long as Augustin holds my heart, I will never again bring up the subject of sex or mention anything that could lead to a rape.* Maybe, just maybe, if I could keep my idiot mouth shut, I could preserve my virginity as well.

Augustin appeared as promised on Thursday afternoon to reclaim his stallion and resume our language studies. Before we turned our attention to English and Ælte Teutonica, I inquired about the events of two nights prior, after he had opened the gate for me. "Did you manage to save that woman?" I asked, curious.

Augustin shook his head at me, his expression discontent as we sat beside one another on a couch in the front parlor, our dictionaries lying on a table before us. "The fools should have summoned me far earlier. By the time I arrived, it was far too late for both the woman and her child."

Disappointment gripped my heart, for I had been under the impression that Augustin could always help Teuton women in childbirth, no matter the circumstances. "What happened? Tell me everything."

Augustin frowned, his face still ashen, and he glanced furtively around the parlor before speaking. When he answered me, he kept his voice low, using English words whenever he could. "Those commoners lived in a stuffy room on the second floor of a decrepit inn. Conditions were incredibly filthy, not suitable for childbirth. The woman lay broken on the boards of the floor, half of her bloated body covered with a tattered rag, her legs splayed out, blood saturating the floor. Her husband was there and he smelled of alcohol, his hair unkempt, his eyes glassy. Her mother crouched by her side, along with a witchy old midwife who reminded me of an ogress, her nose long and pointed, her face scarred from pox.

"The child had already died when I arrived, still half inside her womb. It was a boy, and he had tried to come out feet first, which would have been difficult to correct, even for me. I managed to pull the child's body out of her, along with part of her womb, it appeared, for his tiny hands had grasped at it in an attempt to survive, I suppose. My arms were coated with rancid blood up to my elbows, the smell practically making me sick—*me*, a doctor and a Teuton priest!

"I ordered the midwife to dispose of the child and turned my attention to the woman, who by then no longer had the strength to scream, though she had wailed with gusto when I removed the child from her body. Her skin had grown a repulsive shade of yellow, and her womb continued to hemorrhage, thick blood dripping through the floorboards. I tried to stem the flow at first, quickly finding that her soul had slipped too far, the wound between her legs nigh irreparable. So I took her wan face in my hands, whispering my desolate apologies, though I doubt that she heard me, for her eyes had begun to turn white. Ultimately I promised her an easy death, all that I could grant her in my mercy."

I stared at him as he completed his tale, the egg salad I had eaten for lunch churning in my stomach. I shuddered at the thought of this impoverished family torn apart by the dangers of childbirth, the mother elderly and infirm, the husband a drunkard. "How did you . . . kill her?" I whispered.

He sighed once, leaning forward on the couch, his strong hands clasped in his lap. "I stabbed her in the heart with a knife, quick, simple, painless. The husband did not appreciate my mercy—he threw a bottle at me when I left them to their misery—but the mother thanked me for my efforts. I returned her five Thaler since I had been unable to save either the woman or the child."

I cringed away from Augustin, imagining his devilish grimace the moment he stabbed the woman's heart and the resulting fury of the inebriated husband. *How could anyone, rich or poor, ask for this man's help in childbirth, even if he does have bargaining powers with Wuotan?* Finding my voice at last, I stated shakily, "That's just . . . awful. And depressing."

Augustin favored me with a sour look. "What else could one expect me to do? I am not God. I cannot pull every dying soul back to this world. It could have been worse." His expression grew suddenly fierce.

"How could it have been *worse?*" That seemed unthinkable to me.

He looked into my eyes for a long moment in silence, then said quietly, "That was her first child."

The truth of the matter struck me then with stunning force, prompting me to blink in shock, my mouth falling open. *Her first child . . . then she had no other children . . . no innocent boy to mourn her, uncomprehending, unforgiving . . . .* That must have been the exact reason why Augustin used his medical skills and his demonology to aid women in childbirth—*so no more sons would have to face his pain.* Perhaps when he had chosen to follow Wuotan rather than God, the demon overlord of our people may have gifted him with ability to preserve Teuton blood, to plead for dying women and children. In spite of his malice, Augustin *must* retain the capacity to love, I determined, or he would not bother to save other Teuton children from his own dismal fate.

The Christmas holidays arrived with appropriate fanfare, the whole city of Muniche halting its work for a full week to enjoy the occasion. Freia and I walked the streets almost every day despite the snow that coated the ground, spending time with Joel and Master Denlinger, attending quite a few parties. The ironmaster invited all of us to his family's house on Christmas Eve for a feast. That was the first time Freia or I had ever visited his house, and we both fell in quickly with his three sisters, chatting on numerous subjects while the men boasted and laughed amongst themselves. Master Denlinger's mother graciously welcomed us into her home, remarking with a smile that Freia seemed to be a charming young woman. When we returned to the count's estate that evening, Freia and I exchanged much speculation about the Denlinger family. I suggested that perhaps they would accept her even though she had little Teuton blood. I hoped so, for her sake.

Freia and I attended the Christmas Day service at the cathedral of Muniche, along with Joel and Master Denlinger. Over a thousand candles illuminated the main nave, the reverent voices of the monks and nuns pealing out from the shadows as they sang their chants in praise of the Savior's birth. Someone played the cathedral's impressive organ at intervals throughout the service. I suspected that the organist was likely Prince Otto, for I did not see him amongst the crowd, though I did pick out his Lady Maria. Each of the songs sounded ancient and complex, the style quite different from the Baroque music I preferred to play. The bishop of Muniche read the Christmas story from the Bible in Latin, which would not have done much for the commoners filling the church. Several other Catholic priests spoke dialogues and prayers in honor of Christ, and I recognized one of them as Paulus von Bayern.

The middle Bayern brother spoke in a quiet tenor voice, his entire being appearing far less confident than either of the other two, especially when he lifted the goblet of wine upward during the Eucharist. Though I should have focused on the birth of Christ throughout the mass, once Paulus had begun to perform his duties, I found myself making conjectures on his Teuton blood and his looks.

Out of the three Bayern brothers, I guessed that Paulus' blood had to be the least Teutonic of the bunch. If Augustin was ninety-nine percent, perhaps Paulus claimed a mere ninety-six. He seemed uncertain and frail, even as his thin face glowed with passion at the miracle of the Savior's birth. I could picture him breaking under Saxon torture, giving up the song, betraying our people. I could not fathom why Prince Otto had chosen to confide in Paulus, unless he liked to dominate weaker people. Family problems notwithstanding, Augustin and the Prince would have made a much stronger team, blue fire and red, burning everything in their path. I had no clue what Paulus' element was, but it had to be something stupid. He certainly had gotten the worst of the looks. Augustin far outshined his younger brothers in that department.

When we exited the cathedral at the close of the mass, Joel and I walked hand-in-hand toward the eastern gate of Muniche, planning to spend the rest of the day at the Meldorf estate. He remarked that the service had been good, even though he hardly understood anything. He wished that we could have sung a few Christmas carols as a congregation, even though such tunes did not yet exist. "Why don't we sing one now?" I suggested, skipping to the side of the drawbridge and opening my arms to the icy river below.

Joel came to my side, his own smile uncertain as he watched my eyes turn from gray to blue. "Like what?"

"Your favorite Christmas carol. We can sing it in English."

Joel hesitated, glancing down at the river, its waters growing choppier in response to my ice. He looked around, seeing that we were alone on the bridge, then asked, "Do you know 'O Holy Night'?"

I winked at him and spun around once; then I began to sing in a soft voice, in celebration of Christ's birth. Joel joined me on the second line, and I imagined that I was playing the organ, dancing just a bit as the beauty of music took over my soul. When we reached the climactic moment of that gorgeous carol, my soprano ringing out strong, I threw my element at the waters of the Isar, creating a towering ice sculpture in the form of a star, the Star of Bethlehem.

After we had sung the first and last verses, Joel whistled in amazement at the magic I had worked upon the river. "How long is that going to stay there?" he asked, gesturing at my sculpture with one hand as we headed for the road.

"It's winter; it might be there all day." I grinned at him, and he laughed.

As we walked the path back to the count's manor, we continued to sing a variety of Christmas carols, their heartfelt harmonies filling my soul with delight. Joel remarked at one point that he never realized I had such a beautiful voice. He paused on the porch once we had made it to the estate and remarked that he really felt in the mood for a good holiday now. I smiled and agreed, leaning against one of the posts on the porch, my joy still elevated with the combined glory of music and frigid ice.

Then, to my surprise, Joel moved close to me, reaching out one hand to carefully brush aside a few stray hairs from my face. As I stared up at him in wonder, a rush of uncertainty filling my heart, he leaned toward me and kissed my lips for a brief instant, his hazel eyes aglow with emotion. He gazed at me for a long moment afterward and murmured in a husky voice, "I'm really, really glad . . . that I came on this journey with you, Swanie . . . in spite of everything."

Later that evening, as we sipped mugs of steaming cider in the main parlor while Freia played her flute, my mind began the dreaded task of comparisons, my left hand slipped through Joel's. *Three first kisses. Hans . . . the dance . . . the stream . . . Teutonic glory . . . one passionate moment . . . blissful heaven . . . an old man. Joel . . . the outsider . . . handsome . . . hard-working . . . grateful for my foolish mistakes . . . his lips cautious . . . his eyes betraying love.* And the unavoidable memory, for I felt his hands upon my heart from a fair distance away: *Augustin . . . after he saved my life . . . his lips tender, brushing my forehead, my eyelids, my mouth . . . the excitement in his eyes as he kissed me again . . . no shame, only glory . . . his arms imprisoning me . . . his fire overwhelming me . . .*

passion . . . insanity . . . the rapist . . . my master . . . my love . . . .

I had put myself in an awkward position. While I had not yet managed to feel a romantic attraction to Joel, he had apparently convinced himself that we were destined for each other, at least here in the eleventh century. He had mentioned a few other girls in passing, barmaids and his roommates' sisters, his countenance tending to twist itself into a knot when he spoke of their silliness and ignorance. Of course he would want an educated wife, one who spoke his language and shared his ambitions to conquer what trials this primitive land threw at him. In our own time he had dated my cousin Beth, a creative, sensible woman. Now he had no other recourse but to court me, with twenty-two years of medieval peril looming before us. And I recognized the awful truth, though I longed for a far different partnership. I would likely marry Joel, yet I would always love Augustin.

On New Year's Eve, Count von Meldorf took Freia and me to a party for the nobility at the Bayern castle, hosted by the Prince and his Lady. All of the lords of the estates surrounding Muniche were present along with their families, as well as the masters of the major industries within the city, including the grain mill, the sawmill, the breweries, and the ironworks. Master Denlinger found Freia and me soon after we arrived, the palace servants taking our coats and ushering us into the grand halls decked out in splendor for the holiday. I had not been inside the Bayern castle since that Sunday afternoon when I had played the organ; that day, the halls had been still and dark, hardly a soul to be found anywhere. Now every chandelier glowed brightly, torches lit at every doorway, streamers decorating every ceiling, sweet incense curling upward from the mantle of each fireplace. Music floated from chamber to chamber, festive sounds of pipes, fiddles and lutes, making me want to dance. As Freia and I entered one of the main halls bearing a wide indoor balcony and double staircase at one end, I cast my gaze around the entire chamber, taking in each nobleman and noblewoman chatting in cliques. I smiled to myself at the memory of my father's parties with his business associates. The behavior of the wealthy had not changed in one thousand years.

Freia and I stood talking with Master Denlinger and the count, commenting and laughing at the Christmas holidays and the well-dressed nobility around us. Count von Meldorf had dressed up for the party and looked rather stiff, complaining that he preferred to wear simple clothing like his vassals, scratching at his recently-trimmed beard in annoyance. Freia and I both wore new dresses, hers a deep green trimmed with white lace, mine maroon velvet, tight-sleeved with black ruffles around the neckline and wrists, the skirt dragging the floor behind me. I also wore a pair of my mother's gold earrings and one of her gold necklaces along with my locket in an attempt to make a decent impression on the other ladies. The men I could ignore, since Joel, a common laborer, was not present. As for Augustin, I had no idea whether he would deign to show his face or not, and if I decided to acknowledge him, I knew that my public status would spiral to the floor once more.

A hush fell over the crowd rather suddenly as we all snickered at a comment Master Denlinger had made. Everyone turned their attention to the balcony at the far end of the room, where Prince Otto and Lady Maria now stood to address their company. Both of them were clothed elegantly, decked with jewelry galore, and I noticed that the Prince's scant beard had begun to thicken finally. "On behalf of myself and my family, I bid all of you a hearty welcome and prosperous New Year," Prince Otto began, spreading his arms out toward us. He continued speaking for several minutes and I blocked it out almost immediately, lifting my eyes instead to his companion Maria, the Lady of Muniche. I studied her expression as the Prince talked, trying to discern what she really thought of him, this young child who could have been her son. It must be difficult for her, I decided, having been married to his father, now thrust together with this young boy, her new

Keyholder, not related to her by blood but obviously not interested in her as a lover.

When the Prince finished, stepping back slightly, the Lady Maria addressed us next, thanking all of us for our loyalty to her city and our people, expressing hope that we would continue to serve Muniche well in the future. Her love, I could tell from her words, was for Muniche alone, not for the child who held the keys. Everyone's attention turned to Paulus, who stood to the left of the Prince, clothed in the simple brown robe of the Catholic clergy, his tenor voice asking us gravely to remember the reason for the holiday and give God the glory for our success. My eyes remained on Maria as Paulus spoke, studying her face's pinched expression. I realized unexpectedly that I pitied her and her fate, which she had not been able to choose. Hans had once said that being the Lady of a Teuton city was a privileged position, but looking at Maria, I began to doubt that.

After Paulus finished speaking, there was a short pause, and I looked back at Prince Otto, who glanced this way and that, his expression slightly perturbed. He took one step forward, placing his hands on the rail of the balcony, and said, "Well, my lords and ladies, if that is all, you may—"

"That is *not* all." Augustin's voice cut sharply into the Prince's farewells as he appeared rather abruptly on the balcony, striding forward with confidence to address the crowd himself. My heart pounded at the sight of him, standing above us with his family, dressed as elegantly as them, jewelry included, half of his hair pulled back, his expression appraising as he looked down at everyone. He *had* the looks, and he had my heart.

A tense silence filled the hall while he eyed the guests; his mouth turned upward just a bit when he saw me in the crowd. "As the eldest man of the Bayern family, I am pleased to thank all of you again for your diligence, your loyalty, your service, and your Teuton blood. On behalf of myself and my mother, I welcome you to this celebration, wishing every man and woman a prosperous New Year, abundant with pleasure and glory. I hope that, in spite of our company"—his eyes turned to his right, resting for an instant on the Prince—"you shall fully enjoy yourselves this night." Augustin nodded once at everyone, then disappeared into a doorway to the right of the balcony. The Prince glared after him as I struggled to hold in mocking laughter.

Moments later, we all drifted toward the dining rooms, the tables heaped with delicacies fit for royalty, from roasted swans, geese, and steaks to the usual sausages, along with countless cheeses, fruit preserves, salads, steaming rolls, pastries, and, to my surprise, salted herring imported from Italy. Bottles of wine and tankards of beer stood ready to quench guests' thirst, and I took a glass of French wine along with some herring, fruit, and cheeses to serve as my dinner.

I attached myself to a group of noblewomen including the Ladies Adeline and Hildegard, and Freia occupied herself with Master Denlinger. I smiled and laughed with the women while I nibbled my victuals, and inevitably the conversation turned to Augustin von Bayern's short speech. All of my companions asserted that Augustin's conduct had been positively rude, interrupting the Prince's farewell and belittling him with his final comment. "But have you heard what he did just two weeks ago?" the Lady Hildegard questioned as the ladies around me bristled at his demeaning behavior.

I had a feeling that I *had* heard, and I froze just a bit while the others shook their heads, prompting Lady Hildegard to relate her gossip in a low voice. "Late one night after the city gates had been locked, that wretched man broke into this castle and caught his majesty unawares, demanding a key to one of the gates so he could let one of his harlots out of Muniche."

My eyebrows came together at this label—*his harlot? Me?* The other ladies gasped, and Lady Hildegard went on, "The Prince refused, and his wicked brother struck him in the face, knocking him to the ground, nearly breaking his jawbone, I heard. Then he pilfered the key ring from the

Prince's belt as he lay unconscious, stealing one of the keys and throwing the ring into his majesty's wounded face."

The other ladies exclaimed in horror, and I frowned, certain that it could not have been *that* bad. I had counted just past four hundred before Augustin had reappeared from the castle that night, which would not have given him enough time for a knock-down, drag-out fight. One of the younger, unmarried ladies asked who the offending woman had been, whether any of the night guards had recognized her, prompting me to freeze once more. But the Lady Hildegard waved her bejeweled hand absently. "Who knows, and who cares, my dear? That horrible lord takes a new harlot every night, and he sacrifices all of them one by one."

This was getting ridiculous. "He can't possibly do that *every* night," I said, speaking for the first time. "He must sleep, sometime."

Lady Hildegard chuckled at me, her gray eyes twinkling with foreboding. "My dear Lady Swanhilde, demons never sleep," she reminded me. I stared after her as she drifted away with the rest of the group, several of them commenting that it was high time for a dance. A moment later, a strong hand clapped down upon my right shoulder, and I turned to face Augustin himself.

"Why the dreary countenance? This is a party." He eyed me, concerned.

I shrugged, and he lifted his hand from my shoulder. "They were just . . . talking about you . . . ." I glanced at the retreating ladies, disgruntlement filling me.

Augustin's lips parted into his familiar smirk. "If you continue to pay me heed in public, they will talk about you next," he said. I shrugged again, prompting him to nod sagely. "Come then. I have something to show you."

Chapter Thirty:
A Memorial

As I followed Augustin toward the darker hallways of the castle, I related what Lady Hildegard had said and asked him what had really happened that night. "I found the Prince shortly after entering the castle, reading a scroll before the fireplace in the library," Augustin said. I struggled to keep up with him as he threaded his way through the dimly lit corridors. "I told him in no uncertain terms that I required the key to the eastern gate. Instead of granting me what I needed, he plied with questions. I had no time for that, for I had promised to attempt to save a woman in childbirth that night. Therefore, I acted in the most efficient way possible."

We had approached a narrow staircase, and I followed Augustin downward, practically tripping on my long skirt. "So you punched him in the face?"

Augustin chuckled and paused at the bottom of the stairway to reach for my hand. His eyes glowed with fire to light the way through the basement corridors. I took his hand, and he answered, "Yes, I did, but I did not break his jawbone, nor did I cast the key ring into his face after I had located the correct key. I hit him sharply once and he summarily fell upon the floor, knocking himself out cold, I might add. I returned the key after I had finished with the dying woman and locked the gate once more. I found the Prince in the library still, the time then far past Vigils. He sat in his chair by the fire, his Lady pressing a wet cloth to his cheek, his entire body sagging, frightened, oppressed."

Augustin stopped short in front of a plain wooden door, placing his free hand upon the knob and turning to face me. His eyes still gleamed a fervent blue, looking spectacular in the dark. "Those keys, my lovely Swanhilde, are a curse. Just because his brother had taken one of them without his permission, he sat unable to move, unable to think, scared to death for his key, his gate, his city. In his distress he found comfort only in his Lady, a forty-four year old woman with whom he could never mate. What a piteous life he leads." Augustin's upper lip curled into a snarl, and his right hand tightened around my fingers.

I considered his words for a moment, recalling the look on the Lady Maria's face while Prince Otto spoke his discourse, the absence of feeling, the unwanted devotion. *Unending Faithfulness at Indescribable Cost.* The inscription on that painting in my elderly mentor's apartment surfaced in my mind, and I shivered once at the chains that bound Lady Muniche's heart to her Keyholder, no matter who he was. But I had another question to ask before Augustin opened the wooden door in front of us. "Did you tell the Prince why you needed the key?" I remembered Lady Hildegard's explanation: *to let one of his harlots out.* If Augustin's typical candor had triumphed in this situation, it could spell trouble for me.

He drew me close to his chest and reassured me, "I told him that one of my female guests had overstayed her welcome and needed to depart the city for the night. I did not mention your name." He smiled caustically and released me, then added, "My excuse disturbed the Prince, for he demanded the reason I had not kept the woman at my cottage for the night, like I usually do."

I took one step backward, thinking of another of Lady Hildegard's assertions: *he takes a harlot every night.*

Augustin's acerbic statement did not seem to nullify her declaration, and I wondered what that would mean for me. How had I agreed to let this man bind me to him if he continued to run around with local whores? A trickle of depression began to seep into my veins at the potential repercussions, but I realized that Augustin awaited my comment on his admission. "Well, I'm glad you didn't tell him your whore was me." I curled my lip at him. "What did you say, when he asked why you hadn't kept the woman at your cottage?"

Augustin grinned rather wickedly and glanced once at the door, then looked back at me. "I told him that I had not treated the woman in the usual way. I told him that I had achieved a glorious union that night that he would never experience himself." He laughed a throaty laugh, his eyes shining with conquest.

I had an inkling that the Prince would know exactly to what Augustin had referred, since he also was a Teuton priest. "What did he say to that?"

"He was quite displeased, for he shall never feel a loving heart in his hands with that decrepit replacement as his Lady." Augustin snickered again and stroked my heart in the same moment, likely relishing its tenderness. "I told him that by accepting those wretched keys, he will never know the glory I have found."

I shook my head at my proud priest, rolling my eyes at the animosity that seemed inevitable for the Bayern family. "You really hate your brother," I noted, feeling a brief wash of sympathy for the Prince, bound to a frigid woman.

The hands of Augustin's spirit hardened around my heart, and he rebuked me. "None of that. The Prince needs no commiseration, for he chose his destiny himself. And yes, I do hate him, and here tonight I shall show you why." He turned the knob of the door before us and opened it with a flourish, ushering me inside.

The room beyond the door was small, the walls and floor made of stone, one ornate stained glass window high up near the ceiling across from the entrance. I studied the window for a long moment before looking around the room, seeing that it depicted Christ clothed in white robes, His spread arms revealing the scars in His hands, a light yellow halo adorning His head. I marveled at its design, as well as the fading light of evening seeping through its panes, the room taking on the strange hues of its reflections.

When I finally lowered my gaze to the chamber itself, I discovered that we stood inside a tiny chapel hidden away in the basement of the Bayern castle. A few steps to my right stood an altar draped with a soft purple cloth that cascaded to the floor. Upon the altar stood two intricate wooden crosses and several unlit candlesticks. A beautiful tomb made of black and white marble rested against the wall beyond the altar, and above it, upon the wall, I saw an image of Marelda von Bayern painted peaceful and fair. She wore a gorgeous blue gown, her raven hair curling down around her shoulders, her smile vibrant with youth, her eyes the exact same color as Augustin's.

My mouth fell open, and my ice cooled my veins as I realized that he had brought me to his mother's chapel, her final resting place. Augustin had closed the door behind us and stood nearby, watching me. I knew I should say something, but my voice had left me in the stillness of the chapel. When I finally managed to pull my gaze away from the magnificent likeness of Marelda von Bayern, I saw a single candle burning upon her marble tomb, its wax appearing old and worn, its flame a brilliant blue. *For a solid year following her death, I spent my days in her chapel . . . my own blue candle of memoriam burning always . . . .* It burned still, after twenty-two years, the only light in the room save the fading light of day. He must think of that tiny flame always, somewhere in his heart, or it would have gone out long ago . . . keeping her memory alive through his element, through his fire . . . .

Augustin moved slowly past me to lift each candle from the altar and light them individually, reverently. The room brightened enough for me to read the Latin inscription upon Marelda's tomb: *CMXCVII–MXXII. Marelda Louise von Förster und von Bayern, Lady of Muniche. Precious Daughter, Dedicated Wife, Devoted Mother. May your memory never fade.* Beneath this stood several Bible verses proclaiming the glory of the resurrection.

Tears had begun to leak from my eyes. I brushed them away, ordering myself not to weep for this woman I never knew, to stop thinking of my own mother, the woman whose undying influence had made me who I was. Augustin gently touched my shoulder, sensing my grief, his voice soft as he began to speak at last. "I have spent countless hours over the years in this chapel, weeping and stretching myself upon her coffin. I have prayed to her here, begging her to watch over me from heaven, to whisper to me in my agony, just a breath against my cheek. I still come here from time to time, though no one else in my family does so. I remember her best, her beautiful smile, her gentleness, her love . . . . For many years she has been my life, my everything. My heart and soul died when she did."

I lifted my gaze to Augustin's face and took him into my arms as I saw the emotion working his jaw, his eyes staring blankly, the fire gone from them. I held him against my breast while he sank to his knees, sobs shaking his body, his hands clutching the folds of my dress. I stroked his hair tenderly, my own sorrows having fled, replaced by an innate desire to soothe this wretched child whose mother's death had driven him insane. "Hush, now, hush, my darling," I whispered to him, his sorrow enclosing my own heart. "She is here with you, always, and she loves you. Be still." I kissed his hair, wishing to grant him some of my strength, to give him hope, though he did not want it.

Eventually Augustin raised his tear-stained face from my chest, shaking his head slowly back and forth, his eyes shut against the pain, his hands still clinging to my clothing. "What would she think of me now," he muttered, his voice sounding like he had scraped his throat with metal, "if she saw who I have become? A ruler, the leader of her people, that is what she wanted. But I have become a wraith, a heartless devil, a murderer, a rapist, a soulless beast."

I knelt down beside him, taking his face in my hands, looking into his eyes as he blinked his tears away. "You don't have to be this way, Augustin," I told him, brushing the tears from his face with my fingers. "You can choose to do right, to be a good leader, like she wanted. But to do that, you *must* let go of your hatred."

His face began to harden, prompting me to rush ahead before he could cut me off. "*I* know about this, Augustin, as much as you. I don't know how much you saw in my memories, but I was five when my own mother died giving my brother life. It took me *years* to accept what had happened, to try to move on, to honor her memory properly, to do what she wished, to learn about Teutons despite my father's dislike for such things. Look at what happened to *him!*" The words tumbled from my lips and Augustin gawked at me, his expression suggesting that I had turned into a demon myself. "After my mother died, my father started hating everything to do with Teutons, with our people. He never wanted me to learn about Teuton history, Teuton traditions, because he feared it would kill me like it killed my mother. He buried himself in his work, despising his blood, forgetting what's really important in life. Augustin, you don't want to be like that!"

When I fell silent at last, Augustin answered me, his sorrow having fled, his odium returned with a vengeance. "I cannot forgive him, no matter how much you would bleed for it. Wuotan would not allow it, for my hatred fuels my service to him, reinforces the power he has granted me. And you should remember, Swanhilde, that *your* brother paid the price for his sin—with his life." Malice dripped from his words, his fingers harsh upon my heart.

I wrapped both of my arms around my chest at his ferocity, crouching on the purple drape decking Marelda's altar, agonizing memories tearing me apart. I saw Dane in the hospital bed gasping for breath, crying for a relief that would never come. How could Augustin throw *this* in my face without regret, without sympathy? How could he think to compare *this* with his own brother, the Prince, proud and haughty, raised to prominence as a result of Maria, "the replacement"? He did not move to comfort me in my anguish. In fact, he had risen from the floor and stood several steps away from me at the edge of the altar, his fiery eyes livid, his arms crossed. Choking on my tears, I managed to say, "I . . . I never . . . hated my brother. I *could* not . . . I *love* Dane . . . even today . . . ."

"That is because you are a woman." Augustin's unfeeling voice clawed at my soul, his hands grasping my heart so fiercely that I almost felt physical pain. "You women cling to love as the answer to all wrongs, the triumph over evil. Your heart is soft, while mine will forever be a hard stone, unforgiving, unyielding."

"But you weep for her still," I reminded him, lifting my head to meet his eyes, blinking my tears away. "Just a moment ago, I held you while you cried for your mother. You have *not* forgotten how to love, or you would not have brought me here to face your grief . . . Augustin."

My bitter priest stared down at me, the anger gradually seeping out of his eyes, his hands caressing my heart more tenderly now. "It is too late for me to change, Swanhilde," he murmured, regret tingeing his words. "I have been this way for two decades. No hope remains for Augustin von Bayern."

I shook my head at him and blinked away the last of my tears. "In spite of who you are and what you've become, *I* will love you, Augustin," I promised him, holding his gaze. "If everyone in this world shuns you, casts you aside, I will forgive you and love you still."

Augustin blinked at me, his expression bewildered. He turned away to look toward Marelda's image. "I came here before I created our union," he confessed to me, his eyes now on the blue flame of his ever-burning candle. "I needed to ask her permission, and her help. I told you— weeks ago, in the archives—that the heart-bond of the Teutons is formed of love. I was afraid I could not achieve it . . . without love in my heart. But as I knelt here, begging for her counsel . . . I felt an assurance grow within my soul

. . . that it *could* be done in spite of myself. My mother would have wanted it." Augustin paused to favor me with an uncertain smile, the emotion of his admission softening my heart. "She likes you," he murmured, "because you are the first to have loved me since she left this world."

I shivered all over. Contentment flooded my veins at my bond with this sinful Teuton priest, the one who depended on me for love, I abruptly realized. "I guess I *was* supposed to come here . . . twenty years too early," I mused, finally feeling at peace with the workings of the Torstein, bringing me to 1044.

Augustin's smile widened, and he knelt on the cloth in front of me, sliding one hand down the side of my face, cradling my chin. "Fate shall always bring us to the places we *should* be . . . blissful or damned," he whispered. "You have brought light into my dark world, Swanhilde." He leaned forward to kiss me gently on the forehead, the heat of his lips making me tremble.

I smiled at him and reached up to stroke his face, feeling the contrast of ice upon fire. "So I'll have twenty-two years to teach you love."

"Yes, assuming you do not take yourself away from me prematurely, as she did." He glanced again at his mother's picture and then stared into my eyes, his fiery ones alight with importunity. "You must not die, Swanhilde . . . not until I allow it. Please, my darling . . . I will make it easy for you . . . you must let me do it." His pleading eyes begged for my understanding, my acquiescence. I nodded at him helplessly, unable to speak. A moment later he kissed me, his lips gentle, his arms wrapping around me, his fingers running through my hair.

When we broke apart, I felt my heart racing at his affection, desperately wanting more of his touch, more of his taste. My eyes locked with his, and my fingers traced his face as he watched me, sensing my emotions, his eyes glowing more brightly. Before I could tell myself to stop, I pulled his face to mine, pressing my lips against his urgently, gasping while I thrust my hands into his hair. His strong arms wound around me, bending me backward until my shoulder blades rested upon the altar. Suddenly, he backed away from me, tearing my feeble arms from their hold, his eyes wide with shock and lust, his tongue slowly dampening his lips. "My darling . . . ." His voice was low, husky. "I do not know . . . if this is the proper place . . . for that." He glanced around at the chapel as he spoke.

I came to my senses then and mentally smacked myself. *You idiot . . . you promised yourself that you wouldn't tempt him this way.* "You're driving me mad," I scolded him as I got to my feet, trying to steady myself.

Augustin rose to his feet himself, straightening his garments. "That is my intention," he informed me with a wicked grin. "We had better rejoin the party, however, or all of your noble acquaintances are going to assume that we have been having sex in one of the bedrooms." He glanced toward the door, still grinning.

"Good point." I looked down at my own clothing, smoothing out the wrinkles. "Do I look decent enough to present myself to the aristocracy once more?"

"You look beautiful," Augustin replied simply, his eyes appraising me once. "Now we must go, and we should reenter the halls separately to avoid suspicion." I nodded in agreement, following him to the exit and taking his hand once more. He extinguished the flames of all of the candles save his eternal one before shutting the door to the chapel behind us. "I shall wish to dance with you later," he added while we wove our way through the clammy basement halls en route to the staircase. "Everyone in attendance tonight is primarily of Teuton blood, so there should be extensive elemental dancing following the meal."

I exclaimed in surprise at this, for as yet I had never been to any sort of party at which everyone had danced with their elements, not even at the Teuton festivals of München. Excitement filled my heart at such a prospect, and I could hardly wait. "Will they be dancing inside?"

Augustin snorted at me as we ascended the staircase to the main floor. "Of course not. This castle has an extensive backyard, my darling. I shall find you there later, when you have finished mingling with your peers."

Much later, after drifting from group to group, chatting, laughing, eating, gossiping, and listening to the festive music, I made my way to one of the massive balconies that overlooked the Bayern back gardens, replete with trees, bushes, and vines. A fresh coating of snow dusted the ground, giving the entire scene a white tranquility, reflecting the argentine glow of the waxing moon. I cast my gaze toward the fountains, three of them, architecturally elaborate and entirely frozen, their ice calling to me along with the snow. A frosty breeze from the Alps in the distance caught my hair while I leaned against the stone wall of the balcony, wearing no coat or hat but feeling no cold, an icy blue perfecting my vision.

I ran my gaze over the entire yard and saw that Augustin had indeed been right. Although most of the guests remained inside, huddling close to the blazing fireplaces, three couples danced upon the grounds below me, leaping and flying. I watched each duo in turn. A man of earth whirled with a woman of air, sprinkling dust upon her billowing brown hair. A man of energy raced with incredible speed, chased by a woman of yellow fire, her grasping fingers enflamed. One woman, her body dripping with unfreezing water, bounded upward like a fountain, seeming at first glance to be dancing with no partner. But when I gave her my full attention, I finally caught a glimpse of her partner skulking in the shadows—a man of darkness, almost invisible, engulfing her with his element, turning her water black.

My ice within me sensed Augustin's presence long before he touched my shoulder, but I was too engrossed in the other dancing Teutons to acknowledge him at first. "And what is the purpose of standing here in stasis?" His deep voice pulled me from my reverie, and I turned to face him. His eyes burned bright, the ends of his black hair smoking, his proffered hand a luminous blue. "Let us join them."

I needed no further invitation; I threw caution aside and drew my ice to the fore. It crusted my hair and fingers in frigid perfection, so I grinned, expelling one frozen breath before taking Augustin's flaming hand. We leapt from the balcony an instant later and began our dance.

I do not know how long we danced in elemental glory, but I do know that it was the most amazing dance I had ever experienced at that point in my life. We whirled together with no barriers, holding nothing back. I grabbed the ice in every fountain, gathering its crystals into a veil to surround my head. Augustin set bushes aflame, melting my icy creations while I doused his flaming ones.

We joined the others at one point to dance in a merry group. The water-woman and I attempted to vanquish one another, her unfreezing water beating vibrantly against my ice as we laughed at our failures, our equality. Augustin had a good-natured competition with the yellow-fired woman, each of them throwing their flames at one another, their primary colors duking it out while they chortled together. I had never seen Augustin enjoy himself so much, dancing with no anger, no hatred, only glory and beauty. He was a Teuton, the same as me, and I would always love him.

As our elemental vitality diminished, we drifted away from the others, and Augustin led me beneath the brown grapevines of the Bayern vineyard. I trailed him with a broad grin, my Teutonic nature reveling in the magic it claimed. When we halted in a snug copse, Augustin lifted my right hand with his left and turned my palm upward, bringing his right hand toward it, holding a fist-sized blue flame. The fingers of his left hand warmed my blood as I stared at his small fire, cringing at the realization that he planned to set it upon the palm of my hand. "I can't do that," I said, my ice coursing faster through my veins in self-defense. "I'm not fire. It may burn me."

"My fire will not burn you, my swan princess," Augustin murmured, his left hand rubbing my fingers. "I belong to you, as you belong to me. If I could give you my heart, as you gave me yours, I would. But you can imagine this flame as my heart, granted to you, with all of its wickedness and hatred. It is yours." Carefully, he set the flickering blue flame upon my right palm. It flared as it merged with my icy hand, taking on the shape of a beating heart.

I gaped at it in amazement, sensing its heat, its life. I drew it cautiously to my chest and called my icy spirit forth to welcome it, to allow it to warm me, to complete me. The flame vanished, and heat flooded my veins for a fleeting moment, filling my soul with something new, something alien—*fire*. Lifting my gaze to Augustin's, I exhaled one hot breath of smoke, cerulean flames smoldering on the edges of my vision before my ice reclaimed my spirit.

Augustin smiled at me, looking satisfied, and he raised his head to the sky. "It is the new year, 1045," he commented, appearing content.

That reminded me of something. "Happy birthday," I said, with feeling.

"You remembered." I nodded, and he smiled again before taking my hand and leading us back to the castle. "You are the best present I have ever received," he complimented fondly, prompting my heart to flutter with joy.

In spite of my preoccupation, I noticed, when Augustin and I reentered the castle, that Prince Otto now stood on the very balcony upon which I had watched the Teuton dancers, staring down at us in horror and envy.

Chapter Thirty-one:

Further Studies

Shortly after the new year began, a huge blizzard hit Muniche and the surrounding countryside, snowing in the entire community for two weeks as people from all walks of life worked to remove almost ninety centimeters of snow. I helped the vassals clear paths on the count's estate on the first day, using my element to hold back the cold. I also worked to improve my efforts at blood control, imagining its life-giving flow pulsing through each artery in my fingers while I struggled with the hefty loads of snow. Count von Meldorf requested that I remain inside afterward, for he opined that such work should not be done by noblewomen.

I complied grudgingly and joined Freia in the kitchen during the following days, boiling cider and baking bread for the workers, who took regular breaks in the great hall to warm up before the roaring fireplaces. I spent my free time studying Ælte Teutonica by firelight, pondering my relationships with Augustin and with Joel. Neither of them managed to visit while Muniche slowly emerged from the blizzard, so I had a fair amount of time alone to consider the ultimate outcomes of both relationships.

The matter of Augustin von Bayern plagued me as I sensed his hands upon my heart during our separation. I had gone too far with him already, giving him my heart, allowing myself to love him. Though I had brought a resourceful, hard-working outsider on my eleventh century expedition, my heart now belonged to a wicked Teuton priest, and it could conceivably remain his for the next twenty-one years. My actions with Augustin had been downright absurd. I could not bring him back with me; once I returned to the year 2000, he would be dead for some 900 years. I would never again be able to grasp this fleeting glory, this infernal desire, this unprecedented companionship.

Meanwhile, Joel had made it quite clear through his actions that he wanted us to form a traditional partnership and meet all primitive trials as a team. During the Christmas holidays, we had talked about renting a cottage in the city while he continued to advance in his metalworking, about buying a pair of horses and setting off to see all that medieval Europe had to offer, about asking the count to hire Joel as a vassal so we could build a family together on the Meldorf estate. Though my heart rebelled at the mere idea of forsaking Augustin for an outsider, I knew that in the end I would have no choice. Joel and I were here to become a part of history until the Teuton people fell to the Saxons. I suspected that if he expressed interest in some local maiden, I would react the same way he had when he learned of my study sessions. To protect our perilous secrets, the two time travelers from the future needed to remain together, our preferences be damned.

I seldom saw Joel or Augustin during the months of January and February due to the wintry weather. Once the snow had melted enough to travel safely, another blizzard would hit, dumping an extra batch of precipitation upon what already coated the ground. When Joel did manage to visit, we played in the snow together, building snowmen and sledding down a hill on the count's estate. Augustin called on me three times during those long months, complaining that I should be the one to visit him, since my ice should give me some advantage with the cold. We kept our conversations focused on languages, his English improving steadily while I struggled with Ælte Teutonica.

On the first Monday in March, I rode the count's tan mare to Muniche for the first time since the Prince's party, her hooves clopping softly on the slush mixed with dirt on the streets. After eating lunch with Joel outside the ironworks, I rode to the town hall and tethered the horse there for the afternoon, pointing my feet toward the archives. I found Augustin at his writing desk, clothed in priestly robes, his blue-flamed candlestick granting him light enough to work. He seemed surprised at my presence, and I explained that I wished to peruse the shelf on Teutonic traditions again, since my Ælte Teutonica had improved. He waved me away with a nod, insisting that I call him if I required assistance. Moments later, I located the small book on the introduction of Christianity, one that I had found when I visited the archives as a spirit. I sat upon the nearby cloth stool and scoured the ancient writing from its very beginning by the azure light of the chandelier.

Augustin approached me shortly after Muniche's church bells began to toll for Vespers, signaling the close of the workday. He asked what I had found, a curious smile curling upon his face. I answered that I had read quite a bit on the early days of our people and the changes that were made to tradition after the Christian missionaries had reached us. "It never really occurred to me that the missionaries would not have had the Bible yet, in that era. It makes sense, then, that several of the writings on this shelf relate the story of Christ's crucifixion and resurrection." I returned the tome I had been scrutinizing back to its place before stepping out of the aisle to address Augustin again. "The Teuton scholars from centuries ago went to a lot of trouble to justify the state of our blood."

Augustin chuckled at my observation, his face grim. "Yes, we were Wuotan's people since time immemorial until those Christian missionaries cast their spell upon us. Wuotan has never forgiven us for deserting him, and he disapproves of our continued use of his gifts, now that we no longer call him our god. That is why it is difficult for Teuton women to have children. Our demon lord would doubtless stanch the infernal source of Teuton blood, if he had the authority to do so."

My eyes widened, and a strange chill crept into my chest. "So . . . does that mean that Teuton blood isn't fully . . . human?" I shivered.

"No one alive today knows the terms of our people's agreement with him," Augustin replied, his eyes reflecting the crackling flames upon the chandelier. "As for Wuotan's fiery river of blood, I can merely speculate on its true source. We both know that outsiders are not naturally granted the aptitudes innate to us."

"And Wuotan doesn't make it easy for us to have children . . . because he fears that if we multiply like other races, we'd . . . what? Incite an invasion into his fiery kingdom?" I wrinkled my forehead and rubbed my chin, trying to envision how a battalion of mortals could pose a threat to a fallen angel.

Augustin sighed and looked toward the exit, the fire having left his eyes, an abyssal darkness cloaking him instead. "His reasons are his own; he has yet to share them with me. But the continuation of Teuton blood comes at a price far beyond what most of our people recognize." He fell silent for a moment, as though gathering his courage, and the truth clicked into place in my mind in the instant that he spoke it. "Wuotan has demanded blood in return each time my efforts to preserve Teuton women in labor extend beyond the medical aspect. In years past, I offered him animals, but his demands increase with every Teuton born."

I could not think of how to answer him for a long while, my mind reeling at the implications of what Augustin claimed. *If a Teuton priest had offered human blood upon the altar when my Mutti labored with my brother . . . would she have lived?* "It's not like that every time," I said, willing it to be true. "It can't be. Teuton priests in the future don't sacrifice people to Wuotan, and children are born every day." I could not imagine Hans committing such an atrocity.

"His reasons are his own," Augustin repeated, the candlelight showing his face to me at last. He looked pained but determined. "Since my return to Muniche two winters ago, I have saved thirty-three women and twenty-nine children. Only eight have been lost; thus, my efforts are not in vain, despite what the murderer and his faithful cronies think of me."

I thought long and hard about Augustin's statements after I returned to the manor, trying to balance the situation of the Teuton people on the scales of my mind. Wuotan could not possibly require blood in return every time a Teuton was born. That had to be a lie he told to his faithful servant, the one his family had cast aside. I asked Freia's opinion on it, and she looked stricken when I rehashed Augustin's true reasons for his blood sacrifices. "God oversees the miracle of birth," she said, "though I suppose that devilish forces could work to sabotage it."

"And demons can be in only one place at a time," I put in, my gaze on the moonlit fields outside our window. "Maybe Wuotan has it out for one Teuton child per day. It can't be the only thing he spends his time doing."

"He may not work alone," Freia postulated, which prompted me to curl into a tight ball beneath my blanket, my earlier fears of bearing children in this crude era returning with a vengeance. *But I should be fine if I marry Joel,* I reassured myself, *because his plain blood would render our children below Teutonic levels. Wuotan should have no qualms about kids less than fifty percent, even though he holds a grudge against me.*

As the land slowly emerged from winter's chill, Freia and I spent more time outside helping tend the gardens. An undercurrent of eagerness swept through the entirety of the estate. Everyone shared predictions on the year's harvests, and the servant girls exulted about the return of fresh herbs and honey to the daily meals. Joel stayed at the Meldorf manor for the entirety of the Easter holidays, chatting with various servants in hopes of learning more tidbits about medieval farming. On Sunday afternoon, we sat together in the grass beside the stream, the blossoms of the cherry tree suffusing the cool air with the scent of nascent rebirth. "I'm trying to get up the courage to talk to Count von Meldorf about . . . about us," he admitted at length, his gaze fixed on the chattering stream before us.

I scooted away from him, an instinctive reaction; we had been sitting against each other with our hands joined. My heart rate increased in a rebellious manner, and I chewed on the inside of my cheek as I ordered myself to look at my twenty-first century partner. "So . . . you're going to ask his permission to marry me? You think that's really necessary?"

His ears flushed with crimson, and he rubbed his sandy beard and heaved a sigh. "I mean . . . not really . . . but if we're going to try to integrate into life here in Muniche for the next twenty years, we ought to play by the rules. Or were you thinking we ought to go the adventurer route instead?" His worried eyes met mine.

I looked down, feeling my own blush rising in my cheeks. "It'd probably be easier and safer to stay here," I noted. "As fun as it sounds to ride here and there, we have to make money somehow, and I don't want to turn to thievery. And we'll be getting older every day, every year. Not sure how simple it'll be to jump on a horse and go from inn to inn the older we get."

"Yeah, I think it'd be best to have a home base of some sort," Joel agreed.

"I really don't think the count will approve our marriage," I said, folding my legs beneath my skirt and tracing the blades of grass with my fingers. "He told me once before that I can do as I wish since I'm not of his blood, but I'm pretty sure he sees Freia and me like family now. He's expressed concerns about her and your boss."

Joel winced a little, then picked up a smooth stone and turned it over several times in his left hand. "Yeah, this whole 'Teuton blood' thing is too much. My boss is still trying to convince his father to allow him to propose to Freia, and he hasn't had much luck yet. We joked last week that maybe we should all run off to the lands to the west—Schwabia, I think he said?—so we can elope and then come back later."

"We'd better wait until it's warmer first," I said, my aversion at the subject growing ever stronger. So I jostled Joel's right shoulder and asked, "I know you're a decent archer, but how are you with a sword? If we're going to run off into the wild for a few months, we'll need all the weapons we can get." Thankfully, he grinned and took up the new subject with enthusiasm, spouting off a diatribe about him and his coworkers practicing with the swords and spears in their spare time.

Augustin traveled to Bamberg for a priestly conference in mid-April, along with a few of Muniche's council members. Apparently the northernmost Teuton city had a rash of ineligible men attempting to achieve the Teuton priesthood, and there was to be a debate and trial to deal with the miscreants. Augustin promised to meet me in the spiritual realm to continue our studies during his absence, and I suggested that we discuss the outcomes of the trial instead. I was morbidly curious to learn whether the ineligible men were simply Teutons less than ninety percent, or whether there was something more sinister afoot. On the Thursday before he left, Augustin pledged to share all of the proceedings with me, his cobalt eyes glittering with mystery.

Chapter Thirty-two

Uncovering the Truth

On the following Tuesday, Augustin surprised me while I sat on the front porch, sharpening my twenty-first century knife on a whetstone that belonged to Jarvis. I was singing a Nightwish song to myself, and suddenly I felt the hands of his spirit enclose my heart. Augustin's mental voice entered my mind a second later, just as I began the chorus to "Gethsemane." *I never knew that you were blessed with an angel's voice, my lovely swan.*

The knife slipped from my hands and sliced my left index finger on its way to my lap. "Dammit, Augustin," I muttered, cutting the song short and diverting my attention to my injured flesh. I focused on the capillaries and the arteries that fed them out of habit, summoning the platelets, tapping into the magic inherent in my other-worldly blood. "You can't just sneak up on me like that when I'm messing with knives."

His laughter tickled my brain, and he observed, *It seems that your skill at blood control has grown quite advanced.*

I narrowed my eyes at my finger as the slice crusted over. Just a few drops of blood had managed to escape before I stemmed the tide; now a fresh scab crept across my knuckle. "I've practiced on the servant girls who sew," I related. They had yet to realize that I was the reason their legs tended to fall asleep while they sat at their work. "And I think that my self-preservation instinct has recognized the practicality of blood magic. All Teutons should be taught how to do it, I think."

You had best keep such thoughts to yourself, Augustin advised, and I raised my head at last to see his spirit sitting upon the bench to my right, the fruit trees visible through the transparent flames that encompassed him. My lips curled into a mocking simper at the sight; it was truly odd to converse with a spirit while caged in my mortality. *Unless you intend to take up your initial plan and get yourself executed as a witch, you must hold all that I share with you in the coming days in confidence*, he added, his flaming eyes shifting over the front gardens.

The conference had begun on Monday and was set to continue all week and into the next, he told me. Three priests from each of the major Teuton cities had gathered, including the Keyholders of Würzburg and Passau. Prince Otto himself should have gone, but Augustin said that he was currently proctoring some land dispute near Freising. Two priests from the council—one of whom was Lady Adeline's husband—had agreed to represent Muniche. Augustin did not say why he was chosen to accompany them, although perhaps his status as the Prince's brother gave him some legitimacy. I wondered whether every Teuton priest in Bavaria knew of Augustin's occult behavior or if that was a secret our city kept to itself.

The problem at hand involved an elderly priest by the name of Blasi. He had a negative reputation in Bamberg already, for he had long sold protective enchantments against witches and ghosts. He had also convinced some of the locals that he could speak with their loved ones who had passed on, bringing messages from God. It surprised me that the authorities had not taken action against such a fraud already, but apparently he had friends in high places. When word got out that he had shared priestly knowledge with a cadre of young men who claimed no elemental control, the local nobility finally decided that enough was enough.

He shared his secrets with five men in total, Augustin informed me the next week, after the gathering of priests had managed to round up all of the guilty parties. *Two were Teutons of low blood, eighty-six and eighty-seven percent. Two were the bastard sons of a Teuton merchant, and one . . . the final one that we had to chase after . . . was found to have Saxon ancestry.*

We drifted together along the stream that day, and my ethereal robes grew peppered with white icy flakes at that last revelation. *You had to chase a Saxon?*

Yes, it was quite the contest. Augustin smiled, the flames decking the base of his robes flickering strangely against the water beneath us. *He fled north of course, but we captured him before he crossed the border. That one will likely be executed when all is said and done. I have already offered my skills if needed.*

Did you bring your axe? I questioned, abruptly wondering whether that was the real reason he had been invited to this conference. Perhaps the priests wanted a skilled executioner among their number.

No, just a sword, Augustin said with a smile, *but I do not yet know which method of execution shall be chosen, if it comes down to that. Our people's hold on Bamberg is tenuous, as you may know from the city's history. One of the Saxon emperors is entombed there, and their local dialect is smoother than Teutonica.*

I wonder if the results of this conference will ruffle some feathers, I mused, my gaze toward the stream's confluence with the Isar, visible just a few hundred meters distant. *If the Saxon man you captured has noble lineage . . . .*

The Emperor knows that Teutons handle private matters themselves. He has enough on his plate already and ought not to involve himself with matters of improper sorcery. Augustin's expression appeared quite confident, but I thought about it in the months to come, silently wondering whether our Teuton kingdom may fall due to our own prejudice—and a few men of lower blood status, shunned for their inquisitiveness. I thought about my cousins Trudi and Traudl, Teutons of eighty-nine percent who had not yet worked out the magic of the spiritual realm. Was there an actual connection between blood status and elemental aptitude, or were the numbers tossed around to divide us?

When Augustin returned to Muniche, we resumed our language studies, and he offered me a few extra tips about blood control. Joel continued to visit on the weekends, our chats shifting toward memories from the future rather than plans for our eleventh century life. He seemed to enjoy reminiscing about cartoons and movies, about the privilege of kicking back in a recliner to enjoy a Phillies game. His mood had grown rather melancholy, as though the concept of two decades in the Middle Ages had finally hit home for him. I told him stories about my life in München and my years with Beth, days spent imagining characters for her novels and enjoying the Ocean City beaches. "Sometimes I really don't know what I'm doing here," he sighed one Saturday evening while we sat upon the porch watching the sunset. "And how I'm supposed to just pick up my old life when we go back."

"You and me both," I said, for sometimes I wondered how my American cousin would react once she learned that I had gotten intimate with her boyfriend nearly a millennium in the past. Joel had not brought up that subject lately, and I was not about to introduce the topic when my heart preferred to rest in Augustin's hands. "We'll probably have to write memoirs once we go back." Joel laughed, and we took turns relating titles for such a record, each more ridiculous than the last.

On a Thursday afternoon in early May, Augustin and I set our studies aside to walk together by the stream, listening to the countless birds chirping, the insects buzzing, the water chattering in response to the warmth of the season. Presently, Augustin placed his arm around my waist as we strolled slowly through the grass, his face appearing content despite his position as the town outcast, the hated son, the bitter murderer. He wore the black robes of the Teuton priest that day, the cape fluttering softly in the breeze, wrapping itself around my back while we walked so close, the heat of his fire warming me, completing me, assuring me again that my true place was with him, not with a well-meaning outsider.

In tranquility, we approached a small dell beside the stream surrounded by oak trees and bushes. I realized that we had walked much farther than usual, past the water mill to the eastern edge of the count's lands. Augustin halted at the small grove and sat down upon the grass, beckoning for me to join him. I sat down facing him, arranging my light blue skirt around my crossed legs, and he began to speak in a soft, serious tone. "I wish to teach you something new today, Swanhilde, something that no Teuton woman has ever been taught, to my knowledge." He had my attention immediately, and my eyes widened in anticipation. Augustin studied my face for a moment, then looked through the bushes toward the stream and continued. "For some reason, I have grown certain over the past several weeks that you ought to know how to do this despite its risks, despite its ghastliness. You need to know how to bleed a person."

I froze at his words, my ice enhancing my vision, my mouth going dry. "But . . . but . . . ." I could hardly speak, and I cleared my throat. "I don't . . . know . . . if I should . . . if I *need* to . . . learn that. I . . . don't like the taste of blood."

Augustin looked at me again, half of his mouth curling upward into a disturbing smirk. "It is an acquired taste. The first time I drank someone's blood, I nearly disgorged. Nevertheless, now that your skills at blood control have improved, you must learn how to properly bleed a person for information. For there will always be some things, Swanhilde, that cannot be understood any other way but through the honest memories of the blood."

I choked on my own breath, horror causing my body to quiver at the thought of bleeding Augustin for information. I remembered each time he had bled me—the pain of his teeth, the weakness that first time when I trod the precipice of death, the innumerable and undeniable truths he had pulled from my blood. What would I possibly see if I managed to succeed, to taste my master's blood in search of his true thoughts, the darkness that led him down a demon's path? "Augustin . . . I . . . I don't . . . *want* . . . to drink blood. I'm not a priest. I don't really . . . see the point."

"It is not an issue of wanting it, my dear, it is an issue of compelling curiosity. I *know* you have wondered what terrible thoughts run through the dark recesses of my brain, and this is your chance to find out." Augustin leaned forward, his eyes glittering in the shade. "I have never once offered to allow anyone to bleed me. It is a privilege I shall grant to *you*, and you alone."

I trembled and scooted away from him, but I knew that he had me there. He would *have* to bring up the subject of curiosity, that madness that drove us both. And I had speculated on his true thoughts and feelings, for he rarely spoke of them. "But how would I know what to look for, in your blood?" I asked him, beginning to give in.

"You need not worry about that. You may simply bleed me, seeking nothing, seeing the thoughts that are most important to me." He rolled his collar down to bare his neck, pushing his black hair back around his ears, his eyes summoning me forward. I crawled slowly toward him and crouched to his right, staring at his face, his neck, bile churning within me at the idea of drinking blood. "You need not fear the taste," Augustin noted, guessing my thoughts. "Once my memories have begun to enter your mind, you will ignore the flavor, the dampness."

I shivered and cautiously reached my hands forward. I placed one of them on the opposite side of his face and touched the artery of his neck with the other, as he had done to me many times before. I felt the blood pounding there, and I bit my lip, thinking that Augustin was about to turn me into a vampire. I looked into his eyes one final time, sliding my left hand from his neck to his shoulder, my curiosity overtaking me, like he had known it would. I inhaled shakily, then voiced my final concern. "What if . . . what if I can't stop . . . ?"

"I shall stop you." Augustin sounded positive. He stared into my eyes, his gaze demanding no objections. "Now do your duty."

I steeled myself, chewed my lip once more, then leaned my face toward Augustin's neck. The scent of his skin and hair enticed me, and I squeezed my eyes shut, opening my mouth and sinking my teeth into his skin. That was the first time I had ever bitten someone, and the texture of his flesh upon my teeth disconcerted me. Just as I began to reconsider, his blood burst into my mouth, the taste utterly repulsive. I would have pulled away immediately . . . but Augustin had clamped his strong right hand upon the back of my head, holding me firmly to his neck, forcing me to drink, to *drink* . . . . I swallowed, my stomach roiling . . . .

. . . And I was a child, four years old, scratching my fingers upon a wooden door, screaming, breaking my nails, splinters piercing my skin. My father ordered that I stop, that I calm down. I could not. The cries coming from inside the room cut my heart like a knife, and I felt fire within me, burning me, burning the door, burning the lock, bursting through, burning my father, burning everything. And I fell upon my knees before my mother's bed, her deathbed, smelling her blood, hearing her gasping breath, watching her body twitch weakly, her skin white and cold. Tears streamed down my cheeks as I grabbed her hand, trying to warm it without burning it, failing, agony, heartbreak, insanity. And she opened her blue eyes one final time, bloodshot, turning white, her lips bleeding, smiling, her voice laden with love, with regret, with death: "Augustin . . . I love you . . . ." Insanity.

. . . Hatred consumed me. I despised my family, all of them, they had forsaken my mother, my love, they hated me, they loved the city, the keys, nothing more. I was twenty-five now, fully engrossed in the dark powers Wuotan offered me. I stood at my father's deathbed, the one who had betrayed my mother for another woman, standing at the foot of his bed, ugly, despicable, her eyes

flashing with distaste for me. I felt no love, no sympathy, only revulsion, knowledge of what was to come, hatred, revenge. My father cast his dying eyes toward me, his feeble hand lifting those dreadful keys weakly from the bed, begging me to take them, their responsibility, their curse. My eyes fell upon that wretched woman, resolution flooded me, I turned back, stating without emotion, "I shall not take them. Give them to the son you love." I left the room, fire consuming my soul as I saw the murderer outside the door, his expression horrified at my sacrilege. Realization broke across his arrogant face while I glared at him, wishing my fire could burn him to cinders. "Now she is yours, with all of her faults." Triumph, vengeance, hatred . . . freedom.

. . . With a feeling of grotesque satisfaction, I watched the keys overwhelm the mind of the murderer, taking away his free will, binding him with a chain of iron to the city, to her Lady. I walked through the halls of the castle, passing by the door to the library where the murderer lurked with the replacement. I watched him caress her cheek, he, her child, and she gazed at him in perverse devotion, the one she lifted up, the one she named Prince, the one she chose over me. They kissed, their lips melding in the madness of the keys. Distaste flooded my soul, the murderer saw me, horror crossed his face, and I laughed, mocking. I am free; he is bound. Odium is my life, sensual pleasure my only glory.

. . . A blinding meteor shoots across my sky, knocking me senseless, twisting my mind, awakening something long dead and buried. A woman, hair like a black waterfall, eyes like the gray sky of morning, delicate, beautiful. Sacrifice her, no, she is a Teuton, I cannot. Rape her, destroy her, enslave her . . . but her intelligence catches me off guard, her insight astonishes me, her education, her insatiable curiosity, her thirst for knowledge . . . her skill with her ice. Shock, she is from the future, she does not belong in my world, yet she has come by accident, to me, to me. She will not heed advice, she disregards gossip, she watches my sacrifice, sees my monstrous pleasure,

she trusts me. She loves me. *Impossible. Only my mother . . . how could she love me, an innocent virgin, knowing my depravity, she loves me still. My heart pounds, the stone breaks, the iron melts in her grasp, she has bewitched me. I kill her, realize I cannot, I need her, she has altered my world, softened my heart, I must save her, she cannot leave me, she cannot die. Her death would ruin me, drive me insane, I would do anything for her, give her anything, my life, my heart, my soul. I love her. I had not thought it possible . . . . Emotion, beauty, contentment, glory. Swanhilde . . .* I love her . . . .

Chapter Thirty-three:
The Aftermath

STOP!!

Suddenly, I found myself falling backward upon the grass, punched harshly in the ribs, my teeth ripped from Augustin's neck. My head spun; my stomach churned; I could not think. My eyes wheeled as I rolled onto my side, clutching my hands to my abdomen and my aching ribs, the deplorable taste of blood still on my tongue, stickiness coating my throat. I could hardly breathe, and I choked, certain that I was about to throw up. I crawled away toward the stream, groaning, finally vomiting a geyser of blood, staining the ground red. My shaking fingers grasped at the grass as I expelled the entirety of Augustin's blood, my stomach rebelling again and again, sending simultaneous waves of pain and sickness through my body.

I finally managed to fall at the edge of the stream, plunging my weak hands into its cool waters, shakily bringing a cupful to my mouth to wash away the taste of vomit and blood. My innards gurgled while I lay before the brook, staring at it blankly, panting, my eyes rolling back, new memories that seemed more vivid than my own overwhelming my mind, tugging at my heart. I wheezed, trying to ignore the sting in my ribs, at last plunging my whole face into the water before me in an attempt to wash away his blood, his memories, his insanity, his soul. Two disturbing images I had seen returned to me over and over, causing me to moan, to squeeze my eyes shut, though I could see, forever.

A wooden splinter, ripping the nail back from my index finger slowly, imbedding itself in the tender flesh underneath my fingernail, the pain nothing compared to those cries seeping through the cracks in the door . . . the knowledge that my mother was dying.

That fascinating Teuton woman with her magnificent ebony hair and inimitable gray eyes, glinting blue with ice. Her smile, the tenderness in her gaze, her solemn promise: "I will love you, Augustin. If everyone in this world shuns you, casts you aside, I will forgive you, and love you still." Her heart in my coarse hands, soft and precious, bleeding with love and goodness, pounding with life, a life Marelda no longer had. Her image, her persona, superseding my love for my mother—becoming my everything . . . .

I could not think of this. How could I have agreed to bleed him if *this* was what I must see? I would never be able to forget, I realized; truths read in blood could never be forgotten. *Augustin loved me.* I had not thought it possible, and neither had he. He had claimed time and time again that he had not been able to love anyone since his mother had left him dreadfully alone to face a cruel and heartless world. He had given himself over to evil, practically selling his soul to Wuotan, offering sacrifices to him without a care, without shame, without remorse. But I had changed him already, in spite of his denial. His memories pertaining to me had rushed so swiftly through his blood that I could not process them until now, while I washed my dirtied face at the stream, struggling to make sense of it all . . . .

I saw my spirit through his twisted mind, alone with him in the archives of Muniche, having fallen entirely into his clutches. I saw his desire to ruin me . . . and I saw it all

336

change in a single instant. I saw myself lift my head at him, my icy eyes filled with challenge as I snatched his birth certificate from his hands and read it perfectly. I saw his confusion when he watched me write those phrases upon his paper, proving myself shockingly literate, a novelty in eleventh century Europe. I saw his suspicion engendered, his unshakeable inquisitiveness when he scoured the archives for my birth records, finding nothing. I saw how desperately he had wanted to drink my blood on the day that I told him the truth, how he wanted to understand *why* I had come, why the future could not hold me. I watched myself through his eyes while we studied languages together, feeling the frailty of my fingers in his hand when he showed me how to grasp the pen, experiencing the madman's lust when I told him that I wished to learn Teuton rituals—on which he was an expert. He wanted to claim me for himself.

I felt his shock and horror when he recognized me, frozen in the waters of the Isar, watching him bite into the heart of his Saxon sacrifice. I felt his frustration, his lust, his anger . . . and something alien to him—*guilt*. I had seen something I should never have seen, and now I would shun him like everyone else in Muniche. He would lose my friendship, my wittiness, my trust. I saw his amazement when I chose to forgive him that day in the parlor, my gray eyes gravely searching his face. And I saw that from that day forward, Augustin would never be able to stay away from me, for in that moment, he had begun to appreciate kindness for the first time in twenty-two years.

I watched him drink my blood during my second visit to the archives, the taste of it sweet and glorious, nothing like the rancid flavor of his. I saw my own memories through his mind, the future, the reason I had come, the rationale for my constant fidelity to him in spite of everything—my attraction, my love. We were the same, having the same past, reacting in opposite ways. I watched him rush to save me, as he reached the horrible realization that he had killed me, that I would leave him forever. I saw him cut his palms and mine, locking our hands together, calling just enough of his fire from his soul to allow him to follow me to death's door—a fatal risk, I saw, for his element had not completely covered his body in protection. *He almost died for me.* I saw the full truth now in his memories that would forever be my own. He had offered his soul for mine, not caring if he killed himself in the process. He loved me. He would follow me anywhere humanly possible. *He loved me so much I could hardly comprehend it . . . .*

How in the world had it come to this?

I raised myself from the grass finally, my breaths steady now as I blinked my eyes, wiping the last traces of water from my face. I shook my head rhythmically and stared across the stream for a long moment, certainty consuming me forevermore: I loved Augustin, and he loved me. Somehow, we had to find a way to be together. There had to be a way.

I stood up, my legs just a trifle shaky, turning away from the stream toward the glade of oaks. And to my dismay, I saw Augustin lying prone on the grass, his skin the color of a ghost, his fingers curled stiff, his eyes shut, the wound in his neck still leaking blood. *You idiot . . . you just killed the man who loved you!* I fled to his side and dropped to my knees beside his unmoving body. "Augustin . . . Augustin . . . my master . . . please . . . no . . . no . . . ." I gasped out my desperate pleas, staring at his face, waiting for some response, anything. Nothing. I could not even tell if he was breathing.

Sobs shook me, and I laid myself down upon his chest. Was I the reason that Teuton history revealed nothing about an Augustin von Bayern? Was it because he was fated to be bled to death by a witch from the future? This could not be; I had to be able to do *something* to save him, but my reason had vanished. All I could do was cry icy tears while clinging to the body of the priest who actually wanted me. I had found and lost my most desperate wish in less than a half hour.

My spirit sensed something approaching in spite of my distraction. When the silvery voice threaded into my ear along the breeze, it extracted me from my morass of mourning. "*Zoubaraera Teutona,* grant him your blood."

I raised my face from Augustin's chest to look toward the base of the largest oak tree in the dell. My elemental vision revealed its silvery sheen; I had misjudged it as a white oak. And its delicate *Eihalbe* hovered several centimeters above one of its creeping roots, its kaleidoscope eyes shifting from mine to Augustin's prone form. I blinked at the fairy, recalling my encounters with similar entities in my own era—each time, they had offered advice. This one said to grant Augustin my blood.

"So . . . he's not dead . . . he's just in shock," I realized, mentally smacking myself for not having thought of that already. I averted my attention to the priest before me and turned his right palm upward, its chill frightening me all over again. It twitched beneath my grasp and I detected a slow, pitiful pulse, weak and uneven. I sighed with relief, silently thanking God that he was not dead yet. But the *Eihalbe* advised that he needed blood, and I had no idea whether I could manage an exchange like he had done for me in the archives. Were my skills at blood control good enough to accomplish such a thing? I had to try.

Hastily, I searched through his pockets and found a knife, double-edged and long, disturbing to look upon. I beat back my fears and turned both of his palms upward, ordering myself to focus. I hiked my skirt up and straddled him, locking my gaze upon his pale face to give me incentive. Then I sliced my right palm first, cringing at the pain, holding the blood back while I shifted the knife to my injured hand to cut my left palm deftly. Then I slit the palms of Augustin's hands and cast the knife away as I pressed my hands upon his, directing my blood to enter his veins, to grant him strength, life, vigor. There was fire in me somewhere, *his* fire, and I sweated, clenching my teeth and ordering it to supplant my ice, to give warmth to my master's corpse. Heat rushed through my veins, so I rolled my eyes back and channeled it into my arms and hands. "Do not doubt yourself. His spirit is within reach." I apparently had gained a mystical cheerleader. I pushed my blood further into Augustin's veins, guiding it up his arms and into his torso.

When I opened my eyes once more, I saw that the *Eihalbe* fluttered much nearer now, its eyes trained upon Augustin's face. It had laid a fresh silver oak leaf upon the wound in his neck, since like a fool I had not thought to heal that first. My focus wavered, but I endeavored to continue picturing our blood and spirits as one, my heart vigorous enough to provide life for us both. I saw that Augustin's skin had begun to return to its natural color. The veins in his neck pulsed once more, and his breathing had improved, the movements of his chest discernable. I felt a wash of relief, and my eyes locked with the *Eihalbe's* for an instant. "Thank you," I whispered in a broken voice.

The silver fairy nodded once toward our joined hands and said, "Respect the price." My lips parted into a look of astonishment as the fairy flitted back to its tree. The *Eihalbe* who had led me to the Torstein back in my era had offered the exact same counsel before departing. Was that some sort of code that the fairies wanted me to break?

I sensed myself growing weak as my blood continued to flow into Augustin's hands. *That's probably what the* Eihalbe *meant, you idiot,* I realized. So I shut my eyes to focus on healing the slices in my hands and in those of the priest before me, slowing the arteries' currents, summoning the platelets. I counted to ten in my mind while I completed my task, then lifted my hands from Augustin's and took a look. Long scabs traced each of my palms from the middle finger down to the wrist, no trace of blood escaping. I glanced down at my master's hands next; they, too, had scabbed over. Sighing in relief, I looked toward Augustin's face and discovered that he was looking back at me, his light blue eyes glinting with surprise.

I threw myself upon him then, cradling his face in my hands, shivering as my ice chased his fire from my spirit. "Oh, Augustin . . . Augustin . . . I'm sorry. I'm so sorry." The words tumbled from my lips, and I caressed his hair, the silver oak leaf slipping from his neck to the ground. "I didn't mean to . . . kill you. I would never . . . . I should have stopped. Can you forgive me?"

His lips parted, unease marring his expression. "You . . . bled me . . . almost . . . to death . . . ." His voice was barely audible, his eyes wide.

I buried my face in his neck, tears coming to my eyes. "I know, I know . . . ."

Augustin's hands touched my sides and back, their familiar power noticeably absent. "It was . . . not your fault. I should have . . . pushed you away . . . earlier. I used . . . the last of my strength . . . to break your hold . . . . Forgive me . . . ."

The feebleness of his arms scared me afresh, and I lifted my head from his neck to meet his gaze. "Are you going to be all right? I gave you some of my blood, but I should have noticed earlier that you were . . . dying. I was so afraid, Augustin, afraid of losing you. I . . . if I had killed you . . . I would never have forgiven myself . . . ." My lips trembled while I spoke, passion layering my words.

Wonder appeared in his light blue eyes as they traveled toward my hands, still stroking his cheeks. "You . . . gave me your blood?"

"I did, but . . . ." My voice trailed off as my gaze darted toward the silver oak tree standing tall amid its cousins, trails of ivy creeping up its trunk. "I kind of . . . lost my mind . . . when I saw you lying here." I bowed my head, shame heating my cheeks. "I didn't realize you just needed blood. I thought you were dead. But there's a silver oak just behind your head . . . and its fairy gave me the push I needed." I saw no trace of the *Eihalbe* now, even with the blue haze of ice sharpening my vision. I lifted my head to look toward its branches bursting with green, lobed leaves in a silvery sheen. Perhaps it was hiding there now, watching and listening.

For some reason Augustin's arms grew taut around me. "I see," he said in a flat voice. I looked back down at his face, taken aback by his distrustful expression. "We ought to move on from here." His arms slid away from me as he shoved himself into an upright position, a trace of pallor crossing his cheeks at the effort.

"We can sit here for a while longer. I might have given you too much of my own blood, actually." I settled onto the grass and leaves at his side, clasping his left hand in both of my own. Its warmth soothed me, and I hoped that meant that his fire had begun to reignite within him.

"Very well." Augustin still appeared discontent, and he leaned forward to retrieve the knife I had tossed aside earlier, slipping it into a pocket in his cloak.

I tried to read the tenseness of his posture, the wariness in his eyes as they ran over the crumbled silver oak leaves strewn across the ground where we sat. "You don't like *Eihalbae*, do you?" I gathered, stroking his hand in an attempt to calm him.

His pale lips curled into a sneer. "It is difficult to 'like' spirits who wish to probe into humanity's private matters." His left hand stiffened in my grip.

"Well, you'd be dead if that one hadn't told me to grant you my blood," I pointed out, his enigmatic response not having resolved my confusion in the slightest.

"Strangely enough, I feel warm despite having lost so much blood," Augustin said, dropping the subject after the manner of a Teuton priest. "Should I attribute this to the icy witch at my side?" He studied my countenance.

He must want to keep his opinions on the *Eihalbae* to himself. Maybe a fairy had criticized his demonic obsessions sometime in years past. So I turned my attention to his question, blushing a little as I met his forceful gaze. "Well, you taught me fire," I reminded him, thinking of that wild New Year's dance.

His eyes widened further, and his left hand flexed to grasp one of mine. "You have become a force to be reckoned with," he said. "Few Teuton women know how to manipulate an element other than their own."

A smile crept across my face. "I had to save you somehow," I confessed. "It was necessary. I saw . . . I saw . . . ." I stumbled over the truth, the startling reality I had seen in this murderer's blood.

Curiosity and trepidation warred on Augustin's face as he pressed, "What did you see . . . in my blood . . . ?"

The myriad of images raced through my mind again, but in this moment, only one stood above the rest. I met his gaze, abruptly fearing that he might deny the truth. "You love me," I whispered.

Tenderness softened Augustin's expression, and he brought his right hand forward to trace it down my face. "Yes . . . somehow . . . I do. I *love* you, Swanhilde . . . my darling . . . my life."

I kissed his mouth in the next moment, relishing the taste of his tongue, the warmth of his breath, the way his arms tightened around me protectively. When we parted, he cradled me against his chest, his right hand moving to rest upon my heart, the heat of his spirit permeating me deep inside. I wrapped my own arms around his neck and ran my fingers through his hair while we stared at each other in shared passion, shared desire. And we kissed again, more ardently this time, our love spilling over, filling our world with color. When we pulled apart after an infinite moment, I sighed, shaking my head at the madness of it all. "Well . . . . This really changes things," I commented, wondering how I could possibly set aside this newfound love, this impossible devotion that threatened to wholly transform my destiny.

Chapter Thirty-four:
Preposterous Plans

We spent the remainder of that afternoon discussing what I had seen in Augustin's blood and trying with increasing desperation to fabricate new plans for our future. Our shared truth had struck us like a bullet between the eyes: our besotted hearts rebelled against the mere idea of going our separate ways either now or in twenty years' time. Augustin informed me at one point that he could not bear to consider the pain he would feel if I forsook him for Joel, even if I did so for convenience alone. His anguish engulfed my heart as I struggled to envision some way to break the ties that bound me to my sole twenty-first century companion. How would he react if I told him that I liked him as a friend but not as a romantic partner? Would he take it in stride, or would he tell the Prince of the coming apocalypse, upending the path of my people's history?

Augustin offered the most dreadful solution, one that I could not condone even though it would certainly solve the problem. He said that he could kill Joel himself, sending him back to his girlfriend in the twenty-first century, leaving me free to do as I wished. He hinted that we could move into the Bayern castle, for he still had his own wing there, unused since he had abandoned it two winters prior. I begged him not to do it, even though a part of me yearned to insert myself into the Bayern line, to raise Teuton children with the priest who could shield me from the dangers of childbirth. I feared to face Joel in the future if I allowed such a terrible thing. My cousin's death had not come at my hands, and I could not forgive myself if I offered her boyfriend's life in exchange for my heart's mad desires.

When we parted ways just before dinner, Augustin promised that we would find a solution eventually. He said that he would hunt through some of the olden records to see if the heathens of the past had ever bent time. I clung to his pledge like a lifeline, working to appear content at dinner and afterward, as I helped one of the cooks pluck some herbs to use in the main dish tomorrow. But I spilled the entire story to Freia after dark while we sat together on my bed, for this new trial was one I could not face alone.

My roommate listened intently for the most part, but shied away from me when I admitted to having drunk Augustin's blood. "Swanie, are you sure that's a good idea?" she asked, her green eyes glancing furtively around our dimly lit bedroom. "From what I've heard from Master Denlinger, Teuton priests learn certain ceremonies for their private edification. I've heard that it's forbidden for them to divulge their wisdom to the uninitiated, especially to women."

I shrugged once and reminded her that I had come to the eleventh century for the purpose of learning all I could, including any and all secret rites. "Augustin is the only Teuton priest in Muniche who would enlighten me on such things," I added in a low voice, my ice on alert for activity in the hallway. "He doesn't see me as the typical, uneducated woman, and that's a rare find here in your time. He has taught me so much, but today . . . . Freia, trust me, I really didn't *want* to drink his blood." I shuddered at the memory of the awful taste in my mouth and the thick moisture lining my throat. "I wouldn't have done it at all, but he forced me into it. And honestly, I am glad he did. If I hadn't, I would never have discovered the extent of his love for me. He never would have admitted it, but now the truth is out in the open for both of us."

Freia nodded at me seriously, her expression thoughtful and anxious. "So have you changed your mind about your commitment to Joel?"

I answered her forthrightly, able to suppress the truth no longer. "Yes, but Augustin and I have yet to decide how to properly deal with the matter. I suppose I'll just have to accept the fact that I must break his heart. I can't ignore Augustin's love, for it is far stronger than anything I've experienced before."

Freia sighed, averting her gaze to her hands clasped in her lap, a pained look marring her smooth forehead. "And I suppose I can't dissuade you, for you know that I believe a marriage should be built upon love. It would make it easier for you if you married Augustin," she said, her mouth twisting into a discouraged frown. "Although all of the noblewomen would say that you married the most scandalous fiend in Muniche . . . at least he's a Teuton."

I studied Freia's face, caught off guard by her statement. "What about Master Denlinger . . . and you?" I whispered, fearing that her own struggles with love may actually surpass mine, as an outsider in a Teuton city.

Freia looked away toward the window, her expression discontent. "He loves me, he says, and wants me to be his wife." I gave a quick squeal of delight, but my friend had not finished. She raised her eyes to my face, tears visible in the corners. "But his father doesn't approve, for he says that my Teutonic blood is far too low. I love Heinrich, too. He's much humbler than any of the pompous lords with whom my father wished to pair me, and he's hard-working and kind. But my Rhenisch blood poses a problem. Even his mother disapproves of my heritage, even though she likes me."

I sidled closer to Freia while her tears trickled down her cheeks, placing my arms around her in sympathy. Part of me wanted to suggest that she try to win Joel instead, since he had no trace of Teutonic blood; but she already loved the ironmaster, and I knew firsthand that love rarely responds to logic. "I guess both of us have the tendency to fall for the wrong men," I sighed, knowing that it had started for me at age thirteen, during my first dance with a fiery Teuton priest—a glory I would desire for the rest of my life.

Freia wiped her tears on her nightdress, brushing a few stray blond hairs back from her face. "Heinrich insists that he would take me anyway, even though I'm not a Teuton, but we would have to run away together and marry in another town. That would raise talk, and neither of us knows whether his family would forgive him for such a thing."

I smiled wanly at my best friend and said, "Well, if I honestly decide to marry Augustin, we'll have to figure out what to do about Joel. I have no idea how to solve *that* issue. Augustin says he could kill him, to send him back to my time, but I can't let him do something that awful. We'll probably have to leave Muniche too, if we chose to marry. I've really messed everything up, and it's frustrating." I sighed, shaking my head at the combined grief of our circumstances.

As we prepared to climb into bed for the night not long afterward, I snuffed most of our candles with my ice, gazing for a moment into the one yellow flame we kept burning all night. My golden locket with its picture of Hans lay beside the candle on our nightstand, but thoughts of Augustin consumed me while I stared at the glowing fire. Augustin—my fiery priest, my master, my protector, my lover. And I felt, on that night, that my love for him had finally surpassed my love for Hans, just as his love for me outweighed his love for Marelda. Ancient devotion waned with the honesty of blood—with the passion of two youthful hearts.

Freia's voice called out to me in the darkness when I slipped beneath my blanket. "Are you going to bleed Augustin again?"

I winced at the thought of that, tugging my blanket tight around my neck. "No . . . I don't think so. I'd rather not have to bleed anyone again, for I doubt I'll ever be able to forget what I saw . . . or that horrible taste."

"Good." Freia sounded pleased as she shifted on her bed. "You really ought to stay away from Teuton rituals, Swanie," she added with a yawn. "If someone finds out that you know so much, and that it was Augustin who taught you, both of you may end up facing unfortunate consequences." She had a point there, considering all the times Augustin had stated that the Teuton priests of Muniche would punish him if they found out how many secrets he had revealed to me. But I chose to ignore Freia's concern for the moment, turning over in my bed to face the wall, images of my heathen priest filling my mind while I drifted off to sleep.

I saw Augustin often as the month of May progressed. We discussed a myriad of options for fulfilling our love, none of which would have sufficed. He continued to assert that it would be easy to send Joel back where he belonged through a quick and simple murder, while I agonized over exactly how to break the truth to him. He never seemed to broach the subject of our mutual future anymore when he stayed at the manor on weekends; he preferred to joke about happenings at the ironworks and reminisce on the modern world we had left behind. I tried several times to make myself tell Joel that I loved someone else, that we could remain friends but walk separate paths in the eleventh century. But traces of panic shackled my chest whenever I considered it while in his presence, and I would spill some drivel about gardens and music instead.

On the final Wednesday of the month, Count von Meldorf called me into his office shortly before dinner, having sent Jarvis to retrieve me from where I sat on the porch with Freia, who was endeavoring to learn some of my songs on her flute. She already had Nightwish's "Swanheart" down pat; I had begun to instruct her on "Deep Silent Complete." I told Freia that I would see her at dinner and followed Jarvis into the house, straightening my hair underneath its mauve covering that matched my dress. I figured that the count may wish to discuss aspects of business with me, as he had done several times before. He had proven himself to be a shrewd trader, and I enjoyed taking mental notes on his methods the few times I had been privy to his deals. In some ways, he reminded me of my father.

When we entered his office, the count dismissed Jarvis with a wave of his fleshy hand and requested that I take a seat, for he had some serious matters to discuss with me. To my surprise, once I had situated myself upon a stool across from his desk, he informed me gravely that Joel Hudson had come to him just a few weeks ago to request permission to marry me. My ice stiffened my body at this revelation. I abruptly wondered whether *that* was why Joel had stopped yammering on about our future as a couple—was it because Count von Meldorf had turned him down?

The count cleared his throat after broaching the subject, his hulking body resting upon a bench behind his desk, his blue eyes darkened. "I could not bring myself to grant the boy my blessing, Lady Swanhilde," he said. "No matter what past connections the two of you may have, he is an outsider, and your Teuton blood is strong. He holds a commoner's status, while you have proven yourself to be highly educated and astute at business. As a noble lord with no direct heirs, I could see myself preparing you and a Teuton husband to manage my land once I have passed on. I have thought upon it for quite a while now, you see."

My jaw dropped of its own accord; this was an unexpected proposition. "My . . . my lord . . . I . . . I don't know what to say . . . ." Novel images appeared in my mind: Augustin and Swanhilde, lord and lady of the Meldorf estate. I wrapped my arms around my torso, my feet fidgeting beneath my skirt.

"I do not wish my land to be divided amongst the commoners at my death," the count went on, frowning toward the window and drumming the meaty fingers of his right hand upon his desk. A slight cloud of dust hovered around his hand. "That always leads to dissent; the Prince's recent dealings at Freising are proof of that. But I also could not grant my land to a mixed family; local law forbids it. So if you insist upon matching yourself with your travel companion, my lady, you must do it without my blessing."

But I don't want to "match myself" with Joel. I have a purer, nobler match in mind. "I understand," I murmured, my gaze riveted upon my hands trembling in my lap. I did not know whether the count realized how serious things had become between Augustin and me. He certainly must know *something*, especially since the servants liked to gossip about Freia's and my courtships with the local lords. Emilie had asked me just yesterday whether Lord Augustin had kissed me yet. I gathered all of my courage and raised my eyes to the count's. "I do have . . . another suitor, my lord," I admitted, my entire body tensed against an expected onslaught. "But I'm not entirely sure of his intentions yet."

"You speak of the Lord Augustin von Bayern," Count von Meldorf guessed, his wrinkled countenance appearing cautious. I nodded once. "That lord has not yet spoken with me, but I would advise you to tread carefully," he said, running a hand through his wild gray hair. "The local prostitutes speak highly of him, and he is a gambler. You will have to decide for yourself whether that sort of man suits you. But his Teuton blood is beyond reproach. While I doubt that he would wish to learn of farming, I may be open to his offers, should he approach me."

Count von Meldorf had given me more to think about, and that night I lay awake for a long while in the dim candlelight, looking into the blurry expanse above me. So Joel had asked for my hand in marriage, and the count had turned him down for valid reasons. It made perfect sense that only those of Teuton blood could own the land that surrounded Muniche, but I wondered if Joel had asked to be hired as a vassal. The count would probably agree to that, but I doubted that he would want me to lower my status by joining with one of his employees—in some ways, that harkened back to my Hans problem at home.

But the count had not brought up Augustin's worst traits: his dark sorcery and his murderous tendencies. Did he not know, or did he simply not believe the rampant rumors? Instead he had mentioned two factors that I knew but rarely considered: *local prostitutes speak highly of him, and he is a gambler.* I had seen him gamble only once, at Lady Maria's birthday celebration when we had first met. As for the local prostitutes, I had yet to witness any such tête-à-têtes with my own eyes. That was something we needed to talk about, though. I knew quite well that Augustin was a sex addict, and I did not know whether my Teuton body would prove enough to assuage his yearnings. Could I agree to an open relationship, or would jealousy tear my heart to pieces?

On Thursday, Augustin arrived at the Meldorf estate shortly after the lunch hour, an expression of fierce triumph lightening his face. When we met upon the porch, he invited me to walk with him by the stream, for he had a new idea to open before me, one that trumped the plans we had discarded. I accepted his invitation without hesitation, marveling at the radiance shining in his eyes, and followed him as he set out in the direction of the fruit trees.

Augustin did not speak while we passed the gardeners at work, so I took the opportunity to admire his form and attire all over again. He wore the clothing of nobility, his tunic red and black, his black pants stuffed into shining boots, his outer coat a deep crimson with gold trim. He had tied his black hair entirely back, held up by a rather intricate clip, a black cap decorated with ruby-colored stones set atop his head. He looked magnificent, with his muscular hands clasped behind him as we walked, the uncharacteristic smile refusing to leave his face, making him appear nigh irresistible. No one in Muniche would think him hideous or fearsome, if they saw him like this.

When we reached the stream, we took the upstream path toward the cherry tree, and beneath its boughs Augustin gestured for me to sit beside him in the grass. I did so, crossing my legs comfortably underneath my skirt, turning my gaze upon him as he began to speak, using English words whenever he could. "Last night, as I lay awake in bed pondering our future, I realized that thus far,

I have been looking at our dilemma from a purely selfish perspective, disregarding the *other* option, the one we have not yet discussed." He paused, his eyes glowing mysteriously.

My forehead wrinkled, and I cocked my head at him. "Well, another option fell into my lap yesterday thanks to the count," I informed him, "but I'm curious to hear yours first. It must be amazing or you wouldn't be smiling like that."

His smile widened, and he rubbed his hands together suggestively. "I have finally reached the conclusion that there is one, and only one way to utterly ensure that we can remain together even after your time in my era has passed. You took a great risk to come here to me, your adventure far eclipsing any of mine. Where lies the excitement if you must remain the *only* time traveler in this pair?" He gestured from himself to me, and my eyes almost burst out of their sockets when I grasped his implications.

"You're thinking . . . of coming to *my* future . . . with me," I translated, the concept of inheriting the Meldorf estate vanishing from my mind.

"How else could our future truly be together, my darling?" he asked, reaching to take hold of my right hand. "I should have thought of this from the start, but I was thinking selfishly, as I said before. In my self-centeredness, I believed that we should stay in my time, growing old together here where all is familiar to me. But you, Swanhilde, belong in another time, and I love you enough to give up what little I have here to seek our future there."

My mind worked overtime as the scope of Augustin's love struck me again. My ice lingered along the edges of my veins, his warm touch keeping it at bay. "But how . . . how could we . . . *both* go to the future?" I tried to reason out his plans. "You've said before . . . that you can't follow me there."

"Not in death, but in life I could, if the two of us can get hold of the Prince's song." Augustin looked quite smug, and before I could voice any objections, he held up one finger. "Of course you would need to prepare me for all of the changes that the twenty-first century holds compared with the here and now. I believe I could manage to adjust to your era eventually with the help of your guidance and my intellect."

I stared at him blankly. "Are you suggesting . . . that we should *steal* the song from the Prince? You know he'd never give it up willingly." I could not fathom such a scheme ending well.

Augustin's smile turned wicked. "It would not be too terribly difficult to gain the necessary information," he said, a look of bloodlust igniting in his eyes.

I extracted my hand from his grasp and wrapped my arms around my knees, shuddering as his purpose abruptly became clear. "You're thinking . . . of bleeding it . . . from the Prince . . . ."

"Not from the Prince." Augustin chuckled, a deep, frightening sound, then clarified, "That would prove needlessly complicated, for he is a Teuton priest like I am. He would know exactly what I planned to do, as well as what I wished to find. He would fight me, and it is tedious to bleed a struggling victim. There is one other party who knows the song, a weaker man, one who could not resist."

My eyes bugged, and I clutched both of my hands to my mouth while new possibilities raced through my mind. "*Paulus,*" I whispered.

Augustin laughed again, his tone reminding me of Wuotan's laughter in the currents of time. "Yes, my lovely swan. I could bleed the song from him, locking him away somewhere so he could not squawk about my actions before we could make our escape. Afterward, I could meet you at the Bayern castle, where you could bleed the necessary information from me." I shot him a disturbed look, but he reminded me, "You would have to play the song yourself, for I could not open the gates to the future, only to the past. Then we could leap through the gates together, for you would have to pull me through on your own power to ensure that I could successfully gain access to the future. Once we finish our journey through the dark void of time, we could begin our life in the twenty-first century, leaving this epoch behind us permanently, with all of its deficiencies." Augustin finished his discourse with a nod, his expression pleased.

I held my peace for a long moment as I turned the idea over in my mind. *Augustin von Bayern in the twenty-first century . . . . He would have no trouble learning the languages . . . and he could study modern science and learn how to work with modern technology . . . he would love the accessibility of information . . . the libraries, the internet . . . . He wouldn't be able to kill and rape at random, but maybe the distractions of fresh knowledge could keep his mind from such sinful desires. We could marry . . . raise children . . . manage my father's company together . . . wow . . . .* When I finally spoke, I voiced a foolish question. "And Joel?"

"You could tell him the truth, and we could bring him with us." Augustin's mien implied that I should have thought of that myself.

"That actually . . . might . . . work . . . ." I shook my head again at my master's cleverness, a smile finally breaking across my own face. "Of course, I'll have to prepare you for everything first, before we go. There are lots of confusing things about the twenty-first century, new inventions, new ideas, and you would have to be ready for them. Once we get there, we'll have to fabricate some sort of ancestry for you . . . my father might know some people who could do that . . . ."

Augustin chuckled, rising from the grass and holding one hand out to me. "There is much to consider, but now, we ought to return to the house to take up our linguistic studies. I ran across a few English words this morning that I am not sure how to pronounce." He pulled me to my feet, and we set our course for the manor, my thoughts whirling in excitement. This new idea *would* work; I felt certain. I could hardly wait to begin, to really ponder all of the things I would need to tell Augustin before we left the eleventh century for good.

When we reached the front porch of the Meldorf house, a well-dressed page boy stood before the door chatting with Jarvis. Both servants turned to regard me as I ascended the wooden steps, the boy's expression taken aback at the presence of Augustin behind me. He handed me a small scroll, stating that he had been sent to deliver it to me. Once I had taken it, he sprinted away down the stairs, shooting one final disapproving glance toward Augustin.

I glanced once at Jarvis, who nodded at me and reentered the house. Then I turned my attention to the scroll, breaking the seal and unrolling it. Augustin came to my side as I read its contents aloud: "'My Lady Swanhilde von Thaden, I request that you visit the library of the Bayern castle Friday afternoon at None, to discuss a matter of utmost importance. Sincerely, His Majesty Prince Otto von Bayern.'" I tilted my head, considering, then said to Augustin, "Maybe he's finally changed his mind about the song, and you won't have to bleed Paulus after all."

Chapter Thirty-five

Advice from the Prince

I clad myself in one of my most elegant spring dresses the following morning for my meeting with the Prince. Freia suggested a silver one, its material light and airy, the bodice patterned with tiny white buttons decorating the waistline. The silver skirt swept the floor, their hemlines trimmed with white lace, and the backs of the flared sleeves hung to my knees. I donned a matching silver head covering, tying all of my black hair underneath it into a complex bun. I slipped one of my best pairs of sandals upon my feet and slid a pair of my mother's silver earrings into my earlobes. I completed my look of sophistication with my mother's diamond necklace, which I had not yet worn in public. I had asked Jarvis to drive me to the Bayern castle in the count's carriage, for I hoped that such a conveyance might deter any highway robbers from attempting to pilfer my jewelry.

We arrived at the Bayern castle just as the church bells had begun to clang out their melodies, announcing the arrival of mid-afternoon. A servant opened the castle gates for us, and the carriage clattered over the stone pathway toward the main entrance. A rush of uncertainty entered my veins when I realized that just moments from now, I would be meeting Prince Otto in the library. It would be the first time I had spoken to him one-on-one since that day in the forest, when he had reprimanded me for using my ice against the Gypsies. My opinions of him had taken a downward spiral since I had befriended his hated brother, and I began to wonder exactly why the Prince wished to speak with *me,* the strange woman from the future. If he had really decided to allow Joel and me to use his song to return to our time, he could have called Joel to the castle. Worry gnawed at my soul as Jarvis helped me descend from the carriage and promised that he would wait for me on the front porch. I thanked him with a wan smile, then turned to the front door of the castle, which stood open for me, the Prince's trusty servant Bruno waiting inside to usher me to the library.

Bruno and I exchanged a few words while he led me through the impressive halls, mainly remarks on the season and on the health of the Prince and his Lady. I eyed Bruno covertly as we walked, remembering the other time I had encountered him, that Sunday when Augustin had let Joel and me into the castle to speak with the Prince about his Song of Time. I doubted Bruno had forgotten that incident, particularly since the Prince had ordered him to escort us away from the Bayern grounds once he and Paulus had discovered our pursuits in the music room. I wondered if Bruno believed Augustin to be mad, like most of the servants, and if he had ever actually seen Marelda's chapel down in the basement.

We reached the library after threading through a few stone hallways, and Bruno opened the massive wooden doors for me with a flourish. I thanked him properly and entered the room beyond, my ice-tinted eyes traveling over its contents—I had decided to simply enhance my vision with my ice for this rendezvous today, since my stash of contacts had dropped below fifty pairs. Books and scrolls lined every wall of the library, the shelves reaching much higher than my head. Several dark tables flecked with gold stood in various places in the room, imposing leather chairs resting near them. An enormous fireplace ornamented the left wall, two golden statues depicting the Bavarian lion standing in front of it with their teeth bared, their claws unsheathed. Above the marble mantle hung an exquisite painting of the city of Muniche, her walls and spires grand, the rays of the sun covering her in a holy light.

I noticed, as I advanced slowly into the library, that three elaborate chandeliers hung from the beams of the ceiling, their candles lit with tiny flames of yellow and red. A low reddish-tinted fire also smoldered in the fireplace. Combined with the glowing candles, it cast the entire library in a ruddy hue, contrasting with the pure light filtering through the windows on the far wall. I frowned slightly and halted ten paces from the door, which had been closed behind me. The Prince had likely lit the fire and the candles himself, and I found that I preferred blue fire to red any day. I wondered if enough of Augustin's fire rested within my soul to thrust a few blue flames upon the candelabra, vanquishing red with blue. I snickered to myself at the thought, then averted my gaze to a high-backed leather chair near the fireplace, from which Prince Otto arose to greet me.

He strode forward to meet me, and I studied his appearance in the quick seconds it took him to cross the floor. He wore deep burgundy robes flecked with a light auburn, the buckles on his brown leather boots and golden-tinted belt shining grandly in the firelight. He wore quite a few impressive gold chains, along with a ruby ring on the middle finger of his left hand. His black hair draped just a bit over his ears, and his neatly-trimmed beard had begun to look almost decent, more like a man's. He walked with confidence, his posture erect, his dark blue eyes silently welcoming me to his castle, his kingdom. He actually did appear attractive, when I viewed him as an unbiased subject. I even supposed that quite a few young noblewomen prayed earnestly every night that once the Lady Maria passed away, Muniche would choose them next. But despite Prince Otto's handsome exterior, my attitude toward him had been forever tainted by his brother, the hated one, my master—and I would pick him over the Prince in any circumstance.

Prince Otto stopped about a meter away from me, bowing low and spreading out his hands in a salutatory gesture. "My Lady Swanhilde von Thaden, I thank you kindly for accepting my invitation to meet me here on this lovely afternoon. Your stunning appearance rivals the grandeur of the springtime, it would seem." He smiled brightly as he spoke, his dark blue eyes taking in my outfit and jewelry with a look of appraisal.

I curtseyed low in response, feeling slightly perturbed that the young Prince would compliment my looks so overtly when he held no claim to my heart. I knew that Augustin would punch him in the face for such flirtatious comments. "It is my pleasure to come, *Leitaeri*," I answered him, holding onto my decorum, "although I must admit that your purpose in requesting my presence has remained elusive to me, thus far."

The Prince chuckled, waving his left hand dismissively. "All in good time, my lady. Come sit with me." He turned back toward the leather chair in front of the fireplace, and I trailed behind him, glancing around at the contents of the library again. He signaled me to the chair across from his, to the left of the hearth, just several paces away from one of the lion statues. "I have asked the servants to bring us bread and tea," he said. "Afterward, we may confront our business."

Business. What sort of business would the Prince have with me? I wondered as I settled into the dark leather chair, my buttocks sinking down into its cushion rather comfortably. I crossed my ankles underneath my skirt, sitting as straight as possible in such an immense chair, gazing for a moment at the reddish flames of the fireplace while the Prince sat upon his own chair. I lifted my eyes to the beautiful painting of the city that hung above the mantle, marveling again at its artistry. The Prince noticed my preoccupation and said with a smile, "That is my Muniche in the splendor of summertime, aglow in the light of her heavenly guardians." He breathed a quiet sigh of contented satisfaction.

"It is an amazing likeness, fully evincing the glory of Muniche," I agreed, thinking that I had never before seen such an exquisite portrait of my city, medieval or modern. "Who is the artist?" I inquired, suddenly curious.

The Prince's visage darkened, and he tore his eyes from the painting, staring down at his folded hands in silence before meeting my gaze and stating, his voice grave, "My mother painted it one year before my birth."

My eyes widened at this revelation, and I looked from the Prince to the painting and back again. "Marelda . . . ." I whispered, images of her beauty racing through my mind —the ones I had seen in Augustin's blood.

The Prince looked away from me, staring into the flickering flames of his fire for a long moment, grief evident on his face. "She was like unto an angel of God, I have heard," he murmured, his mouth twitching in sorrow.

I wondered, while I watched Prince Otto struggle for control of his angst at the untimely death of his mother, whether Augustin had ever seen the Prince's sadness first-hand or whether he had ignored it altogether. Apparently my master was not the only one who felt pain at the subject of Marelda's death. I breathed out once, reminiscing upon my own past tragedies, and abruptly heard myself saying, "I lost my mother when I was five years old, *Leitaeri*."

The Prince raised his eyes to my face, his expression startled. "I had not realized . . . . I had believed that your family awaited you in the future, my lady."

I smiled half-heartedly and looked down at my own hands. "Just my father, *Leitaeri*. My mother died giving my father a son." I heard the Prince gasp, and when I lifted my eyes I saw that he had grown rigid in his chair, his hands clutching the armrests, horror and sympathy warring on his face. I shrugged quickly, brushing aside any well-meaning words he may have wished to impart with the remark, "But I'm the only one left now. My father looks to me to carry on our heritage."

Dead silence in the room for what seemed to be a full minute. At length, the Prince sighed heavily, clearing his throat and straightening in his chair. "Please accept my deepest apologies, my Lady Swanhilde. Such grief is a tragic burden to bear." I shrugged again at his words, looking away and thinking of Augustin, of whom the Prince likely also thought, now that he knew of our common ground. "I trust that you have found the eleventh century to your liking, my lady?" The Prince changed the subject with finesse, his eyes alight with curiosity.

My mind ran over the events of the past year in a flash, as I suddenly realized that Joel and I had indeed been in this era for almost a year now. "The eleventh century has been decent," I said honestly, meeting the Prince's eyes once more. "It certainly has been an adventure so far, *Leitaeri*, and I thank you again for your kindness in accepting Joel and me into your realm."

The Prince nodded, a smile appearing beneath his fuzzy beard. "I could do no less for a Teuton woman and her charge, seeking asylum after such a harrowing journey." His eyes flashed with a touch of humor as the servants appeared behind us, carrying trays bearing tea and warm, buttered biscuits. Prince Otto indicated that they should set their goods upon the small tables that stood beside our chairs, and I thanked the plump, mature woman who handed me my teacup for her hard work and generosity. The woman dropped a brief curtsey before departing from the room, and I turned my attention back to the Prince when he queried, "And what of Muniche, Lady Swanhilde? I trust that my city in its formative years stands as strongly as the Muniche of your era?"

I took a sip of tea and gathered my thoughts, unsure how to respond to that question, since I knew that in twenty-one years this ancient Muniche would burn to the ground. It would return in the twelfth century, of course, reborn around a conclave of monks, ultimately taking the modern name München. But the Bavarian capital of my day and this primeval Teuton stronghold seemed hardly the same place, sometimes. I remembered my beloved mentor, the wise Lady Muniche from my time, thinking that she was a lot more long-suffering and friendly than the Prince's middle-aged companion, Maria. But in the end, I bottled up all of my criticisms and replied, "Eleventh century Muniche is undoubtedly the pinnacle of Teuton civilization and success, *Leitaeri*. I am honored to be a part of it myself, observing its prosperity firsthand."

The Prince smiled at my accolade, retrieving a biscuit from the tray beside him and bringing it to his mouth. I took another sip of tea while I waited for him to speak again, still pondering the real reason he had sent for me. After swallowing a mouthful of biscuit, the Prince said, "I would also make the assumption, my lady, that you have ultimately found peace in your heart, even though you entered this era twenty years too early, by your estimation." His eyes watched me sagaciously, his expression suggesting many possible meanings to his words.

I caught his intense look, and it unnerved me as my mind worked to reason out the purpose of his question. The servants had left us in peace, so perhaps he was about to bring up our "business." I nodded at him cautiously, taking another sip of tea before stating simply, "Fate shall always bring us to the places we should be, *Leitaeri*." A second after the words had left my lips, I realized that I had just repeated something Augustin had told me, in Marelda's chapel at the New Year's party.

"It shall, indeed." The Prince's eyes had begun to burn me, the red fire before us flickering just a shade more brightly. I fidgeted in my chair, gripping my teacup a little more tightly, wishing the Prince would just spit out the truth before it drove me insane. "And thus, I must now address the reason I requested your presence, my Lady Swanhilde." Prince Otto eyed me seriously, and I waited, my ice seeping further into my veins, an instinctive precaution. "It has come to my attention that you have developed a rather . . . disturbing . . . relationship . . . over the past several months . . . with my eldest brother."

My ice froze my body in an instant, casting the library in a sharp veil of blue. The teacup trembled in my hands, and I set it down upon the table beside me before its contents could taint my dress or the floor. I had not expected that the Prince had brought me here to reprimand my camaraderie with Augustin. How could I possibly defend myself against *this?* I swallowed once, then pointed out, "I spend a lot more time with Joel than with your brother, *Leitaeri.*"

The Prince looked troubled, and his posture relaxed just slightly, his eyes shifting to the fireplace. "That may be true," he allowed, his forehead wrinkling as he considered my words. He turned his gaze toward me once more and voiced the awful truth I could not counter. "However, my Lady Swanhilde, you are a Teuton woman, and your friend Joel Hudson is an outsider. Your blood longs for another of its kind, one who could fulfill your innermost desires."

My hands had begun to turn a translucent white as my element struggled to protect me from the wretched truth, the verity that I had heard from Augustin's lips many times before. "My responsibility must remain with Joel," I said in a weak voice, even though if our recent plans came to fruition, that issue would be permanently resolved. "I brought him here into this time period, and therefore I cannot forsake him, no matter what longings I have in my blood."

Prince Otto's eyes flashed red, whether in response to the manifestation of my ice or my ridiculous lies, I could not tell. "I saw you dance with my oldest brother in elemental glory on New Year's Eve," he accused, his expression dangerous.

"I have danced with fire in my own era," I retorted, my icy hands digging into the leather armrests. "I consider it recreation, *Leitaeri.*"

The Prince glowered at me for a long moment, the fire in his eyes gradually cooling while they returned to their natural dark blue. "Calm yourself, my lady; you are growing hysterical. Pull your element back before you freeze the entire room. Your display may attract unwanted company." I frowned as the Prince glanced toward the closed door of the library. I had no idea that my ice had begun to alter the temperature of the room. Maybe he was making it up. I focused, ordering my ice back into my spirit, and the Prince went on. "You seem incredibly unwilling to admit to your actions with my brother, which surprises me. I have already spoken with him about this matter and had hoped that perhaps you might take more kindly to my advice, since he forever refuses to listen to me."

I blinked at the Prince, my vision having regained a portion of its natural ambiguity. "Then . . . Augustin has already told you . . . everything?" Prince Otto nodded at me seriously, and I felt a rush of alarm, wondering what exactly that could mean. *Augustin would never have told him about the future. He likely just bragged about our heart-bond, since the Prince could never achieve its glory with Maria.* "Well . . . unlike me, *Leitaeri*, I'm afraid your brother prefers to view these matters as a conquest, one of the few achievements he can claim over you." I eyed the Prince in speculation, lifting my teacup from the table.

The Prince huffed in annoyance. "In that, he is wrong, my lady." I spluttered into the cup, shock filling me when I met the Prince's gaze, seeing torment in his dark blue eyes. "Augustin does not know this, but I once had the same bond you share with him now, one thousand years in the past." A gasp escaped my lips, and I froze in my chair, my teacup forgotten in my fingers, while the Prince related his heart wrenching tale.

"When Paulus and I used my song to travel to the time of Christ, we spent quite a few years in Palestine before traversing Asia Minor, proclaiming the good news of salvation wherever we could. During our time in Palestine, I met a young Jewish woman named Kezia, already a follower of Christ. She was—and still is—the humblest person I have ever met, her heart full of love and grace, always willing to help others, to pray, to comfort. She was beautiful, with eyes the color of earth beside the river and hair as black as the night sky. And I loved her."

I stared, my mouth forming a small *O* of surprise. The Prince leaned forward in his chair, sighing once, twisting his hands. "We were married for twenty-six years. She bore me three children, two sons and a daughter. I told her everything about myself, who I was, why I had come, from whence I had come, and she loved me even though I was a Gentile. Though she had not been born a Teuton, I created the heart-bond with her during the first year of our marriage. Through it I experienced a love I had never known before . . . a love I shall never forget.

"When the Romans began persecuting Christians in force,"—I watched the Prince's face harden as his story transitioned from beauty to tragedy—"Kezia and I realized that our time would be short. She expressed the hope repeatedly that once I returned to the future, the Lord would grant me a woman to take her place, to love me and keep me close to God. Paulus and I were visiting a church several cities away when the Romans attacked our village, killing every Christian they could find. I returned to my house to find my faithful wife hung on a cross in the front yard, her body picked apart by vultures, her heart vanished forever from my hands. They had gotten to our children as well, but Kezia's brutal murder has remained with me always, the image never leaving my mind. When Paulus and I were thrown into the coliseum less than a year later, I remember begging God to let me die permanently then, so I could reunite with my family in heaven."

The Prince paused, turning his back to me so he could compose himself, his shoulders shaking with quiet sobs. Tears welled in my own eyes, and I placed the teacup back upon the table, ordering myself not to compare his story to mine, not to think of what would happen to me one day when my heart-bond with Augustin broke. The severance had dragged the Prince into despair, and he was a man . . . what would it do to me, a tender-hearted woman?

"When the tigers snapped my neck," the Prince continued thickly, wiping his tears away and turning to face me again, "I awoke to find myself here, back in this castle, a young man again, my hands once more grasping the responsibility that had evaporated from me in the past." He reached his right hand into his outer tunic to pull the keys of Muniche from his belt, prompting me to stare. "Without these keys, my heart was free to love whomever it wished," he said flatly, fingering each of the iron keys in turn. "But now, the city binds me to herself, to the Lady who manifests her soul, teaching me accountability, loyalty, and pride. Despite what you may think after hearing my tale, my Lady Swanhilde, I would *not* freely sacrifice these keys to another at any cost. Unlike my eldest brother, I *love* this city and shall gladly shoulder all of her burdens, like my father before me." He clutched the key ring tightly for a moment, then placed it back inside his tunic while I gaped, marveling at the other-worldly power of the keys of a Teuton city.

The Prince lifted his eyes to mine, his expression making him look far older than his twenty-three years. "But . . . I have never forgotten the bond of the Teutons . . . even though the bond of a city is far stronger, unbreakable by man. I still recall the tenderness of Kezia's heart in my hands . . . the benevolence of her smile . . . her dedicated love for God. Time, unfortunately, does not erase all memories. That is why, my Lady Swanhilde, I urge you now . . . as one who has experienced your pain . . . that you ask my brother to break your bond . . . before things get worse."

I considered his advice for a long moment, nibbling a biscuit as my response slowly coalesced in my mind. The Prince meant well; I could see that clearly. He did not want me to have to face the pain he still faced today, the longing for a partner long dead and gone. But Augustin's reminder flashed through my brain: *Glory is ephemeral . . . one must enjoy pleasure while it lasts . . . .*

So I lifted my eyes to the Prince's and replied slowly, "*Leitaeri,* please allow me to offer my sincerest apologies and sympathy for your . . . incredible loss. Time travel introduces many unfortunate complications into life, and love." The Prince bowed his head formally, accepting my condolences, and I decided that I might as well just be as forthright as I could be. "Your advice is sound, *Leitaeri,* but . . . it is already too late for me." I lowered my voice considerably and admitted, "I *love* Augustin, and I loved him before he created our heart-bond. And in spite of what you believe, your brother does, in fact, retain the capacity to love, and his devotion to me has staggered me eternally. It is stronger than anything I have ever experienced . . . ." Prince Otto's mouth fell open in shock when I finished passionately, "So I *can't* ask him to break our heart-bond now, no matter what it may do to me in the future. I can't set aside his love, even though we don't belong together. It is too late." I sensed Augustin's love wrapping my heart in a wondrous shroud as I spoke the truth, infusing me with acceptance, belonging.

The Prince made a sound in his throat, his jaw working in frustration, his eyes glinting red once more. "You have not known him as long as I have, my Lady Swanhilde." His tone was harsh, cutting me like a knife. "He is lying to you. All he wants from you is your body, to fuel his insanity for blood and power. He glories in your submission, in your helpless heart crying for his mercy."

I screamed at his words and leapt to my feet, my contentment vanishing as my loyalty to Augustin prompted my ice to erupt. "You have no conception of the extent of our love . . . *murderer!*" I spat.

Chapter Thirty-six

Joel's Suicidal Mission

Prince Otto rose from his chair himself in response to my ire. The flames crackling in the fireplace turned a darker red while their master's eyes searched my face, fury rippling in heat waves from his chest. "He has you *blinded!*" the Prince snapped at me, his irises the color of blood.

"How *dare* you speak of blindness, *you,* the one whose sight is veiled by the *keys!*" My hair and fingers froze as I rushed to defend my beloved master, ice and fire churning together in my veins. "You should not discredit that which you have not experienced, *Leitaeri*! You had the bond with an outsider, while I have it with a man who is almost fully Teuton! Augustin would give anything for me, his heart, his life, his very *soul!* He would follow me in death, follow me to the future, if he could! How can you even *think* to compare your love for Kezia with *this,* when you have not killed yourself yet in order to meet her in heaven! If you really loved her, *that's* what you would have done the moment you burst forth from those gates, the keys of Muniche be damned!"

The Prince bared his teeth and stepped forward to tower over me, heat from his inner fire threatening to melt my icy shield. "You *forget* that you are speaking to the *ruler* of this city," he growled, his tone laden with reproach.

"The *ruler* of this city should stop assuming his own feeble love can hold a candle to that of his brother," I retorted, my icy fingers curling at my sides while I glared up at my opponent. "Augustin has far more love in his heart than *you*, who lived your life without a care for the precious life you ended at your birth!" I had seen his sorrow earlier, when we discussed Marelda's painting, but in my ire I could recall only Augustin's despair, Augustin's loneliness, Augustin's devotion to his dead mother. "I am eternally grateful that your brother has chosen to grant just a portion of that love to me in the form of our bond, and you should stop judging him as a heartless sinner just because you don't *understand!*"

The Prince cried out in rage, red fire sizzling on his fingernails as he raised both hands in warning. "You go *too far!*" he roared at me. "If you cannot hold your tongue, you will pay the price for your language, for you are speaking to royalty, to the Keyholder!"

I should have backed down, for he had a point there. I should not say such wicked things to the Prince of Muniche when I was one of his subjects. But I realized that I did not care, for I was not from this era. If my vicious defense of Augustin trampled the boundaries of medieval propriety, so be it. We would be leaving the eleventh century behind us soon, if our plans reached their probable conclusion. So I drew myself up straight, lifting my icy fingers threateningly, my eyes glittering blue. "I will *fight* the royal Keyholder if he continues to say that Augustin's love for me is a lie. Perhaps he *should* have killed you years ago."

The Prince screamed at my disparaging words, his hair blazing red, the fire in the hearth and upon the chandeliers blocking every other color from the room. He threw his fire at me in the next instant, and I had just enough time to raise my frozen hands to protect my face. My element pulsed with life as it consumed his fire, prompting it to fall to the floorboards in a smoldering pile of liquid. The Prince sprang atop his chair, which would have looked funny under any other circumstances, but he poised himself there to get a better shot at me. He thrust a ball of red flames at me again, and I dodged quickly aside, toward the center of the library, away from the roaring fireplace that could very well have fought me itself at the Prince's direction. The fiery red ball hit my chair, vanishing before it could harm the leather, and the Prince snarled at me, preparing to attack again.

Up until that point in my life, I had never truly battled another Teuton with the intent to injure. Hans and I had fought for fun several times, and I had sparred with my friends and cousins. Fighting the Gypsies had been childishly simple since they had no elements to counter my ice. But now, as I faced the wrath of the fiery Keyholder, I had the terrible feeling that I was horribly unprepared and would likely fall. *How could ice beat fire . . . ? His skin would be too hot for me to freeze him, and I can't melt his fireballs indefinitely. Is he going to try to kill me?*

I melted another fireball, panting with the effort, and suddenly my self-preservation instinct took over my body when it sensed the Prince's burning fire attempting to find purchase on my icy skin. My unconscious mind delved into my spirit, and the crimson hue of the library flickered, the color shifting, a new force within me altering the red flames of the chandeliers. Before I knew what had happened, a burst of cobalt blue flame exploded from my frozen fingers, meeting the Prince's red fire in midair, the desperation in my soul fueling its vivacity.

The Prince stared at the striving flames in shock, his element slowly calming, his hair returning to its natural black. He crawled carefully down from his perch, his fiery hands cooling, his eyes turning blue once more as he watched the elemental battle play out in the air before him. My own fear also subsided, and my ice sank back into my spirit along with Augustin's fire. I began hyperventilating as my hair and eyes returned to their usual colors, my right hand gripping my chest. Had Augustin seen this somehow through our heart-bond?

The scuffling flames slowly dissipated into smoke and the air cleared, the sunlight again filtering in through the windows. The Prince stood still before me, his hands clasped behind his back while he looked at the place where the flames had fought, then at me, then upward at the nearest chandelier. I followed his gaze and saw, to my astonishment, that an equal number of red and blue flames now burned upon the candelabra. The Prince drew a deep breath and stated tonelessly, "That . . . is impossible."

I had regained my breath, and I lowered my eyes from the ceiling to meet the Prince's, regret and shame marring my self-confidence at last. "*Leitaeri* . . . please . . . forgive me," I apologized, wanting to kick myself for my disrespect. "I . . . I should never . . . have done that . . . or said those things . . . . I'm sorry . . . ."

The Prince eyed me for a long moment, pressing his mouth into a thin line. At length he sighed, lacing his fingers together. "I suppose I shall . . . set aside . . . your rash actions and insolent words . . . for the moment. But, my lady, there is something that you should know, now that we are once more on speaking terms."

I glanced toward the closed door to the hallway, somewhat surprised that no one had come to investigate our brief melee. Perhaps the Prince had kept the noise contained to the library; it had to have been his doing, for I certainly had not held back. I felt thankful that no one had encroached upon our scuffle, for I doubted I would still be alive, if another Teuton had emerged to protect Prince Otto. "So what is this thing that you believe I should know, *Leitaeri?*" I asked.

The Prince's expression grew a tad ferocious, and he responded, "I can state this with complete certainty, Lady Swanhilde, although you shall not believe the truth. My brother could never love you as much as Joel Hudson loves you." He scowled at me, his glare suggesting that I wake up and see the light.

I fought the urge to counter his claim and tried to suppress a frown. "I am afraid I do not understand what you mean . . . *Leitaeri.*"

"Joel Hudson is willing to go to great lengths for your sake, my lady, disregarding everyone's advice." The Prince paused, and I shook my head at him, still uncomprehending. He sighed and folded his arms across his chest. "The boy wants to marry you, and your charms have bewitched him beyond all logic and reason, I fear. He wishes to take your surname and manage the Meldorf estate as your partner, your equal . . . something he could never be . . . unless he performs the unmentionable duty." His eyes, though they remained blue, burned me like the sun.

His implications struck me with the force of an oncoming train. My ice crept back into my veins, and I stepped back, my ankles failing, my hands coming up to cover my mouth in denial. "*No . . . .*"

The Prince nodded grimly. "Joel Hudson plans to become a Teuton by blood alone so that he may marry you as an equal, to save you from the stigma of tainted blood, of bearing mixed children. He loves you enough to change his heritage for you . . . to risk his *life* to grant you acceptance."

I staggered backward, falling upon the arm of the leather chair upon which I had sat not long before, knocking the small table with its tea and biscuits to the floor. "*The . . . blood . . . transfer . . . .*" The words fell from my lips, my voice breaking, abject terror taking root in my soul.

"I shall perform the ritual one week from tomorrow," the Prince said, his expression severe. "You may try to dissuade him if you wish, but your efforts will likely be in vain. His ardor toward you has become his insanity."

"No . . . no . . . no . . . he can't *do* this." I prattled like a lunatic, frozen upon the arm of the chair, my chest tightening in panic. "It will *kill* him. It's *suicide* . . . . And what if it *actually* kills him . . . ? It's a deadly ritual . . . the writings say to stay away from those . . . he could die . . . it would be my fault . . . ."

"With this ritual, one party involved shall probably die," the Prince stated, his tone sounding detached, as though he had conducted many blood-transfers in the past, and this was just one out of many. "I prefer to hope that his donor shall survive, for it is an easier burden to bear—failing to create a new Teuton—than the burden of becoming a Teuton with the awareness that in doing so, you killed your best friend."

I gasped in shock, climbing shakily to my feet. I clung to the back of the chair as I tried to steady myself, to bring myself back under control so I could properly handle this horrific situation. I knew who Joel's donor *had* to be, without question. "*The ironmaster....*" My thoughts raced to Freia, my non-Teuton best friend, the woman who loved Heinrich Denlinger dearly.

"Yes, and I do hope that I shall not kill him, for he is my friend as well. His mother and my Lady Maria are cousins." The Prince eyed me sourly, his expression suggesting that he could not care less whether Joel died or not.

"He can't *do* this," I gasped again, resolution entering my veins. I must at least attempt to change his mind. "I can't let him die . . . . I would never forgive myself. I have to tell him not to do it . . . ."

The Prince sighed, kindness and sympathy evident upon his face as he said, "I sincerely hope that you can deter him, Lady Swanhilde. Nevertheless, I fear it shall come to pass despite our good intentions, for no one truly understands the extent of the blood-transfer until one takes part in it himself . . . and by then, it is far too late to reconsider." I glanced toward the door to the hallway, preparing to depart the castle in an attempt to find Joel— my foolish, naïve lover. Prince Otto waved a hand at me, urging me to go, speaking one final phrase in parting. "Lady Swanhilde, you must not discredit the love of this honest outsider. It by far exceeds the love of a rapist, no matter what he has led you to believe."

I fled from the Bayern library in an icy blizzard, streaking past countless servants standing in the doorways, their grim faces implying that they had heard every word and ridiculed me for my devotion to Augustin. I blew past Jarvis on the front porch, yelling at him to drive us immediately to the ironworks. I heard his "Right away, my lady," reaching me as through a tunnel, my mind whirling while I leapt into the carriage, shutting its wooden door firmly behind me. I bounced up and down upon the cushion, the horses' leisurely pace infuriating me while I watched the Bayern front gardens drift slowly by.

"For heaven's sake, Jarvis, speed up!" I screeched at my driver, prompting him to turn his head to stare at me in surprise. "The ironworks is all the way on the other side of the city, and we *have* to get there before Vespers! *Drive* this carriage with your element!" I ordered, for I had learned that he was energy. Therefore, he could push us with superhuman speed if he had the mind to do so.

Jarvis gaped at me as we exited the Bayern gates, entering the main street. "Drive with my element? Now? In public?"

"*Yes!* Do it!" I cried at him, throwing pieces of my ice toward the ceiling of the carriage to illustrate my point. Jarvis' face hardened in fortitude. He swung to face the horses, energy sparking in his hair when he snapped the reins, his element zooming down the fabric like that of a modern Maypole. Both horses cried out and began to sprint. I grabbed the sides of the carriage to steady myself as it shot forward with the speed of a car on the interstate, careening around animals and people. Jarvis shouted for everyone to split, his element thrusting them to the sides of the streets before they could comply. It was an exhilarating ride, something I had never experienced before, and we reached the front entrance to the ironworks in less than a minute according to my internal clock.

I was out of the carriage and through the doors to the foundry in seconds, my ice seeking Joel's boss, the ironmaster, whose element I had learned was metal—perfect for ironworking. My spirit detected his presence quite readily, despite the many other dead metals crying out from the fires and tools in the hot foundry beyond me. Another worker approached me before I could head in the correct direction. He asked me what I wanted, his dirtied face taken aback by the presence of an obviously wealthy noblewoman in such a polluted place.

I told the man in no uncertain terms that I sought Master Denlinger, and he bowed jerkily at me before disappearing into the smoky expanse beyond. I waited impatiently, tapping my foot for what seemed an interminable time before Master Denlinger appeared, clad in soiled short pants and tunic, his brown hair wild, his usually light gray eyes the color of steel. He recognized me in an instant, pushing me out the main door onto the steps before asking, "Swanie? What is it?"

"Please, Master Denlinger, please . . . could you let Joel off for the rest of the day?" I begged, folding my hands and lifting them to his grimy face. "I realize it's not Vespers yet, but . . . I have to talk to him . . . it's very important . . . please . . . ."

The ironmaster's eyes faded to their natural gray, his expression stating that he knew exactly what had disturbed me. "Of course, Swanie, I can let him off this once. And you need not call me 'Master Denlinger.' You are my lovely Freia's most trusted friend. Please call me Heinrich."

"Oh yes, yes . . . thank you . . . Heinrich." I smiled shyly at him, impressed by his gallantry, wishing anew that he could manage to wed Freia somehow, her lack of Teuton blood notwithstanding. He entered the foundry a moment later, asking that I wait for Joel in the carriage. I followed his instructions, my mind racing to come up with some decent arguments against what he planned to do.

Joel opened the door to the carriage not long afterward, his clothing dirty from work, his blond hair appearing rather dingy, his face smudged. He hesitated a moment before sitting next to me, his expression suggesting that he did not wish to ruin my dress, which likely had already begun to show signs of wear due to my fight with the Prince—I had not taken the time to check. I waved him forward, my eyes holding his, my desperation doubtless evident on my face. I choked out a quiet order to Jarvis, asking him to drive again, anywhere, slowly. Then I turned to face Joel, closing my eyes briefly against the horrid reality before gazing into his hazel eyes, tears clouding my vision.

He blinked at me, watching me struggle to form words, concern evident upon his bearded face. "You asked my boss to let me off for the day . . . what happened, Swanie? You look terrified." He spoke in Teutonica, the phrases uncertain, his earnest eyes searching my face.

"I . . . went to see . . . the Prince," I began, stumbling over the English words. "I thought . . . I thought . . . when he summoned me . . . that he had changed his mind . . . and would give me . . . the song . . . ." My tears spilled onto my cheeks, and I brushed them away with my sleeve. Bloody images filled my brain, sounds of Joel crying in agony, in death, in his attempt to become one of my people. How had he found out about the most deadly Teuton rite in existence? I had never even hinted that it was possible for an outsider to gain Teuton blood.

Realization dawned on Joel's face, and he frowned slightly, nodding once, running one hand through his hair. "He told you about next Saturday." He made the statement in English, his voice dull, resigned.

I stared at him. "Were you planning to keep it a *secret* from me?"

Joel looked at me seriously, regret showing in his eyes. "I didn't want you to have to worry about it. I know you're against trying any dangerous rituals."

Anger flared within me, momentarily pushing aside my angst. "How *could* you *think* of attempting such a thing?" I demanded, my tears still flowing. "You're not looking at it the right way. It's going to *kill* you!"

"The chance of my survival is greater than fifty-fifty," he reminded me.

I recalled the statistics I had read in one of Hans' books ages ago: *In over 90% of known blood-transfers, one of the parties involved dies. In less than 40%, both lose their lives . . . .* "Your chances are *not* that great," I informed him. "And *you'll* probably be the one who dies, not Master

Denlinger. What are you thinking, involving him, anyway? Think of Freia. What if you survive, and he dies? What if both of you die? How do you think she would feel? She loves him!"

Joel averted his gaze from mine, looking at the shops and dwellings to his right as our carriage clattered along the streets of medieval Muniche. "He already talked to Freia about it during lunch break today. He told me she understands, and she'll forgive me if something goes wrong."

I gaped at Joel, my eyebrows coming together in annoyance. "So why do I have to be the *last* one to find out about these things?" I huffed, my tears having finally abated. I remembered that Freia had traveled to Muniche to share a lunch with her beloved, but I had no inkling of the issues they had apparently discussed. "It figures I had to find out from the Prince, not from you! We should have talked about this first, because you have no idea what you're getting yourself into."

He reached for my hand, sidling closer to me on the cushion, massaging my frigid fingers, trying to calm me. "Swanie, listen to me," he whispered huskily, his hazel eyes staring into mine. "I *love* you, and I want you to be my wife. I want to be your partner here, working together with you, running the Meldorf estate. I talked to the count about us last month, and he told me that he's planning on leaving his land to you. But he can't do that if you marry an outsider. It's against the law."

I shook my head at Joel, his urgent explanation falling on deaf ears. "Look, Joel, I really don't care about your blood. I'll marry you anyway, for I love you, too." I bit my lip at that lie, forcing myself to keep meeting his eyes as I went on. "I know I can't inherit any land if I marry you, but who cares? We can just travel around like we talked about before. You shouldn't risk death just for my sake!"

Joel leaned closer to me, grasping both of my hands in his grubby fingers. "Swanie, don't lie to yourself. I know you want to stay in Muniche, and for us to do that, I need to be your equal. You need a Teuton man; I know it from watching the others in the city. The happiest couples are the ones who married their equals, not the ones who married some other type of German. Your people are special, Swanie. They have powers in their blood that no one else can grasp. I never knew such a thing existed until seeing it firsthand here on the streets. You have a glory I can't attain without changing my blood, and I'm willing to try it, even if it kills me."

"But Joel, you're not accepting what the blood-transfer *means*," I insisted, squeezing his hands with the urgency of my message. "The Prince said that no one truly understands it until he takes part in it himself . . . and by then, it's far too late to reconsider. Becoming a Teuton isn't worth the risk!"

"For me, it is, Swanie." Joel's hazel eyes glimmered with sincerity while he explained, passion tingeing his tone, "If we really intend to stay here until the end, to see this beautiful city and its amazing people fall to the Saxons, I don't want to just hang around like an idiot bystander. I want to *fight,* and I'll need Teuton blood to have any sort of impact. I would have an element, and even if it ended up being something stupid, like, I don't know, *fog* . . . I could shove it up someone's nostrils and choke him to death. I want to be able to strive with the Teutons as their equal, not as an outsider. I want to be able to marry you as an equal, giving you children of pure blood to carry on our legacy once we've gone home. You said we're supposed to become a part of history while we're here. How can I do that if I keep being plain old Joel Hudson?"

His arguments were strong. Even in my fear I could appreciate the fact that his intentions were pure and courageous. But the means to such an end were *insane . . . .* "I understand that you want to do this for yourself, as well as for me," I allowed, cringing at the memory of the gruesome sketches I had seen in that ancient pamphlet about the blood-transfer. "But you're forgetting that the blood-transfer is *the* most dangerous ritual still performed in our time. The things I read about the Torstein, before we came here . . . they warned time travelers to stay away from deadly Teuton rituals. I know that ritual suicide is the only sure way of death while in the past, but I doubt that the Teutons who have used the Torstein ever bothered trying the blood-transfer. It could *honestly* kill you, Joel. How could I explain that, if I come back through those gates without you? What am I supposed to say to Beth, when she asks what happened to her boyfriend?"

Joel's expression grew troubled; apparently he had not thought of this. But at length he sighed and patted me lightly on the shoulder. "Hey, if ritual suicide is the only *known* way to die, I should be fine. If I actually died next Saturday, your people would have written it down, right?" I froze, shocked by his logic. "Anyway, I don't think the blood-transfer is going to kill me. Heinrich trusts Prince Otto to preserve our lives, and even I trust the Prince more than any other Teuton priest. They say that trust plays a big part in the success of the ritual. Maybe if the Prince turns me into a Teuton, he'll decide to change his mind and give us the song. I have to try it for your sake and mine, and for the sake of our future."

I tried reasoning with Joel some more, relating to him what I knew of the mechanics of the blood-transfer—the ripping of the arteries, the mixing of blood, the separation of the spirit from the body to complete the procedure. I mentioned that the blood-transfer dealt with Wuotan directly, the demon god of the Teutons whom we had already angered enough by using his powers to travel time. I feared that Wuotan would try to kill Joel before bothering about the ironmaster. But Joel shrugged off my concerns, promising that he would survive and insisting that he could put up with the necessary torture. "Just think, when it's done, I'll have an element like you," he proclaimed, looking elated.

When we parted ways soon afterward, Joel kissed my lips for a long moment, reminding me of his love. And I leaned back against the wall of the carriage as it rolled toward the eastern gate of Muniche, wondering how in the world it had come to this when I had offered Joel nothing more than cursory affection.

Chapter Thirty-seven

Respect the Price

That evening after dinner, I confronted Freia about Joel's plans, relating the entire story from the beginning. My ignorant American lover would attempt to become one of my people whether I liked it or not, and his own reasons for it were strong. I cried for a long time in Freia's arms, my mind completely consumed with images from the abyss. I saw Joel's handsome young body ripped apart, his arteries dangling in the hands of the Prince, his life gradually expiring while I watched. For the first time in my life, my thoughts and heart remained fixed upon Joel alone, and I realized that somehow I *had* to love him, despite my preoccupation with Teuton priests. No priest could give up so much for me, renouncing his heritage for the sake of my purity. Even Augustin's impossible love had been shoved to the back burner of my mind as I pondered Joel's insane devotion. What would my cousin think of him, of me, when we returned? And what if the ritual worked? Would Beth insist upon attempting it herself, if her boyfriend gained Teuton blood?

By the time my tears had run dry, our bedroom had begun to darken. Freia had assured me over and over that she had already spoken with Heinrich and that she fully agreed with what he intended to do for my companion. She understood that the blood-transfer might kill Heinrich and leave Joel alive, but she told me that she would not hold it against us, for the bounds of friendship began and ended with the willingness to lay down one's life for another. She would miss Heinrich if he died, but she would remember him as an honorable Teuton man, one gallant enough to risk everything to share Teutonic glory with a stranger.

We sat in silence for a while upon her bed, Freia gazing down at her hands folded in her lap while I stared into the flickering flames of the candles. I thought of Augustin finally, wondering what he would think when I told him of Joel's plans. Maybe he would suggest that we rush ahead with our own plot, to bleed the song from Paulus and leave the eleventh century forever. Then we could deter Joel from his fool's errand, for he would return to his American girlfriend and likely forget about becoming a Teuton. He and my cousin could build their future in America, and Augustin and I could remain in München, starting our future together. That would be the smartest plan, I realized, for if Joel went through the blood-transfer for my sake, I would have to force myself to love him for his pains. That would be difficult with Augustin in the picture.

I tore my gaze away from the candles, drawing in a deep breath and lifting my eyes to Freia's, intending to tell her the truth, to wish her long and prosperous days in Muniche without me. But she opened her soft lips first to speak the words that I had always feared to hear. "Heinrich spoke to his parents yesterday . . . about me . . . and him." Her lips began to tremble, and tears dampened her eyelids. "His family will not give us permission to marry since my blood is not Teutonic. They ordered Heinrich to find another woman." Tears trickled down her pale cheeks as she blinked at the coverlet beneath her.

Disappointment gripped my heart, and I pulled Freia into a supportive hug. "You'll have to run away together and elope," I whispered, thinking that if they did so, I should go with them and sign as a witness.

"No . . . ." My best friend spoke the word in Rhenisch, pulling away from me, her skin appearing even whiter when she raised her green eyes to mine. In them, I saw the wretched resolution, the same insanity I had seen in Joel's hazel eyes earlier that day, and I choked on my breath. "Heinrich loves me just as I love him, and we wish to be married properly, by Teuton law," she said fiercely. "I'm going to do the blood-transfer for our sakes. If all goes well next Saturday, Heinrich has agreed to give his blood for me, if Prince Otto allows it."

My skin grew frigid at her horrifying proposition, my eyes transforming into a frozen blue, cold air escaping my lips. "Freia, you *can't* do that!" I cried out. "You *can't* do the blood-transfer with a man; it would kill you both! Crossing genders threatens certain death, for the differences in the blood of men and women are too great to surmount. *Those* are the less than forty percent of all blood-transfers in which both parties die! It would never work!"

Freia shrank away from me on the bed, pulling her blanket around her to ward off the cold radiating from my being. "We talked about this at lunch, Swanie," she told me solemnly, her eyes silently pleading with me. "Heinrich and I are both willing to give up our souls for one another, so we may build our future together either here or in heaven. What other choice do I have? If I don't do this for Heinrich, I'll have to return to Eisenwald and marry a pompous prig, a man I do not love." Freia shook her head at me, wiping her tears from her eyes. "If this is the price I must pay for Heinrich, I will pay it, for I love him."

Her impassioned plea struck a knife through my heart, bringing Augustin's memories to the forefront of my mind: *I must save her, she cannot leave me, she cannot die . . . . I would do anything for her, give her anything, my life, my heart, my soul. I love her . . . .* "You're not going to do this with Heinrich," I said, my ice calming as I accepted the inestimable cost of friendship. "It's an unnecessary risk. If you must do the blood-transfer, you're going to do it with me."

Freia blinked at me, shaking her head in disbelief. "Oh Swanie.... I would never ask ... such a thing ... from you ...."

"You don't have to ask. I'll do it for you. You're my best friend here, likely the best friend I've ever had. I'll gladly offer my blood to make you my equal." A touch of dread crept up my spine, but I shoved it firmly away.

"Oh, Swanie," Freia repeated, gratitude evident in her tone. A second later she embraced me, murmuring her thanks, solidifying our friendship.

"I have just one request," I said when we rose from her bed soon afterward, preparing to sleep. The vastness of what I had just pledged to do had not hit me yet. I hoped that it would remain in the distance, or I might chicken out. *The Teutonic blood-transfer* .... I shuddered once, then told Freia, "We need to do this next Friday, before Joel and Heinrich do theirs."

Freia nodded at my words. She stepped to the mirror, washing her face at the bowl and studying her reflection. "I'll speak to the Prince tomorrow afternoon. Heinrich was supposed to send word that I need an audience with him. But why do you think we should do it first?"

"Because when Joel does it, I'm going to watch, and seeing it firsthand might scare me enough to make me reconsider." I smiled frankly at Freia as I pulled my brush through my hair. "I doubt the guys will reconsider," I added, "because men always think they're brave and powerful. Even if it kills both of us, they'll still go through with it."

Freia gave a half-hearted chuckle, and when we crawled into our respective beds after snuffing the extra candles, she whispered one final word to me in the darkness. "Friday?" Her voice sounded small and fearful.

I sighed heavily, telling myself not to be afraid, even though I was about to take part in the deadliest ritual known to Teuton lore. "Friday," I confirmed, shutting my eyes tightly against the awful images of Joel and me screaming in torment, drowning slowly in a pool of blood, dying forever, never seeing our home again.

When Joel arrived at the Meldorf estate the next day after Sext, we ate a late lunch together in the great hall, most of the vassals and guests already having dispersed. I informed him that Freia and I planned to speak with the Prince within an hour or so since she also longed to attain the magic of Teuton blood. He appeared troubled at first but admitted that he could not criticize our decision, since he was about to do the blood-transfer himself. "I guess that'll make us true equals, if we both go through it for the sake of our friends and our futures," Joel noted, looking rather impressed by my bravery.

"Hopefully if Wuotan decides to kill two out of the four of us, it'll be me and you," I said. "That way Freia and Heinrich can have their happily-ever-after here." Joel raised his eyebrows but admitted that I had a point, and we parted ways soon afterward; he planned to talk with the count about his intentions in my absence. I shook my head at my own folly while I rode the count's tan mare down the road to Muniche. Of course, I had no plans to speak with the Prince myself. Once I parted ways from Freia at the Bayern gates, I would ride like the wind to Augustin's cottage, for he needed to know of the madness my friends and I had planned. My steadfast love for Freia had upended my plot to escape to the future with him.

It took me longer than I had expected to locate Augustin. The bells tolled None all over the city as I reined my horse in outside a pub in the wealthy section of Muniche. I had switched horses with Freia outside the Bayern castle, riding one of the count's many dark brown mares in my quest for my master. I had clothed myself entirely in black for once, including a veil that did little to aid my vision, but I had chosen my attire carefully. It was Saturday, and I knew that I may encounter a decent number of familiar noblewomen on holiday in Muniche. Thus far, my relationship with Augustin had stayed mostly under the radar, since he visited me on Tuesdays and Thursdays. Therefore, I hoped to disguise myself enough that no one would take notice of my business with Augustin that afternoon, for I did not wish to become the topic of new rumors.

I went to his cottage first and found Viktor there alone. After some difficulty, he managed to convey the message that his master was not at home but that I could probably find him at the ritzy tavern on the southern side of Muniche. I balked at showing my face in such a place, but I thanked Viktor anyway, ordering myself to be courageous. The importance of the upcoming blood-transfers outweighed any consequences I might face upon appearing at a bar filled with the local aristocracy. After I tethered the count's horse at a railing several stores down, I walked resolutely toward the correct pub, thrusting its doors open with a flourish.

A bouncer of some sort met me at the threshold, requesting five Thaler for entry—a hefty sum, but I had stocked my purse with ten times that much before striking out for the city. I dropped the necessary coins into his greedy hands, and he bowed at me and asked if I required an escort. I told him no, drawing myself up straight, peering through my black veil at the scene before me.

The room was large with two separate bars set up against the right and left walls. Massive kegs lined the wall to my left while a variety of wine bottles stacked the shelves to my right. On the wall opposite the entrance stood a candlelit stage on which danced a jester, his clothing hideous, his antics ridiculous. A small band of fiddlers and flutists swayed to the right of the stage, playing cheerful tunes. Two couples skipped to their music, threading their way around the tables, the men well-dressed, the women looking unmistakably like wealthy harlots.

About twelve tables of various sizes stood between me and the stage, and I recognized the young Count von Reuter at one of them. I looked away quickly and ran my eyes over the giggling women interspersed amongst the men, their painted faces and careless gestures suggesting lecherous intentions. I frowned, thinking that I might be the only decent woman standing on the floor of this tavern . . . . And a second later, my eyes fell upon Augustin. He wore the robes of nobility and sat at a table with three other decently-dressed men, each pair of hands clasping an array of cards, a large hump of gold coins upon the table before them.

A sneaky smile crept across my face as I realized that this was the first time since Lady Maria's party that I had encountered Augustin on a Saturday, the day when he set aside work for pleasure. Now, he sat ten paces away from me, wholly engrossed in his gambling, his expression set in its usual harshness, his mouth pressed in a thin line at his companions' raucous hoots. I stood still, waiting to see how long it would take for him to notice my presence.

Finally, he lifted his eyes from his cards and looked straight at me, his blue irises flaring with disapproval. I froze, unable to step forward to greet him, the denigration in his glare frightening me. His mouth twisted into a sneer, and he rose from his stool, waving his free hand to someone across the room. My own eyes followed his gesture, and to my horror I watched one of the harlots cross the floor to his side. She wore a bright red dress with a neckline almost low enough to show cleavage, her black hair curled into a pile on her head, countless red ribbons dangling around her cheeks. Augustin thrust his cards into her hands with a cursory nod, and she sniggered at him, her sparkling eyes saucy. He said something to his companions when they bombarded him with complaints, then brushed past them, crossing the floor to where I stood frozen in less than a second.

"What are you doing here, Swanhilde?" he demanded, standing over me with his hands on his hips, his eyes burning me to the bone.

I struggled to organize my thoughts, my eyes darting from Augustin to the whore who now held his cards and back again. "I . . . I . . . had to find you . . . ." I choked, my Teutonica failing me. "Something . . . terrible . . . I had to . . . ."

Augustin huffed in annoyance, shooting a warning glance back toward the card players. "Can your crisis wait until I have finished my game? I *was* winning, before you appeared." He glowered at me critically.

I spluttered, closing my eyes as I tried to push aside the terrible truth I was seeing here and now. *Gambling ... harlots ... my unfaithful master ....* Finally, I pulled myself together. "Can I watch?" I asked, my voice hardly audible.

Augustin raised an eyebrow at me, still scowling. "You play cards?"

I shrugged quickly, trying to keep the disappointment off of my face. "Yes, I do, twenty-first century cards, to be exact. And I'm pretty good."

Augustin growled, then strode swiftly back to his companions, waving for me to follow him. I trailed behind, looking around at the other people in the pub once more. Thankfully, Count von Reuter was watching the jester. Augustin retook his seat, taking his cards from the harlot, announcing that he was ready to finish the game. He reached back to grab an empty wooden stool from the table behind him, dragging it to his right side for me.

The card game resumed once more with gusto, the other players murmuring as I shakily sat upon the stool. The eyes of the red-clad harlot were on me the entire time, an insolent smile upon her face. Abruptly, she plopped herself onto Augustin's lap, throwing her bare arms around his neck rather erotically. My master gave her a quick hug while I gaped, then turned his hand of cards just enough so that I could see them.

The four men played three more hands while I watched, sitting stock still upon the stool, trying to ignore the baleful stares of the whore on Augustin's lap. The game bore some similarities to Rook, though it involved ancient face cards, Roman numerals replacing the familiar numbers. After the third hand, Augustin won, prompting his three companions to howl in frustration, chugging their beer as he deftly transferred the entire pile of gold coins into his jeweled purse. "Five hundred fifty Thaler," he informed me proudly, stashing his winnings beneath his cloak. The red-clad whore clapped her hands, her grin suggesting that she planned to claim some of it for herself that very night. "Not too terrible a kitty."

I shook my head at Augustin while his companions begged for a rematch. My master refused, stating that he had more important business to attend. He rose from his stool, setting the harlot upon her feet. I watched in disgust as she took his face in her hands and kissed him soundly on the lips. "Should I expect to see you tonight, Augustin?" she asked, her voice seductive.

He smiled at her briefly, answering with a touch of dark humor, "Certainly, Gisela, assuming I do not receive news of a coming apocalypse." The whore laughed loudly at his joke, and Augustin snickered once before placing his right hand firmly upon my back with the words, "Let us leave this place."

I untied the count's brown horse moments later, my hands moving mechanically, my mind not wanting to accept what I had just witnessed. Augustin appeared beside me when I climbed into the saddle, already seated atop his black stallion, following me as I guided my horse toward the eastern gate of Muniche. I could not speak, and I blinked repeatedly to hold back tears of betrayal. *You knew this . . . you idiot . . . and you still let him seduce you . . . you let yourself love him . . . and he sleeps with the local whores every weekend . . . just like the rumors say. You're such a fool, Swanie . . . why can't you love Joel instead? He's a decent guy . . . a Christian . . . honest . . . trustworthy . . . .*

"So may we discuss your crisis in public if we speak English, or would that be too dangerous?" Augustin's deep voice cut into my troubled thoughts, but I could not answer, nor could I look at him. I rode the horse blindly, the reins slack in my hands. Suddenly, my master drew his stallion up directly beside me, his left leg touching my skirt, his strong hand taking hold of my reins. "Are you jealous, Swanie?" I knew he was staring at me, but I could not meet his gaze. He made a sound in his throat at my silence, jerking my horse forward, holding my reins and his. "Ride with me," he ordered, his voice callous.

My eyes swam with tears, and I hardly noticed as Augustin guided both horses to his cottage, placing them in Viktor's charge, swinging me out of the saddle and leading me through his front door without a word. Once inside, he shut the door behind us, locking it firmly and gesturing me to one of the leather chairs in his parlor. "Sit." It was not an option. I obeyed him, plodding forward as through mire, sinking down upon one of his high-backed chairs. I stared blankly at the polished table before me, at its brass legs carved in the shape of wolves' paws, mentally kicking myself for having fallen prey to a sex addict's charm. I had not even noticed that Augustin had left the room until he returned and placed a glass goblet of dark wine into my hands. He set the bottle upon the table and seated himself upon the chair to my right, clutching his own goblet of wine in his right hand. "Drink, Swanhilde, and speak to me."

My hands shook as I brought the glass to my lips. I closed my eyes to take a cautious sip, my tears leaking onto my cheeks. The wine was strong and fruity, fit for royalty, reminding me of the wine he had given me on the night I had witnessed his sacrifice. The alcohol warmed my throat, and I wondered for a fleeting moment whether Augustin intended to make me drunk, so he could convince me that what I had seen was an illusion. I took one more sip of wine, then said the only thing I could manage to say. "I suppose . . . your brother was right. You're a liar. All you want from me is my body, nothing more. You glory in my helpless submission, in my naïveté." I stared at the floor while I spoke, my voice sounding flat and dead.

Augustin was silent for a long moment; then he cleared his throat and spoke, his tone demanding no disbelief. "I shall be honest with you now, Swanhilde. For over two years, I have been sleeping with Gisela. She is the illegitimate child of a Teuton noblewoman and an Italian merchant; therefore, her Teutonic blood is high enough to hold me back from sacrificing her. She has a kind heart, though her mind is empty, and she is extremely good in bed. You have known from the start that I enjoy sex immensely, so my relationship with a prostitute should come as no surprise to you."

My element had begun to freeze me, my fingers icing over as they grasped the stem of my wine goblet. What had I been *thinking,* granting such a man control of my innocent heart? I had not been thinking; that was obvious. "So she's better than me," I translated dully, still gazing vacantly at the floor.

Augustin rose from his chair at my words, setting his goblet beside the bottle upon the table before kneeling at my feet. I turned my head away, unwilling to meet his eyes. He reached for my face in response, preparing to brush my veil aside. I cringed away and raised my goblet to throw it at his face if he tried to reach for me again. He grumbled in frustration and ripped the goblet from my hands before I could react, placing it upon the table. As I cowered on the chair, my empty hands clutching its leather, he leaned toward me again, the fingers of his spirit suddenly harsh upon my heart. "Swanhilde, look at me." I still refused, gasping in pain when he gripped my heart savagely. He pushed back my veil and placed his strong hands on either side of my face, forcing me to meet his burning eyes.

"Did you see Gisela in my blood?" he demanded, his expression fierce. My lips parted, and I whimpered, all of the languages I knew tangling inside my brain. "*Answer me!*" he roared, his hands tightening upon my face. I shook my head as well as I could in his iron grasp. "Exactly," he stated. "When you read my memories, you saw *what is most important to me.* I cannot lie with my blood. No one can. You saw my mother, and you saw yourself, and you saw that I love you more than I love my mother. You did not see Gisela because she is nothing to me. She is just a game, a way of escape from my tormented life, a way to release my sensual urges. *You* are much greater than that, Swanhilde, and you know it. You are the one who has changed my world, shown me that there are greater things in life than murder and lust. I enjoy Gisela's body and the taste of her Teutonic blood—but I love *you* for your soul. Swanie, you are the *only* woman whom I have befriended for more than a year in my adulthood who still retains her virginity. *That* should give you reason enough to never doubt that you are my everything."

My mind whirled at his impossible words, but I could not forget what I had seen in his blood, in spite of what had happened at the pub that afternoon. He was right. I had not seen Gisela; I had seen myself. I struggled to sort out my feelings, my jealousy, my disbelief. "But how . . . how . . . ." I could hardly recall any Teutonica in my discomfiture, and finally the words came out in Bayerisch, my native language. I do not know whether Augustin understood them or not. "How can I marry . . . how can I *love* . . . a player . . . a heartbreaker . . . how can I *love* . . . ."

Augustin's hands softened upon my face and my heart, his fingers tender now as he gazed deeply into my eyes. "Swanie, when I am married to you, I will not *want* any other woman," he said, his hands brushing away my tears. "Your body will satisfy me as no other . . . for you are a Teuton . . . and I have never . . . in my *life* . . . shared a bed with a woman of pure Teuton blood. You are everything I desire, everything I love. That will never change."

I blinked against a new flood of tears, a stream that did not stem from betrayal this time. Augustin pulled me against his chest and held me tightly while I wept, his voice reassuring me, reminding me again that he was the partner I truly needed. In spite of what Joel planned to do for me, Augustin would forever have my heart. When I finally composed myself, he drew back from me just enough to look into my eyes. "Am I forgiven?" he inquired softly.

"Yes . . . always . . . ." I whispered back, pulling his lips to mine.

Chapter Thirty-eight:
A Devil's Advocate

When we ended the kiss, Augustin did not let go of me at first, his light blue eyes gazing into my gray ones, a contented smile gracing his lips. We were both kneeling on the floor together now, I realized, the leather chair at my back, my master's arms curved around my body, holding me still. At length Augustin sighed, tracing the warm fingers of his right hand softly across my lips. "Your kisses are far better than Gisela's, my darling," he said, his eyes lidded.

A shiver of pleasure ran through me, and my hormones began churning in my veins. "Really?" I whispered, relishing the touch of his fingers upon my mouth.

Augustin chuckled quietly, staring into my eyes. "Kissing your lovely lips is like melding with an angel . . . melting snow in my fire," he said. "And your tongue is far more intoxicating than any wine I have ever tasted."

My heart began to pound, and I took a deep breath, ordering myself to keep my head. "Augustin . . . you're driving me insane . . . ." I reproved him, my eyes traveling to his magnificent lips, the realm of his fire.

My master drew me closer and murmured, his mouth brushing mine, "I will alter your standards one day, my dazzling swan princess . . . ." His lips merged with mine an instant later, and we kissed for an infinite moment, my hands running through his silky hair, my icy breath meeting his fire in blissful glory. He ran his own hands down my spine, bending me backward until my veiled hair pressed upon the leather chair behind me, his tongue memorizing every portion of my mouth. When he finally pulled away from me, I panted for breath, my heart pounding like a freight train. "Have I convinced you yet?" he asked me, tracing his hands down the sides of my bodice.

He had the sinful part of me convinced, but I forced myself to remember that I intended to wait until marriage. "Not . . . yet . . . ." I admitted, though my eyes likely appeared otherwise as they stared fixedly at his lips.

Augustin groaned, his expression becoming perturbed. "You certainly are a hard case, Swanhilde von Thaden," he stated reproachfully, taking his hands off of me and sitting back on his heels. He shook his head once, a caustic smile appearing on his face. "Whenever you *do* change your mind, please tell me immediately. I do not care if you have to drag me away from the archives or interrupt another card game. I would leave everything behind for your sex." His eyes appraised my body, glittering in approval at my all-black dress.

I laughed shakily at his fervor and placed my hands upon the leather chair at my back. "You'll be the first to know, Augustin," I promised.

"Fair enough." He smirked at me, picking himself up from the floor and holding out his right hand to help me stand. I grasped it with a smile, allowing him to lift me to my feet. "But if today is not the day, we may as well confront your crisis," Augustin said, waving me to the chair and retrieving our wine goblets from the table once more. Disturbing images of the blood-transfer erupted afresh in my brain, and I deliberated on where to begin. He handed me my glass with the words, "I suppose I may safely assume that your calamity has something to do with the discussion you held with my brother yesterday, since I doubt that he chose to show you mercy and grant you his song. If he had done so, you could have waited until Tuesday to impart the information to me."

"You assume correctly," I affirmed, then ran through a condensed description of the Prince's warning about the dangers of forming the heart-bond across the expanse of time. I did not broach the subject of Kezia, focusing instead on the Prince's harsh judgments of Augustin's character. My master shrugged, noting that Prince Otto had never appreciated him and that his accusations were nothing new. "Well, I fought him over it," I disclosed, fingering my wine glass.

Augustin's eyes widened at this, and he leaned forward in his chair, both of his hands clasped around his goblet. "With words?" he queried.

I snorted quietly, wishing it had been that simple. "No, it . . . was a little worse than that," I told him, embarrassed by my disrespectful actions with the Prince. "He said that your love was a lie, and that really bothered me. I really started tearing into him after that . . . bringing up the subject of Marelda . . . and his bond with the city of Muniche. He warned me to stop more than once, but I didn't listen. And in the end, he attacked me with his fire."

Augustin's eyes popped open, his body growing rigid. "You fought him *with your element?*"

"Yeah, it was . . . really scary. I've never fought another Teuton before, and I doubt I would have won, except . . . ." I remembered the moment when fear for my life had overtaken my soul, bringing Augustin's fire out along with my ice. I exhaled once, then met Augustin's anxious gaze and confessed, "I was trying to melt his fireballs . . . just three of them, I think . . . but I realized that couldn't go on . . . and before I knew what was happening, *your* fire came out of my hands."

Augustin gasped, his goblet trembling in his usually sure hands. His light blue eyes began to glow with heat. "You threw blue fire at him?"

I nodded and chewed on my bottom lip. "I don't know how it happened. I didn't think I could *do* that . . . I mean, you gave me your fire only once. I united it with my spirit, but I didn't know . . . that I could . . . . I almost passed out with shock when I saw those blue flames shooting from my frozen fingers."

Augustin blinked, his expression disturbed. "What did my brother have to say about that?" he questioned, looking as though he feared the worst.

"Well, he stopped fighting me, thankfully." I thought back, trying to recall every detail. "He climbed down from the back of his chair and watched my blue fire fighting his red fire in midair until the flames evaporated. Right after that, we both noticed that in my elemental desperation, I had altered the color of half of the flames burning on his chandeliers, changing them from red to blue. He said that what I had done was impossible . . . and he said that he would ignore it . . . for the moment." Dread addled me at the potential repercussions.

Augustin sighed heavily and took a long sip from his goblet. "That may indicate trouble for you, Swanhilde. When a Teuton woman successfully creates an element far astray from her own, priests consider that to be sacrilege, a level of knowledge no woman is allowed to achieve, the path toward witchcraft."

I trembled, suddenly fearing that the Prince may break through Augustin's front door to drag me to the main square of Muniche and burn me in front of everyone. I opened my mouth to speak, failing, and Augustin took another sip from his goblet, his eyes still upon me. "If you are lucky, my brother may decide to level all of the blame upon me. It would not be difficult for him to discover that I, in fact, have taught you all that you know. I do not know what penalty he would thrust upon me, although for years he has insinuated that one day I shall have to pay the price for my sins." Augustin grimaced and averted his gaze to his bookshelf on the far wall. "The Catholic clergy have asked him time and time again to have me executed for my murderous tendencies, as well as my fornication. The nobility has begged him to cast me into prison or evict me from Muniche altogether. Thus far, he has ignored their pleas, for he knows that I am the rightful ruler of this city. He fears what might come to pass if he chastises our mother's favorite son."

His words got me thinking in a new direction, and I should have predicted the truth at that point. When I look back upon it now, it is blatantly obvious. But my love for him held me blinded, as the Prince had said, so instead of addressing the issue of Augustin's habitual sins I asked, "Does the Prince think Marelda might come to haunt him if he punishes you?"

Augustin chuckled darkly, leaning back in his chair. "I doubt he fears such a thing, since he knows as well as I know that our mother is in heaven. Those souls who reside there do not prefer to return to earth, unfortunately. But in light of your . . . skirmish with the Prince . . . we should go ahead with our plans immediately and leave this time behind us, before something dreadful comes about as a result of your unprecedented skills."

I swallowed a mouthful of wine, hesitant to bring up the next subject, the one that truly actuated my "crisis." I had a feeling that Augustin would explode once I told him of my plans with Freia, so I addressed Joel's resolution first. "After the Prince and I had calmed down, he finally told me why he had summoned me to the castle. Apparently, Joel has decided to prove his love for me in the most terrible way possible. He plans to become a Teuton by blood alone, with the ironmaster as his donor, next Saturday." I paused, awaiting Augustin's reaction.

My master raised his eyebrows, and a sinister smile spread across his face. "Well, that is certainly brave of him, courageous and incredibly foolhardy. I suppose Master Denlinger has asked my brother to perform the ritual?" I nodded, and Augustin spat out a derisive laugh. "He shall kill one of them; that is definite. It would make matters easier for us if Joel dies, for when we meet him on the other side of the gates of time, you can say, 'You are fated to

remain an outsider. Go back to your previous girlfriend.'"
He laughed again.

I frowned, Augustin's lack of sympathy annoying me.
"I couldn't do that. If he dies because of the blood-transfer,
I'll end up blaming myself for the rest of my life. And if it
succeeds, and he survives . . . I'll have to marry him even
though I will never love him. I can't disparage him once he
becomes one of our people. I would have to reward him for
his pain . . . at the cost of my happiness."

Augustin snorted and ran one hand through his black
hair. "Swanhilde, your pure heart wants to pull you down
into the abyss. You need not feel guilty for the choices of
others. You are not responsible for Joel's destiny, and if he
succeeds in becoming one of our people, you are under no
oath to become his wife. But there is another option, of
course. If we drag him back through the gates of time
before next Saturday, he shall likely forget about the
blood-transfer altogether, once we have returned him to
his own era."

I wished more than anything that I could have agreed,
but I had already resolved to do the same thing for Freia's
sake, and I would not renege. "Augustin . . . I . . . can't . . .
." Words failed me, and I shivered at the thing I had
pledged to do. The priest beside me waited, eyeing me
suspiciously as I gathered my courage. "I can't leave . . . the
eleventh century . . . yet," I whispered, my whole body tensing. "I'm going to do the blood-transfer too, for Freia, on
Friday."

Dead silence in the room, broken by the shattering of
glass upon the wood floor. Augustin's wine goblet had
fallen from his hands, splattering its contents all over the
floorboards, staining his black boots. He stared at me in
horror, his jaw working manically, his hands curling into
claws. "*Are . . . you . . . INSANE?!*" The words burst from
his lips like the cry of a hawk, his blue eyes flaming with
fire.

An instant later, he had leapt from his chair, crossing
the floor to stand over me threateningly, heat from his
blood scorching me through my clothing. I cringed away

from him, pushing myself into the back of the chair. "I *have* to," I gasped, my ice flooding my veins in defense. "Freia is my best friend, and the Denlingers won't let her marry Heinrich any other way. I have no choice—"

"You *DO* have a choice, you fool!" Augustin cut me off, his hands clutching my shoulders so tightly that I shrieked. "The blood-transfer will *kill* you, and I will *not* allow it! No one deserves your Teuton blood. *NO ONE!*" He shook me, his white teeth bared, his expression suggesting madness.

"Augustin . . . I *have* to do it," I whimpered, struggling to free myself from his muscular grip. "I *love* Freia . . . I . . . ."

"*Damn you!*" Augustin roared. His hands abruptly ripped the veil from my hair, shoving it away from my neck, forcibly tilting my head to the left. He bit down onto my artery, and I yelped, wondering what he could possibly be seeking now. His powerful hands pinned me to the chair, his body shuddering as he drank my blood . . . and he pulled away before I could count to ten, wiping my blood from his mouth.

I pressed my right palm against the wound, working to close it myself. I accomplished the feat without much difficulty, although Augustin had likely begun to halt the bleeding himself. I lowered my right hand to my lap, staring at the blood staining my fingers. Then I raised my eyes to my master, who stood bracing himself against the table, his countenance wavering between shock and resignation. "I see now," he said at last, his hands gripping the edge of the table. "You love her, and you want her to be your equal. You have no choice. *I* have no choice . . . ."

I nodded slowly, trembling with belated shock. "Forgive me . . . master . . . ."

Augustin shook his head as if to clear it and shut his eyes. "Do it then, since you love her. But you should know" —Augustin reopened his eyes to stare at me dangerously— "that the Prince has conducted three blood-transfers since my return from Salerno, and I have witnessed each one. He killed one of the participants each time, and once, he killed both of them. His skills at the devil's work are lacking, for he prefers to consider himself a saint."

I shivered again at this, recalling what Joel had said about the aspect of trust as a necessary component of a successful blood-transfer. "But who else could we ask to do this? Freia and I both know the Prince . . . ."

"You could ask any of the Teuton priests in Muniche, and not one of them would be willing to save you if Wuotan laid claim upon your souls. They hold no sway against the whims of a demon, for they are all Christians tampering with the powers of darkness. That is why every Teutonic blood-transfer ends in tragedy, for it is Wuotan, not God, who gives us our blood." Augustin's lips curled into a sneer, and his eyes cindered me. "*I* could preserve both of your lives, if you ask me to perform the ritual," he proclaimed.

My mouth fell open as I considered this possibility. "How many times have you done the blood-transfer?" I asked, curious.

Augustin's sneer deepened into a scowl, and he replied shortly, "None."

I gaped, my mind working to understand his self-confidence. "Then why . . . why do you think . . . *you* would succeed . . . ."

My master stepped toward me, darkness radiating from his aura. "Because unlike the other eighteen priests in Muniche, *I* do not shirk the duties of Wuotan," he said. "He has granted me some sway over the continuance of Teuton blood, a power I have used countless times to preserve the lives of laboring women. Unlike the fools who cringe at the authority of the pope, *I* would not simply stand by while Wuotan dragged you to your death. I would argue publicly for your souls, whatever the cost. For the blood-transfer, Swanhilde, you need a devil's advocate. *That* is I."

I stared up at Augustin, the demonic gleam in his eyes not escaping me. *It would be safer to trust a heathen priest to do this right* . . . . But something he had said in his discourse had taken me off guard. "What do you mean . . . that you would argue *publicly* for our souls? Are you saying . . . ."

"Yes, blood-transfers are always performed in public," Augustin confirmed, prompting me to freeze, my fingers melding with the glass goblet I still held. "The ritual, since it is so incredibly gruesome and devilish, has the tendency to draw a crowd, which is one reason the Catholic clergy detests it so much. Blood-transfers are traditionally done at Sext, so anyone breaking for lunch may attend the ritual, held on the platform in the main square of Muniche. Once the ceremony is complete, a council member officially announces the blood results, and a chronicler documents everything for the city records."

I began to hyperventilate as my thoughts raced back to what Hans had told me about the blood-transfer. *The one ritual that involves Wuotan directly . . . can be carried out anywhere . . . in a home or a forest . . . with no more than a priest, two willing parties, a knife, a bowl, and a fire.* "I thought it was done in private. At least, in my era . . . it's not a public spectacle."

Augustin smiled derisively. "That is likely due to your modern notions of reason and your disbelief in the miraculous. You have told me before that people in your time believe that the world appeared by chance, without God. Why would such agnostics wish to watch a ritual that clearly evinces the presence of demons? In this era, the supernatural influences everyone. Though no one prefers to admit it, the populace at large still clings to the ancient lore. Therefore, many commoners and nobles alike enjoy observing the sorcery of Wuotan, to the displeasure of the clergy." Augustin's smile grew sardonic.

I would have to think about this later, but I doubted that the public nature of this ritual would dissuade me from doing my duty. The idea of allowing everyone I knew to watch my agony while a Teuton priest ripped my arteries from my body was not a pleasant thought, but I had to go through with it for Freia's sake. So I nodded, my ice gradually withdrawing back into my spirit. "So you think we should let you do it, instead of your brother." Augustin nodded seriously, and I continued, "And you'll ensure that both of us survive . . . pulling us back from death if Wuotan tries to take us."

"Yes, I shall, but I must prepare extensively first." Augustin frowned, walking back to his chair, glancing once at the shards of glass and wine staining the floor. "Since I have never done this before, I shall read everything I can find on the subject and speak with every priest in Muniche who has performed the ritual. I do not wish to kill either of you due to my own ignorance."

"I'm going to have to convince Freia," I realized, wondering how I could possibly manage that. "She doesn't exactly . . . trust you . . . but she knows about our love . . . so hopefully she'll agree, for my sake."

"When I see you Tuesday, we shall sit down together, the three of us, and I shall relate all of the necessary information to you, so that you may prepare." My master rested once more upon his chair, his hands folded before him as he gazed toward his bookshelf with a pensive expression. "You must convince Freia to trust me, Swanie, or Wuotan may decide to kill her. Both of you must be willing to put your souls into my hands, so I may bring you safely to the other shore of the bloody river. When Wuotan comes to you, offering you relief from the pain, both of you must be willing to refuse him, enduring the torture, or you will die. I believe both of you are Christians, so you need not fear his power over your eternal resting place . . . but he will likely try to kill at least one of you."

Suddenly another thought occurred to me, and I sat up straight, a Bayerisch curse falling from my lips. "Freia went to speak with the Prince this afternoon, to request that he perform the blood-transfer on our behalf. I'm supposed to meet her in front of the Bayern gates. She probably wonders where I am." My eyes drifted toward the front door of the cottage.

Augustin was on his feet in an instant, motioning for me to get up. "In that case, both of us must depart. You must meet your beloved friend and convince her to trust me for this ritual. I must also ride to the castle this evening and order the Prince to renounce his claim on your blood."

When I mounted the brown horse not long afterward, having cleaned up my appearance considerably, my veil once more concealing my face, I asked Augustin one final question. "Are you still going to sleep with Gisela tonight?"

He grinned at me roguishly, his light blue eyes flashing in the fading sunlight. "Unless you would prefer to share my bed tonight?" I shook my head at him, and he nodded. "Then I shall see Gisela, but now, you must ride. To business."

Chapter Thirty-nine

The Details

Joel met us at the stables as soon as Freia and I returned to the Meldorf estate from our activities in the city. On the ride home, I had rehashed most of what Augustin had told me, trying to persuade her that it would be far safer to trust him to perform the blood-transfer on our behalf. She appeared unhappy with the idea, murmuring that she did not wish to put her naked body in the hands of a known rapist. I laid the topic aside once Joel joined us, for his hazel eyes shone with exultation. He had informed the count of his intentions to become a Teuton, and apparently the count in turn had pledged to reconsider his plans for his land if the ritual succeeded. "He told me that I'd better claim you fast once I have Teuton blood," he said with a grin as he helped me down from my horse.

"The local lords around here are ravenous," I answered, putting on my best show of nonchalance. "Heinrich will have to do the same. The vultures will descend once word gets out that Freia's about to change her blood." My room-mate blushed, and we spent the rest of the evening and weekend chatting with the vassals about blood-transfers they had witnessed, about what to expect. Their tales grew taller with each passing moment. One priest had nicked someone's heart by accident. Wuotan had possessed one new Teuton after the ritual had finished. Ghouls had risen from the graves of those who died during past blood-transfers; local priests had to hold exorcisms. By Monday night, I had begun to regret offering my Teuton blood for such a rite. *You don't have to be scared,* I told myself over and over again. *Most of their stories are just made up. Augustin will do it right.*

The issue of Gisela gnawed away inside of me in my master's absence, and I found myself wondering what exactly he had done with her on Saturday night. Did he go to her every night or only on weekends? He had said that her mind was empty, but how intimately did she know Augustin? Had he shared his sorrows with her, or was theirs a relationship built upon sensual profit alone? His blood had confirmed that he preferred me over any other woman—over anyone, actually—but I had trouble finding peace with the concept of a partner who patronized prosti-tutes.

When Augustin visited the Meldorf estate on Tuesday afternoon, I buttonholed him about it after we sat down upon the porch bench that faced the gardens. He wanted me to summon Freia so he could impart all that he had learned about the blood-transfer, but I told him flatly that I needed to speak with him privately first. "Did you have.. . an enjoyable night on Saturday?" I asked, my narrowed eyes scrutinizing his face.

He looked away from me, his countenance growing inscrutable. "It was decent," he said, his eyes focused on the sky, their irises nearly an exact replica of its hue. "Gisela is always a talented whore when it comes to matters of the bed. She never complains when I hurt her, submitting without protest to my demands. Unfortunately, even she could not clear my mind on Saturday night, allowing me full relaxation and release. This blood-transfer shall plague me until it is done." He frowned and folded his arms.

"What, did Gisela not make you drunk enough to forget your troubles?" I curled my lip at him, wondering whether rough sex was the only type he knew.

Augustin pursed his lips at my humor and studied me out of the corner of his eye. "Even drunkenness cannot erase all memories, Swanie. And I rarely intoxicate myself, despite what rumors you may have heard. I tried, Saturday night, but even then I kept seeing your tears of agony, your body ripped asunder, the burning knife in my hand . . . ." He broke off, his expression pained. "Gisela asked me about you on Saturday night, after she had made me drunk," he added.

"What did you tell her?" I asked, fearing the worst.

"She asked me who you were, and I told her the truth." Augustin waved a hand at me when I froze. "Do not fear her gossip, Swanhilde, for no one listens to a harlot. She said that she had seen you around the city, usually in the company of a blond-bearded metalworker, a commoner. She had heard that you plan to marry him and that the respectable women consider you a coquette." Half of Augustin's mouth curled upward into a wry smile, his face still turned toward the gardens.

I sighed at his words, disgruntled that in spite of my good intentions, apparently my public reputation left much to be desired. "Did she say anything else?" I asked finally, unsure whether I really wanted to know. Maybe he and Gisela just gossiped about other people during their raunchy activities; if so, she did not know his heart.

Augustin turned his body to face me, his light blue eyes glowing just slightly with his fire. "As I lay naked upon my sheets," he began, meeting my gaze, "with her resting atop me nursing her wounds, she looked me straight in the eye and said, 'You love her, don't you?' And I responded—after twisting my hands in her hair for a moment, imagining it was yours—that I do love you." His eyes burned into mine.

I gaped at him, my own mouth dry. "What did she say to that?"

He eyed me seriously, lifting one hand to trace it down the side of my face. "Her exact words were, 'She is a very lucky woman.'"

The enormity of that statement sent a shiver of pleasure through me, a smile of satisfaction playing upon the corners of my lips. *So I'm better than Augustin's whore, and she envies me . . . for he does not love her, and she knows it.* "I hope I'll be enough for you once all is said and done," I said, leaning my cheek into his hand. "I don't really like to share."

Augustin chuckled quietly and leaned forward to kiss me, his lips imbuing my entire body with warmth. "Neither do I," he informed me when he had backed away, laying his hand back into his lap. "And thus we must hope that my brother fails in his attempt to transform Joel into a Teuton. You had best call Freia now, so I can clarify any uncertainties either of you may have about the upcoming ritual."

I found Freia helping the maids with their spring cleaning on the second floor. She hesitated to accompany me when I told her that Augustin had come to share the details about the blood-transfer. "Swanie, I'm really not sure if I can consent to him doing the ritual instead of the Prince," she told me in a low voice, wiping her hands off on an apron that she had tied over her plain green dress. "I'm having trouble finding peace with the idea of the city executioner ripping my body apart in such a way. It might tempt him to treat me like one of his harlots—or a sacrifice."

"He won't sacrifice you once you have Teuton blood," I assured her. "And we'd be better off to let him do it since he doesn't shy away from Wuotan's devices." My roommate pursed her lips, and I beckoned her to the front staircase. "Either way, we should go and listen to what Augustin has to say. He probably has some tips about how to survive."

Freia agreed to this with a sigh, and we stepped onto the porch shortly afterward. Augustin had risen from the bench and stood against the railing of the porch when we appeared. He bowed low in Freia's direction, thanking her profusely for agreeing to meet with him to discuss our plans for Friday. Freia curtseyed uncertainly in response, her cheeks red as she returned Augustin's greeting in a shy voice.

He nodded once at her, his expression just a trifle irritated. Then he waved us to the bench, announcing that he would stand before us at the railing and relate every bit of relevant information he had learned in the past several days. He requested that if either of us had any questions, we should voice them with no reservations. He also added that if we had trouble understanding something, we should say so immediately, so he could explain in Latin, English, or Rhenisch as the situation required.

Freia and I sat upon the wooden bench with our backs to the house. I could tell that Freia felt uncomfortable with our impending chat, so I slipped my left hand into her right one, squeezing it supportively as Augustin began to speak. "I have spoken with the clergy and the council already, and they have granted me permission to perform this ritual for your sakes." He paused briefly, eyeing us both in turn, and I felt Freia stiffen.

Her green eyes met mine an instant later, her forehead wrinkled in reproach. "We're better off letting him do it," I repeated quietly, a touch of guilt seeping into my chest at her reproving expression. I had tried to convince her that Augustin would be a better choice of officiant several times since Saturday, but I had not told her upfront that it had already been settled.

Freia murmured a quiet prayer and clutched my hand more tightly, shifting her gaze back to the priest before us. He looked from one of us to the other, then began to speak again once he saw that we had fallen silent. "The council has scheduled our duty to take place this Friday at the opening bells for Sext, so that anyone interested in observing may do so during their lunch break. The ceremony shall be held in the main square of Muniche, on the platform across from the fountain, where all public rites are conducted, including executions." A dark smile touched the corners of Augustin's lips. I eyed him reproachfully, trying to send him the message that he should stop scaring Freia.

"Upon the platform shall stand two wooden benches, upon which each of you shall lie for the ritual," Augustin went on, meeting our eyes in turn. "A small table shall be placed between these benches, bearing the iron bowl for the mixing of your blood, the stone knife for the opening and closing of your wounds, and the vial of viscous solution for the blinding of your eyes."

Both of us recoiled at that pronouncement. My forehead wrinkled as I tried to recall whether I had read anything in *Der Weg* that referenced such a thing. "Each participant of the blood-transfer must be blinded beforehand, whether they are male or female," Augustin stated, observing our reactions. "The writings suggest that those who retain their sight never survive the journey through the river of blood, for many disturbing things could be seen during the ritual. Thus, they are blinded to protect their souls, that Wuotan's minions may not lure them into eternity."

Freia and I looked at each other again, the fear in her eyes doubtless reflecting my own. "We don't . . . stay blind afterward . . . right?" I asked Augustin shakily.

"Of course not; the blindness is temporary," he said, a look of mockery appearing in his light blue eyes. "A Teuton who has some degree of experience in the spiritual realm could direct their element to break through the blindness and free their sight, though I would not advise doing such a thing."

"So the solution is kind of like contact lenses," I mused to myself in Bayerisch, silently thinking that I might try to remove it just to see how Wuotan's fiery river looked.

Meanwhile, Augustin began to describe the other items that would be upon the platform: an iron cauldron of fire for the invocation of Wuotan and a screen enclosing the sides that faced the audience. "The screen is set up for the sake of public decency," Augustin explained, a wry smirk curling on his lips. "The clergy does not wish the entire city to clearly see your bodies, as you both shall be naked for this ritual."

Freia gasped sharply, and my eyes turned slightly blue, although of course it would make sense that we would have to be naked for the extraction of our arteries. Augustin's eyes glittered as though he imagined exactly how the two of us would look when we lay helplessly before him three days from now. *He's probably getting hard just thinking about it,* I thought to myself.

I felt heat spreading across my cheeks, so I turned my attention to Freia, who cowered against my left shoulder. I slipped my hand from hers and placed it around her back instead. "He's not going to care about how you look," I muttered to her. "He has to focus on the ritual itself."

Augustin discussed the placement of the audience next. The clergy would stand to our right as we lay upon the benches, the other Teuton priests of Muniche to our left, along with a chronicler to record the process for the city records. Behind the clergy and priests would be the women who had chosen to observe, since both Freia and I were female, and in the back, the men, furthest away from our nudity and shame. The audience would be required to keep silent for the duration of the ritual. Any who attempted to come forward for a better view would be beaten back by the knights standing guard. Those who tried to interfere would be punished later.

From there, Augustin began to relate the steps of the blood-transfer one by one, beginning with our arrival at the square before the bells for Sext. There would be some sort of shelter set up behind the platform, where Freia and I would have to remove our dresses and wrap our bodies with a red cloth. "The cloth is intended to protect your privacy until you have lain yourselves upon the benches," Augustin explained, "for if you simply stepped onto the platform naked, the audience would likely see more than they ought. The color of the cloth indicates the nature of the ritual, of course: bloody, wicked, painful, devilish. Once you have stretched your backs upon the benches, you must unwrap your bodies, leaving the red cloth draping over the sides of the benches, offering you some comfort, I suppose, since it remains between your skin and the wood. However, I doubt once the ritual has begun that you shall remember the softness of the fabric, after you have entered the burning river of blood."

I shivered once, still holding Freia in my arms for my own reassurance as well as hers. Augustin paused to declare that the Lady Freia appeared as though she had a concern and should voice it while she had the chance. I looked at my best friend, noticing that her lovely face had turned deathly pale, her green eyes terrified. I whispered in her ear that she ought to say whatever she needed to say, that Augustin would not harm her, although he eyed her with an expression that could burn ice. At last, Freia began to speak, her breath coming in short gasps. "My Lord von Bayern . . . I do not know . . . if I'm comfortable . . . with . . . with . . . the nakedness . . . ." She choked on the final word, her cheeks flushed scarlet.

Augustin's eyes softened and he stepped away from the railing, bending down so he could meet Freia's panic-stricken gaze. "My Lady Freia, the three of us here on this porch are the only three who shall observe your nakedness. And in spite of the terrible rumors you have heard about me, the appearance of your body will be the last thing on my mind, in light of the seriousness of the blood-transfer. You need not fear me; I promise you that." Augustin and Freia stared at each other for a long moment, and finally, my best friend nodded slowly, sidling even closer to me. Augustin straightened, but before he stepped back to the railing, he shifted his gaze to my face and added mischievously in English, "But I shall be *very* interested to see *your* nudity, my darling Swanhilde."

I gave him a hangdog look, wondering in the back of my mind whether that may spell trouble for my tenuous virginity, assuming I survived the blood-transfer. At that point in my life, I had never shown my naked body to a man, yet I knew for a fact that I was something to look at, considering the many compliments I had received from men both young and old whenever I wore tight dresses or bathing suits. My breasts were a decent size, not too large or small, and my legs and hips earned quite a few stares of appraisal when I wore shorts in the summer. I said nothing to Augustin's comment, averting my eyes to the fields behind him. *What will he think of my body when he's seen so many naked whores and sacrifices in the past? Will he find me more attractive than them?*

Augustin began detailing the blood-transfer in earnest during his next discourse, describing the physical process step by step as well as what Freia and I would experience as the victims of this horrid ritual. I realized quite quickly that what little I had known about the blood-transfer was nothing compared to what would actually happen. The things Augustin told us made my blood run cold, but I was grateful that he had chosen to explain everything to us, so we could have one last chance to reconsider.

First, Augustin would speak the opening words of the ritual in Ælte Teutonica, invoking Wuotan's mercy, wisdom, and protection—this preliminary incantation always disturbed the clergy the most, Augustin noted with scorn. Next, as the flames in the cauldron responded to the chant, taking on colors and shapes with the power of our demon overlord, Augustin would blind Freia and me. This would be our first moment of pain, the beginning of what would seem to be infinite torment. Once we had relinquished our sight, Augustin would heat the knife in the flames of the cauldron until it glowed white, all the while speaking more chants to Wuotan. Then he would begin the procedure with me, for my Teuton blood was stronger and more vital. Until Freia became a Teuton, I could bleed longer than her, my master stated flatly, adding that he would endeavor to hold back our blood flow until he had finished all eight of the incisions.

The cuts would start near our hearts, Augustin told us, branching out from there to our limbs. The first cut would reach down to my left knee, the second to my right knee; the final slices would curve upward to the creases in my elbows. He would make similar incisions in Freia's flesh and then lift out our arteries whole, trusting Wuotan to preserve our bodies for the completion of the ritual. Next, Augustin would mix the artery blood in the iron bowl, setting its contents aflame with the cauldron's fire. Once it had burnt out, he would replace the arteries, giving me one from Freia's leg and one from her arm, that our blood's eternal union may be accomplished. He would heal the incisions using both the fiery knife and his skills at blood control, and the ritual would conclude with the typical test for Teutonic blood. My own Teutonic blood should end up stronger, and Freia's percentage should match mine.

Throughout the entire procedure, Augustin informed us gravely that we would notice nothing save the agonizing pain. Our souls would leave our bodies behind without any elemental protection, plunged by Wuotan himself into what would seem to be an endless ocean of blood. We would feel as though we were drowning in our own blood, Augustin said—smelling, tasting, breathing its disgusting substance. Our voices would scream on this mortal world and in the bloody river until our strength waned, until our will to survive dimmed. Despite the gruesomeness of the ritual itself, with its physical impossibility and fatal risks, the greatest danger awaited us after Augustin had closed our wounds, when our souls drifted in dying torment.

"By that time, all either of you will wish for is relief," Augustin informed us solemnly, his expression grim. "You will desire an end to the pain, an end to the fire, an end to the drowning blood. It is then that Wuotan shall come and offer you exactly what you want, an end to the suffering, cessation of pain. He shall come persuasively with the intent to beguile you to follow him into eternity, to death. No matter *what* Wuotan may offer you, you *must* resolve to refuse him. You must not cease fighting for your lives until I close the ritual with the Ælte Teutonica words, '*It is done.*' Then, only then, can you rest."

Freia and I stared at Augustin, then at each other. All of the morbid details of what we planned to do polluted my mind, sickening my willpower. Was I really brave enough to face this terrible thing?

But after a long silence, Freia nodded at me, resolution visible in her wide green eyes as she squeezed my hand firmly. So I turned to regard our heathen priest with the words, "We believe you, and we shall do it."

Chapter Forty:
A Taste of Death

Augustin's face grew caustic at my confident assertion. He sighed once, crossing his arms and leaning back against the railing. "I feared that my reasoning would not dissuade you . . . you foolish, naïve women." He scowled at us, blue fire highlighting the annoyance in his eyes. "I shall freely give my soul for yours during this ritual, using my influence to argue with Wuotan for your lives, should he try to seduce either of you. Yet I had hoped that you would be willing to reconsider, once informed of the bloody details." Augustin sighed again, his expression growing resigned. "But I suppose that my brother is right, that no one truly understands the extent of the blood-transfer until one takes part in it; and by then, it is far too late. Logic and reason are powerful forces, but the intellect holds no sway over the rabid desires of the heart."

I smiled slightly at his words, and Freia squeezed my hand again. We both knew full well that we would do the blood-transfer no matter the cost, for she loved Heinrich Denlinger, and I loved her. There was no other solution but to give our blood for one another, to offer our souls for a cheerful future. "Well," I said, stretching a bit on the bench,

413

"it's a good thing we're planning to do ours first, because if both of us survive, we'll have one more chance to dissuade the guys from doing it." Freia laughed lightly at my joke, though her face still appeared pale and uncertain.

"Both of you shall survive; I shall make certain of it," Augustin pledged, his expression positive. I rose from the bench, prepared to tell Freia that she could go back inside, to give Augustin and me some time to ourselves before he inevitably left to plunge back into research. But before I could speak, Augustin lifted a restraining hand. "I have not yet finished, for I fear that the Lady Freia still holds some doubts which must be removed before we perform this duty." Freia stiffened on the bench, her wide green eyes darting from me to Augustin. Though I had no idea how he intended to convince her to trust him, I nodded at her in reassurance, indicating that she should hear him out. He stepped away from the railing, kneeling onto the porch at her feet and lifting his light blue eyes earnestly to hers.

"Lady Freia von Eisenwald," he began slowly, his tone resonant, his eyes sincere. "I know that I ask a hard thing of you." My eyes flew open when he spoke to her, switching adroitly from Teutonica to perfect Rhenisch, her native tongue flowing from his lips with the grace of one who had spoken it for many years.

Freia's eyes widened as he talked quietly to her, holding her gaze with his, reaching forward carefully to take her hands. To this day I know not what he said to her, for while I had picked up some Rhenisch from my best friend, I knew only the rudimentary phrases, often understanding them within the context of our conversations. But Augustin spoke to Freia with astonishing fluency, his tone persuasive, his eyes begging for her trust. She whispered a few sentences in response, her manner apologetic. I turned away from them and approached the railing to observe the count's magnificent flower gardens, roses, lavenders, and pansies in bloom for early June.

When the murmured exchange behind me ceased, I circled back to face the bench where Freia sat, her hands still imprisoned in Augustin's fingers, her eyes still locked with his. I could tell by looking at her face that the fear in her eyes now no longer resulted from him, but from the ritual itself. As I watched in fascination, Augustin released her hands, lifting his to cradle her delicate face, like he had done to me many times before. He spoke one short question in Rhenisch, his voice deep and pleading, and I had a feeling that I knew what he had asked: "Do you trust me?" I saw Freia whisper a response, apparently the right one, for Augustin's eyes glittered with approval. He murmured to her one final time before kissing her forehead gently.

A contented smile graced my lips while I watched him pull away, seeing the shock and amazement on Freia's face and the satisfied glint in my master's eyes. Before taking his hands off of her face, he said in Teutonica, "Lady Freia, your radiance is like that of the sun, and your hair like a field of barley under the summer sky." Freia gasped, and he let go of her, rising to his feet with a cursory nod. "It shall be intriguing to see what element is granted to you."

Augustin came to my side at the railing, and I asked him if he planned to stay longer. He replied negatively, for he had much more research and preparation to do before Friday. "Unfortunately, we likely shall not meet again until Sext on Friday, my swan," he told me, his eyes burning with regret. He lifted his right hand to my face, tracing it down my cheek and jaw, the heat of his skin causing me to shiver with desire. He bent his head toward me, his mouth a centimeter from mine as he said, "If you still love me after what I must do to you on Friday . . . I shall never have occasion to disbelieve again . . . even after one thousand years." Our lips met a moment later, and his arms wrapped around me protectively.

Later that night, Freia and I discussed the upcoming blood-transfer for a while, relating our fears and taking comfort that we would be tackling this frightening ritual together. I noted that we probably ought to eat and drink more than usual on the day before, to strengthen our blood for the bleeding, though that likely would not help much. As I slid beneath my blanket, I heard Freia shift on her bed and comment softly, "I see now why you fell in love with

Augustin von Bayern. He can be quite charming when he wishes, and his intelligence lightens his fearsome countenance."

I smiled wistfully at her words, knowing she was right. I wished that I could find it within myself to forsake Joel in spite of the blood-transfer, in spite of his insistence that we meet the trials to come as equal partners. "Yes, he's . . . amazing," I murmured back, not knowing what words could suffice my love for Augustin.

"It surprises me that I'm about to say this," Freia whispered, her voice sounding slightly tense, "but I think you should marry Augustin instead of Joel." I said nothing to this, closing my eyes against the ache of love and those alluring hands forever stroking my heart.

Late Friday morning, Freia and I rode to Muniche in the count's carriage with Jarvis in the driver's seat and the count himself seated upon the bench facing us. He had been distressed when he first learned of our plans, but he admired our bravery and decided to accompany us to the main square so that he could observe the cost of loyalty. He told us that he had not witnessed a blood-transfer in over two decades, for he generally found the ritual too grisly to watch. He also feared that one of us would not survive. Both of us plastered false confidence on our faces and reassured him, telling him that Augustin von Bayern would be the officiator and that he would preserve both of our lives no matter the cost. Count von Meldorf vowed to stand as near to the platform as he could, and afterward he would have Jarvis bring the carriage around to pick us up once we had washed ourselves. He had stocked the space beneath his seat with crackers, fruits, and bottles of wine, so that we could restore our strength.

Freia and I both felt grateful that the count chose to accompany us, even though he disapproved of our mad venture. Heinrich and Joel had also promised to stand amidst the crowd, foregoing lunch on our behalf. Several of our noble friends—including the Denlinger sisters, Lady Hildegard, and Lady Adeline—had promised to attend as well. The presence of our friends eased our fears enough for us to mount the carriage that morning, though my ice coursed lightly through my blood in apprehension.

We said little to one another or to the count while the carriage clattered over the dirt road toward the drawbridge. When Jarvis paid our toll, I looked out the window to see Garin Zeuner bow at me gravely. I looked away from him, focusing my attention on the light blue sky streaked with cirrus clouds and the chattering rivulets of the Isar beneath us. At least the weather was perfect today. We need not fear interruption from rain or extreme temperatures.

Jarvis turned the carriage toward the main square after we passed through the eastern gate, and my eyes took in the streets, houses, and shops teeming with life. I watched several peasants pushing carts laden with fabric, a small group of young knights gesturing at each other with their swords in a vain attempt to impress two teenage girls laughing upon a windowsill, knots of children shouting as they played in the gutters, shopkeepers arranging their goods and tantalizing passers-by with their pleas for a sale. A smile curled across my face while I gazed at the activity of my medieval city, comparing it to the München of my era. Not much had changed in one thousand years. Business still boomed, and the people still enjoyed the daily commotion.

Jarvis parked the carriage in an alley at the eastern side of the square, not far from the platform. Freia and I climbed down from the carriage and paused in the shadows of the high-roofed buildings, waiting for the count to join us, our eyes fixed on the wooden platform that might be the site for our execution. It had already been furnished like Augustin had described. My ice-tinted eyes could see the two benches where we would lie side by side, placed perpendicular to where the audience would gather, the screen obscuring their view of our naked bodies. I saw the table between the benches and the iron cauldron not far from the platform's edge. I could not see the items on the table from where we stood, nor could I tell whether a fire already burned within the cauldron. No one was on the platform yet, although a small group of people had begun to congregate just beyond the screen, which looked to be slightly higher than my waist.

"There is still time to change your minds." The count's gravelly voice cut into my concentration, a hint of desperation in his tone.

I summoned my courage and turned to face him, ready to insist that our duty was necessary. But to my surprise, Freia spoke first, her green eyes alight with a valor I did not feel. "We cannot, my lord. All you can do for us now is pray." She clasped my right hand tightly, a solemn promise.

The count made a grumbling noise in his throat, but he nodded at us, then stepped forward to give us each a parting hug, his element leaving just a trace of dust upon the blue dress I wore. "Lady Swanhilde, you must try your hardest to survive, for my sake," he said. "If you die, I will have to seek out another Teuton to inherit my land." I chuckled shakily and pledged that I would do my best.

Freia and I undressed moments later in the small, enclosed area that had been set up behind the platform, hanging our clothing upon two metal hooks and laying our shoes on the ground below. At length Freia whispered, "Just in case we don't . . . survive . . . I have to say . . . that you've been the best friend I've ever had . . . Swanie." Her eyes met mine, her blond eyelashes damp with tears.

I threw my naked arms around Freia, hoping that the ice coursing through my veins did not make our goodbye hug uncomfortable for her. "I can truthfully say the same thing," I whispered back fiercely. "And that includes all the friends I've had in the future, too. You'd better make sure you survive, even if I don't . . . because if this doesn't work, I'll be greeted by the gates of time, not the gates of eternity."

We stepped away from each other and retrieved the deep red cloths that hung on hooks upon the flimsy wall of the enclosure, wrapping the coarse fabric around our naked bodies. We paused beside the exit to listen to the sounds of the gathering crowd, our final hesitation grasping our souls as we realized *what* we were about to do, in front of the entire city. I began shivering although I was not cold, and I clutched the cloth tightly around me. The first bells for Sext began pealing through the square, and Freia drew herself up straight, her expression set. "I trust him to keep us both alive. Let's do this," she said.

I bit my lip briefly and amassed all of my fading courage. "I trust him, too. Let's go."

We ascended the four steps to the platform moments later, carrying ourselves with a poise that I certainly did not feel. We walked steadily to the wooden benches, and on the way I let my gaze run quickly across the square. There had to be five hundred people present, from nobility to the poorest commoners. I did not have time to pick out any familiar faces, but I did see six members of the Catholic clergy standing to our right, attired in vestments, and to our left, the black-clad Teuton priests of Muniche.

My eyes left our audience behind as Freia and I stepped around the table between the benches . . . and I lifted my gaze to our heathen priest, Augustin von Bayern. He stood with the flaming cauldron at his back, his cobalt eyes appraising us, a rather demonic darkness erasing all traces of mercy from his face. He wore black from chin to the ground, his sleeves flared like the robes of a vampire, his hood pushed back to reveal his obsidian hair shining in the sunlight, half of it pulled behind his head as usual. After glaring at us for what seemed like an infinite moment, he waved us to the benches, then turned to address the audience, stating our names and current blood percentages in an emotionless voice.

I glanced at Freia briefly while I lay upon the left bench. I tried to send her a message to not be afraid, that we could trust Augustin despite his alarming façade, which was necessary for this ritual. She was not looking at me, but I saw that her fingers trembled when she slowly unwrapped the red cloth covering her body. I followed suit and stared up at the sky above, trying to concentrate on the beauty of the day, to stop my arms from quaking. Augustin began the invocation of Wuotan, his Ælte Teutonica sounding authoritative and humble at the same time.

I closed my eyes, ordering myself to relax, although my ice did not want to obey. Some of Augustin's recitation crept into my brain while I worked on breathing steadily: *As your servant, I appeal to your mercy to preserve the lives of these two . . . . Give me the power once more over the continuance of Teutonic blood . . . over the souls of these two . . . . Forgive us for our treachery, Wuotan . . . may you use this ritual for your glory alone . . . .* My eyes flew open as the implications of this incantation surfaced in my mind. By performing the blood-transfer—in *public*—Augustin seemed to boast of his demonism and hatred for Christianity. He likely spoke the opening invocation with much greater sincerity than any of the other Teuton priests in Muniche. It was no wonder the Catholics distrusted this ritual.

Suddenly, Augustin's face appeared above me, his expression still devilish, his right hand holding the vial of viscous fluid, preparing to pour it into my eyes. I summoned all of my strength, clutched the bench more tightly, and looked into my master's eyes, shoving my doubts away. He leaned forward, placing his left hand firmly on my forehead, and his ferocity faded for the briefest of instants as his lips formed the English words, "Forgive me for what I must do."

The solution blurring my vision was the first moment of pain, Augustin had said on Tuesday. I fought to hold myself back from shrieking, for I knew worse was to come. While I waited for those final seconds of humanity, my body tensed for the fiery cuts from the knife, Augustin's words whirled through my memory: *Forgive me for what I must do.* I doubted that any other Teuton priest would say such a thing before blinding a woman. I loved him so much, for I knew that he considered me his equal. He would have to hurt me today, more than ever before, but that would change nothing. He was my chosen partner, now and forever.

As these blissful thoughts flowed through my mind, putting a smile upon my face despite the blindness, I felt a sharp pain slice into my chest just below my heart. Fire split my skin apart, racing down my stomach, my hip, my leg. A matching blaze opened my right side, tearing through me with impossible speed, cutting into my ribs, my shoulders, my elbows. Weakness grabbed hold of me while the stone and fire seared my flesh, the acrid smell of blood assaulting my nose, its stickiness choking my lungs, binding me to the ground. And I felt flaming hands of darkness ripping my spirit from my body as I screamed, the agony overtaking every memory, every thought, the terror pulling me into delirium . . . .

And I felt myself plunged into the depths of the ocean, it seemed, every defense failing me, unable to move, unable to breathe. Blood had conquered my spirit, clouding my reason, staining my very being. I could no longer feel the coarse cloth beneath me, the warmth of the sun, Augustin's hands tearing my arteries from my body. My spirit was gone, pushed into a repulsive oblivion without the help of my ice, my eyes blinded, my tongue tasting nothing but blood. I gasped, I cried, I tried to scream, but I was drowning slowly in a river of blood, a fire consuming my soul from the inside out. Was this hell? I could not see. I could not think. My faith in God should have protected me from this.

I was alone. Some corner of my mind remembered the things Augustin had said on Tuesday, that Freia would be in the same position as me after our bodies had been cut apart. She should be here somewhere, drowning in her blood, in my blood, in *our* blood . . . but I could not sense her. I screamed, but I heard no reply. I sensed nothing but this vat of blood, this burning blood scarring my spirit, dragging me down to the abyss, never to see light again, never to know relief. *No one truly understands extent of the blood-transfer until one takes part in it . . . . That naïve Prince. He never understood it himself. How could I . . . how could we . . . this is hell . . . death . . . where is death . . . anything . . . free me from this torture . . . .*

Suddenly, I was no longer alone. As I felt my strength failing, my will to fight slowly dissipating, I heard a voice speaking to me out of the blood, out of the fire. *Swanhilde*

. . . I can bring you to the other shore . . . . It spoke in Bayerisch, my native dialect. I did not recognize the voice; its pitch sounded too deep to be human, too confident, too seductive. I tried to ignore it, to concentrate on fighting for my life. *Swanhilde . . . you cannot fight forever. You do not have the strength. You will fall into death, into eternity . . . unless you come with me. I can lead you to safety. I can relieve your pain. Give in to me, Swanhilde. Come with me . . . you do not belong in a place like this . . . .*

The blood had fully engrossed my soul, the fire burning me alive, the sticky liquid inundating the lungs of my spirit. How had I not died yet? I could no longer scream; my strength had almost vanished. Relief . . . yes . . . I needed it . . . I wanted it . . . heaven . . . anything . . . . *Come with me. I will give you relief, my dear. Do not struggle. Put your spirit into my hands, and rest . . . .*

Though I did not recognize this bass voice crooning in my ear, I found that I could not resist it, either. It offered me exactly what I wanted, and this torment had lasted too long, into infinity. I could no longer recall what it felt like to walk the earth without pain, without a sweltering fire scorching me from the inside out. It was too late for me. All I wanted was salvation from this bloody river, from this fiery torture. *Yes, Swanhilde, rest now . . . allow me to set you free from this pain . . . it is too much for you . . . .* And I stopped trying to scream, stopped trying to breathe, stopped trying to fight. I put my spirit into the hands of darkness, silently begging them to take me away.

The pain faded gradually, and as it dulled I worked to peel back the veil of blindness that obscured my vision. I summoned my ice to restore me as I vaguely began to wonder what it was that pushed me forward, what soft voices hummed around me, welcoming me, praising my bravery. I felt like I was in the spiritual realm now, no longer drowning in a fiery river of blood. Perhaps if I could see, I could find my way back to my body . . . somehow . . . .

The moment my element broke its way through the curtain that impeded my sight, I saw those labradorite gates right in front of me, their doors standing open, the currents of time beckoning me forward. *SWANHILDE, NO!!!!*

That voice I recognized, and I would have paused, but I found that I could not. The truth of the matter hit me fast, and I abruptly recognized my mistake. I had given in to the temptations of Wuotan. He had pulled me from the bloody river too soon, sapping my strength, twisting my will to live . . . and now I would die, and he would laugh at his victory as I rushed back to the twenty-first century. What would my failure do to Augustin? Horror overtook me, reinforcing my resolve, but I still could not turn back. And I heard a horrible argument, roaring voices.

You CANNOT take her. You have GIVEN me the authority over Teuton blood, the power to pull souls back from death. She is MINE!

It is too late for her, my servant. She is just one of many, and she chose her path herself. She will go. You can do nothing.

If you take her, you lose ME! Is that what you want, master? Do you want me to follow her into that black oblivion?!

You cannot follow her in death.

I WILL, one way or another. GIVE her back to me, or you lose everything you have worked for!

Destiny's tide has claimed her. There will be other women, my servant.

NO ONE CAN TAKE HER PLACE! I will DIE with her!

Very well. But you cannot tread both paths forever, Augustin.

Just as the hands of my soul began to disappear into the darkness of time, I felt a blazing fire scorch me again, dragging me back with a force I could not counter. I screamed as the gates of time faded away from me, and my spirit contracted, cast again into the blood, into the agony. But I heard him say, as I drowned completely in the final throes of the bloody river, *Forgive me Swanhilde, but I love you too much to let you die this way.*

Chapter Forty-one:
Final Arguments

Eventually, I regained consciousness, my spirit gradually returning to my broken body. I heard murmuring voices as through a fog, felt the pain of a metal knife slitting my wrist, sturdy fingers holding it still, healing the wound as abruptly as it had come. I breathed in shallow pants, my hands barely feeling the coarse cloth beneath my skin.

The absence of pain in my chest and limbs surprised me, for I remembered the fiery cuts of the stone knife ripping my body apart. Somehow, the sorcery of the ritual had repaired the injuries to an extent not humanly possible. A fleeting memory crossed my brain, an image of my Opa Hobart, who had quadruple bypass surgery several years before I embarked on my adventures with the Torstein. It had taken him months to recover, weeks to feel no pain. Yet here I lay, still as a corpse, having undergone a surgery far more complex . . . sensing no pain in my chest or limbs, just an overwhelming weakness that pinned me to the bench.

I heard Augustin's voice addressing the crowd, stating rather impassively that my blood now stood at ninety-six percent Teutonic and Freia's matched mine exactly. My lips began to form a feeble smile at this news. An animated murmur raced through the audience, and I heard my master speak the closing words with an air of finality: "It is done." *So it worked . . . . Freia and I both survived. We are Teutons joined forever by blood.* I wondered whether my blood would still be ninety-six percent Teutonic once I returned to the future. Technically, time travelers returned unchanged from their adventures, yet I had read something that made me contemplate . . . though I could not recall where or what . . . .

There was a bit of commotion around me, murmured phrases in a language I did not understand—Rhenisch, I realized, Augustin and Freia. Thus far I had not opened my eyes, working instead on gathering my strength, overcoming the weakness of profuse blood loss. Freia's blood flowed through my veins now along with my own, and I imagined that I could detect a difference, a new vitality. I felt the heat of the noonday sun upon my naked flesh, and I flexed my fingers slightly. It was time to live again, to push aside those awful memories of drowning in my own blood, of Wuotan's hands upon my spirit, pushing me toward the gates of time. *Augustin had given me a second chance . . . .*

When I opened my eyes, blinking against the bright rays of the sun, I saw my savior's face hovering above me, his blue eyes aglow with concern. I stared at him in adoration, disregarding the blinding sun. My lips parted, but I found that I could not speak as I looked into his mesmerizing eyes, their beauty rivaling that of the ocean. "Can you get up?" he asked me quietly, his gaze roving once over my naked body before focusing on my face.

I still could not speak. I stared at my master desperately, silently longing for him more than ever before. I wanted to feel his powerful arms around me, granting me their strength. *He pulled me back from death . . . and he argued with Wuotan for my life . . . I love him . . . he loves me . . . .*

My heart throbbed with yearning, and Augustin's lips twisted into a discontented frown as he leaned down to wrap my exposed body with the cloth. "You need not fear anymore, Swanhilde," he told me while he wound the fabric around me, taking my head in his hands when he had finished. "The blood-transfer is done, and it was successful. Both you and Freia are now ninety-six percent Teutonic."

My eyes tore themselves from his face at last, rolling to the right, where my best friend had lain. "Freia?" I choked, my voice barely audible.

"She is fine. I helped her off of the platform. She likely washes herself now, in the basin of water that has been brought from the well. You need to do the same before the blood dries on your skin. You do not want to irritate your wounds, my darling." The touch of his hands upon my face sent my hormones racing.

I did not know whether I could manage to stand yet, so I simply gazed at him, ordering my voice to break free from the weakness. "You . . . saved me . . . ."

He scooped me into his arms, a wry smile spreading across his face. "Yes, I did." A hint of triumph appeared in his eyes.

"You . . . argued . . . with Wuotan . . . ." I could not think of what to say, how to express my amazement at the boundlessness of his love.

"You heard." His smile grew a trifle sneaky.

"'I love you too much . . . to let you die . . . this way.'" I breathlessly repeated what he had said when he had pulled me into the river of agony, that magnificent promise that had carried me through the final moments of pain.

He smiled at me tenderly and traced my lips with the fingers of his right hand. "I suppose I should be angry with you, for almost taking yourself away from me like that. But now, as I stand with your living body in my arms, I feel only relief . . . and gratitude." He paused, having carried me off of the platform to the walls of the enclosure, behind which I could hear Freia splashing water over herself. "You must not do this to me again, Swanhilde, no matter how attached you become to some foreigner. I cannot bargain with Wuotan indefinitely for your soul. I feared today that he would refuse me . . . that I would have to leap through those gates behind you . . . though it would kill me . . . ." Distress clouded his face, and he held me closer.

The passion in his words struck my heart, and I leaned my head against his chest. "Augustin . . . . I want to stay with you," I moaned. Forever after, anytime I faced death, I would return for him, if he called me.

He fingered my lips again, desire burning in his eyes. "And you must," he crooned, "you *must* stay with me . . . for without you . . . I have no hope . . . ." He set me carefully upon my feet a moment later, hovering over me while I steadied myself. I realized that most of the weakness had finally left me. My blood coursed strong and fast, and I needed to find Freia, to welcome her into the companionship of the Teutons. "Once you have cleaned yourself and dressed, both of you should return straight home to rest and regain your strength, to allow your new blood to run its full course," Augustin advised.

I nodded at him, then remembered that I had planned to meet Joel for dinner once he got out of work at Vespers. Freia had pledged to do the same with Heinrich Denlinger. Both of them would want to make certain of our survival, and both of us would have to argue one last time for them to cancel their plans for the next day. "We'll go back, but we have to eat dinner with Joel and Heinrich first," I told Augustin, my voice finally sounding normal.

His expression grew slightly caustic. "Of course. Perhaps now that you and Freia have experienced the blood-transfer yourselves, you may be able to convince those foolish boys to reconsider. I highly doubt that my brother shall go to such *lengths* to preserve their lives, should one or both of them choose the path of death, like you did." Augustin eyed me scornfully.

"You're probably right." I shivered once at the thought. "We're certainly going to try, but I doubt they'll listen." Augustin smirked and turned to go. I took a step forward, reaching one hand out to him from underneath the red cloth. "Augustin . . . ." He halted, and I thought fast, unsure what I needed to ask of him, what I desperately *wanted* of him. When he turned slowly to face me, a glorious demon ensconced in black, I choked out the words, "When will I . . . see you again?"

"Tomorrow," he answered without hesitation, his eyes glittering with expectation. "I never miss a blood-transfer, Swanie, for there is always something to be learned from such ghastly ceremonies. You shall see me there."

I sighed in relief, though part of me could hardly stand to wait that long. By then I would be completely distracted by Joel's mad act of bravery, unable to discuss the events of today in detail . . . ending with my master's valiant dash to save my life. How could I possibly love Joel if this wicked priest would throw such things in a demon's face, disregarding his own soul for mine? "Augustin," I gasped when he turned from me again, "I . . . I . . . thank you . . . for . . . saving me . . . ." The words were horribly insufficient.

He stopped his retreat and flew to my side, his fiery eyes staring into mine as he whispered thickly, "I would pull you back from death a thousand times and again . . . my love." And he kissed me, his arms completely enveloping me in black, our lips taking each other's hungrily, a playful striving of fire and ice, inestimable glory. When he parted from me, returning to the platform to clean up the mess, I ran my tongue across my lips, wishing to taste Augustin forever, whatever the cost.

Freia and I met Joel and Heinrich on the front steps of the ironworks at the first bells for Vespers, both of them bubbling over with excitement at the success of our blood-transfer. We had spent most of the afternoon recovering in the count's carriage, sipping wine and consuming the crackers and fruit, marveling at the lack of pain from our healing wounds, recalling the deep red scabs we had seen on our bodies when we washed. Jarvis drove us to the ironworks shortly before the end of the workday; he and the count returned to the Meldorf estate afterward. The count ordered his servant to bring each of us a horse for the journey back home after we shared dinner with our respective lovers, and Jarvis promised to tether them outside the Denlinger house for our use.

Dinner was festive, though short, the entire Denlinger family present at the table, including Heinrich's sick father. It was the first time I had met the elder Master Denlinger, a gray-haired ghost of a man who coughed frequently, his skin yellow with illness. Despite his obviously poor health, he conducted himself like a model gentleman, congratulating Freia and me on the victory of our blood-transfer, welcoming Freia into the sphere of the Teutons. Heinrich's younger sisters chattered with us constantly. They asked all sorts of questions about the blood-transfer while their mother ordered them to be still, stating that such discussions were not fit for the dinner table. Once we had finished the meal, Joel and I went outside for a private chat while Freia accosted Heinrich. Twilight had already begun to descend, but I was determined to try one final time to dissuade my naïve companion.

"Okay," I began, speaking English as we sat upon the Denlingers' stoop, "I have a lot to say and no time to say it, so you'd better get ready to listen."

"I'm ready, but first, can I ask one question?" I sighed impatiently, and Joel leaned forward on the steps, placing his hands between his knees. I noticed that his fingers appeared a lot more limber after almost a year of hard work at the foundry. Beneath the sleeves of his brown tunic, his arms also looked impressive. *But that's nothing compared with* . . . . "I was wondering why that executioner officiated your blood-transfer. I thought it was supposed to be the Prince."

Of course he would have to bring *that* up. "Well, that's kind of a long story," I hedged, trying to come up with a decent excuse for Augustin's involvement. I had kept my dealings with the eldest Bayern brother a secret from Joel following that organ concert of mine; he had no clue about the relationship we had nurtured in the shadows. At last, I admitted part of the truth. "As it turns out, the Teutonic blood-transfer is, *like I said,* the most dangerous ritual known to our people, because it involves Wuotan directly. Augustin von Bayern doesn't cringe back from devilish rituals like most of the priests around here, so Freia and I decided that it would be smarter to let him perform the ceremony." Before Joel could speculate on this, I added sharply, "And we were right, because in case you didn't notice, we both survived, which happens less than ten percent of the time."

Joel made a snorting sound, then shrugged. "I guess that's good, but I have to say, seeing him up there ripping you to shreds really scared me to death. The whole time, he looked like he wanted to eat your flesh, *seriously*."

I rolled my eyes. "The Prince will probably look at you and Heinrich the same way tomorrow, assuming you haven't had a spark of intelligence and decided not to do it. The priest has to be merciless for the blood-transfer in order for it to work. And Joel, you really, *really* need to reconsider. Honestly. You have no idea what you're about to do . . . *I* didn't know . . . until today." My voice cracked, my lips quivering as I searched for words to explain my newfound horror.

Joel looked into my eyes, his face troubled. He put his left arm around my shoulders and pulled me close to him. "Tell me what it is, Swanie."

I drew a shaky breath, then met his gaze as I spilled my story. "It was the *worst* thing I've ever done in my entire life. It was worse than watching my brother die, and for years I thought that was the most awful pain possible. This was beyond the bounds of earth. I thought it wouldn't be so bad, in the beginning . . . when they put that stuff in your eyes to blind you, it's uncomfortable but not unbearable. Even the first cuts, the fire and stone . . . even those weren't so terrible . . . at first. But once the priest finishes cutting you . . . *that's* when the horror begins . . . when your soul leaves your body—"

"Wait a minute," Joel interrupted as I shuddered at the memory of forsaking my body with no elemental protection, "are you saying that your soul *actually* leaves your body . . . for this ritual?" His face looked slightly nauseated. "That's not possible . . . according to the Bible . . . for to be absent from the body is to be present with the Lord . . . our souls can't *do* that . . . ."

"The souls of outsiders can't," I corrected, wondering how to properly deal with this issue. "You know about the powers of the Teutons. You've mentioned the elements and the blood control. Well, one of the other things Teutons can do is to separate their souls from their bodies, leaving their elements behind. And that's what makes this blood-transfer *really* dangerous. I think it may be Wuotan himself who pulls the soul from the body without protection."

Joel drew back from me, his expression disturbed. "This is more serious than I thought," he muttered, a bit of uncertainty crossing his features. He glanced toward the pair of horses tethered not far away, his lips twisting into a grimace.

"It's *far* more serious than anyone thinks," I agreed, warming to the subject now. "Wuotan pulls your soul from your body and plunges it into a river of fiery blood, and when you're there, you can't *think* of anything else. You feel like you're drowning in blood and burning in the flames of hell at the same time. You can't remember what life was like before you ended up there, because the pain is so terrible. You want it to end somehow, anyhow, even if it means death. *That's* the danger, the worst aspect of the blood-transfer. Once you think you've been in that horrid blood and fire for all of eternity, you'll take any way out, no matter *who* offers it. And Wuotan is the one who will come to you, offering you relief. But his definition of relief is death, not success."

Joel gawked at me when I paused for breath, fingering his beard nervously. "Did he . . . did Wuotan . . . do that to you?" He sounded horrified.

No reason to deny it. "Yes, he did," I said, drawing my arms tightly around my body at that dreadful memory. "And I thought I was ready. I thought I knew enough to refuse him. But by then, all I wanted was relief, an escape from that bloody torment, a quenching of that fire eating my spirit. So I believed him. It was the stupidest thing I've ever done. He dragged me from the blood too soon and shoved me toward the gates of time."

Joel gasped at this admission, his hazel eyes bulging. "You mean . . . you saw those gates . . . the ones we jumped through to get here?"

"I did . . . and I couldn't turn around, even though I tried."

"You nearly went home to Beth," Joel murmured, a faraway look in his eyes. "I wonder how she'll react if I return home with Teuton blood like you."

"She'll probably try to convince me to offer my blood for her. She's already tried that before." I cringed. "But I could never do the blood-transfer again, not for her or anyone else. It's going to infiltrate my nightmares for years, I think."

Joel held his peace for a while, and I chewed on my lip at the thought of my cousin learning that I had done the very thing I had urged her not to do ever since I had first told her about my Teuton blood. She would doubtless feel betrayed. If the ritual succeeded tomorrow, and Joel achieved the magic she longed for . . . . "If you were so close to those gates, how did you manage to come back?" Joel's question brought me back to the present, though now I feared the results of the upcoming blood-transfer either way.

I sighed at his query and kept my answer as simple as possible. "Augustin pulled me back, because he has some sway with saving Teutons from death. That's another reason you shouldn't do this tomorrow, Joel," I said, nodding at him significantly. "You and Heinrich are planning on having Prince Otto officiate, and he doesn't dabble in heathenry. If Wuotan decides to kill one of you, he's not going to do anything to stop him. You're going to have to save yourselves, and believe me, it's nigh impossible when you're drowning in that burning blood."

Joel sighed, his eyes studying the darkening sky. Freia appeared in the doorway a moment later, speaking her farewells to Heinrich. Joel and I stood and stepped onto the street to give them some privacy, pointing our feet toward the horses Jarvis had brought. "If Heinrich hasn't changed his mind, I'm still going to do it," Joel said when we halted beside the tan mare. "I *want* to be a Teuton no matter the cost, and if both of us resolve to not listen to Wuotan, we should be fine." He took my face in his hands and leaned down to kiss my lips. His gentleness inspired nothing in my bound heart. The selfish part of me thought that it might not be so bad if the ritual killed him tomorrow. Then Augustin and I could go ahead with our plans to bleed Paulus and flee this era for good.

After Freia and I mounted our horses, I faced Joel one final time. "Guess I'll see you tomorrow at Sext," I said in parting.

"No, actually the Prince moved the time to None." I started in surprise, this news taking me off guard. "He sent a message to Heinrich while we were working this afternoon, saying he has other business to accomplish first," Joel explained. "That might make things better for us, since most of the trades don't stop on Saturdays. There may not be such a big crowd."

I frowned thoughtfully, recognizing the truth of this. Maybe Freia and I could get a better view with fewer people in the crowd, since as women we would be confined to the outskirts. Despite my misgivings, I was insatiably curious about what the blood-transfer would look like as a spectator. I had not really seen much of it thanks to the blindness. We parted ways from our respective counterparts shortly thereafter, guiding our horses toward the eastern gate of Muniche.

When Freia and I undressed for bed later that night, I stood at the mirror for a long while viewing my naked body by candlelight, tracing my fingers down the scabs on my chest, legs, and arms. Augustin had said on Tuesday that they would soon fade to scars, the edges of which would vanish with time. But he said that the four lines closest to the heart would remain as permanent reminders of our ultimate act of friendship. I wondered if those would disappear in the currents of time, or if I would have Freia with me always.

The two of us dabbed a poultice of herbs mixed with silver oak leaves onto our scabs before crawling into bed.

Gretchen had recommended it to quicken the healing process. I came to sit beside my best friend on her bed once we had clothed ourselves in our nightgowns and snuffed most of our candles. "I want to see something," I told her seriously, looking into her beautiful green eyes. "Don't move."

I focused on my ice, bringing it forth from my spirit while she watched me, reaching out to her, *seeking* . . . and I found a glowing warmth, a radiant luminosity brighter than the sun, pulsing with Teutonic life. I smiled, calming my element, and met Freia's gaze. "So you are *light*."

Chapter Forty-two

The Fate of the Foreigner

Saturday dawned with clear skies and cool temperatures. A soft breeze drifted down from the distant mountains, birds warbling as they flew amongst the plants of the Meldorf estate. Freia and I spent most of the morning bustling about the manor in a vain attempt to take our minds off of what would inevitably come that afternoon. We dusted the spotless furniture on the first floor, swept the already-clean porch, helped several vassal women trim the flowerbeds and harvest radishes from the garden. We spoke little, focusing on our work, fearing the events that would begin at None, each bell clanging in the distance a new knife piercing our souls. I told Freia at lunch that I would have to teach her how to properly use her light to its greatest ability. My best friend smiled wanly at me in response, her green eyes troubled, her heart unwilling to reply to my attempt at gaiety. Fear for the lives of our lovers consumed our thoughts, giving the chicken stew an insipid taste.

Count von Meldorf decided not to attend Joel and Heinrich's blood-transfer. He said that he had seen enough the day before to fill his nightmares for the next several months. He accepted the fact that we both had to go, but he warned us that observing the act of the blood-transfer may be more horrific than taking part in it ourselves. Freia and I shared a private glance at this. Of course the count would never comprehend the extent of the blood-transfer, but we thanked him for his concern. We promised that we would return home shortly after dark at the latest, but that he need not wait up for us, for we planned to spend the afternoon and evening in the city. Freia had some shopping to do, and I hoped to accompany her, assuming the ritual met with success.

The count lent us the usual mares for the trip to Muniche, Freia seated atop the brown one as I rode the tan one. Each of us wore airy dresses of lighter linen due to the balmy weather, Freia's a lovely pattern of bright green and tan, mine a deep violet trimmed with black lace. I had braided my hair into two long pigtails pinned around my ears, a deep purple veil covering my head. For once, I had chosen not to bother with jewelry, my golden locket included. We went to the city today for the sake of our foolish lovers, not to impress the local aristocracy. We both carried handbags stuffed with fifty Thaler apiece, among other things. I knew that Freia intended to purchase some new soaps and sewing needles. I planned to scour the selection of flower bulbs, for I had noticed that the count's gardens boasted not a touch of blue, my favorite color. I hoped to find some seedlings that could fix that.

Garin Zeuner was not at his post that Saturday, so we did not pause to exchange words with the toll taker. The knights beside the eastern gate bowed at us when we passed through, and we nodded at them politely before turning our mares toward the main square. We passed by Augustin's cottage two streets from the gate. I did not see my master there, but Viktor stood atop the porch, his posture stooped, his gray hair wild as usual. He swept the three steps leading to Augustin's door, the bristles of his broom scraping the stone rather forebodingly. He looked up when Freia and I rode past, and our eyes met for the briefest of moments, recognition breaking across his grizzled face. I nodded once at him, not knowing what sort of greeting would suffice, since I spoke no Magyar. Viktor bowed his head at me in response, speculation in his eyes.

Freia and I tied the horses to a railing opposite a barber shop at the western edge of the main square. A rather large crowd had already gathered in the space beyond us, consisting mostly of commoners. Most of them looked like other men from the ironworks, coming to see the fate of their employer. I found it difficult to see the platform with so many people standing in my way. In the eleventh century, most of the women were around my height, but the burly ironworkers blocked my view as Freia and I trotted around the outskirts of the crowd, seeking a decent observation point.

We met the Denlinger sisters and mother at the right of the platform. They had staked out territory as close as the women were allowed, some thirty meters from where the Teuton priests gathered. Since today's blood-transfer involved men rather than women, any females who chose to observe were consigned to the back to protect their innocence. I thought such restrictions ridiculous, but I grudgingly accepted the fact that I would be banished to the outskirts, my foolish lover far out of reach while he performed this idiotic act for me.

Freia and I stood with the Denlingers so that she could comfort Heinrich's mother, who was obviously distraught at what was about to take place. His youngest sister Kathe drew close to me, taking my hand as the bells for None began to clang throughout the square. I held her to my chest and stroked her light brown hair in an attempt at reassurance.

The crowd grew silent as all attention focused upon the platform, which I could hardly see over the heads of the men in front of me. Raising myself up on my tiptoes, I peered between two rotund noblemen, managing at last to take in the top of the screen and the brim of the flaming cauldron. I could not see the benches at all, which made me huff in annoyance. What was the point of attending a blood-transfer if we could not *see* it? Prince Otto addressed the throng, relating Joel's name in full—pronouncing it rather badly—then moving on to Heinrich's. I frowned, dropping back onto my heels, and glanced around at the square behind us. My ice-tinted eyes picked out the shape of a half-barrel in the gutter several meters away.

I whispered to Kathe to hold my place and raced to retrieve the barrel, pulling it from the muck gingerly and dragging it to where the Denlingers stood. Freia shot me a weak grin for my ingenuity as I climbed upon it, lifting Kathe to stand in front of me for a better look herself. Now I had a decent view, and I let my gaze rove over the crowd while the Prince began the invocation. About three hundred people had gathered for the event in my estimation, fewer likely due to the working hours. The crowd stretched from one end of the platform to the other, the men in front of me about eight rows deep, no women taking up the empty space behind us. I saw the black-clad Teuton priests of Muniche poised in front of the group of men, and I eyed them for several moments, trying to pick Augustin out of their cluster. Most of them had their hoods up, hiding their hair from my sight, although I did see the Old One from the council, the one who had the long beard that looked like a wizard's. I exhaled once in disapproval, knowing that my eyes could never find my master . . . although my icy spirit likely could . . . .

I allowed my spirit to reach out just a bit, calling for him, then turned my attention back to the platform. I could just make out the benches now from my elevated perch, discerning the forms of Joel and Heinrich outstretched upon them, silently awaiting their doom, their bodies blurred by the screen. I looked at Prince Otto, who stood like a god before the fiery cauldron, his youthful face both solemn and fierce as he called for Wuotan's aid, the fire before him flickering red, black, and green in response, its flames contorting into sinister shapes.

While I listened to his incantation, studying his face and proud stance, it occurred to me suddenly that the Prince did not believe one word of what he said. He spoke the ritual scornfully, out of necessity, his tone sounding like he would rather avoid this part. I remembered the humility in Augustin's voice when he had recited the spell on the previous afternoon. Realization struck me that *this* was why Prince Otto never fully succeeded in this heathen ritual. Wuotan meant nothing to him; he used his gifts merely for his own selfish gain. Fear gripped my heart, and my eyes widened in horror at the probable consequences of the Prince's sacrilege.

After Prince Otto finished speaking, he strode away from the audience to the table, preparing to blind Joel and Heinrich for the ceremony. I averted my gaze once more to the group of Teuton priests standing directly in front of the platform. And my ice-tinted eyes locked with Augustin's, for he had turned from his fellows to stare directly at me, his cobalt fire answering the call of my ice. Though I could not properly communicate with him from this distance, I ogled him in desperation, trying to send him the message: *Your brother does not realize the gravity of what he's about to do. One of those men is going to die, and he's not going to save whoever Wuotan deceives. It's going to be Joel. I know it.* My master raised one eyebrow at me, the fingers of his spirit encircling my heart as a rather nefarious smile broke across his face. I could imagine his answer to my thoughts: *Who cares if Joel Hudson does not survive? You love me, not him.*

I clutched Kathe closer to my chest, tearing my eyes away from my callous master, fear for Joel's life blocking all other thoughts from my mind. What could I do if he died? How could I forgive myself for leading him down this rabbit hole? I watched while Prince Otto finished heating the stone knife in the wild flames of the cauldron, its blade transformed into a glowing white, horrible to look upon. Kathe gasped and hid her face in my skirt. I wrapped my arms around her, not wanting to watch, unable to look away. Freia stepped closer to me, placing her blond head upon my right arm, whispering under her breath that I must tell her the moment something went wrong, since I had the best view. And that was the moment when the Prince plunged the knife into Heinrich's chest, his teeth bared in ferocity, his eyes flaming red—I could actually *see* the fire in them from where I stood. I heard Heinrich cry out in pain, and I winced as memories rushed through my brain . . . *the fiery stone, the scent of my own burnt flesh, the hands of darkness . . . .*

My stomach churned as I watched the Prince lift four arteries from Heinrich's body, dangling them in the air for a moment before placing them in the iron bowl. Blood spurted everywhere, so it appeared. He raised his knife above Joel's body next while I stared in revulsion. The innocent foreigner I had dragged into this mess screeched in agony as the white knife ripped his flesh apart.

What have I done? My eyes remained riveted on Joel's body, which jerked in torment, sinking finally into stillness when Wuotan tore his soul away. *I should have stopped him . . . .* There was blood everywhere on the platform. It gushed from the motionless bodies and dripped from the Prince's hands. My stomach gurgled again, and I felt a fleeting instant of gratitude that the wind was blowing away from where I stood.

Prince Otto mashed the eight arteries in the iron bowl, muttering more chants in Ælte Teutonica, his expression grim. Then I noticed that a black figure now stood to my left, his arms folded, his face suggesting intense concentration. "Macabre, isn't it?" Augustin murmured softly in English, his eyes trained on the activities upon the platform. He had no trouble seeing over the crowd.

For once, I felt little relief at his presence. "I swear, Joel is going to *die*," I hissed at him. "Your brother has no idea what he's doing."

Augustin's mouth curled into a fearsome smirk. "That is true, and Wuotan shall not be merciful two days in a row."

My ice had practically frozen me solid at this point. Kathe cringed away from me, jumping down from the half-barrel and running to her mother. Freia remained at my side, her eyes darting from me to Augustin. She likely wondered what we were saying, since she did not understand English. Out of the corner of my eye, I noticed that Lady

Adeline had joined us and stood talking in quiet undertones with Mistress Denlinger while all of her daughters clung to her dress. Heinrich's mother blotted her face with a handkerchief as she tried to comfort her daughters, obviously fearing for her son's life. I watched the Prince set fire to the arteries within the bowl, my own fears focused on Joel alone. "What are we supposed to *do* if Wuotan decides to kill Joel?" I whispered to Augustin, hoping for some sort of encouragement.

Augustin snickered darkly. "Watch," he replied.

I sighed in frustration, and I would have smacked him on the shoulder, had my body not been mostly frozen. I focused briefly on abating my ice, the blue veil over my vision dissipating just a bit. Meanwhile, the Prince moved to return the burnt arteries to the two corpses upon the benches. When he raised the first one from the bowl, I saw, to my surprise, that it appeared healthy and red, no trace of fire evident upon it.

I turned my attention back to Joel's body, wondering wildly whether he may actually survive. If he did, what sort of Teuton would he become? How high would his blood be? What element would he be granted? He had wanted to be fire, and I hoped that he would get his wish. After all, I had always had a weakness for fiery Teutons. My first love had been an old man of black fire, and now my iniquitous master of blue fire stood at my side, my heart forever in his hands. *This is going to be such a problem . . . if Joel lives, we'll have to bring him back to the twenty-first century right away, before he proposes to me here.*

While Prince Otto finished replacing the arteries, closing the wounds with a light trace of the stone knife—which had returned to its natural color—my gaze remained upon Joel. I wondered how long it would take before his spirit reentered his body. This was the most dangerous point of the ritual, Augustin had said. I had a feeling that it was about this time that Wuotan had come to me in the river of blood, offering me the relief I desperately needed. How had Augustin known that I was dying? Had he transformed himself into a fiery storm to come after me, or had he done it without his element, like after he had bled me in the archives? What had the crowd thought of his madness . . . what had the clergy thought . . . what had the Prince thought . . . . Frightening speculations raced through my mind with the speed of a whirlwind, and I would have plied Augustin with questions in the next instant, had the conversations around me not snared my attention.

The two noblemen standing in front of me muttered together, taking bets on which of the two would survive. "One of them is bound to die," the heavier one whispered loudly to his companion. "His majesty has no talent for this sort of thing, unlike his sinful brother."

The words of Lady Adeline and Mistress Denlinger reached my ears then, the older woman groaning in sorrow. "I fear the devil is going to take my son . . . ."

"You cannot be sure of that, my lady," I heard Adeline replied softly. "Soon their bodies will begin to move once more, with life. Do not fear."

And while I stood upon the half-barrel with my eyes fixed upon the forms of the bloodied victims, I heard the rotund nobleman say to his companion, "Which one is Wuotan going to take?"

"The foreigner." Augustin's blunt words, his Teutonica contemptuous, his mouth twisted into a derisive smirk, his smoldering eyes appearing to pierce the realm beyond this world.

A squeak of dismay escaped my lips, and weakness washed over me. *No . . . no . . . what have I done . . . Joel . . . what have I done?* I began to pant, staring as Heinrich's body quivered with life, while the body of my foolish lover remained still. *What have I DONE?!* I whirled to face Augustin, almost tripping but somehow managing to stay atop the half-barrel. "You can't just stand there and watch! *Do something!*" I cried to him in English, my reason swept away in panic.

My master turned to face me, his visage set into a pitiless mask. "What am I to do, Swanhilde? This is not my blood-transfer; I cannot interfere. And what is he to me? I pulled you back *only* because I love you." His eyes burned me, his scowl appearing to come from the depths.

I shook my head and pushed away Freia's comforting hands. "But if Joel dies, it's *my* fault! We can't let this happen! How could I face him in the future?"

"Swanhilde, he made the choice himself." Augustin's retort stabbed me like a razor, its truth finding no purchase against me although I bled. "Joel wanted to be a Teuton, disregarding all advice, and he must pay the price allotted."

Resolution flooded me as I swung my head around to face the platform once more. I saw the Prince staring down at Joel's corpse, doubtless about to say those wretched words to wash his hands of responsibility: *I can do nothing for him.* My hands curled into fists, and I hurled a curse at the Prince. "If you won't save him, *I* will!" I snapped at Augustin. Then I flung myself into the crowd, thrusting the men aside with the strength of my ice, carving a wintry path to the platform.

I heard gasps around me, felt hands shoving me, heard Freia cry out for me to come back, but I ignored all of it. My mind was working overtime, recalling the times when Augustin had pulled me back from death. He had gone to the spiritual realm to do it ... he had been touching me ... he had used his fire to overtake my spirit, to drag me to life, away from the gates of time. Part of me knew that I had no idea how to mimic his redemptive actions, but desperation fueled me as guilt for Joel's life consumed my senses. I had to try, even if I failed, even though everyone around me would see. Joel was more important than my reputation, more important than stupid medieval chauvinism. I had brought him here, and he never would have done this otherwise.

Once I had pushed my way to the front of the group of men, to the place where the black-clad priests stood in a coterie, I knew that I could go no further. The Teuton priests would certainly hold me back, and I was not skilled enough to fight them. I heard a knight speaking to me angrily from somewhere close by. He ordered me back, saying that women could not be so close to the platform. I paid him no heed, shoved aside all of the restraining arms one final time, shut my eyes, and coated myself with my ice, my spirit leaping into the atmosphere.

I blinked my eyes and looked around at the cloudless sky, knowing that I had only seconds. I had to locate Joel before Augustin came after me. I screamed his name, sending my spirit's ice out in every direction with all of my senses, my robes shifting from blue to white to a clear translucence and back again with my effort. I imagined that I could sense his presence somehow, although I had no clue what his element would be. I cast my spirit toward a portal of obscurity that materialized some distance away, knowing deep within that I would find Joel in a place far removed from the earth below.

Sultry voices murmured around me as I flew through swaths of vapor into darkness, voices that reminded me of the ones I had heard the previous day when Wuotan had pushed me toward death. I began to catch fleeting glimpses of magnificent women, their appearances outshining any mortal, their eyes red, their hair aglow with a variety of elements. *Wuotan's sirens?* At last, I heard his frightening laughter when the darkness eclipsed everything else, and I rocketed forward with impossible strength, crying out for Joel.

An instant later I saw the gates of time poised upon the edge of a towering cliff, their black walls shot with greens and blues creaking open. I pulled myself up short, knowing that I may be in danger of falling into them myself if I continued to fly forward. The current carried me that way, I discovered, and just ahead I could see Joel's spirit. He looked feebler than Heinrich Denlinger's father, his robes a ghostly gray streaked with blood, his face pallid, his eyes clouded.

I screamed at him with the voice of my spirit, crying for him to turn back while he still had the chance. But I heard Wuotan laugh again in a sinister tone, and the current that drew me toward Joel grew stronger, sapping my own strength with the suddenness of throwing a switch. Out of nowhere, Augustin was beside me, a fiery blue demon in the darkness, his eyes scorching me, his expression furious. *Swanhilde, you CANNOT do this. Come back with me NOW!*

For the first and likely only time in my life, I heard myself retort, *NO! I have to save Joel!* Augustin ignored my outburst, his fiery hands delving into my spirit with overwhelming power, his grip upon my heart so tight it hurt. But I fought him viciously, enclosing my spirit in an icy shield, using all of my energy to reinforce it against his blazing fire. Our outrageous struggle pushed us through the currents even faster, bringing us almost to the same point as Joel's weakened spirit, the gates of time looming larger before us. *Augustin, I won't turn back without Joel!*

You WILL turn back for ME! I am your master! He burned my heart with his fire, and I cried out in pain, my icy shield rippling.

As I strove with Augustin, I noticed that Joel drifted forward directly in front of me. I shoved Augustin away with a force I did not know I had, reaching my icy hands out to Joel . . . and grasping nothing but air. *NO!!!!* The burning fire upon my heart drained my vigor, pulling me to my knees. *SAVE JOEL!* I begged.

A mocking voice addressed Augustin from the darkness. *Twice in two days, my servant? I believe you ask too much this time.*

You have no authority to take her, and you know it! GIVE her back to me!

But she will not obey you without her lover.

I heard Augustin scream, his hands cindering my heart to ash. *HE IS NOT HER LOVER! I AM HER LOVER! And she WILL turn back for ME!* His fire scorched me again, dragging me against the current, away from the dying Joel.

Then I shall take the foreigner, for he meddles too freely with my devices.

So be it.

I ordered myself to rise up and fight again, trying to find my ice somewhere within me, though all I sensed was Augustin's fire. Sorrow consumed me when I realized that it was no use against the bargaining demon and his servant. *Please . . . please . . . Augustin . . . save him . . . you're killing me . . . please . . . .*

To my utter shock, I felt his fiery grip loosen just a bit as my distress touched his soul. He could not ignore my grief, for we were joined with a bond too profound for words. Abruptly his fire stopped burning me, and he addressed Wuotan again. *Master, I must take both of them.*

The authority is not given to you, Augustin. The foreigner is mine.

What do you require from me in exchange for both of their lives?

There was a pause, then one phrase uttered in Latin: *Damnatio aeterna.*

Another pause as the extent of that requirement struck me hard. *So be it.*

Wuotan laughed more frighteningly than ever before, but then I found myself shooting forward in a straight trajectory for Joel, his spirit gradually slipping into the currents of time. Augustin leaped out beyond me, his fire striking Joel's spirit . . . and finding no purchase. *Damn it, Swanie, he is wind!* I watched in horror while my master's blue-flamed hands reached for Joel's whirling robes, passing through them once more. *I cannot save him alone, but perhaps two fires could pull him back!* He stared back at me, his eyes glowing with an impossible demand . . . .

And somehow, I summoned Augustin's fire from deep within, transforming my robes into a blistering storm. Augustin and I clasped hands, our blues combining, and our united force dragged the dying Joel away from his escape, his wind blowing our flames in wild array. I followed Augustin's lead, ushering Joel's spirit back to that bloody river. I caught glimpses of smoke seeping from its crimson flow as I watched Joel's spirit sink beneath its currents. Then Augustin said, his mental voice sounding incredibly weary, *He will live. Now we must go, or I shall die. You have ruined my strength, Swanhilde . . . you inane, merciless woman . . . .*

Chapter Forty-three:

The Nameless One

I opened my eyes to the brilliant sun beating down from a cloudless sky. I lay prone on my back, the uneven stones of the square digging into my ribs, my still-frozen arms splayed at my sides. My breath came in short gasps while I attempted to clear my spinning mind, to let go of those terrifying seconds of eternal fire and the visible frailty of Joel's spirit. I could not comprehend, as I lay there trying to recover, what exactly had pushed me to such great lengths to save the life of Joel Hudson, my cousin's boyfriend, the man for whom I felt no love. It must have been guilt, some sort of time-travelers' comradeship. *You inane, merciless woman . . . .* Augustin was right; what was my problem? I should have let Joel die.

As I began to move my eyes around, slowly twisting my neck to make sure it still worked properly, I noticed that something pinned me to the ground, something heavy, something that could not have been simply my own weakness. With a low moan, I forced my head up from the stones, ordering my ice to return into my spirit, my body gradually melting its elemental protection. And I saw the black hair of Augustin's head a fingerbreadth from my nose, smoke rising from it still, his muscular form flung like a dead weight upon me, his hot hands sizzling the thawing skin of mine. Of course he would have done this. How else could he have pulled me back from my suicide mission to rescue Joel? *Now we must go, or I shall die . . . .* Aside from the smoldering heat emanating from his being, he appeared dead. His body was so heavy. I could not move, and I could hardly breathe.

"Augustin?" I did not know whether I had actually heard my voice or not. I tried again, swallowing first. "Augustin?" I tensed my muscles beneath his weight, wondering if I could somehow push him off of me. Certainly the crowd would have a field day talking about this . . . a woman transforming into an ice block in public . . . a fiery tornado throwing itself on top of her . . . the powerful body of a man now holding her to the earth in what could be misinterpreted as an intimate pose . . . his hands covering hers . . . in public . . . *in public* . . . . Dread washed over me as I wondered what the punishment for this may be. The Prince had seen us . . . and all of the other Teuton priests of Muniche . . . . *Uh oh* . . . .

"Augustin?" I tried again, my voice pleading, my right hand finally tearing itself away from his fiery skin, reaching up to touch his long black hair. His body shuddered at last, and he groaned once, weakly lifting his face from my throat to meet my gaze. He blinked several times in rapid succession, his light blue eyes still appearing to be lost in the spiritual realm before they finally focused on mine. I sighed in relief, as much as I *could* sigh with him lying upon me. "Oh Augustin . . . thank goodness. I thought you were dead . . . ."

His lips twisted downward just a little into a feeble frown, and he answered me, his own voice breaking, "I am not . . . dead . . . yet . . . . But I am . . . beginning to believe . . . that you shall be the one . . . to kill *me* . . . you foolish woman . . . ."

I smiled tentatively, pleased that he had recovered enough to rebuke me. I stroked his hair gently, patting it back into place. "Augustin, I . . . I really don't know what made me do that . . . . But somehow I just couldn't . . . let him die . . . . Forgive me . . . please . . . ."

Augustin's frown deepened, his eyes darkening. "Swanie, you really should *not* have attempted that," he reproved me, his voice sounding stronger. "You do not have the ability to do that. That is my gift alone."

I placed my head back upon the stones, tearing myself away from his gaze, looking once more at the sky. "I guess I should have known that," I sighed, absently watching a pair of rooks pass by overhead. I lay for a few moments without speaking, a burning curiosity suddenly rising within me. "How did we manage to save Joel?" I remembered what had happened—allowing fire to unseat my ice, merging with Augustin's flames to drag my elusive lover away from his portal to the future—but *how* had it been possible?

"I could have pulled you back without difficulty, since I was touching you," Augustin stated, finally releasing my left hand and placing his upon the ground. "Grasping Joel should have been nigh impossible since his mortal body lay beyond our reach here." I met his eyes again, watching the thoughtful expression cross his brow, indicating that he would have to ponder this fully at some later time. "I would hypothesize that it was your will to save him, combined with my power over this sort of thing, that successfully drew his windy spirit into our clutches. And, of course, the deal I made before chasing after him." Augustin's visage grew callous, his body growing rigid upon mine.

I recalled the closing words he had exchanged with his demon lord, and their implication prompted me to shudder. "*Damnatio . . . aeterna . . . .*"

Augustin snorted quietly, not meeting my gaze. "It was nothing, Swanhilde, nothing," he said, his mouth still set in a harsh frown. "We speak oaths like that one all the time . . . although not usually in Latin." His scowl deepened.

Fear pulsed through my veins afresh. I wondered if that desperate promise might come back to haunt Augustin, possibly in the form of public retribution for our actions. "Everyone saw what we did," I pointed out, switching from

Teutonica to English, my eyes passing over the few people lingering about the square. Most of the crowd had already dispersed. The Prince had likely completed the ritual at some point while I had lain slightly conscious, regaining my strength. I realized that I had no idea whether Heinrich and Joel had both survived, for I had completely missed the part where the Prince had announced their new percentages of Teutonic blood. I wondered if Joel's blood stood higher than mine.

"Yes . . . unfortunately . . . everyone *did* see." Augustin rolled off of me at last, his expression vigilant. I stretched my stiff limbs and raised myself up onto my elbows. I allowed my gaze to rove around the square, mimicking Augustin. Prince Otto and one of the other priests were cleaning up the platform. Several knots of commoners and noblemen standing in separate alcoves talked animatedly. Four of the black-clad priests still gathered at the base of the platform not ten paces from where I lay, conversing in guarded whispers. I did not see Freia or the Denlingers anywhere; they likely sought Heinrich somewhere behind the platform.

Thus far, no one had accosted us upon our return from the spiritual realm, although the group of Teuton priests shot glances in our direction from time to time. Augustin's gaze was fixed upon them, his expression distrustful. "You may be lucky, Swanhilde, for they shall undoubtedly excuse you for your actions, leveling all of the responsibility upon me. They consider you to be a naïve woman easily influenced by masters of evil." His tone dripped with contempt.

I managed to push myself into a normal sitting position, and I winced as I tucked my legs underneath my skirt. I did not really want to ask the next question, but my curiosity forced me into it. "What exactly is . . . the punishment . . . for what we just did?" I wrapped my arms around my body, nervous.

Augustin sighed once, his mouth pressed into a thin line. He looked from the group of priests to the platform where his brother was finishing his work. "That will depend upon how the Catholic clergy decides to regard the situation," he said, lifting himself upward into a sitting position as well. "What we did goes against Teuton law, naturally, but if the clergy chooses to label our actions as sorcery, both of us may end up at the chopping block...or the stake." He frowned.

I quailed, drawing into myself like a pile of burning leaves. "Maybe...maybe I should have...let Joel die...." I whispered, staring at the ground.

Before Augustin could respond, I heard authoritative footsteps approaching, and a dark silhouette abruptly blocked out the sun. I lifted my eyes to see Prince Otto standing over us, his form rigid, his jet black robes blowing slightly with the breeze, his flaming red eyes locked upon Augustin's face. In a menacing voice, he repeated the same question he had asked when he had encroached upon my organ concert. "What *have* you *done?*" His bared his teeth at his brother.

Augustin met his glare calmly as I slid closer to him, fearing the multitude of penalties that might spill from the Prince's lips. "I did what I had to do."

"And you *brought* that woman into it!" the Prince roared, his body seething with ire as he stared his brother down. "She used her ice to enter the spiritual realm alone at *your* direction and practically killed herself in a vain attempt to interrupt *my* blood-transfer! Both of you spat in the face of Teuton law, in the face of tradition, in the face of the ruler of this city, to do such a thing *in public* under the eyes of *everyone!* Do you honestly believe, *Augustin,* that you can continue to do such things indefinitely, without repercussions?"

I cringed away from the Prince and grasped Augustin's left arm. He silently met his brother's gaze, finally muttering the words, "I suppose not."

"This cannot go on, Augustin." The Prince's tone had grown more ominous now, the fire in his eyes cooling. He glared at his eldest brother with the look of an unforgiving judge. "You cannot continue to remain here, in a Christian city, while you worship the demon overlord our people spurned nine centuries ago. I heard what you pledged to Wuotan for the sake of the souls of these foolish children, and now you must accept the consequences of your pledge. *Damnatio aeterna.*" The Prince began speaking Ælte Teutonica, condemnation darkening his face. "I shall cut your blood off from our people, and write your name out of history."

I gasped sharply, my ice flooding my veins, my eyes turning completely blue, my fingers digging into the stones beneath me. I heard the Prince walk away, and I heard Augustin's scornful snort of disbelief. But I could not respond. My mouth dropped open slowly, tediously, like the opening of the gates of time. When I tried to find my voice to say something, anything to erase the horrible realization that had come over me at the Prince's words, I found that I could not speak. The Prince's threat played on repeat in my brain: *Cut your blood off from our people . . . . Write your name out of history . . . out of history . . . . No . . . . It couldn't be . . . .*

Augustin observed my reaction, and he took my shoulders in his hands, ordering me to speak, to explain, to control myself. My eyes filled with icy tears as they stared in the direction the Prince had taken, then at Augustin, watching his gorgeous face transform into the pale wretchedness of a cursed demon, a wraith with no name . . . . *No . . . .* He shook me, demanding that I speak, insisting that his brother's words meant nothing, that they were an idle warning intended to invoke fear. And the truth struck me hard in the face: *Augustin, the city chronicler, did not know about this . . . .*

I tried to pull my voice out once more, choked sounds escaping my lips, no words forming in any language. Augustin ogled me, frustration evident upon his face. I had to tell him what I *knew* was going to happen. How had I not seen this from the start? How could I have been so blind? Why else would Teuton records hold no trace of his existence?

I still could not speak, and in desperation I lifted my icy hands to my collar, folding back the black lace, indicating with gestures that Augustin should bleed me and see the truth for himself. I heard him huff in frustration, and then he leapt to his feet, lifting me bodily off of the stones of the square. He carried me to the nearest alley and pressed me against a brick wall, holding me still with the force of a devil. His teeth sank into my neck, and I forced myself to ignore the pain. I relaxed my ice as my mind replayed a conversation with Hans from long ago . . . .

. . . I was thirteen, and it was summer break, a cloudy day in München. I sat in the gazebo with Hans, who was dressed for work, wearing a short-sleeved gray button-up shirt and matching pants, while I wore jean shorts and a red tank top. A priest's book lay open on Hans' lap, and I worked on using my ice to cool my body, my elemental abilities pathetic at that point. And Hans lifted his dark blue eyes to mine, his tone laden with foreboding as he said, "Today, I wish to explain to you the various curses that a Teuton can level upon his fellows or upon a city, beginning with the worst of all: the filial curse.

"This curse is the most horrible act a Teuton can perform upon another. It is leveled only within the bounds of family blood, which is what gives it its name. I've told you that blood is the strongest tie that binds Teutons together, but the truth of the matter is, Swanie, that even this tie can be severed. If a family member commits unforgivable wrong that brings shame and dishonor to his surname, the head of the family may choose to curse his name, permanently cutting off his blood from his kindred. This curse is rarely carried out due to the gravity of its consequences and the strong ties of filial loyalty. Those who are cursed seldom believe they deserve such a dismal fate. For in leveling the filial curse, the victim's heart is consigned to Wuotan himself, his life cut off from his people, eternal solitude his only destiny.

"The act of the filial curse involves blood, fire, and metal, the most powerful of the Teutonic elements. The condemned one must appear before the head of the household, and any other close family members must also

be present to give their unspoken consent to the ritual. The head of the family speaks the traditional words in Teutonica; you have likely seen that they are written in Der Weg. While the curse is invoked, a cut is made in the forearm of the condemned one, measuring about ten centimeters long, directly upon the artery. As you may gather from this, it is extremely difficult to survive the act of this curse. Medically, one with a slit artery should die in less than a minute. Throughout our history, only Teuton priests have survived this curse, giving rise to the Black Priesthood, the Cursed Ones, the ones required to give their hearts eternally to Wuotan, to learn his dark arts, to forever reject the mercy of God.

"Once the curse is spoken and the artery has been severed, the blood from the condemned one is collected in a bowl, usually held by one of the other family members present. Most people who face this ritual die before the curse has been completed, but those priests who manage to stem the flow of their blood must next write their full name out upon paper, using their own blood and an iron pen. Then the head of the family casts the paper into the fire, speaking the closing words, proclaiming that the name of the Cursed One never be spoken again.

"Thereafter, the nameless one must leave his family house permanently, forsaking all friendships of this world and joining himself with Wuotan and the other Black Priests. Usually, there are very few Black Priests in existence at one time due to the nature of the dark powers granted to them by Wuotan. Their most fearsome gift, Swanie, the one that holds them back forever from worldly acquaintances, is the gift of death. A Cursed One can kill with his mind whenever he is angry, and those who choose to seek advice from a Black Priest must face the danger of this uncontrollable gift. It is forbidden for Teutons to have dealings with Black Priests, or to read their writings, for fear of angering Wuotan.

"Once the curse has been completed, the name of the Black Priest is written out of history entirely. All records of his existence are destroyed. His birth records are burnt, *and any papers bearing his name are either burnt or altered to make the name unreadable. The Cursed One must choose a new name for himself, creating a new and secret history for himself in the annals of the Black Priests, in which he shall remain for eternity, consigned to hell, never again to be recognized by his fellow Teutons, forever cast out of his family."*

. . . Augustin broke away from me, closing the wound in my neck in seconds, wiping my blood from his lips, his light blue eyes wide with horror and disbelief. He took several steps back from me and shook his head, shock and betrayal breaking across his face. I remained plastered against the brick wall as I observed his shifting emotions, my ice fully abated, my clammy fingers gripping the bricks behind me. At length, Augustin opened his mouth, then closed it, his eyes darting to the square, then back to me. "I . . . cannot . . . believe this . . . ." He stared at me with a look of a student who had failed an important test.

I stared back at him, tears seeping into the corners of my eyes. "I should have seen it from the start," I whispered, everything suddenly clear in my mind. "It *all* makes sense now . . . why I had never heard your name before, when I first came here . . . the ultimate punishment for your dealings with Wuotan in a Christian era . . . he's going to curse you." I choked on the words, my tears leaking onto my cheeks. "He's going to write your name out of history. *That's* why I'd never read anything about an Augustin von Bayern. I should have *known* this . . . ."

"How could he do such a thing?" Augustin's voice came out low and hoarse, his expression pained. "I would *never* do this to him, even though he killed our mother. And I would never do it to Paulus, either, even though he is fated to betray our people, resulting in the destruction of this city. How could he *do* this to *me?!*" Augustin clasped his throat, his agony clawing at my heart as I blotted my tears on the sleeve of my dress.

"And we can't do anything to stop him," I stated dully, my mind realizing the whole wretched truth. Part of me wanted to beg Augustin to bleed Paulus now, right away, so we could escape to the twenty-first century before the Prince could level the curse. *But it was already written in history . . . .*

"I don't know how much you saw in my blood, but I remember reading somewhere, in one of Hans' books, that the first time the filial curse was performed, it was done in the early days of Christianity," I related. "There were four priests of Wuotan who refused to convert to the new religion. Their families cast them out with the curse, and they migrated north to Scandinavia. According to what I've read, the filial curse wasn't performed again . . . until the eleventh century."

Augustin eyed me grimly, nodding at the horrible logic in my words. "No one could perform this ultimate breach of family loyalty again until now," he said, his expression disgusted. "That damn Christian Keyholder," he spat.

I was still putting two and two together, and I suddenly recalled something else. "*Of course* it would be you. Before I came here, when I read all of that information on the eleventh century to prepare myself, Hans brought me a few pages written by a Black Priest named Wolfgang, information on the Torstein written shortly after its creation. I studied those pages for hours and found out a lot of horrific facts about time travel . . . and Wolfgang's handwriting *looked exactly like yours*." I looked up at Augustin in consternation.

"So I am to spend the rest of my existence writing ridiculous facts about the accomplishments of the Prince." Augustin scowled in disgust. "At least I chose a decent name for myself. Wolfgang. A good Teutonic name with no ties to that hypocrisy called Christianity." He nodded once, looking thoughtful, then said, "But how did the Prince learn of this? I had never known the particulars of what became of those four rebellious priests until I saw it in your blood."

Both of us paused, trying to reason things out, and the inspiration struck us simultaneously. We gazed into each other's eyes and spoke our conclusion in unison: "The archives!"

Augustin's face hardened in resolution, and he grabbed my left hand firmly. "Come. First we must purchase some food and drink to restore our strength. Then we shall go and see this for ourselves."

Chapter Forty-four:
One Glorious Union

We ate a hasty meal of cabbage, bread, and sausages at an outdoor café halfway between the main square and the town hall. As I stuffed fresh red cabbage into my mouth, I concluded that the Prince must have discovered the information on the filial curse during his preparation for the blood-transfer. Although he had officiated the rite several times before, he likely felt threatened enough to study the writings about it again, after watching his demonic brother perform one perfectly the day prior. If Augustin saved both parties involved in his blood-transfer while the Prince let one die, the Prince doubtless assumed that the townspeople would belittle him. Therefore, I decided that he must have scoured the shelf on Teutonic Traditions. Perhaps that was where he had stumbled upon the curse.

Thoughts of Joel did cross my mind as we finished up, Augustin chugging a stone mug of beer while I washed my sausage down with mead. I knew that Joel had survived thanks to my mad efforts. By now, he and Heinrich had probably gone to the Denlinger house to rest. Freia would likely be with them . . . and Joel would wonder where I was. Had he heard any of my argument with Augustin . . . had he heard Augustin's bargaining with Wuotan? I needed to find Joel, to congratulate him on his new Teuton blood and ask what percentage he had gained. But I knew that I would spend the rest of the day with my master, searching the city archives for any and all information on the filial curse . . . and after that . . . ?

I heard Freia's voice call out to me from nearby when we rose from the table, having finished our meal. I saw her astride the count's brown mare a short distance up the road, a bag of groceries hanging from her saddle. "Swanie, I've been looking everywhere for you," she exclaimed. She reined in beside me, her eyes shifting from my face to Augustin's.

I glanced at my master's face for a brief moment, silently indicating that I needed to have this conversation, even though it would delay our mission. His mouth turned sharply downward, but he bowed at Freia politely and took several steps back to give us some privacy, his expression suggesting that I had better not take long. So I focused my attention on my best friend and whispered the most important query. "How are they . . . Joel and Heinrich?"

"They're resting now at the Denlinger house, recovering from the ritual. Both of them are rather proud of themselves for having survived." Freia smiled, a wry curling of her soft lips; then she added, "Joel has been asking about you. The Denlingers are planning to have a large dinner at Vespers to celebrate. Joel wants you to be there." She looked at me seriously, her delicate hands gripping her reins more tightly than necessary.

I sighed heavily, shifting my weight from one foot to the other, knowing full well that I could not leave Augustin now, no matter what Joel may think. I stepped close to the horse and lowered my voice even further. "I can't come to dinner. You saw what I did . . . with Augustin." I nodded at her significantly, and her face paled. "I fear we may be punished . . . for our actions. And we need to find out, right now."

Freia read the worry in my eyes, and her own widened. "Do you think . . . that they might cast you into prison?" she whispered nervously.

I shook my head once, shivering all over. "No. I think it might be far worse than that." I paused, glancing back at Augustin, who stood about a meter away, his arms crossed underneath his black robe, his expression severe. "Don't wait up for me," I begged Freia, turning back to face her. "I'll come back home, but I don't know when. Don't tell anyone. Please . . . just make some sort of excuse for me."

Freia clasped my hand in hers for a brief moment, squeezing it in confidence. "Be careful, Swanie," she advised. I turned from her and raced back to where Augustin stood, practically tripping on my long violet skirt in my haste.

As we ascended the steps to the main entrance of the town hall soon afterward, I suddenly remembered that I had left the count's tan mare tied outside the barber shop at the edge of the main square. Augustin shrugged once when I mentioned this. He said that the horse would be fine, that I could retrieve her when I departed Muniche for the night. Since the town hall lay directly opposite from the eastern gate, I would indeed pass through the main square again later. So I shoved my concern for the horse aside and turned my attention to our predicament.

When my master and I burst through the door to the archives, we found one monk sorting through some files. He gawked at us in fright when we marched resolutely into the murky room, Augustin throwing his blue flames upon the aged chandelier without preamble. He ordered the monk to leave, summarily thrusting the poor man into the corridor and slamming the door in his face while I waited beneath the candelabra, gazing around at the dusty shelves. "We may have little time before *someone* comes in to disturb us," Augustin said, stalking past me in a wave of black. "I shall search through the oldest files on Teuton history from the earliest days of Christianity. You may look where you wish." He disappeared down one of the long rows of shelves in an instant.

I spun to face the shelf on Teutonic Traditions, my intuition telling me that the information we sought would be there. I squinted at the multitude of dusty scrolls, boxes, papers and tomes, pulling items off of the shelf at random. I flipped through many pages I could not read due to the faded ink or the odd shape of the letters. My desperation drove me doggedly ahead, my eyes seeking the fateful words in Ælte Teutonica: *Black Priest, Cursed One, Filial Curse* . . . . At last, I retrieved a thin, flimsy volume from the top shelf, its cover less grimy than its companions, suggesting that perhaps it had been recently consulted. I cracked the binding when I opened it to the title page, which read in Latin: *Forbidden Sacraments*. The rest of the book was written in Ælte Teutonica, and I quickly discerned that the volume contained information on the oldest heathen rituals of the Teutons, the ones that were banned by the Catholic Church.

My eyes widened as they flew over the words, halting just long enough to read each individual heading: *Invocation of Demons, Blood Sacrifices, Fertility Rituals, Divination, The Bending of Time*. My fingers froze just long enough for me to process the variety of possibilities of such a heading. So the workings of time did have something to do with Wuotan . . . and maybe Prince Otto was not the first Teuton to ever experiment with such things.

I shook my head once, ordering myself to concentrate, my fingers flying once more . . . and halting over the caption: *Teutonic Blood-Transfer*. There were three whole pages dedicated to the particulars of the ceremony, and smudge marks on the sheets indicated that someone had recently handled them. A frown creased my forehead as I turned to the back of the book . . . and found myself reading the heading: *Retributions*. One page over from that, I saw the subheading: *Filial Curse*.

My eyes opened wider and wider when I read the accompanying lines detailing every aspect of the curse, the spell written at the bottom of the page. I slammed the book closed, holding the spot with my finger, and leaped into the center of the archives, seeking my master. I found him standing over his writing desk with several large historical tomes open before him. I darted over to him and flung the book on top of his hands, flipping to the correct page. "Here it is. I found it."

I stared at Augustin in muted horror while his light blue eyes focused on the page before him. He took it carefully from my hands, his expression growing more and more distressed the longer he read. He narrated the awful truth in a soft murmur, his tone sounding resigned. "The four rebellious priests . . . cursed on the Lord's Day . . . in the Lord's holy Name . . . their blood severed from their people . . . their names forever condemned . . . the inalterable curse . . . forced servitude to Wuotan . . . bringing eternal death . . . ."

I shuddered at the history of the filial curse, its implications shattering my faith in my own people. How could they devise such a terrible thing, refusing to forgive, turning their backs on the mercy of God? Even if four priests chose to reject the new religion, how could their peers wish such a thing upon them, handing them over to a demon? *How could the Prince do such a thing to his brother . . . ?*

At length, Augustin shut the book, laying it down atop the historical works, his strong hands grasping the edges of his writing desk, his shoulders slumping, his mouth twisted into a grimace of agony. Tears burned in my eyes at the sight of his despair, and I placed my arms around him, trying to grant him some form of comfort. "Oh Augustin . . . my love . . . I wish there was something . . . anything . . . I could do . . . ." My voice broke, for my desires were hopeless. Now we finally knew Augustin's fate, written with the iron pen of eternal death.

Augustin shook his head, not relaxing his agonized posture. "And he shall perform this act upon me tomorrow, on the Lord's Day, casting me out of the Bayern family, banning me forever from the city of my birth . . . breaking my ties with the Teuton people . . . cutting off my blood from my mother's . . . ." Augustin's face contorted with grief, his hands curling into fists, tears leaking from beneath his eyelashes. "Marelda . . . oh Marelda . . . I have failed you." He moaned softly, his teeth sinking into his lip until it bled.

I held him more tightly, his sorrow striking my heart, making me wish for the impossible, making me want to change history, in spite of the consequences. "Augustin . . . the curse . . . it won't change anything . . . for me . . . ." I whispered fiercely, my love for him growing stronger than ever before.

He lifted his hands off of the table, wiping his tears away on the sleeves of his robe. He straightened and turned his head to give me a dismal look. "You realize, Swanhilde . . . that they will force us . . . to break our bond."

I gaped at him, horror flooding my veins at the mere suggestion. "*No . . . .*"

"The Prince would not allow you to remain tied to a cursed priest," Augustin said, his face appearing devoid of vitality. "They will likely stage some sort of trial, to lay my sins out before the council . . . and you will be compelled to watch . . . and they will order us to sever our heart-bond to erase your guilt. I should never have taught you so much, Swanhilde, for you know enough to be legitimately labeled a witch. But if we break the bond of our souls, they might show you mercy and level all of the punishment upon me."

I shook my head fiercely at his words. My heart throbbed at the sensation of his hands upon it, clutching it as though he never wanted to set it free. I did not *want* him to set it free. I loved him far too much to say goodbye, even if he was to become the first Black Priest in nine centuries. "They can't *do* this to us," I insisted, grasping onto denial. "How could I ever know love again without you?"

Augustin reached his right hand out to touch my face, his fingers warm as they traveled gradually across my cheek to rest upon my dry lips. "We shall have to break the bond ourselves, willingly, when they order it," he said, "for it would be far less painful . . . than if the Prince or one of the other council members rips us asunder. That would be unbearable torment for both of us . . . my love."

Tears welled in my eyes, and I concentrated on the softness of his touch, on the devotion binding our spirits together. How could I ever agree to let Augustin go? He had saved me from death, rescued me from a childish love for an old man, entrusted me with his own sinful heart, treated me as his equal, loved me more than he loved his mother . . . . "Then . . . then . . . is this . . . the . . . end?" I choked on the dreadful words as Augustin's fingers left my lips behind. I stared into his eyes, unwilling to relinquish the most glorious union I had ever known.

I watched his light blue eyes grow moist, the final bells for Vespers echoing throughout the murky basement, each tone counting down our last moments. "My . . . love . . . I . . . I . . . cannot . . . ." Augustin's jaw worked with passion as he struggled to express himself, his usual profoundness escaping him.

And suddenly, I realized that the finality of this impending curse filled me with an unfamiliar resolve, a fierce yearning that I could no longer push aside in spite of my commitment to purity, to my virginity. *I'll never see Augustin again after this day, after this night . . . and I want him more than anything . . . .* I grabbed my master's right hand with both of mine. "Augustin," I gasped, "if this really means that it all ends today . . . tomorrow . . . then there's one more thing I want . . . one last thing . . . *tonight* . . . ." My heart pounded with hunger, and I am certain that he must have felt the shift through our spirits' bond.

Augustin gawked at me in shock. He dropped his hand to his side, breaking it from my grasp, his eyes glittering as he shook his head at me firmly. "Swanie, you cannot mean that . . . you do not know what you ask . . . ."

"I *want* it, even if you hurt me, even if you kill me!" I cried out, leaning toward him and folding my hands. "*Please*, Augustin . . . I *want* you!"

For a short second, everything froze as I stood before my master, silently begging him to ravish my body, to teach me all that I did not yet know. He stared back at me, his eyes burning hotter, his hands flexing, his lips parting to reveal his bared teeth. "Then I shall *take* you!"

Before I had time to react, he had snatched me bodily into his arms, pressing me into the robes at his chest. He flounced out of the archives, extinguishing all of the blue-flamed candles before the door banged shut behind us. He took the steps to the ground floor three at a time, holding me close while he paused outside the door with the Latin sign: *Muniche City Records*. He glanced this way and that, and, seeing no one, transformed himself into a fiery cyclone. His demon arms bound me to him as he shot from the town hall onto the street, crossing Muniche in the fading light of day to his front door in less than a minute.

I barely had time to think while he carried me in his storm. My body somehow escaped his burning flames, though my ice did not course through my blood. Perhaps my desire for him had ignited his fire within me, merging us into one scorching elemental blaze with the prospect of one final night together without boundaries. The better portion of my brain questioned my intentions. Did I really want to grant my virginity to a man about to be consigned to a demon, a man that I could never marry? But it was too late to change my mind, for Augustin's lust for sex far outweighed mine. Now that he had imprisoned me in his arms, I could no longer refuse him.

We burst through the front door of his cottage, almost tripping over Viktor, who stood at the entrance to the hallway wiping his wrinkled hands on a rag. My master halted, cooling his fire with rather impressive suddenness, setting me upon my feet without actually letting go of me. He leveled a vicious glare at Viktor, prompting the old servant to cringe backward, and he barked out a slew of sharp orders in Magyar. Viktor said something tentatively in response and stepped out of Augustin's way. Then my fiery priest pulled me down the short hall past the room with the couch, thrusting me through the last doorway and closing it firmly behind us.

At first, I could not make out the contents of the room, but it did not take Augustin long to light eight candles with his blue fire, each of them set upon various shelves. My master finally released me, turning back to lock the door with an air of finality, placing its silver key somewhere within his robe. I blinked several times, letting my eyes adjust to the dim bluish light, then gazed around myself in wonder at the realization that I stood in Augustin's bedroom.

The door and walls were made of dark paneled wood, the window upon the far wall blocked by heavy black curtains. On the wall to the left of the door stood a gray-stoned fireplace, the mantle of solid black marble, four glowing candlesticks sitting atop it along with rather Gothic-looking goblets and sculptures. Beside the fireplace stood an oaken writing desk laden with pens, inkwells, and papers, a leather chair poised before it. To the left of the window on the far wall, I saw a massive wardrobe, its larch doors sealed tightly, likely the place where Augustin stored his priestly robes as well as his noble attire. To the right of the window stood a decent-sized mirror and washing table, somewhat similar to the one Freia and I shared in our bedroom at the count's estate. To the right of the door, not two paces from where I stood, was an imposing book-shelf stacked with papers—*Augustin's secret writings*. I stared at the shelf for a long moment, my curiosity gnawing at my bones . . . and then I turned my gaze toward the four-post bed, its headboard pushed against the right wall, its mattress laden with midnight black blankets.

The implications of what I had begged him to do to me in my moment of desperation struck me hard as I focused on Augustin's bed—a large expanse of darkness seeming to signify the altar on which I would sacrifice my innocence forever. Four plush pillows lay at the headboard, two of black and two of a deep blue. When I lifted my eyes upward, I saw that a rather impressive mirror had been nailed to the ceiling, allowing those who lay upon the bed to observe their activities in full. My mouth dropped open as my mind made wild speculations about prostitutes . . . and my master's voice reached me then, deep and firm. "If you are not out of that dress by the time I turn around, I shall tear it to shreds. That is a promise."

Nervousness washed over me in a flood. I tore my eyes away from Augustin's bed to see him standing before his wardrobe, its doors open now, his back turned to me, his nimble fingers working to remove the traditional clip from his hair. *Oh . . . shit . . . Swanie . . . you are going to die . . . .* I turned around myself, focusing blindly on the paper-laden shelf, my fingers working shakily to unwind the ribbons of my bodice. I breathed shallowly while I carefully loosened all of the stays of my dress, my shaking hands preparing to lift it over my head. Then I remembered the purple veil covering my hair, and I mentally smacked myself, realizing that I would have to undo my braids unless I wanted Augustin to rip my hair out by the roots. I pulled the pins from my hair one by one and dropped my veil to the floor. Next, I slowly tugged my dress over my head, allowing it to fall to the ground in a pile of violet and black. I shivered when I slipped my feet out of my sandals and hesitantly removed my undergarments, my eyes traveling to the blatant red scabs marring my torso, legs, and arms from yesterday's blood-transfer. *He's not going to think you look beautiful . . . he's going to think you look like a poor man's whore . . . .*

Uncertainty grabbed hold of me, and I stepped shakily away from my pile of clothing, lifting my hands to unwind my braids, my fingers stumbling as I let my hair down. My chest rose and fell swiftly with my breath, and I looked down at my naked body again, biting my lip once more at the sight of those scabs. *Even my legs won't impress him, though they've earned many a stare in the past. What are you thinking, Swanie? Augustin has had his share of women, most of them much better than you. He's going to eat you alive . . . .* I grabbed some of my black hair, slightly wavy after a day in braids, pulling it forward to cover my breasts, totally unnerved and unwilling to show myself to my master.

"Turn around." His voice sounded much closer than I had expected, his tone demanding no disagreement. I summoned all of my failing confidence and obeyed him, closing my eyes, bracing myself for a barrage of reproach.

"Look at me." I could not refuse, though I feared to open my eyes. I stared at the floor for a long moment, then gradually lifted my head, intending to meet Augustin's gaze, no matter how disparaging it may be.

But his naked body seized my attention, and I found myself gawking at his cock. It stood erect and waiting, and I wondered wildly how often it had stood like that for me already. Had my reserve tortured him all this time? *You need to look at his face. He said to look at* him, *not at his penis.* I chewed on my bottom lip and lifted my head, distracted next by his muscular chest. My eyes widened, and my heart pounded at the sight of his impressive physique, his magnificence, his power, his Teutonic glory. *His face, Swanie.* When I finally managed to do as he had asked, I saw that his gaze was fixed upon my body, which I knew looked incredibly pathetic compared with his amazing figure. *At least you're not the only one distracted.*

Very slowly, he walked around behind me, and I watched his every movement, my whole body trembling. I felt his fiery hands upon my neck, drawing my hair back, pulling away the last of my protection. His hands continued to rest upon my neck, stroking it gently, his warm lips breathing upon my left ear. "I never did tell you . . . what I was thinking . . . yesterday afternoon," he murmured, "when you lay before me, completely at my mercy . . . your eyes staring bravely into mine . . . their color akin to the glorious gray sky before dawn . . . ."

My heart pounded, and he came around to stand in front of me. He traced his hands carefully down my throat, down my chest, pausing to fondle my breasts. My eyelids slid closed, and my lips parted of their own accord. "You looked like the pinnacle of Teutonic splendor in the light of the sun," he intoned in a sultry voice, "your beauty surpassing that of Aphrodite . . . your body absolute perfection . . . as it is now . . . yes . . . even with the scabs . . . *perfection* . . . ."

I should have said something, praised his own magnificent body, its muscles undulating with power, but I could not find my voice. His fire coursed through my veins at his touch, my yearning increasing with every passing moment. *I love him ... I fear him ... and he thinks I'm beautiful....* His hands slid upward to cradle my face, and he drew closer to me. I opened my eyes to stare into his, which glowed with rapture. "You fear me." His lips bent down to briefly caress my own.

I could not speak, but my tremulous shivers gave me away. He wrapped his arms around my body, pulling me against him. "I will hurt you, Swanhilde," he said quietly, his tone almost apologetic. "But that will pass. My fire burns within you, and it shall rise to meet mine, our ecstasy outshining the sun, filling this world with our glory, with our final union. Do not fear me, my darling, for I love you, and that will never change."

His incredible words revolved in my head, chasing my fears away, and I finally brought my own arms up to encircle his neck as he kissed me, my passion awakening, my strength pulling me to him. And he pushed me upon his bed, upon his black coverlet, my head sinking into one of his pillows while his sinuous hands made their way to my pelvis. His lips drifted downward to the hollow of my throat as his fingers manipulated my body more expertly than I had ever envisioned. I moaned, my eyes squeezed shut as I surrendered myself to this wondrous master, a man who thought to satisfy me first before claiming my most precious gift to assuage his own desires.

And afterward our bodies and elements wholly entwined as he taught me all that I had ever desired and everything that he had promised—the height of pleasure and pain in one infinite night. Augustin guided me to a heaven I had never known, a Teutonic glory that I would crave for the entirety of my existence.

Chapter Forty-five:
My Resolution

I know not how long I lay upon the blankets of Augustin's bed, intoxicated with satisfaction and wonder. My mind blissfully replayed every moment since he had first put his hands upon me when I stood shivering with fear and uncertainty. Now I marveled that I had been afraid at all, for everything had been so perfect, so amazing, an unforgettable ideal. I had felt pain when he had first penetrated me, but the grandeur of passion had swept it all away. Now, as I rested with a smile on my face, I remembered only the glory of giving myself entirely to the man I loved, the one who *could* be kind, like he had said so long ago in the archives . . . .

Presently, I heard him exhale in contentment, and I lifted my gaze to the mirror above us. He lay comfortably beside me, his hair looking quite disheveled, his hands clasped behind his head, a rather mischievous smile playing upon his lips. "So," he said at length, his tone saturated with fulfillment as he met the eyes of my reflection, "do you horribly regret granting your precious virginity to the worst of men, my beloved swan princess?"

I smiled back at his image and stretched a bit. "No, not really," I replied, "though I suppose I should regret it. I should feel guilty." My contentment faded slightly at the awareness of what I had just done, committing fornication without remorse with a man destined to become a Cursed One before tomorrow's sunset. I knew that I would never forget the perfection of our sex, and that would likely come back to haunt me once I married Joel. For the rest of my life, in the eleventh century and in my own era, I would think of Augustin any time I got in bed with my husband. But when I lay upon his bed that evening, hearing the bells tolling in the distance, indicating nightfall, I did not lament my actions. What else could I have done, since I would never see this man again after he had been cursed? My virginity belonged to Augustin alone. I should have seen that long ago.

Augustin chuckled, sounding satisfied. "You are not a good Christian, my dear swan," he said with a snicker, turning his head to the left to smile at me beguilingly. "You should feel incredibly guilty for breaking God's law, yet here you lay beside me with a blissful smile on your face . . . my charming seductress."

"I think you're the one who did the seducing," I corrected him, turning my own head to the right to meet his gorgeous eyes. "'The pinnacle of Teutonic splendor . . . beauty greater than Aphrodite.'" I quoted his accolades, shivering all over at the memory of his hands upon me, his sonorous voice whispering such praise in my ear. "I love you . . . *so* much . . . ." Nothing I could say would ever suffice.

Augustin hummed in satisfaction, his eyes traveling briefly to his bedroom window, blocked by those thick black curtains. "It appears that you shall not be exiting the city tonight," he noted with a smirk, listening to the bells for Compline.

I sidled closer to him upon the bed, my eyes half-closed. "I'm not leaving you tonight," I whispered. "I will stay with you as long as you allow me." I wished that it could be forever, despite the Prince's nefarious plans for tomorrow.

My master sighed at my words, a touch of pain crossing his handsome face. "Enjoy pleasure while it lasts," he murmured, quoting the words he had spoken on the night he had created our heart-bond. He lifted himself off of the blankets a moment later, rolling to his side and leaning on his left elbow as his light blue eyes scoured me from head to foot. He frowned slightly, the candles in the room burning brighter at his silent direction. "I hurt you," he said, his visage hued with anguish.

I looked down at my naked body and discovered that Augustin was right. My shoulders and limbs were marred with burns and bruises just barely visible in the candle-light. I probably had quite a few bite marks on my neck, for I knew that Augustin had bled me in the throes of elation. Some of the scabs from my blood-transfer had broken away from my skin, leaving marks of tender scarlet in their absence. I had hardly noticed his violence, for I had been too overwhelmed by ardor to register anything but delight. "It is nothing, my darling, nothing," I assured Augustin, flexing my limbs to ward off any impending stiffness. "At least you didn't kill me," I added with a roguish wink.

Augustin shook his head with a sigh, appearing slightly annoyed with my careless response to his brutality. "If I had killed you, I would have taken my own life next, before the murderer makes that wretched mark in my flesh. I fear that your wounds may require attention, however. I suppose I should have held myself back, knowing your inexperience . . . please forgive me."

I rolled onto my side to face him, touching his face gently with my left hand, desperately wanting to erase his tormented expression. "You are forgiven, always. Please don't worry about me, Augustin. I'll be fine. I can use my ice to heal the burns later, and the bruises will fade. What you did to me during the blood-transfer was far worse. Don't fear for me now."

My lover sighed again, closing his eyes while I stroked his face, his right hand coming up to encircle mine, the warmth of his blood enticing me afresh. I felt him caressing my heart as I reassured him, his love solidifying our bond, ensuring that its severance would torture us both eternally. When he opened his eyes, the extent of the sorrow and devotion pouring from them caused me to tremble again, my mind not wanting to confront the inevitability of the end. "Do you need anything, my love?" he asked me, his voice still sounding concerned for my health. "Food, water, wine? I can call Viktor. He would bring us anything I ask."

I considered his offer for a short minute, realizing that I did feel somewhat hungry, after all that had passed between us. But I could eat later. Right now, as I lay at my master's side with the warmth of his inner fire caressing my skin, I wanted only one thing. My lips quivered when I tried to answer him, my voice hardly audible. "No, Augustin . . . you don't need to call Viktor . . . ." I broke off, dropping my gaze to the blankets, fearing that he might think me a nymphomaniac if I admitted that I wanted to get intimate with him again so soon.

His light blue eyes widened, the fire within them beginning to smolder as he sensed my desire. He slowly unwound his fingers from my hand and reached forward to stroke several locks of my hair. "What then do you need . . . my precious darling . . . my beloved Teuton princess . . . my perfect angel? What do you ask of me . . . your iniquitous master . . . forever enslaved by your allure?"

He already knew what I wished, and his low voice hypnotized me, causing me to tremble all over again. "Please take me again," I begged him. "Put your hands on me . . . master . . . ." And he obeyed me without hesitation, his eyes sparkling in the candlelight as he kissed me, his hands once more pinning me to the bed.

At some point, the bliss of ecstatic gratification pulled me into a peaceful slumber, my spirit floating away in a dream, wishing that my union with Augustin von Bayern could last forever, the intentions of our adversaries notwithstanding. I found myself treading softly upon the grass at the banks of the Isar in the darkness of night, the stars twinkling above me, the cool breeze toying with my hair, the waters of the river lapping quietly at my bare feet.

Presently, I sat down upon a hillock at the water's edge, not taking thought as to how I had come to this enchanted place. I knew only, while I rested upon the springy grass, gazing across the river toward the stone walls of Muniche in a mixture of contentment and sorrow, that my love for Augustin outweighed everything else in my life. Our one glorious night together, immoral though it may have been, had confirmed the fact forever in my mind and heart.

"Am I disturbing you, Teuton princess?" A familiar voice cut into my reverie, and I turned my body just enough to see my lover standing beside an oak tree not far from where I sat. He wore robes of cerulean that glowed mysteriously in the dark of the night, his black hair highlighted with flecks of cobalt, fire glimmering in his fathomless eyes. He stood watching me with a smile playing upon his lips.

My eyebrows came together slightly as my mind struggled to reason out his sudden materialization in this tranquil night, his appearance reminding me of a shining star—or a Teuton spirit. I shook my head, glancing again at the serenity of nature around me, hearing the nightingales calling among the shadows of the forest. Then I murmured quietly, "I am dreaming."

"*We* are dreaming," my lover corrected me with a smile, stepping onto the grass, drawing near to where I sat. "You certainly must recall what I told you the first time you asked me about the heart-bond of the Teutons." He gestured at my own clothing, his fiery eyes glinting with amusement.

I looked down at myself, noticing suddenly that I wore robes of deep green that matched the midnight waters of the Isar before me. My eyes opened wide, and I stretched my hands out to stare at their translucent sheen. *I will be able to feel you, and you me, though we be separated by great distance. We shall have the privilege of meeting in the realm of the spirit at any time, even in our dreams. . . .* Augustin's words came back to me, filling my heart with tranquility and wonder at the same time. "Then we . . . are both asleep . . . together in the spiritual realm . . . in our dreams?"

My lover smiled at my perceptiveness and sat down beside me on the grass. "You are correct, my darling." Augustin's burning eyes locked with my icy ones, and he lifted his left hand cautiously to trace it down my face. I could not feel his touch, for I was a spirit, and his fingers passed through my skin.

I fantasized that I could feel him anyway, closing my eyes briefly at the imaginary contact of a glorious angel clothed in blue. "Why have you never come to my dreams before?" I asked him, opening my eyes once more, my mind running through all of the possibilities that we had missed. I would rather dream blissful realities with Augustin than playful fantasies alone in my head.

My lover's expression darkened just a bit, and he dropped his left hand to his side. He brought his right hand from his robes, the heart of my spirit cradled securely in his fingers. "As a narcissistic fool, I believed that our union would last some twenty-one years, never thinking that my aberrant obsessions would bring us to ruin. And thus, I have squandered the time that could have been ours, allowing you to dream freely without my interference. But now . . . we have no time left . . . ." Augustin paused, his face crumpled with grief while he stared at my beating heart, clutching it close to his chest. "This night, there is one duty that I must perform before the sun awakens us. But aside from that . . . I shall not let you go." He raised his eyes from my heart to meet my gaze, and abruptly the scene swirled around us, pulling us away from the idyllic banks of the Isar, coalescing into the dim light of Augustin's bedroom, the blue-flamed candles burning low.

I took half a step back, ordering myself to recover from this abrupt change of location, unsure how my lover had managed it. There before us, lying upon the sheets of Augustin's massive bed, I saw our sleeping bodies, one blanket thrown over our nakedness, my master's arms curved around me protectively. I marveled at the peaceful appearance of my face, my aura shielded in contentment. "We look . . . so happy . . . ." I observed, feeling as though I were about to cry.

"And we are," Augustin murmured, his spirit drawing closer to mine, his blue robes melding with my darker ones. "This is the first time I have shared my bed with a Teuton woman—with the woman I *love*—and she has given me everything I have ever desired . . . ." My heart pounded at his words, and I tore my eyes away from our sleeping bodies to gaze into the eyes of Augustin's spirit. "My swan . . . my precious darling . . . how madly I love you," he whispered.

Longing streamed from my spirit into his, prompting both of our bodies to shift in their slumber. Augustin moaned softly in his sleep, and his arms tightened around my body. "We ought to wake up," I said, annoyed that I could not touch my lover in the realm of dreams. I desperately wished to kiss him, to unite with him again.

Augustin chuckled, his fiery eyes drifting from my face to our resting forms upon the bed. "No, unfortunately we must not disturb them in spite of our desires, for our bodies must rest now, considering what shall befall us after sunrise." Dread washed over me at the knowledge of what was to come, and an instant later the scene shifted again. My lover carried our spirits to the halcyon glade at the riverbank, pale moonlight shining on the rippling water. Augustin stepped before me, his feet hovering above the water, his fire infusing his spirit with more beauty than ever. "Dance with me now, my lovely Swanhilde, and sing to me your songs of the future . . . that we may forget our troubles . . . just for a moment."

So we danced in elemental rapture while the moon traveled across the starlit sky. Our feet united with the water and the earth, our spirits leaping into the air to play upon the stone walls of Muniche, the city that would be Augustin's for one last night, before his name was ripped from him forever. Whether anyone detected the fleeting dalliance of our spirits, I know not, for we completely ignored the knights on guard upon the walls and at the gates, focusing entirely on our mutual adoration. I sang many songs to him in our dreams that night, from popular American ballads of the late twentieth century to my favorite European Gothic melodies. I wanted that night to last forever so I could sleep eternally with Augustin, my fiery priest, my master, my lover, my everything.

When the gray of dawn crept slowly from the eastern horizon, Augustin murmured that he had to part from me to complete one final task before rising to face that dreaded morning. I hesitated to let him go, begging him to take me with him, though he insisted that he needed solitude for his last undertaking. "I shall wake you when I have finished," he promised me with a sad smile while we dawdled at the banks of the Isar, the eastern drawbridge not far downstream. "Now, I must say farewell to those other eyes that have guided my life, and yours must merge with the gray morning sky. Dream in peace, my swan." He leaned down to kiss my hair, his lips passing through its swirling strands, and then he vanished.

His words repeated themselves in my mind while I stood bereft at the riverbank, staring blankly at the place where he had disappeared. *Those other eyes that have guided my life . . . . Of course. He's going to say goodbye to Marelda . . . who will no longer be his mother once the curse is complete . . . .* Sorrow gripped my heart, along with a wretched fury directed at the Prince, that pompous fool who disregarded the tie of family blood due to his own insane jealousy. I wished to rip Prince Otto's heart from his chest myself, crushing it with my hands and trampling those ridiculous keys to the ground. I realized that I wanted to watch Augustin say farewell to his dead mother, even though he had requested privacy. Maybe if I was careful enough, he would not notice me. So I closed my eyes and pictured the gloom of Marelda's chapel, imagining myself there in my dream . . . .

And I was there, my caution clothing me in mist, my feet resting upon the stone floor in the dark corner beside the door to the hallway. Hardly a ray of light seeped through the stained glass window in the early hour before dawn. I willed my spirit to meld with the gray stone wall as much as my ice could allow, my blue eyes detecting no light save the flaring fire of Augustin's ever-burning candle atop his mother's tomb.

And I saw the groveling form of my master, his arms stretched out upon the marble casket, his spirit's radiance wholly extinguished, his cobalt robes appearing as black as the chapel itself. He wailed, his head pressed against the marble before him, words spilling from his tormented lips in every language he knew, many of them unintelligible to me. I heard him begging in Latin, in Teutonica, in Ælte Teutonica, in English . . . crying for his mother to forgive him, not to forget him, to punish the treachery of his brother, to allow him to die in his sleep, that he need not face the treason to come. His tragic appeals struck my heart in a mortal wound as his fingers clawed at the marble: "I am your child . . . your child . . . I *love* you . . . I *love* you . . . and he would tear us asunder . . . he would sacrifice me to Wuotan himself . . . do not leave me . . . *please . . . do not leave me . . . .*"

Resolve filled me as I fought against all of my instincts, ordering myself to remain in the shadows, to stand apart from Augustin's grief. Somehow, some way, I would *not* let them break our bond. Seeing my lover's anguish convinced me, for I knew that despite his pleading prostrations, his connection with his mother's blood would run dry that very day, his eternal flame extinguished. He would lose his name, his honor, his city, his mother, his chance at heaven. *But he would not lose Swanhilde von Thaden.* I could not let this misunderstood child degenerate into a lonely wraith who knew no love. I would have no time to consult any writings, to discern a way for the woman to cling to the heart-bond even if the priest severed it. But I resolved that I would do it somehow even if it killed me, for I loved Augustin even if he must become Wuotan's slave forever.

My eyes opened to the bluish glow of Augustin's bedroom, my gaze toward the shelves laden with his secret writings, the last bell for Lauds dying away in the distance. It was Sunday, and dawn had broken behind the black curtains hiding the window. Today, everything in my world would come crashing to the ground. I groaned softly, stretching my arms and legs, feeling the dull ache within them from my activities of the previous night . . . and Augustin's arms tightened around me, drawing me close to his warm skin. I rolled carefully onto my back to meet the eyes of his reflection in the mirror above us. Then he rose to hover over me, his disheveled black hair brushing my face as he leaned down to kiss my lips. "I missed you, my darling Swanhilde," he said after he ended the kiss, his light blue eyes gazing kindly into mine, his hands gently cradling my head.

I smiled at him, stretching once more underneath the blanket. "How could you have missed me?" I teased him, fluttering my eyelashes. "I sang to you practically all night. I'm shocked that I have a voice left this morning."

He smiled at me knowingly, pressing his body upon mine and wrapping his hands around the back of my head. "Yes, you did . . . and it was beautiful." Our lips met once more, his tongue entwining with mine briefly before he moved his face to my neck, breathing deeply, savoring the scent of my skin and hair. I felt his teeth pierce my skin a moment later, drinking my blood one final time, his lips kissing the wound away once he had finished. "I shall miss this so terribly," he sighed, his fingers twisting in my hair. "Seeing your love for me . . . tasting your sweet blood . . . feeling your trust, your devotion."

Tears welled in my eyes at his words, so saturated with regret, and I pulled him closer. My fingers rubbed the muscles of his back, and I felt him relax at my touch. I could find nothing to say as the misery of the future filled my mind, and I buried my face in Augustin's neck, my body shaking with silent sobs. How could I let go of this magnificent man, in spite of his shortcomings? How could I make myself forget his love, his intelligence, his charm, his generosity? We lay for a long time holding one another in sorrow while the birds chirped joyfully outside the window, ignorant of the tortured pair upon the bed within.

At length, Augustin spoke again, his deep voice sounding troubled. "I have not been good to you." His hands grasped my heart while he made his confession, his light blue eyes wet with remorse. "I promised that I would be good to you, and instead I have ravaged your heart, stolen your virginity, injured you with words and violence. I have failed you." His visage contorted with grief, and tears trickled down his cheeks.

I shook my head firmly, bringing my hands forward to wipe his tears away. "Please, Augustin, don't cry," I whispered, pulling his face to mine and kissing him softly on the forehead. "You did the best you could. You taught me everything, showed me glory, gave me your heart. I love you." He held me closer in response, laying his head upon my chest, and I stroked the locks of his ebony hair, my devotion to this condemned priest forming a bond I resolved not to break.

My mind turned to the particulars of the filial curse, running over its frightening details as Augustin raised his head to look into my eyes. "Are you afraid?" I asked him tentatively, knowing that I certainly would be, if I were in his place. The idea of stemming the flow from a fatal wound unnerved me, and I doubted I could accomplish it. I recalled discussing the filial curse with my Teuton girlfriends back home; we had considered the medical aspects of a sliced artery. Erika had declared that it ought to be called "filial homicide."

My master shook his head, his expression appearing resigned. "No, Swanie, I do not fear the curse," he replied, his mouth twisting into a frown. He looked away from me, casting his gaze toward the black curtains covering his window. He said nothing more for a few moments, his mouth twitching thoughtfully, and then his arms tightened around me again. His blue eyes glowed with sickened passion as he met my gaze. "What I do fear . . . is losing you . . . forever."

I gasped at the emotion in his words and pressed my lips to his again, my body quivering with urgency, my mind and heart cataloguing Augustin's taste and the warmth of his fire. "You won't lose me," I vowed fiercely when we paused for breath. "I will always love you, and I will always be yours."

Eventually, Augustin sat up upon the bed and sighed, glancing toward the window. "You must leave me now and return to Count von Meldorf's estate," he said. I opened my mouth to protest, but Augustin raised one hand to cut me short, his voice firm. "It would be far worse for you if they discover you here, having spent the night in my bed, when they come to drag me to my trial. They shall come for you as well, but they must find you at your home, innocent and safe, a witch perhaps, but not a harlot."

I groaned, accepting the truth of this, and crawled down from Augustin's bed, crossing the floor to his washing table to clean up my appearance. He followed me to the basin and drew one of his own combs through my long hair while I washed, working out its tangles and pulling it back with one of his best clips. I retrieved my clothing from its pile moments later, donning it primly and smoothing out the wrinkles, setting the purple veil again upon my head. I slipped my feet into my shoes and plodded to the bedroom door with legs of iron. I knew that I needed to say something profound now, in our last private moment, but I had no idea what could possibly suffice. At last I looked toward my lover, who stood by his now open window, silently staring up at the cloudy sky. "Augustin . . . ." I broke off, working my way around the lump in my throat. Then I promised, "The curse means nothing to me. I will love you still, and forever call you by your name."

And he answered without turning, "You will always be everything to me."

Chapter Forty-six:
Our Sins Laid Bare

One of the priests of energy from the Teuton Council of Muniche came for me at the Meldorf estate shortly after Sunday mass had begun. By then I had changed into a different dress and spilled the entire story to Freia. She had offered what support she could, her Teutonic light strengthening my spirit just enough to face the trials to come. I asked her to send Jarvis to find me if I did not return home by sunset, and she vowed to pray for me and for Augustin, her usually sunny face darkened with disappointment in the people she now called her own.

The priest brought me to the meeting place in the forest, the same venue where the council had welcomed my companions and me to their city nearly a year before. Today's ceremony was the exact opposite of that, and my feet stumbled on the roots of the trail as I plodded into the clearing, the priest looming darkly behind me. He ordered me to kneel on the ground in a corner of the clearing furthest from the river—not surprising that they would place me as far from my primary element as possible. They must really think me a witch, or a woman with a death wish. Did they fear that I might ask the Isar to fight them in order to delay the curse? I shook my head at the insanity of it all, then lifted my eyes to see the stage set before me.

I knelt with the opening of the trail to my right, the priest of energy planted behind me along with one of the other council members, the forest at their backs. To my left was the traditional fire pit, its crackling flames a mixture of red and yellow. Directly across from me I saw the waters of the Isar, its currents appearing choppy with the impending rain. Between the fire and the river stood a rather long table laden with more papers than necessary, along with the iron bowl, an iron pen, and a rather wicked-looking knife. Paulus von Bayern, dressed in the brown robes of the clergy, stood behind the table, his hand clasping a feather pen; apparently he had been commissioned to document this atrocity. At his side I saw the bishop of Muniche, having forsaken Sunday mass to witness this punishment. Between the table and the river, the eldest council member, Lady Maria, and Prince Otto stood in a tight cluster, each of them clad in black, their faces devoid of mercy.

And when I tore my eyes away from the menacing forms of our judges, I saw my lover on his knees some twelve paces away from me, the two burliest council members planted steadfastly behind him, as though they feared that he might attempt to flee. But when I met Augustin's eyes, he smiled at me in what looked like scornful acquiescence, as if he knew what I wished to do and intended to help me do it.

The Prince stepped forward, turning his back to the opening of the trail to address the ten Teutons before him—five council members, two of the Catholic clergy, the Lady of his city, and the guilty pair kneeling upon the ground. When he began to speak, I realized that every member of the Bayern family was present for this horrible ceremony. I wondered if the Lady Maria would hold the iron bowl into which Augustin's condemned blood poured, or whether Paulus would do it himself. I suspected that Lady Maria would have to do it. Paulus looked like he would pass out at the sight of blood.

"Now that we have all gathered at this place, allow me to offer a condensed explanation for the duties we must perform on this Lord's Day." I turned my full attention to the Prince, who stood with his hands clasped in front of him, his dark blue eyes observing his audience. "Each of us standing here today acknowledges the fact that my eldest brother has proven himself to be an enemy of God since the years of his childhood." My eyes darted to Augustin's face, and I saw that he looked at the Prince rather disgustedly while he voiced his judgments.

"When I accepted responsibility for this city from the hands of my dying father—after my eldest brother rejected this duty—" he shot Augustin a reproachful glare "—I have since been approached time and time again by my councilors as well as members of the clergy. All of them have begged me to mete out punishment upon my brother for his sins. In my mercy, I chose instead to grant my wayward brother another chance at goodness, hoping that he would one day accept the salvation of Christ and forsake the ways of the devil."

The Prince was lying through his teeth. Augustin had never told me that his youngest brother had begged him to become a Christian. I doubted that their hatred for one another would allow for such a thing. The mockery in Augustin's eyes as he stared at the Prince seemed to verify my assumption. "The clergy has reminded me in recent days that a ruler cannot grant mercy forever, for the unrepentant sinner must ultimately face the penalties for his deeds. I can no longer allow my eldest brother to continue in his iniquity in this city, after what all of us saw on the past two afternoons."

His eyes ran over the council members as well as Paulus and the bishop, and I tensed, for I had not realized that everyone in the clearing had been present for both blood-transfers. "I cannot silently condone the public display of such sorcery, for fear of leading the innocent people of Muniche back into the heathenry from which they were redeemed nine centuries in the past. Therefore, the Lord Augustin Abelard Ulrich von Bayern must meet his final condemnation on this Lord's Day; but before I reveal the specifics of his punishment, the Old One and I shall bleed him to lay his sins bare before you, that all of you may understand the reasons for his sentence."

I had not seen *that* coming. My body grew frigid, and I dropped both of my hands into the pine needles beneath me, remembering my master's words on the day I had uncovered his love: *I have never once offered to allow anyone to bleed me. It is a privilege I shall grant to you, and you alone.* Now, both Prince Otto and the head of the council would bleed him, and after that, that pompous Prince would slit his artery. How could he possibly have enough blood in his body to survive such treatment?

But of course he would live ... he was Wolfgang ... I had read his writings . . . history would not change. I ordered myself to remember these truths while I shoved my ice back into my spirit. I needed to keep myself under control, or that energy priest behind me might sap all of my vitality using his element. I needed my strength to preserve the bond.

I watched while the Prince and the gray-bearded Old One approached the place where Augustin knelt. The Prince crouched first, nodding once at the burly priests with the words, "Hold him still." I saw Augustin sneer at his brother before one of the priests grabbed his hair and tilted his head to the left, baring his neck. The other priest held Augustin's arms in an iron grasp while the Prince sank his teeth into his brother's neck. I heard Augustin moan softly, his eyes rolling back as he clung to his control. I knew that he wanted to push them all away, to burn them all with his fire. But I doubted that even he could defeat the entire council of Muniche. As I watched the Prince drink his brother's blood, it occurred to me that the two priests that held Augustin down were using their elements as well as their strength to render him defenseless. The one that held his hair bared his teeth at my master, his eyes glowing yellow—*fire,* keeping Augustin's own fire at bay. And the other's eyes sparked with energy, his hands gripping Augustin's arms in a hold too powerful to break.

The Prince released his brother after I had counted to thirty, waving the wizard-looking priest forward and wiping the blood from his lips. The elderly man bled Augustin for about forty seconds while I sat biting my lip, wishing I could do or say something that would convince them to stop. When the Old One released Augustin, rising to his feet with a grunt and coming to stand beside the Prince, I saw my master clap his right hand upon his neck the moment the two priests let go of him. His face looked deathly pale, and he sank forward a bit as he worked to close the wounds in his neck. *I wonder how long I actually bled him, that day by the stream . . . he looks awful . . . and this time, I can't give him any of my blood to restore his strength . . . .*

The head of the council and the Prince exchanged a few whispered words, and Augustin removed his hand from his neck, which no longer bled. His eyes opened once more, tinted with odium. The Prince turned around to address the onlookers again, and I noticed that the Lady Maria was glowering at Augustin, her wintry blue eyes aglow with hatred and triumph.

"In the blood of my eldest brother, we have found more than enough sins to condemn him this day to the darkest fate that awaits Teutons who consort with the devil," the Prince announced gravely, motioning the Old One to stand beside him as they related Augustin's memories. I glanced again at my master, and our eyes met for the briefest of instants, his familiar smirk reassuring me that he still did not fear his fate. Then, to my shock, Prince Otto and the gray-bearded priest began to speak in unison, their glazed eyes suggesting that they were watching Augustin's memories at that very moment.

"In the year 1028, at the age of ten, Augustin von Bayern began to study the ancient heathen writings in secret, though they were banned by the church. In the year 1033, at the age of fifteen in the city of Vienna, he committed his first sexual sin with a Magyar slave girl. He committed his first murder following a loss at gambling in the same year. In the year 1035, at the age of seventeen,

Augustin von Bayern passed his initiation into the Teutonic priesthood after concluding a secret pact with Wuotan, pledging to use his gifts to serve the devil. One month after this, he sacrificed a Schwäbisch child to Wuotan following a rape, collecting the child's blood for use in sacrilegious rituals.

"Since 1035, Augustin von Bayern has staged one hundred forty-eight blood sacrifices at Wuotan's direction, the majority of the victims being female, each of them being raped as a prelude to their murder. Since 1043, Augustin von Bayern has created a name for himself in Muniche as the one to consult for devilish rituals. He has seduced thirty-nine women to cry for his aid in childbirth, taking from them their innocence in return, calling upon Wuotan to lead them astray."

The two judges paused for breath while I gaped, their accusations swirling in my brain like cars caught in a tornado. *Could Augustin have really done all of that? But it has to be true . . . they read it in his blood . . . the worst things . . . none of the good things. They didn't bother to see the reason for his wickedness . . . the hypocrisy and rejection he's faced since his mother died . . . they didn't look for his love . . . our love . . . . I doubt he's done so many sacrifices since he created our bond . . . .* I shook my head once, trying to erase the doubts that their hideous words had placed in my mind.

I averted my gaze from the Prince and the Old One to my master, where he knelt amongst the leaves and pine needles with his jailors standing impassively behind him. He looked straight at me, his light blue eyes silently begging me for mercy, for forgiveness. I felt his hands upon my heart at that moment, gentle and pleading. *Do not condemn me as they would!* I could practically hear the cry bursting from his heart. I managed to smile back at him weakly, knowing that I could never hate him, for our love outweighed all rational bounds. *You are not what they say. I forgive you . . . .*

Then, both the Prince and the Old One turned slightly to level their stares directly upon me, prompting everyone else in the clearing to do the same. As they began to speak their last condemnations, I felt as though I were sinking into quicksand. "Augustin von Bayern has used this foolish woman, Swanhilde von Thaden, as his unwitting partner in devilry since she fell under his spell shortly after her arrival in Muniche in the summer of 1044. He has revealed the secrets of Teuton sorcery, both the acceptable and unacceptable sort, to this woman, including but not limited to: the use of elements other than her own, the techniques of blood control, the reading and writing of the language of the heathens, the impudence to attempt to confront Wuotan over the souls of the dying, and the devilry of elemental harlotry."

What?! I struggled to maintain my composure while part of me screamed with laughter. Unfortunately, most of my mind had latched onto the horrid truth that they had seen every single sin I had ever committed with Augustin. How could we possibly believe that they might show me mercy?

The elderly priest stepped back to his former place beside Lady Maria. The Prince continued to stare balefully at me while I shivered in fear. "The horrible sins that my brother has committed with this woman were brought before the eyes of the entire city during the recent blood-transfers. All of us watched my brother's satanic act of desperation when he pulled this woman from the clutches of Wuotan on Friday afternoon in an attempt to prove to his audience that his priestly abilities outweigh mine.

"We also saw this woman enter the realm of the spirit at Augustin's direction on Saturday afternoon, interrupting my blood-transfer in public to argue with Wuotan for the soul of Joel Hudson. My brother has transformed Swan-hilde von Thaden into a witch, seducing her with sights not meant for the eyes of women. He has freely admitted that during the winter months, he created the heart-bond of the Teutons with this woman in order to make her a slave to his will, bringing her under the influence of Wuotan, the demon he names Master."

I felt the eyes of everyone in the clearing burning me to cinders as I stared at the pine needles beneath me. Tears trembled on my eyelashes, but I ordered myself to be strong, to keep silent and cling forever to Augustin's love no matter what our accusers threw at us. I heard the Prince's footsteps cross the clearing to stand once more before his brother. "Let the accused now speak his defense, if he can formulate any justifications that would prove valid against the truth in his blood."

I lifted my eyes from the forest floor to see the Prince standing directly in front of Augustin with his hands upon his hips. What would Augustin say now that he had the opportunity to speak? I craned my neck to the right, trying to see my lover's face around the Prince's body.

There was a lengthy pause, and when Augustin answered the Prince, I saw that he looked directly at me. "I have no defense to speak against the truth in my blood, but perhaps if you ask the Lady Swanhilde, she could relate her position on your accusations."

My mouth practically hit the ground while Augustin's blue eyes stared into mine. Both of us knew full well that anything I might say would do no good. Prince Otto huffed in annoyance and spat, "You would ask your harlot to speak for you?"

"Yes, for her education and intellect far overshadow those of the majority of us gathered here." Augustin's face hardened, but he still held my eyes with his.

Abruptly, the Prince grabbed his brother's chin in his right hand, twisting his head sharply upward. "Look at *me*, you wretch! You know full well that our laws do not recognize the appeals of the weaker sex."

To my astonishment, I heard Augustin riposte in a voice dripping with contempt, "Then perhaps Teuton laws should be altered in light of the future, for educated men and women should be held on equal ground."

"Sacrilege!" Prince Otto barked, slapping Augustin across the face. A wash of pleasure rushed through me at my master's words. *I am his equal, and he believes it, even though he sacrifices outsiders to Wuotan.* "If the accused has nothing better to say save ludicrous speculations on the position of women, all of which he wishes to rape and murder, we shall turn our attention now to the punishment."

The Prince returned to his place at the opening of the trail, relating every aspect of the filial curse and what it implied in grand detail. I could tell that both Paulus and the bishop were incredibly interested in the curse, likely making silent conjectures on whether it would suffice as proper retribution for Augustin's sins. The other council members also paid rapt attention, some of them looking like they had never read anything on the subject. A wicked smile crept across Lady Maria's face while the Prince spoke, and I realized that she was probably already in on the plot, since she would have to give her unspoken consent to the curse.

After the first few phrases, I completely blocked the Prince's description from my mind, focusing instead upon my condemned master, my depraved lover. He still knelt only twelve paces away from me, his expression resigned, his body appearing extremely weary. He lifted his eyes to mine as his brother spoke, a sad smile gracing his lips when he caressed my heart, savoring our final moments. I tried to convey a message as we gazed into one another's eyes, concentrating on our heart-bond while our judges reviled us: *Thank you for sticking up for me . . . and for all educated women. You are far better than any of these bigots.*

A moment later, the Prince finished his diatribe and turned slightly to face me. "In light of what we have seen and heard this day, understanding the innocence and inexperience of women, we must therefore erase the guilt of Swanhilde von Thaden by severing the bond she shares with this iniquitous servant of Wuotan before we impose the filial curse. Once she is released from his clutches, she will obey the will of God once more, consigning her tormentor to the fate of eternal damnation." The Prince gestured at the priests guarding both me and Augustin, indicating that they should bring us to the midst of the clearing, so the duty could be carried out under the vigilant eyes of everyone.

They forced me to my knees at the center of the glade, and my heart began pounding in a mixture of terror and denial. I was not ready for this. I had yet to reason out a way to preserve our heart-bond while the entire council of Muniche hovered to ensure that it would be properly severed. My lips quivered, and in desperation I would have begged and pleaded with the Prince to allow me to remain with Augustin, even if it meant that I must become an outcast handed over to a demon. How could I live without Augustin's love, never again feeling the touch of his hands upon my heart?

He stroked my heart again while panic seeped into my lungs, and I lifted my eyes to his as our judges arranged themselves around us in a circle of darkness. They had thrust him to the ground within centimeters of me, and I could have reached out a hand to caress his face had my fear not frozen me solid. The Prince spoke a few more statements regarding what was to be done, and I looked into Augustin's eyes, the English word *no* forming on my lips.

My master shook his head at me almost imperceptibly. Anguish gleamed in his fiery blue eyes as he mouthed the English words, *we must.* I began to wheeze, unable to draw in a proper amount of air, miniscule shards of ice creeping upward from my pores. My reason was slipping away. I fought to control myself, for I needed to be able to think once Augustin carried me to the spiritual realm. *Focus, Swanie. You can breathe. You can breathe, and you have to fight . . . .*

Suddenly, the Prince appeared behind Augustin, dropping a glass vial into his lap with the command, "Now blind her and do your duty. Four of us shall follow you to make certain of your obedience."

All six of the Teuton priests on the council stood around us, and a corner of my mind wondered which four would serve as witnesses to this wretched division. Augustin had been correct from the very beginning; the Prince was a murderer. He had taken love out of his brother's life from the day of his birth, and now he would take away the love of my life without thought, without care.

I mouthed the word *no* again as Augustin looked gravely into my eyes, his hand slowly lifting the vial from where it had fallen between his legs. He hardly seemed like himself for this ordeal, for he wore leather trousers and a brown linen tunic, not the usual priestly robes or noble clothing. *Dressed for the journey of an exile . . . .* I hoped he had asked Viktor to prepare a bundle for him, so he might not leave everything behind . . . and I wished that I could have given him something of mine to keep with him forever, like I planned to preserve the black clip he had placed in my hair that morning.

Augustin leaned toward me, his expression resigned. He glanced briefly at the cloudy sky, silently indicating that I should look upward, so he could blind me for our final act. It disgusted me that the Prince wished me to face this severance in obscurity; his chauvinism knew no limits, it seemed. I inhaled a shallow breath, shuddering once, and looked toward the sky.

When Augustin squeezed a drop into my right eye, I thought I heard him say so quietly I could hardly hear, the English words, "Forgive me for what I must do . . . my love." I bit my lip and struggled to ignore the pain of the solution upon my eyes; it was a necessary evil that I would have to excise once we entered the other realm. Then I called my ice out of my spirit in union with Augustin's fire, and we flew to the ether together one last time, both of his hands touching the skin of my face.

I recognized the contented gliding of my spirit in the moment I entered the atmosphere. I focused without delay upon the scales covering my eyes, channeling my ice there to free my eyesight. I heard the Prince speaking somewhere behind me, the voice of his spirit sounding distasteful. *We are here, and we shall pull her back ourselves. Set your slave free, Augustin, while you yet hold the name, for she must not share your fate. Seduce her no longer; send her back to God.*

I threw the blindness from my eyes in the next second, blinking to see Augustin hovering before me. His spirit was clothed in resplendent sapphire, his eyes pure flames of fire, his angelic face broken with agony as he stared at my heart, beating in his hands. I knew that the other four priests who had followed us—the Prince included—drifted somewhere in the clouds nearby, but I did not bother to search for them. My eyes were riveted on my heart, resting blissfully in my master's hands, throbbing with love, wordlessly begging him not to let it go. His lips parted, revealing his teeth bared in anguish. He stroked the index finger of his left hand tenderly down the center of my heart, his boundless love filling it with life. My eyes rolled back at the sensation his fingers infused upon my being. I may have gasped once, for I knew that he was about to obey the commands of his brother, and I had no clue how to stop him.

He began reciting the ritual words in Ælte Teutonica, his mental voice barely audible, his tortured eyes fixed upon my heart. *No bond is eternal ... no love unending ... even that which was fashioned in the spirit may not persist unbroken ... mere human ties must crumble in the face of destiny ... the priest must free the heart of his beloved ... that she may forget his timeless faithfulness . .. that she may seek her future without his influence ... an unchained soul ....*

I shook my head during the entire recitation; I did not agree with this. Severing our heart-bond would not make me forget Augustin's love. It would drive me mad, make me wish for death. He could not do this. *We* could not do this. But I could not back away when my master met my gaze, the sorrow in his face steeping me in melancholy. His right hand gradually approached my chest as he prepared to place the heart of my spirit within me once more. My robes grew translucent in response to my fear, and the word *no* spilled mechanically from my mind, a voiceless prayer, a desperate cry. But Augustin's expression hardened into impassiveness, and he reached his right hand into my chest, passing through my ghost-like body to set my beating heart in its rightful place.

I hung on to those ephemeral moments, my mind and heart fusing together as Augustin relinquished his claim upon my spirit, freeing me permanently from naming him master. Tears of ice seeped from my eyes when I felt his fingers recede, leaving my heart beating alone in my chest, his face stricken with hatred and loss. There passed one interminable second where I registered the fact that I was *crying* in the realm of the spirit, a misty place of contentment where such misery should not be possible. I heard Augustin say the final words, the dreadful words that put irrevocability upon every Teuton ritual: *It is done.* His eyes flamed with loathing and torment. And then . . . .

My heart raced . . . my mind whirled . . . an overwhelming weakness sapping all of my strength. Right before me, as clearly as though it happened in that very moment, I saw every memory I had made with Augustin in a tidal wave of emotion: *the man of darkness, the non-existent one, the angelic dancer, the scholar, the archivist, the murderer, the power-hungry sadist, the linguist, the teacher, the heathen priest, the rapist, the death-dealer, the doctor, the bitter son, the hated brother, the vampire, the savior, the thinker, the master, the lover, the selfless one, the madman, the advocate of Wuotan, the sexual expert, the kind-hearted partner, the broken man, my insanity, my darling, my equal, my mentor . . . my everything . . . my heart . . . my life . . . my love . . . Augustin!*

I screamed, a piercing cry of betrayal as lunacy flooded my veins. I would never have him again. I would never feel him again. The bond was broken. But I loved him still. This could not be. I could not think. I could not speak. The hands of my spirit curled into claws, and I shrieked with a vehemence that could have split the sky apart. Behind me in the clouds, I sensed that three of the others had already gone, returning to the earth to reunite with their bodies. And I felt the fiery hands of the remaining judge, the one who had torn me from my beloved. He ripped his nails through my spirit, that murderous Prince, dragging me back to hell, disregarding my screams of madness.

. . . And I knew that I had less than a second.

. . . And I knew that I would love Augustin forever.

. . . I had gone insane.

. . . And the instant before the Prince pulled me from the spiritual realm, I tore my own chest open with my icy hands, grasping that deceived heart of mine, that organ that could not pump without its master's touch. I rent it from my breast and cast it down, down through the clouds, through the heavens, to the ground, to the abyss, to death, for I could not live without him.

And as the blackness of death enveloped my sentience, I saw abject horror upon the face of Augustin's spirit. He had not yet left the atmosphere, and he had seen my insanity. And my last vision before oblivion took me was that of his right arm, reaching out like lightning to span the heavens, catching my heart before it could break upon the earth, before it could cancel my life.

Chapter Forty-seven:
This Malevolent Recompense

I opened my eyes less than a second later, finding myself once more in my body, crouched on the pine needles and leaves in the forest glade, the black-robed priests standing over me. My heart throbbed within my chest, and my ice coursed fast through my veins, wiping away all traces of that priest whose devilish red fire had ripped my spirit to pieces. He stood to my right, heat waves still seeping from his body, his fists clenched. My tormented lover knelt just centimeters from me, his deathly pale face lifting slowly to meet my gaze, his mouth quivering in horror, his eyes alight with cobalt flames, burning my bones to embers. And as I stared back at him with the eyes of a madwoman, I watched him carefully turn his right wrist so that it faced downward, dropping it with concentrated deliberation onto the forest floor. Only a moment before, his palm had faced the sky, his fingers curled inward with a fierceness that caused the blood in his veins to pulse visibly.

He had saved me. He was still my master.

There was dead silence in the clearing, and simultaneous waves of triumph, relief, and fright washed over me.

Had the Prince seen what I had done, or had he been too busy trying to drag my spirit back to earth? He could not have seen. We could not let him find out. I had to distract him . . . .

I contorted my face into an expression of lunacy. My voice burst forth with a psychotic shriek, my fingers raking through the rotting leaves beneath me. I no longer cared what they would think of me; let them assume I had gone nuts. Just let them not see that our bond had been restored in my moment of desperation. I heard the Prince's spiteful voice while I ranted, ordering the two priests who had guarded me earlier to drag me back to the corner of the glade.

The dirt of the ground stained my summer dress as they pulled me from Augustin's side, the pine needles piercing the skin underneath my fingernails. But I found that I could not stop crying. My tears flowed like frigid rain, some of the droplets freezing upon my bodice. I know not whether I wept from joy, from sorrow, or from madness. But one truth clung to my heart once the priests had thrust me into my former place: *my heart-bond with Augustin had been preserved, against all odds . . . and now I would have to watch that wretched Prince curse his name.* It did not matter; I realized that then and there. His name would be Augustin eternally, and he would be forever mine. No one could tear us asunder, not even Wuotan himself. Our love was too strong; our devotion transcended all rational bounds.

Finally, I managed to calm myself enough to lift my tear- and dirt-stained face from my lap, my icy eyes blinking in dismay as I watched the tragedy play out before me. The Prince had finished with his heartless preambles while I had raved like a lunatic. Now he stood several paces from the table with Augustin standing before him, his shoulders slumped, his eyes on his boots. The three other priests on the council—the ones who had not been commanded to guard me—hovered not far away, their merciless stares locked upon the two hate-filled brothers. The bishop and Paulus remained behind the table, Paulus' hand now gripping the iron pen, a small sheet of parchment lying in front of him on the table. And poised between the Prince and Augustin, her eyes filled with freezing revulsion, her black dress swirling around her with the force of her wind, stood Maria von Bayern, the pitiless Lady of Muniche, her hands clutching the traditional iron bowl.

This was the worst treachery that a Teuton could commit against a family member—the most malevolent recompense for which our laws allowed. I could not comprehend how anyone could do this to their child, to their sister, to their brother, no matter what wrongs the offending party had committed. How could the Prince have no sense of blood loyalty, no sense of decency, no remorse for this terrible act of treason? How could Paulus just stand there in silence, his face betraying no emotion? How could Lady Maria, the woman who was supposed to embody my city, the blood of my Teuton people, their willingness to forgive . . . how could this woman who should have sought to be Augustin's mother in Marelda's stead choose to cast him aside with such malice, her eyes shining with victory?

Tears burned my eyes as I watched the Prince lift the knife from the table, his expression looking like it came from the pit of hell. "Let us be done with this," he stated callously. Augustin raised his eyes to meet those of his unforgiving judge while the Prince took his brother's right arm in his fingers, turning his wrist upward. He lifted his eyes to the cloudy sky and recited the words of the filial curse, his Ælte Teutonica laden with sick passion, his beatific expression suggesting that he believed himself to wield the scepter of God by carrying out this act.

"Due to the unpardonable sins you commit in excess . . . forfeiting the honor of your family's blood . . . due to your lack of remorse and unwillingness to turn to the path of righteousness . . . in the Name of the Most Holy God, on this Lord's Day, I do curse your name . . . I cut off your life from mine . . . strip your identity from you . . . as has been done from the beginning . . . casting you out from your people until this earth perishes in fire . . . consigning your soul to Wuotan for all of eternity . . . that this fate may be assigned to you with all of its sorrows, you must write your desecrated name with your own blood . . . cursed for all of time . . . ."

The horrible words imprinted themselves upon my heart, and I winced at the betrayal evident upon Augustin's face. I noticed that during the recitation, the Prince used formal grammar in reference to his brother, the first step in officially naming him an outcast, a wraith with no family, no Teuton blood. I bit my lip when the Prince's knife cut into my master's flesh, the bright red liquid bursting forth with the force of an artery. Augustin moaned once as his blood poured into the iron bowl. He closed his eyes in concentration, endeavoring to keep himself alive. They should have shown him just a touch of mercy and allowed him to sit for this part. I found myself focusing on the hemorrhaging artery from where I knelt, reaching out with my own abilities at blood control to come to Augustin's assistance. *You cannot die. You must survive this . . . for me . . . for you . . . for the future . . . .*

At length, Augustin braced himself upon the table, his skin as white as a ghost. He clamped his left hand upon his wounded forearm, the angles of his face set in intense concentration as he abated the flow. When he pulled his hand away, I saw that it was stained with dark blood, and on his right forearm, a rather awful-looking scab had begun to form. Bile churned in my stomach at the acrid stench of blood, and I pressed one hand to my mouth while Lady Maria carried the bowl rather ceremoniously to the table. It brimmed with blood, viscous and coagulating, and she eyed it with a wicked smirk, her face akin to that of a triumphant witch.

Several of the council members murmured amongst themselves as Prince Otto rounded on Augustin, where he leaned against the edge of the table still trying to recover. "Quickly now, write your condemned name one final time, that you may realize the full recompense for your sins." The Prince shoved Augustin toward the bloody bowl with a sneer.

I sat frozen in horror as Augustin weakly accepted the iron pen from Paulus' hands, dipping it into the bowl and scrawling it across the parchment. I imagined the exact words he would write, the sealing of the deal, condemning himself into the annals of the Black Priests for all of eternity: *Lord Augustin Abelard Ulrich von Bayern*. Maybe he even added his mother's maiden name just to leave nothing out: *von Förster und von Bayern*. Part of me felt almost as though this was all just a terrible nightmare, that I would wake up at the count's estate and laugh at my wild imagination, sighing in relief that such a horrific thing could never really come to pass. But it was written in the stars, written in the currents of time, written in the history books —written in the papers of Wolfgang, the Black Priest from the eleventh century who had taken down little-known facts about the Torstein, recording them for posterity in the glorious Carolingian miniscule of my master.

At last, Augustin laid the iron pen once more upon the table, sighing heavily, bowing his head and gripping the wood beneath him as though it was the only solid thing left in his world. The Prince snatched the paper from the table with an air of finality, carrying it to the blazing fire pit while Augustin watched, his mouth turned downward in disgust. The Prince halted before the fire, spinning around to face his audience. He waved the paper in the air and spoke the closing words of the filial curse in an authoritative tone: "May the name of the Lord Augustin Abelard Ulrich von Bayern be burned, and may it never be spoken again!" He cast the paper into the flames with a flick of his wrist, the fire taking on the impossible colors of green and blue and a deep red.

There was a short silence after the fire had calmed. Dread took over my soul as the irrevocability of what I had just witnessed hit me hard. My lover had been cursed with the worst fate known to my people, by all accounts damned permanently to hell, the grace of God forever beyond his reach. Depression seized hold of me at the notion that although I had managed to preserve our bond, death would eventually separate us for eternity—for I was a Christian, bound for heaven, and my master was consigned to perdition, given over to Wuotan. That demon would never allow him to accept God's forgiveness. He would poison him, blind him, drag him down to where those four original Black Priests likely shrieked in torment. How could we salvage our relationship when our fates pointed in opposite directions?

I shivered at the possible consequences of what I had done in my insanity. I had cast myself back into the hands of Augustin, the Cursed One, the Black Priest, the servant of Wuotan. He loved me now, but that wretched demon would twist his love, transforming it into something dark and terrible, a desire to ruin, a yearning to degenerate. *But the laws of the Teutons mean nothing. I do not believe in the curse. Augustin is still my lover, and he still has a chance. I will not give up on him, and neither will God. I don't care what everyone else thinks. The Prince was wrong . . . this curse is nothing . . . it won't break us apart . . . .*

While these tumultuous thoughts raced through my mind, the witnesses in the clearing prepared for departure, the priests extinguishing the fire, throwing the waters of the Isar over the ashes. Paulus and the bishop began to collect all of the papers on the table into a pile, probably intending to file them the next day—and meticulously burn or blot my master's name from all written records. The two priests who had stood behind me moved to sort the other items on the table, and the Lady Maria carried the iron bowl down to the river, casting the remainder of Augustin's blood into its dark waters.

As for my master, he stood near the opening of the trail, his expression downcast, his posture suggesting that he wished to stay just a few moments longer to exchange a few final words with me. But the Prince marched over to him and said in no uncertain terms, "Get out of here, you bastard. What's done is done, and there is no point in your standing here, silently bemoaning your fate. Muniche's gates are closed to you forever. Go to your master and find yourself a new name. I never wish to see your face again."

Augustin nodded mutely, his light blue eyes locking with mine for a moment so brief that I was not sure whether it had actually happened or not. In the next instant, he disappeared into the forest, vanishing like a ghost, like an outcast. And I crawled forward on the pine needles, stretching one trembling hand in the direction he had gone, my eyes brimming with tears. "*Augustin* . . . ." I gasped.

A fiery hand slapped my face harshly, jerking my head backward, prompting me to crumple onto the ground. "DO NOT speak that name!" the Prince roared at me, his eyes glittering red as he drew his right arm back to strike me again. "I am the Prince of this city, the authority over you, and you WILL recognize what has been done this day! Do you understand me?" I groveled at his feet, squeezing my eyes shut against the truth. And the rain began to fall, obscuring my sight while the others departed, misery overtaking me in a dark curtain I could not lift.

End of Book II

~*~

Turn the page for a small taste of hope after such a tragic ending—trust me, I'm crying too!

His Name Was Augustin
Book III excerpt
© C.L. Carhart

Chapter One:
Pulled from the Mire

I do not know how long I lay prone upon the decaying leaves and needles, the rain soaking me through, grime caking my fingers, staining my dress and hair. The full weight of what I had done had dragged me into dejection. As I wept icy tears, I knew that in spite of my efforts I would never see Augustin again. He was a Black Priest now, a Cursed One, an outcast, forever forbidden to enter Teuton lands. No city would welcome him; no one would offer him acceptance. He would never again walk the streets of Muniche in the mortal world or in spiritual form. He would be forced to crawl on his knees before Wuotan himself, facing the fate of eternal damnation, the very deal he had made for the sake of my life and Joel's. His name would be erased from all writings, burnt from the records, ignored in Teuton history, cursed for all of time.

And I would never stop loving him, for I had preserved our bond.

Many thoughts churned in my mind while I groaned in torment on that rainy afternoon, not giving a thought or care to the passing of time, to how drenched my body had become. For a while I wished that I had never come to the eleventh century in the first place. Everything I had planned to do in the past had gone completely haywire, from that first half hour when I had watched my cousin die before my eyes. I had arrived twenty years too early, lost the Torstein due to my own inattention, killed a Gypsy, befriended the most hated man in Muniche, ignored the potential of love with a decent man, forsaken him for a wretch, a demon-worshipper, a devil, a rapist, a sadist, a curse . . . .

At some point, a horrible realization hit me. Perhaps if I had *not* used the Torstein, perhaps if I had stayed in the twenty-first century where I belonged . . . maybe Augustin would never have been cursed. It had all come about because he had taught *me* forbidden secrets; it was all a result of my foolish curiosity. If I had not come, someone else could have stepped in and taught him a better way, someone from his time, someone with a pure and virtuous outlook. Perhaps his cruel heart could have softened, and he could have forgiven the Prince one day. *And then . . . ? Maybe if Augustin had not been cursed, Muniche would not have fallen . . . .*

I wanted to die. I wanted to just lie there in the dirt until death sent me back where I belonged. I had written myself into history whether I liked it or not, since my inquisitiveness had cursed the one man in the Bayern family who seemed to have common sense, the one who undoubtedly could have held the Saxons back. I had ruined everything. I had corrupted my people's future . . . I had spoiled all hopes of their recovery . . . .

Suddenly, something yanked me from the ground with the intensity of fire, forcing me to confront reality again. I staggered for a moment, my eyes darting around the deepening shadows of the forest, seeing the rain pouring from the sky though I no longer felt it. Confusion took hold of me as I turned my gaze upon the River Isar. Its choppy currents lapped at my bare feet, which, I noticed, resembled sculptures of ice. Frowning, I looked down at myself and saw that I no longer wore my dirt-stained light pink dress. Now, dismal robes of grayish green enveloped my body, their dull hue matching the waters of the river. And when I circled around to face the trees, my eyes widened at the sight of Augustin standing beneath a lowering birch, its branches sagging with wet leaves. He wore the vibrant cerulean of the spiritual realm, and he was glaring at me.

"If you continue to lie that way in the rain, you shall unquestionably make yourself sick, Swanhilde." His tone sounded coarse, and he jerked his head toward the forest behind him.

I was too busy having a heart attack at his unexpected appearance to notice anything but the magnificence of his spirit. "Oh . . . Augustin . . . ." I gasped, stretching my arms out toward him. I ran to where he stood—and found myself clutching the birch tree while he stepped gracefully aside.

"You cannot touch me here, Swanhilde," he reminded me as I backed away from the tree in consternation. "We are in the spiritual dream world, for you have wept yourself into an agitated slumber." An instant later, I found myself standing before a crumpled woman curled into a ball on the forest floor, her dress in tatters, her hair muddy, her face a mere shadow of my own. Her eyes were squeezed shut, and she moaned plaintively in her sleep. I sensed Augustin's presence behind me while I stared blankly at my mortal body, disgusted by its revolting appearance. "You should not torment yourself over me, my darling," Augustin whispered in my ear, his concern flowing into my spirit. "You are going to become ill, and I cannot restore your health from a distance."

"But it's my fault this happened," I confessed to him, lifting my gaze to my lover's gorgeous spirit. "I was thinking about everything before I fell asleep. And I realized that the Prince may not have cursed you at all if it hadn't been for my idiocy at Joel's blood-transfer. I should never have come to the eleventh century, because if I hadn't . . . maybe you could have fought the Saxons in 1066, instead of being banished . . . and maybe our people wouldn't have fallen . . . it's all my fault . . . ." My sorrow burst out from my spirit, and I turned away from Augustin in shame. I trod down to the banks of the Isar and summoned its waters to merge with my feet, swirling my dull robes around me.

"My darling, I told you once before that you must not think in those terms," Augustin reproved me. He walked onto the river himself to eye me seriously as my tumultuous thoughts threatened to pull me deeper into depression. "What became of me today had nothing to do with you. The Prince would have discovered the particulars of the filial curse eventually. I have committed more than enough sins to warrant this awful punishment."

I shook my head at his words, my guilt infusing my spirit with weariness. Augustin sighed and stepped close to me, lifting his right hand to trace it slowly down my face, though his fingers passed through my form. "Come sit down with me and hear the truth. You must not blame yourself for this, and if you insist upon doing so, I shall force you to heed my advice." His mouth quirked into a sly smile. He slipped his right hand beneath his fiery robes to touch my heart with a degree of reproach, a wordless reminder of the power he held over me. Then he led me to the riverbank and gestured that I should sit upon him, though our spirits could not touch in our spiritual dream.

I obeyed him in silence, my heart still steeped in melancholy. The fact that I appeared to crush his legs when my spirit sat down did not improve my mood. He requested that I meet his eyes, and when I did so he began to speak softly, his smoldering blue eyes gazing into mine with a depth that rivaled the ocean.

"Swanhilde my love, for one who travels time, you have the tendency to view major events within the bounds of a small box. You must not make assumptions about your place in history, in the past or the future. Our paths are laid down by our Creator, and He knows every choice we shall make, right or wrong. I have become convinced that our destinies cannot be altered through the use of the Prince's song or the Torstein, or through any other means. Seeing the future in your blood has persuaded me forever.

"You must not assign the faults of 1066 to your account, for they have already been inscribed upon the currents of time. What difference could it have made if I had not been cursed and could have fought alongside the Prince for the preservation of our people? The Saxons shall still have the song and shall still raise an invincible army, whether I am there to scorch them or not. It is not given to us to know the future, for although you have traveled to the past, you have no inkling of what may happen upon your return to the twenty-first century. Perhaps that is where the true change shall occur, for you shall return as one who has seen events not meant for your eyes. Perhaps you shall be the one to pull our people from the mire one thousand years in the future."

The possibilities of this proposition grabbed hold of me while I stared into Augustin's earnest eyes, bringing light into my thoughts afresh. "But what could one woman do to change the future?" I wondered, shaking my head at the enormity of such a suggestion. "I don't know what I *could* do to get the Teutons of my era to reclaim the glory they lost in the past. No one cares about that sort of thing in my time. Most people would rather just immerse themselves in mainstream culture." I frowned a bit as something else occurred to me. "What our people *should* have done was to rise up after the Saxon conquest and take Bavaria back. But I haven't read much on the centuries directly after our defeat. Few Teuton writings were set down in those days due to the scattering of our people."

"Then perhaps we should both resolve to do what we can, following the failure of 1066." Augustin's eyes glimmered, and a wraith-like smile stretched across his face. "Perhaps with my new . . . position . . . I could bargain with Wuotan more freely and convince him to use me as a scourge against the Saxons. I do not know, for as yet I have no concept of the extent of this curse." Augustin fell silent, his smile darkening into a grimace. He looked down at his right arm, its skin hidden beneath his cobalt robes. "I fear that I may be damned to hell, Swanie . . . but what can be done?" He drew his sleeve back and there, to my chagrin, I saw a jet-black scar about ten centimeters long upon the forearm of his spirit, the mark of the Cursed Priest.

I ordered myself not to back away, to remain seated upon his lap, to view the scar calmly, without fear. "It still means nothing to me. There is always hope, Augustin."

He unrolled his sleeve to hide the mark from both of us and eyed me scathingly. "You should stop calling me that."

I shook my head, smiling in spite of his fierce expression. "You will always be Augustin von Bayern to me."

He growled and slid himself out from under me, folding his arms as he brought his knees up to his chest. "And you once seemed so respectful of Teuton traditions. Now listen to your blasphemy, refusing to acknowledge the first Black Priest in nine centuries for what he is. It is no wonder you were destined for this misery, doomed to watch our people fall, to lose your mother at so young an age, to yearn for a fiery old man, to forever love a Cursed Priest, one who will ultimately come to despise your goodness. And I was fated to be cursed, yes . . . fated to lose my name, my family, my blood . . . fated to stand by and watch while my city falls, unable to help, unable to interfere. Fated to lose everything I ever had . . . everything I ever wanted."

"Everything but me," I finished quietly, unwilling to allow him to wallow in despondency himself.

He stared balefully at me, rising to his feet and reaching his right hand into his blue robes to retrieve my beating heart from where it rested at his breast. I climbed to my feet as well, a hint of triumph rushing through me when I looked at my heart, held once more in its master's hands. "How could you have done such a thing?" Augustin whispered, his gaze riveted upon my heart. His right hand grasped it tightly, and he raised the index fingers of his left hand to stroke it in wonder.

I closed my eyes to concentrate on the security of our bond, the gentleness of his touch, the devotion that poured from his spirit into mine. "Because I love you," I whispered back, a contented smile gracing my lips. "I couldn't let you go . . . no matter what they did . . . no matter what *you* did. I love you too much . . . and I can't live without you."

"And that love shall become your torment." Augustin's expression twisted into anguish as he placed my heart beneath his robes. Lifting his eyes to mine, he said flatly, "I shall rip you to shreds, my darling, for Wuotan does not recognize love, only hatred. He shall cause me to forget, induce me to treat you as my slave, not as my beloved. And our destinies must part ways for twenty-one years, never to touch again, a permanent separation."

The truth of this clawed at my spirit, but I pushed it aside and asserted with a mad confidence, "But you will always be mine."

"That remains to be seen, Swanhilde." Augustin's face grew caustic, and he cast his gaze back toward the trees. "Now you must awaken, and I must continue my journey, an exile until someone grants me asylum."

I knew that he would force me to awaken, but before he could I grabbed at his left arm, my fingers finding no purchase. "But we'll meet again here." My spirit trembled with silent longing.

Augustin smiled at me, a half-hearted curl of his lips. "I shall be the specter in your dreams, my swan princess." He leaned down to kiss my hair, and a moment later, I opened my eyes to the dirt and rain and leaves, my entire body soaked through and coated with mud. I heard Jarvis' voice calling in the distance, somewhere in the misty forest. So I lifted myself from the ground, brushing the strands of wet hair away from my face, and gathered all of my strength to face the broken shards of my destiny.

To be continued . . . .

Book III comes out in September 2021
Order now from your preferred platform!

C.L. Carhart would be thrilled if you would leave a review for this book. Reviews help buoy an indie author's career, as well as her spirits. She appreciates your feedback!

Sign up for C.L. Carhart's newsletter for an inside look at her author undertakings, along with information on new releases and the occasional secret deal.
https://sendfox.com/clcarhart1066

Check out C.L. Carhart's website to see how Inessa Burnell brought her characters to life, and commission her for some fantasy art of your own.
https://www.clcarhart.com/characters

Mystic Passage is available on library platforms! Ask your local library to order it in eBook and paperback so that C.L. can reach more readers.

Follow C.L. on social media:
https://www.facebook.com/CLCarhartAuthor
https://www.instagram.com/c.l.carhart.author
https://www.minds.com/clcarhart/

Teutonica Translations

Aelte Teutonica - old Teutonica, used in the B.C.E. years
Bluotgifuog - blood-transfer
Der Weg Teutonisch - The Teutonic Way
Eihalbe/Eihalbae - singular/plural, fairy of silver oak
Fiorzoubar - elemental magic
Leitaeri - Prince/Keyholder of a Teuton city
Leitalra - Lady of a Teuton city
Louni - humor/mood
Niofirgeban - The Unforgiven
Teutona - female Teuton
Teutonica - old Teuton dialect
Thaler - medieval Teuton currency
Torstein - stone of the gate
Wegstunta/Wegstuntae - an hour's walk, about 2.3 miles
Wuotan - demon lord of the Teuton people
Zoubaraera - witch

Medieval Hours of Muniche

Vigils – midnight
Matins – 2 a.m.
Lauds – sunrise
Terce – 9 a.m.
Sext – 12 noon
None – 3 p.m.
Vespers – lighting of lamps/dusk
Compline – before bed (dark)

Pronunciation Guide
(for names and commonly used words)

Abelard – AB-uh-lard
Adeline – Ad-uh-LEE-nuh
Augustin – Au-GUS-tin
Bayerisch – BEYE-rish (eye is pronounced like eyeball)
Bayern – BEYE-urn (eye is pronounced like eyeball)
Dane – DAH-nuh
Der Weg – Dare Veg
Eihalbe – EYE-hahl-buh (eye is pronounced like eyeball)
Fonsi – FON-zee
Freia – FREYE-yuh (eye is pronounced like eyeball)
Ina – EE-nuh
Isar – EE-zahr
Jarvis – YAR-viss
Leitaeri – Leye-TARE-ee (eye is pronounced like eyeball)
Leitalra – Leye-TAHL-rah (eye is pronounced like eyeball)
Muniche – MYOO-nih-khuh
None – Nohn
Swanhilde – Swan-HIL-duh
Thaden – TODD-n
Thaler – TAHL-er
Torstein – TOR-stein (stein is pronounced like a beer stein)
Traudl – TROW-dool (trow is pronounced like cow)
Teutonica – Too-TAHN-ih-kuh
Wuotan – VOH-than

About the Author

C.L. Carhart has been writing since the age of 4, dabbling in everything from children's books, to fantasy, to historical fiction. Eventually, her lifelong interest in European history inspired her to create a paranormal fantasy realm based on the Teutonic people groups. The *His Name Was Augustin* series provides a first glimpse at this other-world—a place rife with ancient mysteries and dark magic.

Born and raised in southern New Jersey, C.L. spends her free time hiking with her husband, enjoying metal music, snuggling her feline familiars, and dreaming of the wonders of Germany.